BLOOD

AND

MERCY

RESTORED II

V. S. HOLMES

AMPHIBIAN PRESS

*To all those who shouted into the void
and heard it answer back*

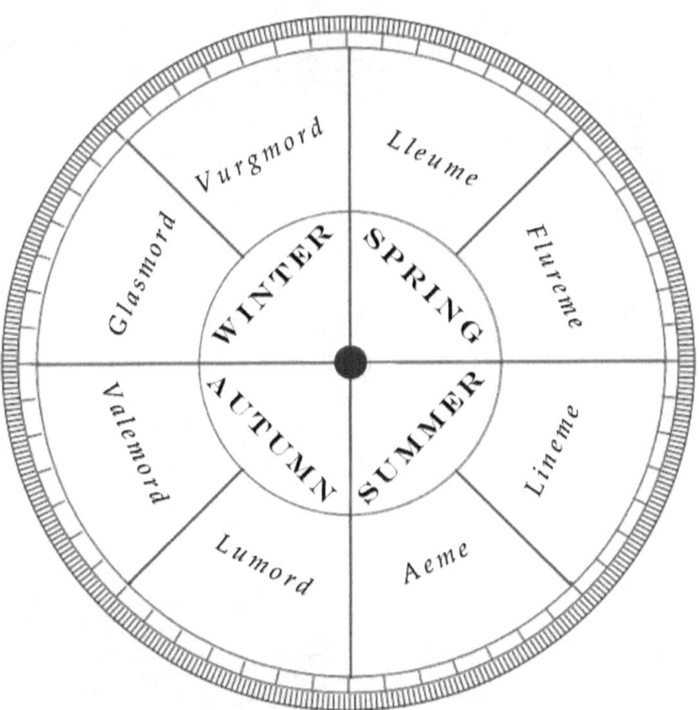

WINTER
SPRING
AUTUMN
SUMMER
Vurgmord
Lleume
Glasmord
Flureme
Valemord
Lineme
Lumord
Aeme

The World Of
BLOOD OF TITANS
N
The Icelock
NORTHLANDS
Neneviir
The
Ilmar
MIRIK
Mirik
Claimiirn
Ceir
Athrolan
Iron Sea
Ceir
Felden
Fort X Stone
X Fort Shadow
Arc of Zunu
Zunu
Eastern
Ocean
X Fort Hero

THROLAN
Fort Hero
Ceir
Bodian
RoBal
BAN
The Hartland
Feld
Ceir
Pardelan
de
Berne's Eye
Berne's
Teeth
Berrinal
Juniaal
Jade
Forest
Barran
Seyn
Ag
VALE
Vielrona
Oth de Dahtaina
NAD
ANEN
Cehn
SUNAM
Sashn
Seas
Burning
Waters

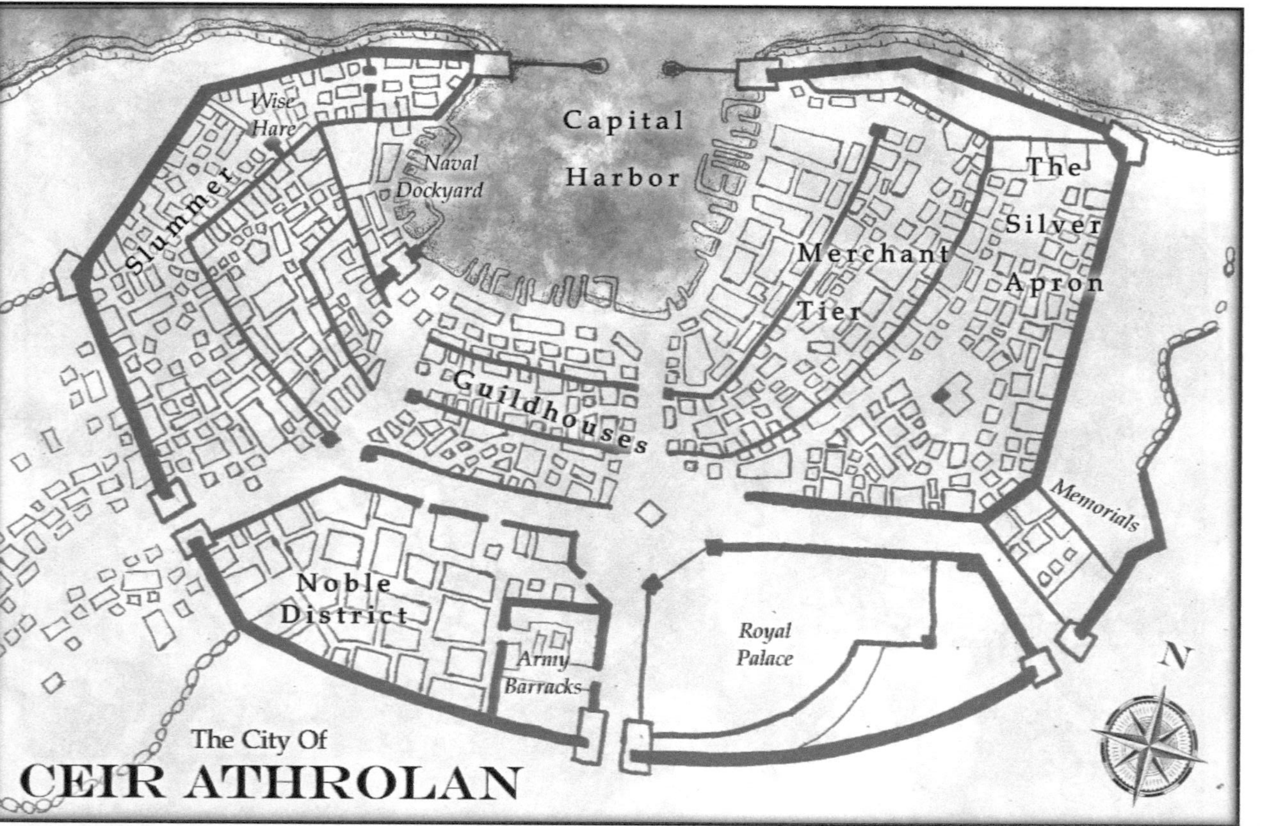

N
Capital
Harbor
Wise
Hare
Naval
Dockyard
Slummet
The
Silver
Merchant
Apron
Tier
Guildhouses
Memorials
Noble
District
Army
Barracks
Royal
Palace
The City Of
CEIR ATHROLAN

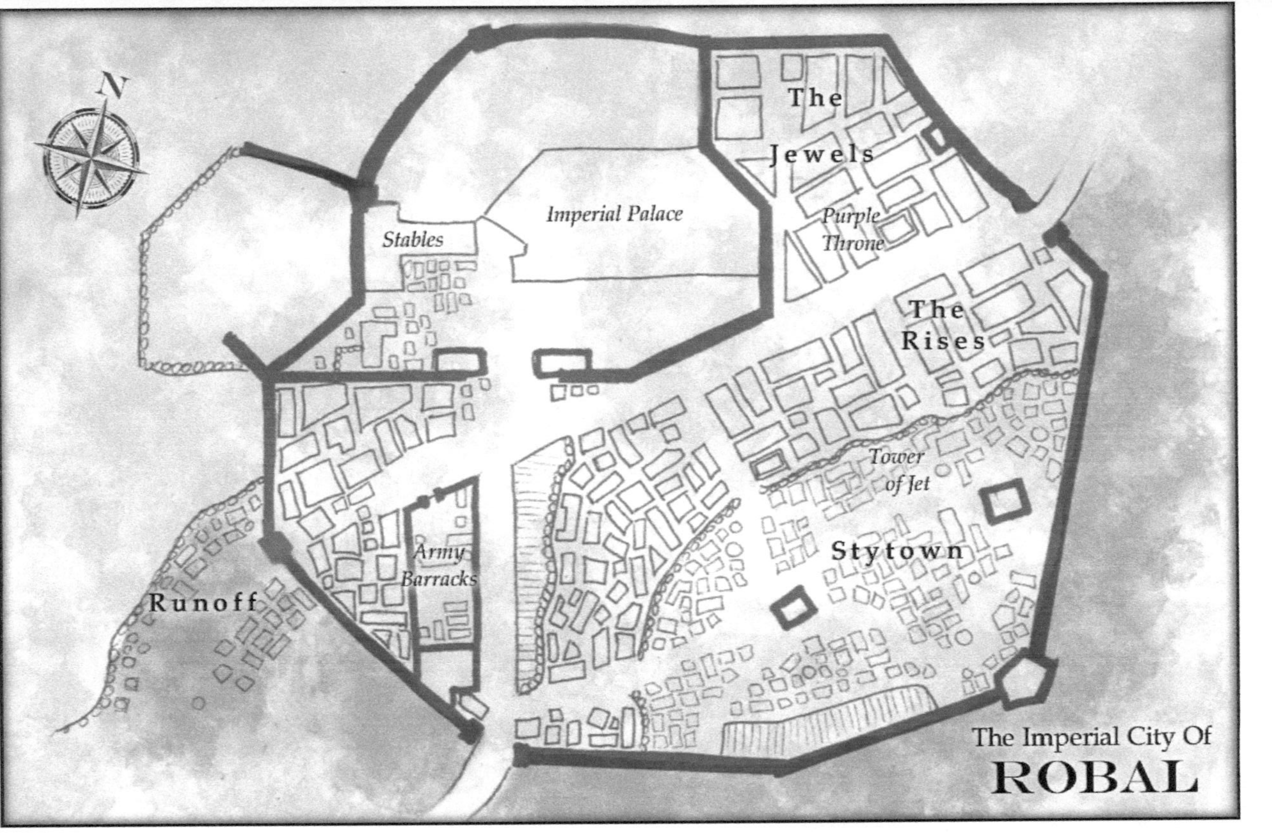

N
The Jewels
Purple Throne
Imperial Palace
Stables
The Rises
Tower of Jet
Stytown
Army Barracks
Runoff
The Imperial City Of
ROBAL

The Truth of God

CHAPTER ONE

37th Day of Lumord, 1272
The Eastern Banis Prairie

THE FOURTH NIGHT ON the trail, wolves circled the tents. At the camp's edge, where cookfires burned, they crept even closer. Rih leaned over, peering past the licking flames at the bright eyes blinking at the edge of the firelight. Already the weather was colder, the air carrying teeth as sharp as those glinting several paces away.

"You'd think they'd be frightened, with this many people," she signed to the woman beside her.

The guard spared a glance for the predators. "War makes everyone hungry. It's been centuries since wolves were seen this far west. They've probably come to eat our dead." She turned back to her bowl with a shudder.

Rih winced and looked back to the camp's boundary. The glittering eyes were gone, just a memory lit on her eyes when she closed them. It would take another week to reach Athrolan's capital, more if the river crossing tomorrow went poorly. Even marches as a foot soldier didn't take this long, thousands of pounding feet beating their steady way across the dusty grasslands. It was hard to manage the transition from soldier to dignitary, but the differences in the march made the gulf between the two yawn wider. When she saw that Bimet was through with her food she leaned forward. "I have something to ask of you."

"Are you certain that's a good idea?" Bimet's gaze moved from Rih to the looming tent of the emperor's ambassador. Vi-baln's shadow paced the tent wall, pausing when a runner appeared.

Rih raised the spear beside her. It was mostly decorative, but the blade was sharp. "I'll be quick." Her fingers curled with ease, forcing casual comfort into the conversation to ease her guard's worry.

The guard's shoulders heaved in a sigh and fell into step beside Rih as she set off through the camp. Fire lit the makeshift road between the linen tents.

Once out of eyeline of Vi-baln's tent, Rih ducked between the gently waving fabric walls of the larger barrack tents. Guards paced the edge of camp. Already she caught sight of armbands, caught glimpses of a fist, rising, opening. Liberty. She settled on the outcropping, legs tucked beneath her, and raised her face to the soft air. There was little time to acquaint herself with the surrounding women, but there would be chance enough upon arriving in Athrolan, where they would be watched more but understood less. Bimet found an outcropping still within whistle distance of the camp, but outside the reach of firelight. Of Rih's half-dozen attendants, Bimet was the only one she had known before any of this. Their troops had worked together often, and the red armband she donned on the second day of their march told Rih enough.

"I don't like this," Bimet signed, lips pursed.

Rih shrugged. "There's no other option. I can't trust letters yet, not until I am safely in Athrolan. There're too many eyes on me. And not only Vi-baln's."

"Then I assume it's important?"

"Fourth Riding is being transferred to a nearby town," she said by way of answer. "A little one I can't remember the name of."

Bimet watched the glowing orbs in the trees bob and slink for a moment. "And?"

Beneath Rih's hand the rock was rough, ragged, and gray. Gone was the smooth red of home, the earth stained red by rust or blood. Her fingers curled in the crags, a tether to this changing world. "They're led by Baniol Desfal, of the Third Arc. I don't want him to leave the town alive. I know there are sympathizers there." She fixed Bimet with a pointed expression. "Understood?"

"Understood. I'll get the word out now. It'll go out with the morning progress runners tomorrow at dawn." Bimet rose, hand pressing the small of her back when she straightened. "I'll walk you back to camp."

Rih shook her head. "I can manage myself. The messengers' tent is on the other side of the camp from ours."

When Bimet was gone, Rih's attention drifted to the darkness before her. A small piece of her wished, fleetingly, that she could disappear in the makeshift roads and slip away into the night. She would not, no matter how inviting the dark woods and winding trails might be. But for a few moments, she could pretend. In a fortnight's time she would be in a different type of forest, one of cold white stone and looming duties.

Already she missed Ki-elte. Already her heart ached for home. *A woman will bleed and die for Ban.* She would see them again in a year, perhaps two, on the field of battle. Somehow, she would find a way, find those who would join their cause.

In Athrolan, isolation would be their greatest ally. She just hoped she could survive it long enough to see her rebellion through.

Coarse grass pricked her feet through her silken slippers as she wound back to her tent, beside Vi-baln's. She turned the corner and froze. Vi-baln stood in the opening to his tent. Lanterns glowed behind him, gleaming off his broad, bare shoulders. His attention was fixed on her. "You'd best mind your slippers," he called, gray eyes never leaving hers.

She risked a nod, knowing he knew few, if any, of her signs.

"Wolves and all."

It was only after she had ducked into the illusion of safety inside her tent that she let herself shudder. Bimet was right to be cautious. The emperor's reach was long. Even here his ambassador served as sharpened claws. *This is temporary.* He would be gone once she married. Even as Athrolan's bride, however, safety was not guaranteed. Not for the first time, she wondered what His Majesty looked like. How he might act. Would she wish to sew his mouth shut as she wished so often of the baniol? Would he learn her signs? Would he be kind? She drew a long, slow breath. She was a soldier and marriage was war.

Φ

38th Day of Lumord, 1272
The City of Ceir Athrolan

Keplan staggered into his room, rain puddling on the wool carpet from his coat. A void opened in his chest, swallowing his nerves, his terror, the blood staining his hands. He looked down. A shred of tissue, remnants of a trachea perhaps, clung to the edge of a ragged nail. His empty stomach convulsed. His sleeves, too, were black with blood.

His tore the garment off, tossing it into the hearth with shaking hands. It was too damp, however, to do much more than smother the sullen flames. "Toss it!"

Even Azimir's swears felt like an inadequate response. The wooden box weighed in his purse, and he fished it out. He moved through the parlor to his study and sank into the chair without bothering to light a lamp. What he had become? He did not want the weight of his people on his mind. He did not want the grotesque mantle of divinity, nobility, on his shoulders. He wanted only peace and Firas and the distance to escape what he had just done. If holding the world's thoughts in his mind allowed him to end lives, then he would silence them.

All my dreams.

A part of him, the part currently struggling to keep its head above the churning guilt, told him this was not a solution. Not a true one. The box clattered open on the desk's polished top. Inside was a plain waxed pouch, a wide bamboo straw and a slim, sharpened stave the length of his thumb. Once each was arrayed across the king's desk, he leaned back. Firas never tolerated his patrons using drugs—dust or its gentler cousin, black leaf. But it was hard to escape in the Slummer. The beggar had not told him how to use the substance, nor had he bothered to ask or even wonder until this moment. *Fates.* This was a mistake, he was sure, a cliff jump from which he could not recover. Azimir's face flashed through his thoughts, followed by Firas's. His lover's expression morphed from tenderness, however, into the knotted snarl of fury, of grief, the one loneliness Keplan could not comfort. Keplan blinked. Blood. Skin and sinew rending beneath his grasping hands. He reached out, awkward but certain as he tapped the powder onto the gleaming wood. Before Firas's echo could talk him out of it, he bent over and inhaled.

He knew enough to pace himself, to circle his room and lock each door before returning to his study. He hated the portraits on the wall, the looming figures he would never live up to, the exhausted gaze of the queen now reduced to burnt bones in the mausoleum. He paced the balcony, emotions flashing through his chest like cannon fire—immediate and violent and inconsequential.

One after another he tore the portraits down, the hard, ancient wood of their frames clattering together. His gaze was caught by a landscape hanging just above his fireplace, and he paused. A forest. *Like home.* The frantic energy faded, replaced by something bright but too sharp for relief or happiness. He sank back into his chair, lidded eyes picking out each detail of the painted tree trunks. A thousand thoughts crashed through his mind, plans and ideas and fears, but not one lingered. Instead his battered psyche was left in unfamiliar silence.

Φ

38th Day of Lumord, 1272

Fog still clung to the stone, allowing the sleepy night and seedy activity to continue a few hours later than usual. Hylier shrugged into his jacket, wishing, briefly, for the old-fashioned cloaks he grew up wearing. Jackets were more practical, but nothing beat the dampness of the city better than being wrapped in thick wool. In a decade they might have silk-lined coats and horsehair decorations from Ban.

A crowd stalled his hurried steps as he turned a corner to the Lily and Alphonse. Guards swarmed around a fountain—one that was a popular gathering spot for the dandies and flirts of the Silver Apron. Someone had shut the fountain's valve, and the basin looked as if filled with wine.

The sickly smell of sweet blood hit him as he shouldered through the crowd. Murder in the streets was nothing new. One look at the man's face told Hylier this was no murder. This was a message.

"Back! I've had enough of you sick gawkers—"

Hylier flashed the emblem on his chest. "King's Guard." It was not truthful, exactly, but it was the best excuse he and Keplan had chosen for the occasions he would need one.

The man peered at the sigil. "Sorry, sir. Had too many trying to make a name for themselves." He heaved a sigh, pulling a stylus from the damp wrap around his head to make a note on the wax tablet in his hand. "Inspector Greton. Been following Peraan for some time now. Didn't expect to see him bloated in the square this morning."

"Understood." Hylier rolled his shoulders back. He did not have to fake the concern on his face. "This man was connected to crimes against the Crown—private information, of course. I'm just reporting to His Majesty." Hylier wasn't a spy, not in the conventional sense. He just knew people, fell into easy conversations and was forgotten other than a vague sense of friendliness. A journeyman inspector would glean more from the scene than he, but he ought to bring something back, some report. *An enemy of my enemy isn't always my friend.* "You think it was a mugging?"

Greton snorted. "Bag is missing. And he was an affluent man. You have a minute to take a look, just don't disturb anything."

Hylier thanked him and stepped closer to peer at the body. It was hard to tell what would be missing, but Peraan was rarely without his drink, especially in the evening. "Have you any thoughts on the matter?"

"Looks like an argument gone foul—clearly tensions were high. Just look at the man's throat."

Hylier crouched, taking care to touch nothing save the fountain's rim to steady himself. What throat? Windpipe was crushed, gleaming shards of bone jutting from where the thin U-shaped bone ought to be. The rest of the flesh was gnarled and torn free. Several pieces bobbed in the bloody fountain. He had never liked Peraan. The man was not likable even from a fanatic-supporter standpoint. Hylier lifted the edge of the man's coat. Spilled purse. No pack or writing kit. "I think I have all I need. See to it that the Palace Guard gets a writ of everything you find."

Greton seemed to speak in sighs. "I'll have it to you in three days. We're barely through with all the murder and looting that happened during the unrest. But I'll see it done, sir."

"Thank you," Hylier answered, slipping back into the crowd. Unrest. It was a sanitary term for tearing oneself apart. It was how his stomach felt now that danger weighed it, now that murder ran rampant. *And Daymir's involved.* The man had given Peraan names. Was this simply cleaning up after letting the fanatic snip loose ends? How did one break three decades of friendship? Before he knew it, his boots had brought him to Daymir's door rather than Keplan's.

The regent was in his seat by the window, where he had been the day before. Were it not for the different shirt, Hylier would have thought he had not moved.

"Haven't seen you much, though we're just a few city streets away," Daymir remarked, sharp lips becoming a smile.

Hylier returned it and gestured to the couch across from the regent. His hand shook. "May I?"

"Surely. I can call for tea."

"I had breakfast on my way up, though don't let that stop you."

Daymir rose, rang for a server and asked for his breakfast and tea. When he sat again, it was with a groan. "So why are you here?"

"To visit an old friend."

Daymir chuckled. "I'm old, but I fear I have fewer friends here than I did while exiled in Marl Black."

Perhaps you've burned too many bridges. Or murdered them. They had never been close enough for Hylier to voice his true concerns, but he had not come so far without knowing how to twist conversations whichever way he needed. "I'm concerned for His Majesty."

Daymir's gaze hovered somewhere between distant and vacant. Today its focus was on the harbor and the white tips of the waves. Hylier's guilt at choosing Azimir's safety and his confusion over Daymir's apparent betrayal soured his breakfast in his gut. If he were a tea drinker, he would have downed three cups in an attempt to quell the churning. *My job is to trust and obey.*

"Concerned?"

Hylier shrugged. "I heard one of the people he used to stay with while he was in the city was murdered."

"In the city. It's odd, we've always said it that way, for as long as I can remember. But it implies the palace, our barracks, all of this, isn't Ceir Athrolan."

I'm starting to think it isn't. "Odd indeed. But Master — sorry, sir — His Majesty is at risk."

"I was hoping to discuss the new trade routes with you. We'll need more swords on the roads —" His words died when he glanced over. "Ah. Hylier. Forgive me, I've been deep in thought and for a moment I thought you were the general."

Hylier forced a grin onto his face. "Of course. We've all had a long few months. Would you like me to send for the general?"

Daymir shrugged. "I'm sure I can send a note. It ought to be discussed with the House of Commons, I suppose." His voice waned to a mutter. "General Aneral should be back from her inspection of Fort Shadow soon."

"I'm sure." Hylier looked away. Arguing would only make the regent angry, and whatever was left of their relationship in his mind, Hylier wanted to preserve. Besides, there were other names on that list, ones that had yet to be crossed out. "I have a lead on some of the threats against the Crown, from Peraan. I'm going to look into them. Is there anything you might know? He wrote you often enough, even if his prose was unbearable to read." He wondered if Daymir knew of his supporter's death already.

"I know little of the man. I wrote to him once, in the beginning, when I did not know what type of man he was. I did not use my name, of course. He did not need that knowledge."

"Dam Ornsen."

Daymir glanced up, eyes clearing of their fogged memories for a moment. The calculating glint was a knife in Hylier's gut. "You know that name?"

"It was my job to read your correspondence. Even when you took care for us not to know it was yours."

Daymir's gaze lingered on Hylier's, nudging through the soldier's expressions in search of something. Betrayal, perhaps, or honesty. Of course, he would find neither. Hylier did not know where his loyalty lay anymore. After what seemed like a serviceable minute, Hylier rose. "I'd like to look into this, both for you and for His Majesty. If there's nothing else, of course."

"No," Daymir whispered, attention fading from the room and returning to some point between reality and the past. "No, there's nothing."

Hylier sagged against the wall outside the regent's door.

"Captain, is all well?" the regent's door guard asked.

"Well as can be," Hylier responded without thinking.

"His Highness the regent asked for General Aneral earlier, before you visited."

Hylier drew a breath. It was only a matter of time before the entire palace realized Keplan was not the only madman controlling their fate. "I think he's just tired. It's been a long time since he had to shoulder the responsibilities of court. Let him rest for the day, perhaps."

"Of course, Captain."

Hylier wished he could just return to bed. Perhaps if he did, the day would begin with something other than murder and madmen. Instead, he took a moment on the bench between the regent's chambers and Keplan's. A breath and another. Later he would go to the training halls and force his anxiety from his body with sweat and exhaustion. First, however, he had to explain how the Peraan situation had grown suddenly more complicated.

"He awake?" he asked the guard outside the king's door.

"I heard him rattling around early this morning. Shift before mine said he came back late, looking like death. Though it's hard to say if he ever doesn't, begging your pardon."

"I'd keep that thought amongst yourselves," Hylier commented. "I'd like to see him. It's about his safety."

Cold air drifted out when the door swung open. Hylier frowned and shut the door behind him. "Your Majesty? It's Captain Hylier."

"Study," the rasped answer drifted from a half-open door. The walls were bare of every portrait, only the landscapes remaining. The paintings were stacked in a corner, covered by a moldering cloak.

Hylier's hackles rose. The double doors of the king's bedroom were open, as were those to the balcony. He nudged the study door open to see Keplan seated at his desk, bare feet propped on the top, smudging what looked like official Banis scrolls. This was the only hearth that was lit, and the sullen fire did little to counter the early morning draught.

Keplan's hair was lank, the kind of greasy that came from too long in hot water. His clothes were pressed and fresh, but the deep bags under his colorless eyes spoke of a sleepless night. His body trembled, alert despite the clear lines of exhaustion. The guard was right. He looked like death.

"You've not been sleeping?"

"I hired you to listen, not gossip with guards."

"You hired me to help keep you safe, sire." Hylier reminded. It was a stretch of the truth, but not one Keplan could really argue with, he hoped. "There've been some developments with your friend's murder. The network of spies and soldiers who wanted Daymir on the throne is alive and well. Quieted by peace, but not converted. You asked me to find out more, and I found a list. Your cousin's name was on there. Azimir. It's a bold network that would attack an ambassador's son in his own home. And they were very nearly successful. And I'm concerned they'll try for you next."

Keplan barely moved.

"Lord Azimir is safe."

"I would have heard it sooner if he weren't," Keplan noted.

It was callous, even for Keplan. Perhaps shock would rouse the man's concern. "Peraan is dead."

Keplan's gaze wavered, but not to Hylier with curiosity. Instead, his eyes flicked to the hearth and back. Fire smoldered there, reluctant to catch on the damp scrap of fabric.

Hylier bent closer. It was a sleeve, decorated, and Keplan's size. Whatever drenched it was acrid and red. Had

Hylier not seen the fountain, he might have thought it wine. "Fates."

Keplan did not respond. His wide eyes were dark, pupils blown from shock or adrenaline or whatever made his whole body shake.

"There's an investigation. I saw it myself this morning. They know it wasn't a robbery. What if they find out?"

Keplan lifted a shoulder. "People won't suspect a king."

"They will if someone saw you. It's the Silver Apron. Someone always sees." He examined the blood-stained sleeve again. "Velvet doesn't burn well."

"I noticed." Keplan's distant gaze rolled to Hylier's. Bloodshot vessels tangled the blue. "I didn't plan to. I meant it, I suppose, but I just—it just happened. You understand?"

Hylier did not understand. He was a soldier, sure, but one during a time of relative peace. Even when the civil war broke out, few were willing to kill their neighbors. But he had never looked at someone the way Keplan looked at Firas. "Of course."

"I can see the Banis camp from here. They'll arrive tomorrow, I suppose. It'll be a distraction from who murdered that pond scum."

"Even for you?" It was pointed and above his station, but Keplan rarely seemed to care about insubordination. "I'll try my best to make this go away, but I can't erase your memories. I'm told it's hard."

Keplan frowned. "You've never killed someone?"

"No. I hope I never have to."

"You're a soldier, isn't that the job?"

"The job is to keep the Athrolani death toll as low as we can. Sometimes that means killing, but lately it hasn't. Hopefully, with you on the throne, that will remain the case."

"It'll be forgotten soon."

"Of course," he whispered again. "I'll see to it this is swept away with distraction. The city does have much to do as it recovers from the crimes during the unrest." Even he heard the strain in his parroted words. *Except I expressly asked them to look into it.*

Keplan hummed indifferently. Despite his lolling head, his thin throat flashed with a pounding pulse.

Hylier hadn't expected the secrets he would manage would be the king's. "There's an inspector, his name is Greton. I don't suppose that means much to you at this point."

Keplan's glazed gaze narrowed a minute before rolling onto his. "Someone of that name frequented the Hare. Usually on nights when a storyteller would bring news from other places. Ban, mostly."

"I imagine so. They've been in the business for generations—even before Her Majesty Tzatia implemented inspectors in Ceir Athrolan—those employed by the city treasury and not the Crown, that is. At any length, sire, they've been in it since the beginning and they breathe lawfulness."

"What does this Greton have to do with the price of wool in Mirik?"

"He's investigating Peraan's murder." He waited until Keplan's eyes seemed fully focused on his. "And he knows it wasn't a simple robbery."

Keplan's face paled further, and his mouth worked as if suddenly dry. "Did you speak to him? What did you say? Can you influence him in any way?"

"I'm clever, but he's just as, if not more, and he's studied this for his entire time in the position. I could do a bit, push his course a bit, but not turn him about. He's tacking against the wind but still a seasoned sailor."

Keplan frowned. "Tacking?"

"Ah, I have a cousin in the navy. It means alternating directions slightly, moving at an angle when the wind is against you. You go back and forth until you've reached your destination." He waved a hand. "It's no matter. I spoke to him just before I came to tell you of Peraan's death. Which, of course, you already knew about. No one seems specifically concerned, but that time will come."

"You think I should confess?"

Hylier drew a long breath. He did not like Keplan. Not as a friend. The man was complicated in the worst ways. But even after a long comradery that bordered on friendship with Daymir, he would never argue that the former exile would make a better monarch. Athrolan was at peace, if tentative, and won on the backs of a dozen lies.

"I think you should do whatever is best for Ceir Athrolan. At this moment, I don't believe that's confessing. And I'm not saying that because you seal my pay. I'm saying it because the most terrible part of the civil war wasn't watching this kingdom attack herself, but seeing the people turn on themselves. I can't stomach watching the people turn on each other, tear one another into pieces." He forced himself to meet those uncanny eyes. "If someone is going to tear themselves apart, even if it's only from guilt, I'd rather it was you and not the city."

Keplan seemed to sink back into the sea of distance between himself and apparently every living thing. After a long moment his attention returned. "When you were there, did you see anything—anything that could point Greton in another direction—any other direction?"

"Nothing comes to mind. Nothing that would help at least, that I'm sure of. There's something, but I—" he sighed. "I need to look into it more."

"Is it something I could help with? Our minds are very different and sometimes that helps."

"I think not." *And tell you your regent may have caused the murder of a dear friend?* He glanced at the tremble in the king's hands and the bloodshot haze over his eyes. "Will this become a habit?"

Keplan frowned. "What?"

"Murdering. Will it become a habit?"

"Hardly. I don't think I have the bones for it. I'm not Domariigo."

The uncertainty was sickening, the distance, the disinterest. It happened once. It might again. Hiding the fact that a serial murderer sat upon Athrolan's throne would not be easy. "I'd hope not."

Something in his voice must have reached Keplan. "I'm not wallowing in apathy over here, Hylier. I'm horrified."

Hylier was abruptly reminded of how much younger the king was than he — a decade separated them, but the shadows in his eyes were darker than Hylier ever feared his own would be.

Φ

41st Day of Lumord, 1272
The Eastern Banis Prairie

The next move was crucial. Her teeth ground on her lip for a moment. Perhaps Bimet spoke, but she didn't look up to check. Her fourteenth tile slid into place beside Bimet's fourth. *Lotus takes all.* She grinned and slid her final one in beside it.

Only then did she look up.

The guard's eyes narrowed on the set, scanning for any error. There was none. "Good game, Your Luminance."

Rih had given up enforcing the use of her name a week ago. The pale tiles rolled in Rih's dark hand. "And you, Bimet. Thank you."

A shadow fell across the tent and Bimet's head turned. She rose and peered out before turning back to Rih. "Someone's come for you — a soldier, said she marched beside you."

Rih gestured for her to enter, sweeping her tiles into their bag at her belt before sitting back. When she glanced up, Kahma stood in the entry. Rih's heart faltered, then burst into an aching flurry. "Kahma!" She surged to her feet, arms around the other woman before she remembered her new station.

"Will you need an interpreter?" Bimet asked.

"Hardly, thank you, though. Would you mind bringing tea for us?"

The guard disappeared and Rih settled back on her cushion. "It's so good to see you!"

"And you, it's been a while." Her hands curled into easy signs, despite missing two of her smallest fingers on her left hand. "Since, when was it, Juniaal?"

"Battle of Nad," Rih corrected with a smile. "Fourth wave. What are you doing here? I thought your Arc was sent north, not east."

"I'm in the Fifth Arc, Jade Riding, now."

Then why are you here? She had not sent word of the rebellion to Kahma. Not yet, at least. And with the loose wrap around her shoulders it was impossible to tell whether she wore an armband at all, let alone what color. "I heard they were riding for a village in the southeast."

A grimace marred Kahma's otherwise delicate features. "That's why I'm here. I got your message."

"Liberty?"

Kahma repeated the word, hand trembling just a bit. "I don't know if it's brilliant or nonsensical to try this. But I think we must."

"If you know—the baniol," she faltered, avoiding the sign for assassination. "What happened?"

"He found out about the plot just hours before. Thought it was coming from Mirik, of course, the villagers were supposedly indoctrinated by Mirikin insurgents. Not a one knew what we were on about, of course. Doesn't matter to the baniol. Had to do the work regardless." Her jaw worked in an effort to keep from shouting, or perhaps from weeping.

The work. Rih knew what that meant, what deeds stained Kahma's hands as deeply as they still did hers. She almost reached out to the other woman, but stopped herself. Maintaining that composure was never easy, and a single touch might shatter it. Comfort came later, when war orders no longer loomed.

"It's a wonder any of us got out alive, when the baniol has his head so far up his shitehole."

Rih rolled her eyes. "It's a wonder any of us survived infancy, frankly." Still, her heart sank. Perhaps she did not have the head for plotting and treason. Surely it was a harried plan, but her nerves were aflame with urgency to do something—anything—to spur her cause onward.

"I hope you know what you're doing. His Eminence sees so much."

"It goes so much further than simply the emperor." Rih's fingers jerked around the words, mouth tightening. "He is a symptom—a dangerous one, one that masks the true illness in our empire, but a symptom. We destroy him another will rise—tumors, one right after the other."

Kahma's expression faded to exhaustion. "I know." She shrugged and her hands dropped to her lap.

Guilt pinched in Rih's chest. Hope was as necessary as honesty. "We need all the allies we can get. Speak to those you trust."

Kahma's smile flashed. "I'll send word if I do." A shadow sank over her features.

"Will you get a chance to go home, soon? See the rest of them? You've been on march for over a year now."

"Bet was my home."

"Bet?"

"The village he made us burn yesterday."

Rih's heart ached. Guilt uncurled that she had not even bothered to learn the town's name. *Bet.* She was no better than the baniol. "I am so sorry, Kahma. If I'd known—"

"This is war. It would have happened regardless, thinking the town housed insurgents. At least your secret is still safe." An echo of strength steeled the woman's frown. "Rih—Your Luminance, I'm sorry—I've got some family on the border. And friends in Mirik, perhaps."

Rih frowned. "In Mirik?"

"My wed-sister has a cousin there. And I'm sure if she spoke to my younger brother, he would support us too. He's a quick-tempered creature but bears no love for His Eminence. We've not always seen on level, but—"

Bimet ducked in, tray in hand, and set the tea between them, hair hiding her speech for a moment before she glanced at Rih directly. "I was apologizing for my tardiness. Fire's a sullen dam with this rain."

Kahma barely glanced at the clay pot and stood. "I should go back to our edge of camp. It was good of you to share your campfires, but you know how little the captain likes us to dawdle. I'll talk to my brother and his wife."

"I hope you find dreams tonight," Rih signed, fingers curling kindness into the words.

Bimet's eyes followed the other woman's exit, then flicked to Rih. Her lips opened, then pursed, but she did not speak.

The soldier's shadow disappeared from the tent wall. Banter and taunts served to distance them a fraction more. But pain surfaced when campfires flickered low across the prairie and stars glimmered in the blackness. In the end, they were all women burning down their own houses, lest they be forced inside the flames.

Φ

43rd Day of Lumord, 1272
The Town of Tut Kunis, Berr

"What does it feel like? For you?" she asked.

Arman glanced up. "I know it looks like sickness, it feels like it too, a bit, but..." He trailed off, eyes fixed out the window of the hut. "It also feels like a relief."

Alea's luminous eyes were steady on his, as attentive as they usually were distant. "I think I know what you mean. It feels right. Familiar."

"It's a relief. But I'm still scared, a bit. Of what it means. I was afraid, years ago during the battle, of what I would become. I saw the Rakos, their twisted forms, their stone flesh, their mania. And I didn't want that. Not for me. Not yet."

"You still became it, though."

"In part. I surrendered. It's odd that we never spoke of this, except in passing. Never processed it. Fates, this has been so lonely. These years, two decades of being alone. Together." His words came faster now. Urgency spurred his tongue. He remembered the Rakos, their stilted words, if they still had them at all, and their calculating animal gaze. If that is where he headed, he needed to speak as much as possible before the power of speech was lost to him entirely. "Before the battle I thought, as your guard, my role was one of fighting. When that didn't work I hiked into the hills behind Athrolan and succumbed. Surrendered. This feels akin to that, just," he faltered. "More. The next step. The final step, perhaps."

Alea's eyes were once again fixed on some point he could not see. "I think there's one more to come. After this. This feels like relief. Coming home. Becoming whole."

"Before I accepted it. This, though," he agreed, "this is closer to welcoming."

The door downstairs banged and her gaze flitted to the ladder leading down. "Speaking of welcoming, I think we're no longer welcome here."

He snorted. "I doubt we ever were."

A small spread was laid out in the front room. Again, outside the windows the town appeared deserted, save for the smoke drifting into the still wind from each chimney. The chief already sat across the table, a steaming mug in one hand.

"You came here seeking a woman—a crone, by your own words."

"Is she ready to speak to me?"

"I was untruthful before. Many have come seeking her, but she never spoke to any. You said she came to you in your dream?"

"It wasn't what I'd call a conversation. A warning. A plea, perhaps, but I could not say whether she knew she'd reached me. Perhaps it was I, and not she, who was trespassing in the dream."

"She was our ward. Since the Gods' War. She arrived wounded and lost twenty-four years ago. Fleeing the Mirikin army. She was unconscious, though her rest was not peaceful. Berrin are devout people, always have been. Many of us worshiped the gods, but many here worshiped the Laen just as much. There was only one place we could think of to bring her, hoping it might make a difference. Heal her or let her pass on to whatever awaited her. Then one morning the wind began to howl. The mountains groaned, weeping boulders.

The wind was hot, whipping our skin until it chapped. And the ocean rose, something between a typhoon and a mist. It whipped and howled over the mountain and was gone. When it was gone, she was awake."

"Is she dead?" Alea knew the words were harsh but could not find the energy to care.

"Hardly. The words she used, her premonitions, visions, whatever you wish to call them, entranced many among us, but none more so than Orabon Marum. He was devoted to her. Others were too. Driven by her words and his own determination, he set out to spread her wisdom. First north, then west. I hoped you would leave without bothering us further, but," he shrugged, "like you said, when you dream of her, it's a warning."

Alea leaned forward, her desperation drawing fuel from the faith of this unknown man. "How far behind are we?"

"Months. It was in early spring."

When Keplan left us. Arman glanced at her. If there was any doubt their son bore their power or something even greater, tied to the world itself, the words dashed it to slivers.

"He's from here?" Alea pressed. Lines formed at her eyes from the effort of speaking for so long.

"No, a border town to the west. One that worshiped the gods."

"How did he end up here, a town that worships..." she faltered.

"You?" His dark eyes bored into hers. "He was seeking new faith. When he heard her message, he found it."

"'Gods' Blood?'" Alea quoted.

"There's more to it. Far more. Were she anywhere else, we'd chalk it up to madness. But what she spoke of were legends passed down through generations. Stories we whispered with sanctity in the dark nights of winter. The only faith we could possibly keep through a hundred generations."

"And the citadel—Lymorda—it's still there?"

"Untouched."

She turned to Arman. "Do you think—"

"Perhaps it wasn't her we came to find. Perhaps it was that."

She whirled on the chief. "Will you take me?"

"No." He set down his cup with finality. "But I will show you the trail."

Φ

Lymorda, Citadel of the Laen, Berr

The mountains were not fit for horses, the trail closer to a stone ladder most of the way. Instead they hauled themselves, hand over hand, for the entire afternoon. When they reached the level outcropping, neither could draw full breath from the altitude, and the city below was a smattering of dark spots. Alea's focus paused on the salt flats far below and the map the chief had handed off before they departed.

"I can't say this is inviting." Arman's hand traced gouges in the stone. A yawning black maw led into the mountain, quickly winding away from sunlight. It was nothing like the smooth metal tunnel that led into the Northlands. Instead it was filled with dust and broken support beams. Alea was certain idealism and misplaced faith were the only things holding the mountains from crushing her. The air inside was different. Cold decay and salt replaced the crisp chill of the slope outside. Despite the damp, not even mold encroached upon the walls. The tunnel stretched on, winding through what must have once been a wining vein. "This wasn't hewn with pickaxes or hammers. It was with hands," Arman whispered as they pressed deeper. "Rakos hands."

Alea nodded. She did not dare to speak yet. A light appeared in the distance and the sound of open air echoed from ahead. She forced her steps to stay measured, though panic screamed for her to run for open air. She stepped eagerly into the light. Rock skittered from the narrow ledge under her boots and she scrabbled at Arman's jerkin. "Fates, if they're not trying to kill us with the crushing rock, then they'll just drop us off a cliff."

Arman nodded absently, his wide eyes scanning the view before them. They were tucked in the shelter of an extinct volcano's yawning mouth. Rippling rock curled up the sides, massive designs carved by Earth Shaker hands. Where Elanal had been quietly somber, this was a testament to titanic power. The citadel itself stood in the center of the caldera. Alea recognized echoes of Le'yne's architecture, but this had been built at the height of the Laen's power, not its end. The city was built in concentric squares, the curling rooftop of the citadel itself rising above, pierced by the black obelisk. Bones decorated the city, save for the central building, but these were the bones of giants. They were of some great animal, bulbous skulls sprouting four tusks twice as long as Alea was tall. Their sloping backs supported the bone columns of the main gate. Pillar-like legs crooked like human elbows and knees, as if poised to charge. "Lymorda. I never thought about the meaning of the name."

"Great Dead."

"You said the Rakos were forgotten, hidden in cities like this. You never came here?"

"I followed the glimmer of their souls, and while they were far flung, none were this far northeast."

"I wonder why. It's beautiful here. Preserved."

"Perhaps the familiarity was too much. Besides, surrounded by wards made of the bones of your own kind is a bit macabre, even for madmen."

They hiked farther. The sound of bone dust under boots and moaning wind were the only greetings. The energy of the place was still but sentient, empty sockets as watchful in death as in life. The citadel loomed closer, great barred doors still impregnable. Alea stopped at the doors. They were unmarked, save for two handprints stamped in the stone. One bore scorch marks. Alea pressed her palm into the right hand, nodding for Arman to do the same. Their hands marbled black and white, ice and fire, wind and earth. The stone groaned, hinges cracking into use after two centuries of stillness.

The room beyond was dark, empty. They entered together, hands brushing but not clasped. The walls writhed with murals, stories picked out in a thousand tiny colors. Alea's throat tightened. Once, the Laen had been as grand as Athrolan. Once they had a rich history, feared and revered by nations. By gods, even. She moved across the room, eyes roving from one scene to the next. Each square panel was as tall as she. Here, among the whispers of ghosts, she might be able to touch her power, mend her connection. She moved deeper into the room, stopping finally before a mighty dais. Instead of an altar like in the other citadels, temples to fallen deities, there were two thrones. She stepped up and settled herself into the seat of black metal. It was unnaturally cold. Her head rested against the hard bowl of the back. She glanced to Arman once before closing her eyes.

She recognized the echo of power, the droplets of black ocean that once brimmed from her veins. They skittered from her grasp, running through her mind like quicksilver. Once, long ago, she had looked on the world through her power, sought the gleam of Arman's golden soul. She sank into the power now, drawing it over her head until everything was black. *I don't have to use it. Just look through it, use it as a spyglass to find the gods' souls.* The latent power in this place promised her there could be another, whispering with the gods' magic.

The world glittered before her, the brown-red of the humans' souls scattered in the town below. She drew back, rising from her body, from the mountains. Athrolan stretched ahead, Ban to her left. Webs of red covered the world, a bloody network of souls and people, impossibly tenuous, impossibly connected. *Blood clogs the city streets.* She had never wondered at the deep color of human souls before, at the richer, brighter color it echoed. Now the curiosity rooted in her mind. Her mental gaze swiveled toward Athrolan, seeking whatever difference that would mark her son's soul. Her vision stung at the brilliant beacon seated in the heart of the great city. It was the burnished copper she recognized. Even from leagues away, through the blanket of Laen power, she could smell the blood. She knew that color, that scent. They were burned in her mind from rending the gods' souls from their bodies.

Her throat ached and the sound of screaming burrowed into her mind. Hot hands gripped her physical shoulders. Her grip on the power faltered and she plummeted back into her body. "Arman!" Her eyes flew open. His brow was pressed to hers. Through her own gasps she heard his sobs.

CHAPTER TWO

46th Day of Lumord, 1272
The City of Ceir Athrolan, Athrolan

GOLDEN NOON LIGHT DAPPLED the silk cover of her carriage. For the past two days it had been awash with the shadows of leaves and branches. Each lurch over the strange, bumpy roads sent another spike of pain up her back. Weeks on the road did no one any favors.

Her long fingers curled around the cup. It might not have been a rough army mug, but it was still far from the delicate glassware of the palace. *What would Athrolan use? Would she be expected to eat as they did? Drink their bitter tea? Or their alcohol?* She shook the nerves away as best she could. Mosil trained her. She knew what dishes they used. Reality, of course, was always shades different. But she was not going into this skirmish with ignorance. *Just apprehension.*

A shadow bloomed across the golden silk and she flinched. In silhouette, Vi-baln's shoulders seemed to span the breadth of her carriage. There must have been wind outside, for his lengths of black hair eddied around the arching headdress he had donned that morning. She watched his shadow hand rise, grasping. Fear flickered through her chest until she realized he must be gesturing at something far ahead. *Athrolan.*

The warm air in the carriage turned cloying. She turned on Bimet. "Roll back the covering. Please."

Bimet ducked out through the back, graceful even in the formal Royal Guard's leathers over billowing cotton. Silk retreated, drawn into precise folds, Rih stood, one hand gripping the naked carriage ribs. Adrenaline was fire in her limbs.

Ocean wind yanked at her clothes, pulling silk taught against the delicate chains. She raised her chin. Vi-baln glanced over, watching for a moment before pointing at the box at her feet. Her own headdress waited inside. It too had feathers, but hers were given by the emperor himself. Vi-baln had plucked his from a falcon he felled earlier. Rih had to step over the thrashing thing that morning. She glanced at the box but made no move to don its contents. *Not yet.*

The wagon lurched beneath her as they descended the foothills to the outer limits. Ceir Athrolan spread below her, glittering and stark.

Black water stains marred the soft marble, and though the gutters were free of refuse, the faint scent of mildew clung to the street sides. Aqueducts arched over the city, water misting through chinks in the ancient stone. They lurched onto the uneven cobbles of the main road. The gates hung open before them, the metal and bolts dark against the massive blocks of the city wall. RoBal's gates served as a demonstration with their spikes and cages against stylized depictions of history. These were plain, though no smaller.

Clusters of musicians and heralds dotted the street corners among the turquoise and gray of the guards. How different was their music? Within her ribs, her heart beat with Banis drums half remembered from her dancing class. It faltered with every wheel-bump on ancient paving stones.

Manors rose to her right, tucked behind their tidy, ivy-hung walls. She glimpsed a dozen flags of various Athrolani noble houses. Mirik's vermillion and green whipped above one of the large houses. Violet draped the Banis ambassador's towers and balconies. The color was garish without the backdrop of rich red clay and black wood. Even more striking was the brilliant turquoise hung from each official building. For an otherwise bland city, the nobles seemed intent on color.

Rih missed the days of entering cities on foot, shoulder to shoulder with her sisters. At least then she could meet people's eyes, she could smell the cooking food and feel the packed clay under her sandals. Here, everything was removed, distant, reaching her through a padding of silks and the scent of horse sweat and leather. Only the sharp bite of ocean salt wound through the haze of her Banis wagon train. She always dreamed of arriving at the head of a march. She never expected it to be as the coddled princess in a wagon.

Vi-baln's fingers gripped her wrist and he jerked his head at the box. He did not need signs when he did not care if she answered.

Her shaking hands fumbled the headdress out. It was a traditional net but covered with hundreds of glass and metal beads. Gemstones dripped from dozens of chains, the end of each finished with smaller, delicate feathers. A few still bore tiny flecks of blood. Jaw clenched, she draped it over her shorn scalp.

Something between fear and anger flamed in her bones, and she forced her chin higher. This would be her city. These would be her people. Whatever the next year brought with war and rebellion, she would learn to find happiness here.

The wagon swayed into an open square filled with onlookers and vendors. A fountain, small by Banis standards, glittered in the center. The rich scent of baking bread was almost akin to the grasslands in summer, but here it was cut by the crisp salt air and the stench of lamp oil. Despite the alien city, the strange pale faces and paler stone, she found dark Banis eyes among the crowd and bright dyed patterns between dark neutrals and eastern embroidery. *I will show them you mean peace.* She did not mean peace, but today she could pretend.

She raised a hand in greeting.

An answering wave rose, then another, then a dozen.

Bimet brushed her arm. "The palace is just ahead."

A swollen bubble of a dome topped the modest, if large building. Rooftops and roads angled down toward the harbor. Every tier was dotted with domes, some flattened, others drawn into a point. Arches cut through each wall, curving stone worn round by rain.

A few dozen nobles and soldiers gathered in the open courtyard. Ivy and ferns clustered in pots and raised marble beds around the fountain. Guards paced the walls, preventing most who tried to climb for a glimpse of the meeting. *Gallants. Their baniols are called gallants.* A thrill shot through her at the sight of a tall, muscled woman in naval garb and an important insignia. A wiry man with gray hair and beard stood dressed in deep blue beside the general. Her gaze lingered on the silver-capped horns of the Ageless warrior, tracing the wrinkled tattoo. Her hackles rose despite the thin arms and paunch under his leather and uniform.

As a child, she and Mosil often snuck into the rear of the smaller palace theater to watch the elaborate wooden puppets portray ancient epics or news from other nations. She knew a puppeteer when she saw one.

Mosil appeared at her elbow, one hand surreptitiously making the sign for "memory."

I rehearsed this, she reminded herself, and stepped from the carriage. The worn marble was cold under the thin soles of her slippers. Vi-baln recited his introductions and flattery, Mosil translating into Trade. Rih dragged her gaze from the general to catch the tail end of Bimet's signs.

"...of the Hartland, King of Athrolan and the Topin Hills." A boy stood a step before the Ageless general, with a modern Athrolani jacket and old-fashioned long hair. Rih swore her pulse stilled. It was not his beaked nose or bloodless face. It wasn't even his obvious youth. *Interrogator's Kisses.*

He swayed. Was he unwell? Drunk? The acrid scent of alcohol underscored that of damp stone. *"He spent some time in Ban, apparently."* Mosil's words during their meeting with Vi-Baln the day before were lead in her churning gut. She did not remember every white traitor or slave her riding took in for questioning, but she remembered the long hair and colorless eyes rolling in the wagon and the muttering of gods and fate and blood.

If he was not already acquainted with madness, interrogation might drive him there. *Does he remember? Does he know my face? Or am I just another brown face to him, just as they are a sea of marble skin?*

Vi-baln's narrow gaze and Mosil's nervous glance nudged her into a faltering curtsy. The king's smile was vacant, and he bowed.

"I look forward to our negotiations and your great empire," he addressed her in Banis, though his accent concealed some of the words. Then it was over. Vi-baln and Mosil fell into step beside the king, Rih and her entourage following them down the narrow, low halls. Athrolan may have been a few centuries older than the Banis capital, but its corridors were far less opulent. Rih's body demanded she run, urging her to forget her duty, forget her dreams of freedom for her sisters and take to the surrounding hills.

Instead, she gripped her hands before her and the tears blurring her vision did not fall.

There was no formal audience or grand entrance. Perhaps that would come later. Mosil had mentioned a ball. Instead, an old man, a steward, perhaps, or serving man, appeared, gesturing down various halls and bowing far too much for Rih's taste.

Her other serving woman, a young girl named Nehla, joined them a moment later as they were escorted down another low, narrow hall. It was dark, despite the pale walls, and decorated with occasional murals.

The door they stopped at was pale wood, lacquered until it shone like glass, and with a heavy lock and handle.

The steward unlocked the door, speaking to Bimet. Rih stepped into the room, scanning the strange architecture. Every door was arched, every window filled with thick glass made wavy with age. Air puffed past her and she turned. The door was shut, and she was alone with her two serving women.

Bimet handed the key to her. "They gave me this," she said, eyes downcast. "His Majesty invites you to explore or rest as you wish today, and requests your presence at the ball honoring your arrival tomorrow evening after negotiations."

Adrenaline trembled in Rih's hands and she sank into one of the parlor chairs. It was plush, but the fabric looked well worn. *How many arses imprinted this thing before now? Where they as scared as I am?* She was beyond even nervous laughter.

Nehla perched next to her. Though she seemed kind, she did not know many signs, relying on Bimet for the majority of their conversations. "Would you like to look around your room? I can help you unpack?"

Rih glanced around, looking for an annex. "Where are your rooms?"

"Below yours. Servants' quarters. But there's a stairwell behind that angled shelf. I guess it's how most ladies in waiting live here."

They were an entire floor away. Her guard and serving woman. Her only voice in this new world. Her stomach pitched. "I think I can unpack tomorrow. I need to rest, I'm not feeling so well."

Nehla searched her eyes, her own pinched with pity. "Are you certain—"

"Please, I'm quite tired. I'll call for you both in the morning." She hesitated, looking around again. "How do I call for you?"

"A bell by our door." Bimet squeezed her hand, but Rih could not find the strength to squeeze back. When she looked up again, save for a dozen trunks, the room was empty.

They tried to decorate it with Ban in mind, it seemed. Landscapes of grasslands hung on two walls of the study, but their craggy outcrops and gray-green slopes belonged to the Felds of southern Athrolan, not the gold Banis prairie. Ban may have boasted ebony wood, but Athrolan's rooms were dark with soot stains from lamp oil and faded blue wallpaper. Instead of a large single chamber divided with screens and built for airflow on hot summer days, her chambers were a series of tight rooms, ending in her bed chamber, which, at least, had two large windows and a balcony door instead of the usual single window.

She drifted from room to room, at a loss. Even the deep sunken bath in her private privy brought nothing but apathy. She would not even have the socialization of a bathhouse, it seemed. A locked door was the only solace when she thought of the king and his young, scarred face.

Though it lacked familiarity, she returned to the privy. Travel—even via a glamorous wagon train—made her reek of sweat and horse and soil. *Sometimes I wish I was born without smell instead of without hearing,* she thought with a small smile.

A minute's fiddling brought water rushing from the metal tap. Two dishes beside the tub held what smelled like soap and something that bubbled delightfully when she mixed it with the water. She left her finery in a pile on the bench by the narrow window and slipped into the water with a grateful sigh. It was not as hot as the thermal pools in Ban, but the day was warm enough she did not mind overmuch. Her eyes lidded and she let herself drift in the lack of sensation. Tomorrow she would attend the exhausting negotiations. Tomorrow she would unpack. Tomorrow the rest of this life of hers would begin. The real work. The framing of her rebellion against the empire she both loved and hated. But that was tomorrow.

Φ

46th Day of Lumord, 1272

A fist banging on Keplan's door disrupted what little sleep he hoped to get that night. He tugged on his robe and padded to the door. Would he ever grow used to having multiple private rooms? He opened the door a crack.

Brentemir stood in the hall, looking as harried as Keplan felt. His hand was raised, ready to unleash another onslaught on the heavy wood. He blinked, bloodshot eyes narrowed in something close to surprise. "Keplan."

"You expected someone else to answer my door?"

"No. Hoping maybe." His gaze roved about the room. "Might I come in?"

Keplan shrugged and gestured to the simple room. It felt odd to have an ambassador, a man of legends, act with deference. "You arrived this evening?" He glanced at the squat clock on his wall, counting the space. "Yesterday evening, I suppose, now."

"I did. Azimir came with me, but I didn't want him here for this."

"And what is this?" Keplan took the seat, watching Bren pace before the fire. "Is this where you beg me to see reason, convince me that all the doubts I've been fighting for the past two weeks are right?"

Bren shook his head. "No. Maybe. I don't understand why you're doing this, why you're throwing your future away. You could come to Mirik, be family, bring your parents, even. Why choose this? Is it because of my sister's promise to Her Majesty all those years ago?" He did not wait for a response, but fell to his knees on the flagging. "Keplan, please. You're all I have left of her. Forget An'thoriend. Forget everything he wants you to be. Those aren't your dreams."

"You want me to give up Domariigo's dreams to acquiesce to yours? Tell me, Bren, when did you decide to take Mirik up?" He slumped back in the chair, wishing there was tea strong enough to ease the pounding in his head and the weakness in his limbs. Apparently dust had a backlash.

"Just before the final battle."

Keplan shook his head. "No, I mean when exactly. In which moment was your mind made up?"

"I saw Athrolan tearing her apart. I saw all of my father's failures and knew that in giving her up to Athrolan, I would be no different."

"Exactly."

Bren's pacing stopped. "She was doing the damage to herself, though. And not because of Arman's failures. And Athrolan isn't your home."

"Isn't it? It's where I sought sanctuary. It's where I've found friendship. It's where the man I love lives. I'm not going to watch it fall to pieces either."

Bren shook his head and looked down. He collapsed into the chair. "I guess I was wrong."

"About what?"

"About who you were. I thought all you wanted was a normal life and family with us in the city. I made the same mistake with your mother. You want the same thing as she — peace and solitude. I thought you sought me out through Azimir because you knew, because you wanted to be welcomed into our home."

"It's a pretty thought."

"Why, then?"

"You won't believe me if I say friendship, I suppose. It's what I told Azimir."

"I might believe it. Azimir's trusting, though, and I think you're a good liar."

Keplan's face smoothed. "I didn't know you were my blood, but I knew you were on the verge of war with Ban, and before I wanted peace, I wanted blood. Part of me still does. I sought out Azimir because I saw him disembark with you in Athrolan and I knew I needed to get to you. You've seen war and don't want it again, but I've seen slavery. I wanted to destroy the Banis and you were my best chance."

"And now?"

"Athrolan is my greatest priority now. But I have not forgotten Ban. And I certainly will not stop your wife's war with them. I may want peace for Athrolan, but all of Ban could burn and I would dance in the light of the flames."

Ice slid down Brentemir's spine. First he had recognized the features of his sister, of Arman. Then he had seen the drive, the intelligence. Now, though, now he saw Arman's determination and Alea's calculation. And in the ice-chip eyes, he saw Azirik's mania. "Are we invited to the ball? Tonight?"

"And the wedding within a few weeks, assuming negotiations are finalized properly today."

"Seems rushed."

"Ban's at war. They have other issues to contend with than a thinly veiled attempt to control a new boy king." The pounding increased in Keplan's temples and he pressed two long fingers against the throb. "Could we discuss this another time, if at all? It's barely dawn and I have a monstrous day before me."

Bren sighed, staring at his boots before rising. "I'm sorry. I'm sorry I didn't understand you better. I'm sorry I couldn't relieve this burden for you."

"I know." Keplan watched him go, watched the wrought bolt fall back into place. Apologies and promises surrounded him, most stemming from pity. He did not want pity. He wanted understanding. He wanted companionship. The bells began their tolling of dawn, and he winced. *I want fucking silence.*

He did not receive silence. Instead, the glaring dawn light crept farther up the walls of his bedroom. Even when he slipped into his study to escape it, sun lanced across the floor and painted the shelves opposite his desk with its brilliance.

Today they would formally ally with Ban. It was already agreed upon, he supposed, but he had read enough history to know nothing was ever as certain as it seemed when it came to nobles. He tried to recall the face of the woman who descended the carriage in the courtyard. He had not thought much on her, save for a few fleeting moments. Frankly, he had thought of little beyond just making it through the day, the minute.

She was tall. Shorn head. He thought he saw dark eyes under the elaborate decorative chains draped over her head. *That could be half the women in Ban.* He longed for someone whose every step and smile and thought he knew like the lines of veins in his own hand.

He was still in his bathrobe staring at the cheap wooden box on his desk when Daymir appeared in the doorway.

Fear and shame shot through his veins.

"We meet in half an hour. You were supposed to see An'thor with me an hour ago to prepare."

"I know." Keplan's voice was a rasp against stone. "I'm sorry, I just—" He shook his head. How could he explain that every time he tried to move, his body seemed too weak to rise, rooted to his chair and the tiny bubble of solitude he still had.

Daymir settled in the seat across the desk, tired eyes all too understanding. "That happens to me too. I'll follow a thought too far, watching the world turn beyond my window until it's nightfall and I've never even had my morning tea."

Keplan blinked. "But you still come back. You can still follow your trail back?"

Daymir frowned, gaze resting on the box.

Keplan glanced between the drug and his regent. If he scrambled to hide it now, all would be lost.

"I do, every time," he finally answered. "But sometimes when I do, it's not to this time. Or this place."

Keplan's nerves settled. "When I visit wherever it is my parents went, that I, too, can see, I'm not worried I won't come back. A bit, perhaps. I'm more worried that when I do, something will follow me."

Daymir nodded, gray hair bobbing. "It helps—when everything seems too heavy—to have something to return to. A reminder of why you're here. Why we need you here. When I was heir I had a shelf on my desk that held my seal, a letter from Her Majesty from decades before, and a few other trinkets. Those were my reminders." He jabbed a finger at the box. "The general keeps his reminders in a box like this too. More ornate, of course."

Keplan flushed. The contents of that box were not why he was here. They were not his reminder. He did not know what was. There was nothing he owned of Firas's, nothing even of his parents. Moly was sweet, but she was happily stabled by the barracks. "I'll try that, then."

Daymir rose with a low groan, wincing as his knees popped in protest. "And try being timely, Your Majesty," he suggested. "State affairs will happen regardless of whether you arrive on time or not, and you might as well get the ordeal over with."

The regent laughed at Keplan's grimace. "I'd hurry, too, if you want to look the part. The Banis are all about the ritual and performance, if I recall."

The door clicked shut behind him and Keplan retreated to the room beside his bedroom and opposite the privy. Brocade, a few silks, and several masses of delicate cotton hung along one side. The other held a dozen boots and shoes with carefully folded jackets and more traditional cloaks. He could not bring himself to look at the two outfits awaiting the ball this evening and the wedding. He rubbed his temples. How could he look a part he did not even feel?

Above, the bell tolled.

Φ

47th Day of Lumord, 1272

Keplan's borrowed euphoria lessened when he turned the corner to the meeting hall and collided with his future bride. She glanced from him to the two women beside her. Both were Banis and dressed in fine silks, but the older of the two wore a leather breastplate over her attire.

His nerves sang through the gentle comfort of dust, but the flickering images in his mind remained mostly peaceful. *I'm safe.* He forced what he hoped was a smile onto his face and bowed. "It appears we're both a bit tardy. Care to walk with me?"

The woman had yet to meet his eyes, her gaze fixed instead on the armored woman. He watched her hands form a flurry of motions. A second later the princess responded with a dozen new ones.

"That would be lovely," the armored woman said. "Thank you."

By the time Keplan formed his question in a way he hoped was neither awkward nor offensive, they had reached the meeting hall in silence. His titles were recited and he found his seat beside An'thoriend.

"How thoughtful of you to join us," the general hissed. "It's not as though our kingdom's future rests upon these discussions."

"It's not as if I can actually contribute," he whispered back under the guise of adjusting the fur hat on his head. "I'm just the mask you all wear to hide your actual faces."

An'thor glared but gave up the argument. "Now that His Majesty is able to join us, shall we begin?"

"Indeed." The heavily muscled man directly across from them leaned forward. "We appreciate you taking the time from your busy day to discuss these matters yourself, Your Majesty."

"Thank you for your patience," Keplan began in Trade. Between the constant drone of translation to and from Banis and the flurry of hands, scratching pens, and whispered conversations, his head was too busy to focus on anything beyond his native language. "As we discussed in our letters to your gracious empire, we are happy to offer an alliance in exchange for peace, trade goods, and continued correspondence and transparency."

"Sealed, of course, with the marriage between yourself and Kajimet Rih-elte, chosen daughter of His Esteemed

Excellence, His Eminence Emperor of Ban and the Jade Forest, Jamun-Ilta the Holy Emerald Throne, overseen by myself and Hand of the Empire, Vi-baln of RoBal and the Emerald Tier." The man who spoke was an ambassador, Keplan recalled, though the difference between his role and the larger iron-eyed man was lost on him.

Political hostages hidden under the title of marriage. He imaged the woman across the table from him felt as much a victim as he. Keplan faltered, realizing all eyes were on him to respond. None of this was rehearsed, not in the traditional sense, and even if it were, the lines fled his mind at the mettle behind the eyes of the Emperor's Hand. "I hope," he began, his voice emerging as a croak. He cleared his throat, but Daymir's hand pressed against his forearm, stalling any further floundering.

Daymir's smile was a flicker of light in the sea of tense frowns. "Indeed. And this meeting is simply a formality, one that allows us to smooth any issues and sign this alliance together, as a symbol of our nation's lasting friendship."

Vi-baln gestured for a small chest to be brought forward and opened. To Keplan's surprise it did not contain a mass of gems or precious metal, but scrolls. The Hand drew out each in turn, reading the official words detailing the Banis gifts to the Athrolani crown.

Keplan's thoughts barely focused on the lists of hunting dogs and war cats, of riches and one immaculately bred riah. How could Athrolan possibly compete with such wealth? Though none spoke of it, he knew he traded Athrolan in favor of security and peace. If Ban disliked a single step he took, the might of their empire would fall on his head.

A folded paper slid down the Athrolani side of the table from the Head of the House of Guilds. Keplan unfolded it and skimmed the words.

Correspondence mentioned grain.

Though the hills behind the palace were awash with brilliant leaves, the fields beyond were sullen. When Vi-baln next paused for breath, Keplan spoke up. "Our prior negotiations discussed grain from your fields. We cannot feed our people with gold or your horses—as fine as they are."

"Though we are honored by your generosity," An'thor interjected, shooting a sharp glance at the young king.

Color flamed on Vi-baln's cheeks. The tension around his mouth said it was from anger, not embarrassment. "It was decided that—given that our resources are focused on our army—wealth would suffice as a substitute."

"And the blight?"

Keplan winced. He did not have to be a political mastermind to realize admitting they struggled to feed their own people was a terrible tactic. "Our wheat suffered in the past few years. And I recall the fields of golden grain sweeping across the northern expanse of Ban. This is something we require."

The Banis ambassador whispered some rant in Vi-baln's ear. The Hand's gray eyes leveled on Keplan. Unwavering.

Keplan held the gaze, tilting his head to Admiral Fess. "Perhaps if I tried my hand at flirting with him?"

Fess's lips twitched. "Don't rule out that option. Our kingdom appears to be on the executioner's block."

"We will include a shipment of seed wheat of our strongest stock, on one condition," the man answered when the whispers had died. "Agree to war against Mirik's madwoman of a Hetmir."

No. Keplan's gloved hands curled into fists. He no longer cared about the polite dance or smiles that veiled teeth. "I'm hardly interested in antagonizing one of the oldest kingdoms this side of the continent." Keplan snapped.

Vi-baln's lips thinned. "Mirik may be old, but she is hardly strong. Our empire does not need your aid."

Euphoria fell away, followed by the thrum of energy that was not quite his own. Keplan scoffed. "I spent months embroiled in civil war. No one is interested in diving back into battle. Ban may make her money from bloodshed, but we do not."

"Then we are better at war than you." It was a bald threat, and Keplan bit back his next bitter words.

"We simply focus our economy elsewhere. We have the largest production of wool and timber. We've survived—and won—every war we've joined in the past century." He felt his mouth curl in a smile, but by the pinched expression on the Banis faces, it was not a friendly one. "The most recent of which was against the gods themselves."

"Banis forces joined you in that, and if I recall it was not Athrolan that won that war."

"No. But it was my blood." The room fell silent. Pens no longer scratched parchment. Keplan laced his fingers together and peered at the Hand. "Your emperor may claim divine blood, but I'm the only one who can prove it. Perhaps Athrolan is not what she once was. Perhaps you boast more gold and wheat and bodies and bloodthirsty plots. But there are a thousand terrible truths in my mind alone, and I promise neither you nor your emperor wishes to test them."

The ambassador's jaw worked as he ran figures and tallies in his mind. An appraising look tempered the chill of the Hand's eyes.

The voice was the princess's guard, but the words were Rih's and her eyes pinned him. "I understand you hope to maintain peace for the beginning of your reign. Ban respects that. However, we are at war ourselves. Our war machines need building. Our soldiers need clothing. You mentioned timber and wool."

"I did. Oak would build you machines. Mutton and wool from our flocks would aid your army." Keplan dared not risk a look to An'thor to confirm before barreling onward. "We have access to Nenev technology in the mind of our own general, An'thoriend Domariigo from the ancient legends. Whatever he knows, we may share with you."

"Then we have peace." Vi-baln's deep voice cut off whatever Rih's interpreter began to say. "And an alliance to celebrate. I suggest a wedding at the turning of the month — it is the first day of the raining season in Ban, a time of fertility and health."

Keplan blanched, jaw clenched. "That's in three days."

"Indeed. The match is made, and our alliance secured." Vi-baln's eyes bored into his. "Waiting only gives time for mistakes."

Daymir glanced from the Emperor's Hand to the king. "Perhaps the twenty-fourth of Valemord. If you are able to stay for the next few weeks, I think it would give not only our bride and groom time to acclimate to one another, but our great nations would have time to enjoy each other's culture a bit more before you return. It's the first day of the harvest season here, which carries the same weight as the first day of your rains."

Vi-baln conferred quietly with Mosil, then nodded once. "A fitting day indeed."

The knot in Keplan's gut lessened only a little. Four weeks, three days, it was no matter. In the swell of voices and shuffling scrolls and papers to be signed, Rih caught Keplan's eye, head dipping in a tiny nod. Keplan did not trust Ban. He barely trusted his own general. But Rih's eyes were as calculating as his own. For whatever reason, she wanted peace as much as he. For the moment, that was enough.

Φ

Rih's door burst open an hour before sundown. Vi-baln's face was tight with rage as he strode across her parlor. Rih scrambled to her feet. Instinct shifted her weight onto her back foot, hidden by her skirts.

"What in the name of all the Holy Emperors were you thinking?" His mouth was wide in a roar, and spittle flew through the air between them. "You were not even supposed to attend negotiations, you were to stay here in your chambers until called for, until the pomp and frivolity of the ball this evening. A wife has no place in matters of state!"

Fear thrummed through her body, but on its tail burned something else. She gripped the back of her chair. If he came closer it would be her first and only defense. She barely understood a shouted word, but dared not take her eyes off his twisted face. In the low light of her room, the faint metallic green and gold paint on his chest and shoulders turned him sickly.

"What do you have to say for yourself?"

Bimet signed a few of his key phrases for her from where she hovered near the servants' entrance. Nehla was nowhere to be seen.

Rih's resolve trembled in her spine. "I was thinking we needed a compromise, and they would accept it better from the woman they will see every day. I was thinking His Eminence sent us here for negotiations," even as she signed her fingers were closer to claws, "and not a declaration of war."

"You presume to know what His Eminence thinks?"

"Was I wrong?" It was not a question, and she prayed the bitterness in her eyes told him as much.

His mouth moved, a hawk panting in the heat. Then his jaw snapped shut, muscles working. When he spoke again it was conversational enough for her to read his lips. "You would do well to remember your station. Even here.

Especially here. They may let their common folk cavort with the nobles and let a pauper sit the throne, but that is not how order is maintained. You know that. An empire cannot rule that way."

She saw a glimmer of an excuse and seized it. "I thought if they trusted me, if they saw me as an ally first, then we would be that much closer."

"Closer to what?"

She glanced at Bimet, but her translator's wide eyes were fixed on the Emperor's Hand. "Controlling the boy king. Is that not His Eminence's plan? When we are no longer distracted by Mirik?"

Vi-baln's gaze turned thoughtful, and his finger traced the butt of the decorative atlatl hanging from his sash. "Regardless," he finally stated, "you have been insubordinate and irreverent. To Ambassador Mosil and to me, and therefore by extension, His Eminence."

A chill sank into her bones. Cold control was terrifying compared to shouted rage. She dipped her head. "Forgive me. I only sought to serve."

His hand was hot under her chin as he lifted it, turned her face one way then another. Searching for cracks, perhaps, clues as to what might lie beneath the layers of muscle and skin. "I know your kind. And I've broken countless people like you. You might sit as consort to a king here, but until I return to our capital, I have you in my sights." He stepped away then and paused by the door. "I'll see you at the ball."

When he had left, Rih collapsed into the chair, shaking. *Weeks.* She had hoped to get the wedding over with and send her entourage back to RoBal. Instead they were here for another few weeks. *Weeks under his bitter eyes.*

"That was too close, Your Highness," Bimet signed, fingers flying in her checked panic.

Rih shook her head. "He doesn't know. He thinks he does, but he has no idea. Not truly."

"You can't know that. You ought to focus on your role here for a time. Let the prairie dust settle."

Nehla appeared from the servants' stairs, glancing between the two of them. "What is it?"

"Vi-baln, he came to reprimand me. I think he suspects —" Rih began. A step behind the younger serving woman, Bimet shook her head once, sharply. Rih shrugged. "I spoke out of turn."

Nehla's dark eyes softened and she knelt at Rih's feet. "This isn't an easy time for any of us. Even a glimmer of hope can't be trusted. I often found it hard to navigate different courts' protocols."

What do you mean by hope? Rih forced herself to her feet. "I ought to get ready for this ball."

Nehla's expression brightened and she almost skipped to the dressing room that someone had filled with her trunks' contents during negotiations.

Bimet glanced at Rih, amused. "She just said, 'You must be excited.'"

Rih snorted, following the younger woman. "Hardly. I've never been to one, not since I snuck into them as a child with the other palace children."

Nehla launched into a rapid recounting of her last ball, one in a small city on Ban's western coast. There were hanging glass globes, if Rih understood Bimet's translations, hastily signed between gathering silks and sashes.

A wave of homesickness washed over Rih. Except she did not miss RoBal. She did not miss the barracks, even. She missed Ki-etle's quick wit and determination. She missed Il-fald's faith, and the burgeoning community she had built in the Purple Throne.

Bimet was too cautious. Nehla was too new, not well known enough to trust with anything more trivial than palace gossip. Perhaps her translator was right, and she should keep her head low, stay her course until everything settled. Until Vi-baln's falcon eyes were safely in RoBal and off of her activities.

The bright mirror reflected Bimet's steady hands, her steady eyes, as she looped gemmed rings through Rih's piercings. Rih drew a breath. It would be struggle enough to survive the next few hours of dancing, introductions, and politics without rebellion on her mind. She squeezed her eyes shut. *Do not think the word "rebellion."*

Φ

"I'll never recall these names," Rih lamented. "The man in the alcove by the fountain. He stood beside the king and conferred with him. Is he a consulate?"

Nehla's painted lips curled in a smile. "That's Daymir Blackhouse, regent to the crown and former heir," she explained before taking a long sip of the punch. "Left the court abruptly after being disowned and stripped of all titles following an accusation of swindling and proposing marriage to the Dhoah' Laen."

Rih's brow shot upward at the last piece of information. She knew little about the Dhoah' Laen other than the stories they were all raised with. Still, those stories were not told with the wonder and excitement of legends, but the solemn reservation of a local folktale. It was too real, and those who lived it were still alive — some of them, at least.

"Can you imagine the hubris required to think you could marry Destruction?" She watched the old man's distant gaze follow the dancers about, disinterested, as if watching wind sweep over the prairie. "How was he allowed to return?"

"I heard it was required due to the civil war. It was the only thing that stopped the war."

Bimet's eyes were not following Nehla's colorful descriptions or her waving hands. Instead, they were narrowed on the other woman's face. She did not seem as entertained. A moment later, when Nehla disappeared to retrieve more punch, the translator glanced over at Rih. "Do you know her well?"

"No, hardly at all. Why do you ask?"

"She knows much about Athrolani court."

"That's why Mosil chose her, I believe. He felt she would help me learn these surroundings faster." Rih caught the pinching around Bimet's eyes and turned the question on her. "Do you know her?"

Bimet shook her head. "Only by name. Our herds are from different hills, if you will."

Rih nodded in response but did not press the matter further. Bimet's expression was not one of differing social circles. It was one of distrust. *I need caution as much as I need new allies.*

Bimet's hand pressed to her arm and the interpreter nodded her head in the direction of a young man. Rih turned, frowning. She barely had enough room in her head for remembering the steps to whatever dance she would be required to perform, let alone several dozen Athrolani names with their harsh sounds and arduous length.

"This is Azimir," she introduced.

Azimir offered his hand, a crooked smile adding warmth to his bow. Unlike most of the palace folk, his skin was a light brown and his eyes walnut.

"Just Azimir?"

His smile faltered, but he soldiered on. "Or Azi. Half the time I don't recognize the rest of it."

It was then that she realized he spoke Banis. Well. "I'm Rih-elte."

"Yes, I know. My wishes on your marriage." He nodded to the music. "Would you like to dance? Not sure if you like this tune, but I enjoy the faster ones."

"I'm Deaf," she noted.

His face fell, and his curved lips flapped with what looked like a sincere if halting apology.

She found a smile of her own. "So, I don't know if I like it either. But I'm a bit worried I'm not familiar enough with your dances for a fast one."

"It's easier to hide missteps when your feet skip." He spotted a tray of candied fruit passing and grabbed two from it. "But I'm wholly content to gorge myself if you'd rather wait for another."

She took the proffered food and tried a corner. Two candied kiwi slices sandwiched a spicy cured meat. *Southern Ban.* It was something adopted—or perhaps shared, now knowing their ancestry was one and the same—from the Vales.

"It's slower now, if you'd like," he noted, jerking a thumb at the musicians again.

She finished her food and, bracing herself, nodded.

His hand was light but sure on her ribs; the other found hers. After a moment she realized his twitching finger must be tapping out the song's beat for her.

He babbled on, and she understood an occasional word, but she swore at one point he lapsed into Athrolani. He did not seem to care, however, that she barely responded. And she found neither did she. It allowed her a slow wheel around the ballroom, time to memorize half-remembered names of those they passed. It afforded a moment of peace in the warmth. The thud of feet on marble was faint but echoed in her own steps.

"How much did you actually understand of that?"

"You mentioned the dome once, and seemed very animated about something involving a cow?"

"Toar, I'm sorry!" His head fell back as he laughed, swearing in Trade before returning to Banis. "No, I was curious about your horses. I'm an awful rider. I suppose I should have figured you'd be hard-pressed to understand me with all the moving and bouncing. I'll do better next time, promise you."

Even as he spoke she noticed he held her gaze better. Perhaps not all Athrolani were foul-tempered.

He was younger than her by a few years, but something in his easy smile and warm eyes made him seem both innocent and wise. "I'd offer to dance again, but it'd be selfish on your first night here, keeping you to myself."

She rolled her eyes, gesturing to the ballroom. "I hardly think I have a line awaiting me. But I feel far more on a level battlefield here. Food I can manage without much embarrassment."

"Ah, Your Highness," he fell in beside her, leading the way to the arrayed tables, "food is my specialty."

Φ

"These get worse with age," An'thor confided.

Fess snorted and knocked back another glass. "I disagree. When I was younger I had to work. I'll never miss the long nights as a page trying to sneak food and wine between platter runs." She shuddered. "You people never had pages? Squires?"

"Something similar, but we also never had balls. Requires far too much heat to make large rooms comfortable. Instead, we had game evenings, sporting festivals in the spring, when the snow retreated a bit. And we had hunting parties."

"The idea of sporting festivals—hundreds of you on the tundra—is ominous."

"And I didn't even tell you what our quarry was." It was his turn to snort. "As usual, we were mostly just bloodying up each other."

"The best part," Fess decided, "of having been to many of these is that I know all of the good hiding places and which food is honestly not worth the stomachache." She belched. "Or which drinks. Fates, I cannot stomach the sweet punch the way I used to."

An'thor's lip curled and he looked away. He disliked Fess's jovial nature, the cavalier tone she used even when speaking with her subordinates. She argued it made for better morale. *They won't listen when you give orders they don't agree with.* It was why the army and navy splintered when he and Raven were at odds. And war required distasteful orders. War itself was often a distasteful order.

A flash of royal turquoise caught the edge of his gaze, and his attention shifted from the jesting naval commander to an alcove across the room. Usually, the alcoves held tables and hidden instruments for smaller court proceedings or scribes recording audiences. Now they were filled with seats and cushions. Others were hung with plants he had never seen before. *Something from the Banis, then.* Soon, the delicate vines and fat, moist leaves would wither in Athrolan's crisp, salty air.

The color flashed between the waving fronds of some monstrous potted plant. "I've found our errant king," he interrupted Fess's analysis of her fruit pastry. Ignoring her frown, he shoved from the wall and slipped through the nearest service door.

The narrow servants' passage wound through the palace's thick walls with as many tiny rooms for those awaiting a ring for service as the rest of the palace had mosaics and broad halls. He dodged a frazzled page toting a tray of meat and trying to quickly swallow a bite without being caught. A turn, a set of stairs down, then up, and he found another door, marked with a tarnished plaque:

Xavier's Mount

He nudged it open, emerging between the large plant and a delicate fountain crafted in the shape of the former king's warhorse. The king sat on a bench to the right, almost as hidden as the door itself. "Kind of you to join us, this being your ball."

Keplan shot a glare at the general, but he did not seem taken aback. "It's hardly mine. Hers, maybe." He jerked his sharp chin in the direction of the Banis princess.

An'thor did not follow his gaze. "You need to dance with her. At least once. Others already have and if you wait much longer, the rumors won't cease until Midwinter."

"I'll give them something truly dramatic to whinge about."

An'thor glared. "I don't want to hear it."

"I don't dance."

"Neither did your father, but he took a turn around this very floor with your mother when she asked."

Keplan frowned at the embroidered hat in his hands. "He dances all the time at home. I suppose I did too, there and in the Slummer."

The ache in the boy's voice was contagious, and An'thor settled on the bench beside him. "I know what you mean. It's been decades since I danced. At least, somewhere where people could see."

"Somewhere other than someone's grave, you mean?" Keplan quipped. Perhaps it was the music, or perhaps he was too tired, but the barb lacked its usual bite.

An'thor turned to watch Rih stiffly following Azimir's graceful steps. "Ah, there's the first rumor now. I can already hear the street barkers that your boy-cousin sauntered in, manhood swinging, and claimed your bride's heart before you ever rehearsed your vows."

Keplan made a show of gagging at his choice of words. "I'll dance with her if it means you'll never speak like that again. Small wonder Dorcal turned cannons on you after listening to that for two decades. I doubt I'll last as long."

An'thor watched him edge around the room, stopped every few paces to accept a greeting or avoid another. The boy's tone was as joking as Fess's had been earlier while discussing her ale-sick. *But his eyes are colder than Nenev ice.*

War was familiar to An'thor, and to that end, he preferred it. He recognized it was ridiculous to be dissatisfied with the very peace he worked so hard to forge or with the king he forced upon the throne. *The king I killed for.* The dramatic thought was made ridiculous by the fact that he lost count of how many people he ended. Even with all his touted declarations that he understood madness, even facing Alea's own terrifying stare, his skin crawled when he looked upon her son.

He dumped the rest of his punch in the plant and retreated through the servants' door. This time the path included another two flights of stairs and a few quick strides across the gallants' hall.

"Official business. King's orders," he muttered to the guards flanking the door.

Neither spoke, but one shot the other a skeptical look as he unlocked the heavy oak. The foyer within was dimly lit and the room beyond even darker. An'thor flopped into a worn chair. Silence. He fished out his flask and took a small, slow sip.

"You come here just to brood?" Raven leaned on the bars installed in his former doorway. The only feature hollower than his cheeks were his eyes. "I know we've never been great at conversation, but my parlor seems an odd place to sit in silence."

An'thor chuckled. "Perhaps yours is the only company I can stand anymore."

"Because I know who you are better than any of them."

An'thor shrugged. It was a habit he picked up from Keplan, and not one becoming a legend. He did not care. "I'm worried."

"About what?"

"That you might have been right."

Raven's thick lips curled in a smile, but it did not seem to be a revelation that truly pleased him. "Go on."

"Keplan's clever, he's got the blood, got the vision — no pun intended — but he's unstable. He's young. He's not built to be king. The joy of a monarchy is usually the heir is of middle years by the time the king or queen dies." He glanced over. "Daymir would have been."

Raven sighed. "Don't walk that path, General. It's dangerous and speaks strongly of treason."

"Treason? You turned cannons on your own city. Is this how things will be? Any who speak out against him will be traitor?"

"It's how it's always been, An'thor. Why are you concerned now?"

"He's driving himself too hard. He rarely sleeps. I fear for him," An'thor confessed.

"Is he mad?" Raven's eyes were cold and level.

"He's always claimed that descriptor, surely, for himself."

"But is he truly? I know I hate his mother, his father, they scare the shite right out of me. I would die before I saw either one rule Athrolan. But even I wouldn't argue they were mad."

"I thought it was his power. Lightning and flames aside, his father heard the minds of others. His mother saw the world differently." The general rose, twirling his flask in his hand, eyes fixed on the tooled leather. "But as much as they were strange, we knew what they were. There's never been a creature like Keplan. Not in any history, not in any tale."

"Hasn't there?"

An'thor whirled. "What do you mean?"

Raven ran his blocky hand up the bars of his door then back down. "What other creatures knew men's fates? What other creatures saw the future, saw the past, as we see the present? It's something I've thought on a lot during my weeks in solitude. You might want to as well."

An'thor nodded, though his mind had long since left the conversation and whirled down a dozen dark paths. He let himself out without saying goodbye. The general's gut twisted. Creation and Destruction both had their costs. They all assumed the price would only be taken from Alea and her guard. *When you break the world, mend it again, there are going to be scars, big ones. Ones we didn't plan on.*

The Laen may have been the oldest, the Rakos the strongest. But the gods, the creatures created before humans, they were clever. Conniving. *Gods' Blood.* He locked his door, poured a drink, and knelt to rummage through his desk. The letter had almost been forgotten in the weeks following the coronation and was overshadowed completely by the Banis negotiations. He found the stack of mail from that week and flipped through it. The letter mentioning the One God was distinctive, written on old Berrin vellum. And it was not there. Perhaps he tucked it away in a drawer? Or a chest to not risk Keplan finding it. His glass was all but forgotten as he tore the desk apart. Next came the small box on his bookshelves. Usually it held a flask and a few secret correspondences, along with trinkets from the people whose lives he took in the Crown's name. His last letter from Eras rested in there beside a box of bullets from his revolver. But no fanatic's letter.

Perhaps it had been given to Keplan, perhaps it had been lost. Except An'thor did not lose things. "I'm the general!" His voice pitched off the stone of his room, skittering over the flagging like claws over ice. "I decide what he reads, what he's privy to. I keep him safe!" The iron toe of his boot dented the desk's wood and alcohol splattered over the surface. All the other chapters of his life were written, twisted out of truth decades ago. Athrolan's general was all he was now. He could not lose control, even to a boy. Even to the king he crowned.

CHAPTER THREE

49th Day of Lumord, 1272
The City of Ceir Athrolan, Athrolan

THE CEILING DRIPPED. KEPLAN blinked, watching the rust-stained droplet form, easing from the plaster, cold and fecund. It hovered a moment, then splattered across his brow. He giggled. His skin steamed with fever. The ache of alcohol in his skull had diminished after another small sniff of dust.

I promised myself only once a day. Only when I couldn't sleep. Only when I needed it. He needed it more than he realized. The evening before was a blur of colors and conversation. An'thor's jabs, his spin around the floor late in the evening, Fess as his partner. His laughter bubbled again. Fess was as terrible a dancer as he, especially when drunk. Sea legs made for poor waltzing.

Something else nagged at him, something beyond his fading ale-sick or the part of him screaming in panic that he could never turn back on this addictive path he currently skipped along.

I didn't dance with Rih. An'thor had ordered him to, but that was not the reason. Her eyes picked out every detail of his face. Surely, to try to read his words. It was not a courtier's careful analysis or a future bride's nervous curiosity. *She's sizing me up. A soldier in her ready stance.*

Thunderous knocking interrupted his musing, and he hollered for his guards to open the door. Belatedly, he realized his potential visitors could include the Banis ambassador or the Emperor's Hand. *Or Rih herself.*

Thankfully, the figure that stomped into his chamber was his general instead. "What's got you brooding now?"

Keplan glanced at him but refused to sit up. "I'm not brooding. I'm recovering."

An'thor's dark eyes took in the king's naked sprawl, following the dripping to the crack in the room's ceiling. "I'll have the head of household fetch the masons this afternoon. Kings shouldn't sleep under failing roofs."

Keplan shrugged. "Perhaps if the royal chambers hadn't been host to flies and rot, I'd not have to."

An'thor heaved a sigh. His shaking hands said that if he had begun drinking at all, it had not been enough. "Must you?"

Keplan smiled. "Why are you here? Other than to inspect my chamber walls."

"You're supposed to escort Her Highness Rih-elte about the palace gardens this morning. You have a quarter of an hour to be ready."

"Isn't it raining?" Keplan asked, frowning at the water stain rapidly growing over his ceiling.

An'thor followed his gaze silently, then cleared his throat. "No. And I don't believe that's water, Wardyn."

Keplan sat up with a groan once the man was gone, fingers wiping the liquid from his face. He rubbed it between his fingers. Water was not leaking from his ceiling. It was blood.

He shuddered and paced into the privy. Visions were one thing. Visions he could push aside as figments of his own disturbed imagination. If others saw them he could ignore them no longer. Blood stained his sheets. Leaked from his ceiling. Was it Peraan's? Perhaps, with nowhere left for their spirits to go, the dead stayed close, cluttered the air around the living until they, too, could no longer breathe.

Steaming water eased his muscles and washed away the offending red stains from his skin. Pinked by warmth, even his scars faded. By the time he emerged, his servants had laid out the outfit sewn for the day, made for slow movement and casual walking. He longed for a hike.

Dressed, with his hair tamed into a silver clasp and several colors of face paint on his features, he looked less like a dock urchin. He eyed the ceiling. It no longer dripped, though the crack remained. *Domariigo didn't seem concerned. Or surprised.* He supposed the man had done enough to have more than a few disturbing bloody visions of his own.

Φ

Rih pored over the negotiation transcripts stacked tidily on her desk. There were so many details that went into a simple agreement. An alliance, for all its frills, was nothing more than a wary handshake between travelers lost on the same prairie. *I won't hunt your grouse if you don't eat my gopher.* Except in this version of the metaphor, she noted, she was the grouse.

Nehla's hand slid across the desk, and when Rih looked up, she signed, "You look troubled."

Rih sighed. Was it worth telling her if Bimet did not trust her? She glanced at Bimet, whose steady gaze revealed little. "I'm just tired. Overwhelmed."

"I'd imagine," she answered with a nod. "I hope you'll have time to rest and get to know these halls soon. And surely you've begun to think about who you'll take into your entourage."

"I'm not sure they have the same ideas here. Cliques, it seems, but it seemed that most women in court have only one or two women who attend them," Rih observed. "Though I could use more friends. Perhaps Fess?"

Bimet's brows shot up, signing quickly, "I'm not sure befriending the naval commander is subtle."

Nehla followed the movements, frowning. "I ought to learn your signs, Your Highness. What was that?"

Bimet flashed a tense smile. "Just that perhaps His Eminence wouldn't approve of socializing much with the military."

Nehla sniffed, lips tightening slightly. "Not unless you informed on their every move, I suppose."

Rih appraised her lady in waiting. It was a pointed comment, one that would bring pain if overheard. *She's brave, at least.* Or perhaps, some friendship of Nehla's own gave her enough privilege to not risk punishment. *And that would make her far more dangerous.*

Both women turned to the door, Nehla bouncing up to answer whatever signal had been heard. The king waited in the hall, accompanied by half a dozen lesser nobles and the aforementioned commander. Nehla bowed and glanced back at Rih. "His Majesty is inviting you on a walk. In the gardens."

Rih rose, offering a bow of her own. "Of course, sire. Bimet, would you find my cloak?"

The translator obeyed, appearing a moment later with the garment. The layers of silk and cotton lent the illusion that she wore a sunrise over her shoulders, though the soft peaches and orange hardly accented the purple of her dress. Hoping he did not notice, she wrapped it around herself and took up a place beside him. Bimet walked a step in front, on his other side, so Rih might see her hands.

"I thought you might like to see how different our gardens are from yours. Our land is not as green, but we have some incredible trees." His gaze was distant, eyes seeming to look through her.

Was it she or he who was not quite there? Rih tried a false smile of her own. "I've never seen the Banis gardens either, though I hear they're stunning."

She glanced back at the others. If they listened in on the awkward conversation, they gave no hint, absorbed with some debate. A pang of jealousy shot through Rih's chest as one of the women laughed.

When she looked back, Keplan was watching her. "Can you hear at all?" It was a blunt question and would have been rude without the faint curiosity on his features.

"Not unless the sound is very loud and close. When one of my army sisters blew her whistle beside my ear once, I heard it. Sharp. High." She shrugged, not sure why she tried to describe a sound to someone who could hear it far better than she.

"Army? I thought you were a princess."

Heat flooded her cheeks. Was she supposed to lie? "Any unmarried woman serves the empire, either with her blood or with her body," she demurred.

He looked away but did not seem offended. He seemed not to feel much of anything at all. He seemed content to walk in silence as they stepped through a curved lattice and into a sloped garden. Large chunks of the white stone jutted from the ground, their tops covered with overflowing ivy and mosses. The air had the clear movement of running water. A sweet, biting scent rose with each step. She glanced down, working her slippers deeper into the dense, tiny leaves surrounding the small cobbles of the walkway. White trees with peeling curled bark dotted the slope, delicate branches a mimicry of the massive boles on the hills beyond the city.

They rounded a bend and Keplan whirled. His pale eyes went wide. Rih turned to follow his gaze. Guards and a number of men dressed in brown rushed down the path, arms waving, mouths agape in foreign shouts. Adrenaline ignited in Rih's limbs. She stilled, scanning the landscape. Were they running toward or from something? A snide voice in her mind remarked that this was not RoBal and Athrolan was not at war, but her heart refused to stop hammering.

Bimet's hand gripped her arm as she dragged her out of the way. "It's a dog!" she signed, laughing. "One of the hunting dogs we gifted the king."

Flashing golden fur disrupted the careful, tidy plantings. The animal raced upward toward them, massive paws ripping at the dry earth. Keplan was shouting something at her as he scrambled off the path. Then Rih's legs moved beneath her, skirts lifted in fists as she ran too. A dozen paces, a score, and she was at the nearest gate in the massive wall. Rih glanced back to see the guards gesturing at her, perhaps asking her to catch the creature or beware. She did not care. The animal's eyes were wide and white.

Her fingers found the wrought latch. It was a small door meant for gardeners and groundskeepers, but today, in a time of relative peace, it was unlocked. She pressed and flung the door wide. A rush of golden fur and slaver burst past and then the dog was free.

Rih followed, thighs burning after disuse. Up they ran, past the gouged earth from decades of war, up toward the spindling fingers of white trees. The animal raced in circles, hindquarters bunching as she wove through the grasses, through the trunks. A laugh welled in Rih's throat and she let it free, clapping her hands with each round the dog made. A few more loops and she trotted to a halt. Still the dog's eyes were wide and white. Still Rih's chest heaved, but it was filled with fresh air and, like the dog, her teeth were bared, but now in mirth.

She crouched, hand out. In Ban she often worked with hunting dogs, albeit those trained to hunt people. Still prey was prey, and the commands were the same. "Here," she signaled.

Tail wafting, he approached and sat. Rih ran a gentle hand down the sleek flank and noted absently that the dog had birthed at least one litter within the last year. "Pretty girl," she signed.

Bimet finally caught up to her, eyes crinkled with mirth that she kept, with some success, from becoming an actual smile.

The guards arrived panting a moment later, far less amused. One spoke in Trade, his gestures making it clear he was complaining.

"She was just having fun. We're used to dogs in our city," Bimet explained, signing for Rih's benefit as she spoke in Trade.

"Well she can care after the bitch then, if she's going to let it run about like a wild thing."

Rih's temper frayed. She disliked pulling rank, but if they insisted on speaking over her, she had no interest in manners. "You realize this creature was a gift from me to your king. Dogs are revered in Ban—second only to horses."

The guard, who sported an officer's sigil on his breast, pursed his lips and finally offered a bow. "Forgive me, Your Highness, I didn't think."

"Obviously," Rih retorted, rising. She commanded the dog to follow and moved back to the garden, heart pounding. It was odd to be obeyed, odd to be revered. *Perhaps that's how His Eminence began. A moment of control gone to seed.*

When she returned to them, Vi-baln was glaring but seemed to be unwilling to castigate her in public. Realizing the king might also disapprove of her actions, she turned to find him. Keplan was nowhere to be seen.

Fess's hand brushed her arm, and she mimed having indigestion.

Bimet asked a question, then turned to Rih. "She says His Majesty felt ill and hopes you'll forgive his sudden departure."

Rih frowned, eyes following the path he must have raced down to escape her as she rushed for the hills. "Of course," she answered.

Fess flashed a smile. "I've got to meet for training otherwise I would offer to walk the rest of the way with you. Perhaps another time."

Rih's curiosity flamed. "Training?"

"We've a little group that practices every other afternoon in the officers' hall," Fess explained.

"That sounds lovely!" After a second of biting her lip, she asked, "You said training halls—are they open to anyone? Or are there ones where I might be welcome?"

Fess's heavy shoulders bunched as she crossed her arms in consideration. "Aye. You train?"

"I was a soldier in His Eminence's army until this past year," she repeated, realizing the woman must have been talking over Bimet's translation earlier.

The commander's smile was honest now, and welcoming. "I'll ask the others today, but if they don't mind, why don't you meet us there next time. They're a nice bunch. Mostly. Sometimes our tongues are sharper than our blades nowadays."

Something greater than relief, than desperation burned through Rih's body. She ignored Bimet's signs detailing Vibaln's protests and bowed to the commander. "I'd be honored."

Φ

The 2nd Day of Valemord, 1272
The Village of Jai, Ban

"Peace!" Reka raised a hand to the guard at the top of the wall. She pushed the braids from her face, letting her take in the old scar and older tattoo. Her outfit was painstakingly devoid of green or vermillion. Still, her heart quickened. A moment passed, then the gate groaned open, just wide enough to permit her. She flashed a smile and slipped through.

A different guard met her on the other side, sliding the bolt home before fixing her with an invasive stare. "What's your business in Jai?"

"My cousin lives here. Ikel." Though not truly related by blood, the two were mistaken for cousins often enough as children. How different they had become that she was unrecognizable.

The guard narrowed his eyes on her tattoo again. "Ah. Border folk. She said you might be by. Monarak something?"

Reka laughed. "Monareka Elang — Reka."

"And you'll be staying how long?"

Until the revolution is won. "For a while. I find myself at a crossroads."

"Where did you ride —" He stopped himself, glancing down the long, dusty but horse-less road behind her. "Where did you travel from?"

"Athrolan, your newest allies. I picked up odd jobs there, but I'm looking for something more fulfilling now. And family."

He frowned at the obvious lines on her face, probably noting that she was well past the years of easy childbearing. "Family?"

"It's been a long time since I saw familiar faces, even in a trade city such as Ceir Athrolan."

"And the Mirikin Hetmir, you know her?"

I bore her children. "Much of what I remember of Mirik is from the Gods' War. I know of the Hetmir a bit—everyone does there, neighbors and all. I couldn't pick her face out of a crowd, though." Reka added a shrug for good measure. "I'm told she's tall."

He did not speak for a moment, eyes inching over her tattoo again.

Reka scratched lazily at the base of one of her braids, inspected her nails, then glanced back at him, unhurried. "Everything all right, sir?"

He nodded, seeming to force the gesture from his distrusting body. "Seems so. Can't be too cautious with the war on. Mirik is everywhere."

How true. Reka made a face. "I'm hoping I can help with that problem, in time."

"Reka?" The voice broke through the guard's questions.

She turned, hand shielding her eyes against the sun-bleached road.

A figure raced through the humble market, people and hens scattering with disgruntled exclamations. Her cousin waved one hand, skirts gripped in the other fist. "Reka!"

Years washed from Reka's heart at the sight. For a moment the street was a mirror, a glimpse into a different life Reka may have led. "Ikel!" The raised hand turned from shield to wave.

Reka's laugh burst like a sob from within her, and her arms locked around her cousin's soft body. *Home.* It was not a sensation she was familiar with, not for a long while yet. "Fates, I missed you. I missed you so much, I forgot what it felt like."

"Oh…" Ikel's voice choked on the emotion and she pulled back, gaze alighting on Reka's scar, her faded tattoo, the myriad lines around her one blazing eye. "We missed you too."

We. In the two decades of her employment with Mirik, her friendship with Bren, there had never been a "we." A "me," surely, with all the complex emotions he could never seem to let go of and all the distance Kemmer forced from her own shame. But there had never been a "we," not since she left her father.

"If she's all through here, I'll sponsor her. In my house, of course," Ikel told the guard, glancing back at Reka. "She's family."

The guard waved them away, mouth a thin line. "Just be sure Jani's here 'fore dark."

"He'll be there early I'm sure, just to escape us two chattering grass squirrels as we recount our decades apart!"

Reka snorted. No matter what paths she took in life, she never thought of herself as a chattering grass squirrel. Her callouses pressed against different ones, but just as weathered, on Ikel's hand as they navigated the market. The lizard tattooed across the dun skin of her left cheek and brow had faded to brown and olive.

She would come back to peruse the wares and listen to gossip, but that would be tomorrow or the next day. "Jani's taken up a guard post? Last you wrote he was still working for the inn. Caravan guard for hire?"

"He was," her cousin agreed, shouldering a basket she must have dropped in her dash to greet Reka. "Not enough caravans to make a proper living. He was home half the days. And mind you, it was nice to have help with the children, but the man makes such a mess being home so much and gets underfoot worse than a litter of puppies."

Reka tried to take the basket to help, laughing at Ikel's determined wave.

"I'm not the one who walked here from another kingdom." The lines of her smile tightened slightly. "Then the matet decreed everyone not a farmer or trader be put on the walls, guarding against Mirikin invasion."

"Fat lot it did. I'm walking right in," Reka muttered, scanning the town as they walked. Guards with non-issued weapons. Old spears, battered bearers. Ankle sandals instead of knee-high armor. Now she regretted not having a moment to find her bearing when she arrived. The signs of war were stark in a town this small. Half of the guards were male, it seemed, but whether that was from proximity to the border or necessity, Reka was not sure.

"Rek?"

She glanced over, realizing she had missed Ikel's last few comments. "I'm sorry, it's been a long walk. All of it, I suppose."

Ikel's fingers squeezed hers. "I'm sure. Let's get you settled." She drew up a moment later at a rel on the corner of a narrower road. Here the street was packed brown earth, not the tidy red cobbles from the marketplace. Poles jutted from the doorway's upper corner, woven grasses provided a sunscreen for the entrance. Someone had woven the fluffy tufts of the grasses into a symbol in the center. Reka tilted her head. It was an antelope. Smile renewed, she stepped down into the kitchen. The windows ringing the portion of the house that stood above ground let in soft, hot sun, filtered through stiff grass curtains. Reka closed her eyes and breathed. Baking. Warm earth. Buzzing insects. A faint crackle rose from the fire in the deep central pit when Ikel shoved a pan into the coals.

When Reka opened her eyes again, a young boy stood in the doorway, tugging on one earlobe. He stopped the moment his mother glanced up from the hearth, hand disappearing into a pocket.

"Who're you?"

"Kas, don't be rude. I told you your aunt would be here soon. This is Reka. Our mothers were sisters."

Reka raised a casual hand. She never knew how to deal with children. They were like horses to her—both too knowing and oblivious at once. "Hello, Kas. Thanks for letting me stay."

He did not respond, so she turned back to the pan. "Haven't had Banis tea in a long while. Though it's becoming more popular in Athrolan now. Trends of fashion and food are subject to alliances as much as anything."

Ikel snorted. "Or perhaps it's just better than that bitter dirty water the Marbleheads drink."

Reka's brows rose at the slur. She loved the Athrolani as much as she loved anyone—that is to say not at all. But not because they were Athrolani. *People are not my favorite.* "Things haven't been easy?"

Ikel's gaze flicked to her son and then back to the tea. "There have been many travelers of late. Ones with information. Others with spears. It's why I wrote to you. Something is coming." She stirred the thick contents of the pan with a broad spoon. "Family ought to be here, lest we fall on different sides of these new walls."

Reka's nerves sparked at the words. She had not walked from Ceir Athrolan and every ally she knew to be on one or the other side of some metaphorical wall. "What have you heard?"

"Kahma wrote me, just a few weeks ago."

"Kahma? Kahma's coming?" Kas asked, bouncing on the balls of his bare feet.

Ikel's lips thinned. "Kahma is in the army, we don't know when we'll see her next. Why don't you go play with your sister?"

"She's weaving and told me I should go eat horseshite—"

"Then go play by yourself," she sighed, frowning as he disappeared deeper into the house. "And don't say that word!"

"Kahma? Someone from Jani's family?"

"His sister. We'll discuss it later, once little ears have gone to bed."

Reka laughed softly. "I don't know how you do that."

"Do what?"

"Deal with them. It's not something that ever interested me, parenthood."

"You never met someone," Ikel answered, as if it was the most obvious thing in the world.

"I've had people whose company I enjoyed more than some. Many even. Pleasure. Conversation. I just never," she shrugged, "fell. Never missed the lack of it, either."

Ikel hummed as if she did not quite believe her cousin, but pressed the matter no further. Instead, she tugged a drawer from the underside of one of the steps leading down to the hearth and pulled out two mugs. A handful of spices went into each, then she poured the pale, thick liquid over each before handing one to Reka.

The Spy Master inhaled the steam. *Lest we fall on different sides.* Had she made a choice against Mirik? Against Athrolan? She combed her fingers through her braids. *I'm not a traitor.* How could one be a traitor if they walked into their employer's study and demanded leave? And he was an ambassador, not the hetmir—he had not been hetmir in decades. *Besdies, I'm not even Mirikin.* She was not sure what she was. The Border nations were all but dissolved, split by the new borders of empires and kingdoms, scattered from past wars, married into a dozen other cultures.

"You all right?"

"Feeling a bit..." She searched for the word. "Lost? Uprooted, I suppose."

"'My blood is the river, carrying my feet across mountains.'" It was an old Border saying, one that spoke to their staunch belief that choice and change were inherent.

"I've let my blood stagnate. I need to remember its pulse and flow."

"Is that why you're here?"

"You wrote me a letter."

"I know why I invited you. Doesn't tell me why you accepted. I thought I'd have to wait a year, two, even, to see your face. You're always speaking of how busy you are, how your jobs take you far and wide."

"Hardly. I mostly roam between cities. Finding people. Losing others." She thought of Hylier and his earnest trust in Daymir, in the order of good and evil. "Making friends."

"And you were able to just leave, you must have high standing."

Reka knew Ikel's verbal fishing was out of love and concern, but Reka disliked being on the receiving side of questioning. Empathy flashed for all the people she wheedled for information. "I suppose. My employer is trusting, sometimes to the point of ignorance. I told him I had a job here, following information. By the time he realizes my reports have stopped, my trail will be long cold."

"What else, then? Beyond work or war?" Ikel settled beside her, hands working on a loaf that must be for their dinner later. Always busy. Always a task. Reka took the bowl of dough from her and began to knead.

Ikel's smile softened and she pulled down dried roots to chop.

Reka had not thought much beyond either work or war in a long while. Five years of living in Mirik, in the small town across the island. Her body, pregnant and full and aching in places she hoped she had not had, was not hers. Meat. "I don't know who I am without work and war."

"You're performing the ruak."

Reka snorted. "Hardly."

"Aren't you though? You've gone so long without yourself, you must reclaim them or declare your new true self. And so long without your people too. You don't recognize it."

"I've never not been me, this sack of bones and blood," Reka protested. She had always been so sure of who she was that the ruak—a rite of transition into a new role or identity— had never seemed necessary.

"What you are changes. New water and stone dust have replaced the blood and bone of you. You're the same—ever changing."

"You're like a library," Reka countered with a smile. "All your thoughts sound pretty but there are many. I don't always agree with them and rarely do they agree with each other." Reka smirked. "That's if I read them at all."

"Just think about it." Ikel swatted at her. "I'm happy you're home."

"I'm happy you're my home."

Φ

The 2nd Day of Valemord, 1272
The City of Ceir Athrolan

The room was large and open, taller than Rih was used to. The variety of weapons was exciting, if only because some were unfamiliar to her. A dozen target quintins lined the back wall, and another room to the left held grappling mats and ropes and walls for climbing. Two men already sparred in there.

Fess's invitation had mentioned a main training hall, but it was unclear which that meant. She glanced back at Bimet, who shrugged.

"I hear women's voices in the next room."

Rih followed her across the sawdusted floor to another broad, open doorway. Fess glanced up from her seat on a bench and waved. When she had finished lacing her soft training boots, she jogged over.

"I'm glad you're joining us." The commander jerked her sharp chin at the men on the mats. "That's Pomodan—the blond—and Jep. Pomo's captain of the guard in the Silver Apron. His partner, there, is the Lord Provost Qaral. Menna and Colonel Curiel are the women by the wrestling rack most interested in drinking their tea."

Rih laughed, and the women glanced over. One raised a hand, the other a skeptical eyebrow. Rih felt heat in her cheeks but steeled herself and went over. "Good morning. Commander Fess was kind enough to invite me to your training session." She offered her arm in the Eastern casual greeting. When they didn't take it, she added a few signs. "You can call me Rih."

The woman who waved took the hand and turned to the translator. "Tell her I say hello and she can call me Curiel."

Bimet smiled patiently. "Just speak to her, like you would anyone else. I'll do the rest."

Curiel's pale cheeks flushed red, and she looked back to Rih. "I'm sorry, that was probably rude. We're not so used to…ah, differences, in the military here."

Rih glanced at the entirely white faces and able bodies and smiled. "I gathered." She turned to the other woman. "You're Menna?"

The woman glanced at Rih's hand as if it was covered in horse dung and turned back to her friend. "Why don't we practice riding? Somewhere where the air is fresh."

Curiel winced. "Maybe later. You can ride alone—I could really stand to practice my grappling. Shoulder's finally feeling better."

All pretense of polite conversation disintegrated. "How can you? How can you practice war with their queen, their figurehead? She's brought nothing but pain to this city!" Menna's gestures flew wildly, composure broken. "She'll bring nothing but death!"

Sawdust puffed in the wake of the door, and no one seemed willing to speak.

Rih's nerves hummed, burning in preparation of violence. *But I was invited.*

Curiel's expression wavered between strained and awkward. "Perhaps just give her time. I know Menna. Her words, though cruel, are often taken back when she's had some time to think."

Rih did not feel particularly charitable. "I will still practice here, as this is my home."

"No one's asking you to leave, Rih," Fess offered. "I'm sorry for Menna. She's a good woman, just hard sometimes."

Rih's hands tightened on the case of her atlatl. "I know many women like that—more concerned with tearing one another down for the coveted favor of men. Most of those I know, those I call my friends, know that's not how we succeed. It's how we lose."

"I think it has more to do with you being Banis," Curiel hazarded, rising to follow them to the benches to don her training vest.

"I wondered. In Ban we have soldiers from all over our empire, all shades of brown and white and black." She flashed a bitter grin, setting her case on the bench. "All equally crushed under the officers' sandals."

Rih knelt to unclip the latches on the wooden box and flipped the lid open. She hoped the conversation would veer from justifying Menna's words in an attempt to comfort her.

Someone knelt in the sawdust beside her. It was Fess. "I've never had the chance to see one up close."

Rih lifted the atlatl from the formed silk and slid away the covering. "This one is new to me. My practice ones were a bit lighter. I admit, I'm far from a master."

"What is your best weapon?"

"The spear. But I promised my teacher I'd practice, so though she might not be watching over my shoulder now, I imagine if I ever see her again it will be the first thing she asks." Rih grinned. "And I've never been good at lying to her."

The atlatl was heavy and smooth, the wood polished rather than worn. The grip was bound with leather, rough side up to help her grip. Copper rings bound each end of the grip, the one at the very base bearing a ring for emblems of luck or prowess. Rih fingered it, wondering what she might bind there. The darts were massive, a hand-span longer than those she was used to. *A proper war dart.* If they only knew they had sent the leader of a rebellion away, unsupervised, with such a weapon. It lessened the sting of Menna's racism.

Curiel's fingers flexed as she observed the beautiful weapon. She glanced at the door where Menna had disappeared. "Perhaps one day you could teach me?"

"I'd like to." Rih bit her lip. "Maybe in turn you could show me the grappling."

Φ

The 13th Day of Valemord, 1272

Incense and the faint odor of tepid tea filled the throne room. The walls were wheeled back into place, shrinking the room to the usual size. Even with the velvet cushions, the throne was dark, and the stone bit into his thin legs until they tingled. He shifted, hoping his expression of vague interest did not slip.

"What can we do, Your Majesty?" the farmer at his feet asked.

Keplan gnawed on his lip. He had not heard the last few lines the man said. *Something about crops and blight.* "Our growing friendship with Ban offers a solution to the blight, Master—" He glanced at the herald standing by the dais's edge.

"Master Wimsen, sire," the boy whispered.

"Master Wimsen. By next spring we will be planting Banis wheat in place of our own weaker crop."

"Banis wheat is fine, sire, but what about this winter—"

"I'm afraid His Majesty can only hear one concern apiece during each audience, Master Wimsen," Daymir interjected. "Please return, and we may have more answers and time to hear your further thoughts."

Keplan did not want further questions, but the man's concern nagged at him. *What about this winter?* He could barely think beyond the next few days, let alone an entire season away. *In that time your kingdom may be on the brink of starvation.* The bright light lancing through the glass dome belied the mercurial weather, but he felt the discord in his bones.

The man was ushered out and the throne room was finally quiet. Keplan pinched the bridge of his nose. His nerves spiraled into the trembling artificial adrenaline as the dust faded from his body. "Is that the last of them?"

Hylier shook his head. "I'm sorry, sire, there's another half hour before your audience ends. Just some discussion left."

"I expected the questions regarding Ban," the consulate noted, "but fates, I hoped they would involve more about what we'd gain and less…" she faltered.

"Blatant hate?" Keplan supplied, flipping through the pages of his personal notes scattered on his lap desk.

Daymir hummed in agreement. "Even if we don't have the knowledge to address the issue now, that last man raised a fair point about winter."

A commotion rose in the hall and Keplan's nerves sang. His memory flashed with images from his coronation, the crown new and heavy on his head. His ears still rang with the sharp smacks. He blinked. His gaze fell to An'thor's hip and the weapon that rested there. The general picked filth from under his cracked yellow nails. Guards still argued in the hall.

The consulates petered into silence, giving up the pretense that nothing happened outside the double doors.

"It's an open audience! I demand my right at audience!"

"Mistress—"

"I'm a 'miss,' you sorry sack of pigshit!"

Keplan bit back a giggle, ignoring Daymir's sharp glare. He enjoyed a good barb.

"Miss, then," even through the door his voice dripped frustration, "you will need to compose yourself prior to going before His Majesty the King—"

The doors slammed open. A woman burst in, face swollen and red from weeping.

Hylier's hand dropped to his sword, stepping down from the dais.

She staggered forward, falling to her knees before Keplan. "Your Majesty, please! My friend, my beautiful patriot of a man, was cut down in cold blood, and you refuse to do a thing. A thing!"

The barmaid. Even through the mask of grief, Keplan recognized her harsh features. Distaste billowed in his gut. "You mean the traitor Peraan?"

"He weren't a traitor!" Her whole body shook.

If dust left Keplan capable of empathy, he might have pitied her. Instead, his pen sketched the frazzled lines of her hair, the wrinkles at the corners of her bloodshot eyes. He added a mole for dramatic effect, though upon glancing up he realized she did indeed sport a beauty mark just below her left eye.

"Why won't you do something? He was an honorable man, one who dreamt of better for us, just as you claim to."

A boot nudged his sharply beneath the table, and he forced himself to focus. "What do you propose we do, miss? We're recovering from a war—a war your Peraan figure-headed, I might add. In war people die. We extend our condolences, but we are in the midst of negotiations and heading into summer with hardly anything to show for our fields' harvest. Your friend's murder is hardly our first priority."

Rih leaned forward, hands flashing several signs. Until that moment, she had been still, learning only. Her translator quickly rose. "Your Majesty, we offer our tracking dogs, skilled in hunting not just game, but human marks as well. Murder on your streets is hardly the way to begin an alliance, let alone a time of peace."

Dogs? Keplan opened his mouth to reply.

"The scent is surely gone," Hylier interjected, "with all the smells in the city. I hope with our continued relationship with Ban, our guards can learn to use tracking dogs, however."

The woman's eyes narrowed on him. "I know you! I know your face!"

"Of course you do, I'm the one Peraan spoke out against. And your king." Panic fanned the flames of Keplan's temper, and he waved for them to escort the woman away.

Daymir leaned forward. "A guard will take your statement, and if we have further news, we will request to see you during our next audience in three days."

"Two days, Your Highness," Hylier whispered.

"Two days from now," he corrected himself.

Keplan watched them escort her out, barely hearing her continued screaming. He could not marry the man she spoke of with the fleshy face he watched life flee from under his own hands. His stomach clenched.

"Sire," Fess leaned forward, "I know she's grief-stricken, but murder in the city is a bit much to ignore—especially someone as influential as Peraan."

Keplan's gaze flicked to her. "He was a pile of horseshite and we all know it. Influence or not. Before I ascended, I had the misfortune of crossing his path not once but twice. Whoever killed the man did us a favor."

"That may be, but retaliation might be a concern." Hylier's voice was low, and the stare he fixed Keplan with was heavy. "The city might be busy investigating other things, and rightfully so, but perhaps a double guard until we determine how far Peraan's influence reached."

"You seem to have a fair idea of his group, Captain," Keplan countered, failing to keep the taunting edge from his voice. "Report back in a week on the Peraan situation—both his actions and the end he very much deserved to meet."

Hylier's bow was sharp, and he did not wait to be dismissed before stalking from the room.

"I'm not certain this meeting is getting us anywhere." The Head of the House of Nobles sighed. "My reports from the Western Provinces aren't good either. Their farmers who were able to plant the Banis seed still struggle. Their fields were slow to sprout. At this rate we'll be harvesting at least two weeks late. More, I fear."

Political intrigue was his bane, but crops and gardening he knew. "Late? I thought the Banis wheat was immune to the blight. Or resistant to it, at the least."

The Consul of Agriculture rubbed a hand over their weary face. "Blight's not the issue now. Banis wheat is used to long, hot days. Little rain. Even in the west, where it's warmer, we've had nothing but clouds and wind since you ascended the throne, sire."

Keplan faltered. *It strangles the world.* "This isn't just an Athrolani problem, is it?"

They shrugged. "I can hardly know. We could ask our allied neighbors, but I would advise against it. While we've enjoyed a few decades of peace with Berr and far longer with Sunam, showing how poor our current hand is would be a dangerous choice when we're already seen as so weak. One more political storm and Athrolan is finished."

Finished. Like most of his thoughts lately, it was fleeting but left fingerprints across his mind. Stains of every idea he no longer dwelled on cluttered his thoughts so thoroughly that nothing was clear. He could forsake love and safety and take a throne to prevent civil war and accept his bloodline and all its burdens to make a kingdom listen. Or he could breathe dust until his mind was quiet for a moment. But no one, save the gods, could change the weather.

"Wardyn!"

He blinked and looked up.

An'thor's black eyes bored into him. "If you're too distracted to focus on your kingdom starving, then perhaps you ought to leave the decisions to us."

"If you're so impatient that you won't allow me to think of a solution, perhaps you're not fit to be a general," Keplan snapped back. Tension rolled over him, and Fess heaved a sigh.

One of the commissioners rolled their eyes.

Honesty. "You can tout my titanic blood all you wish, Dormariigo, but even I can't part the clouds and force the sun. I know our shipment is slated for next year. Did they plant all that was allotted them?"

"Each farmer was given a certain portion, based on their usual yield. It was our hope that in a year or two we could have crossbred the two species, but if we get too little yield, we'll be forced to grind every bit just to survive the winter."

Above the bells rang.

It was all Keplan could do to stay seated while they tolled. Once silence fell again, he rose. "I need to think on this. The Agricultural Guild should research the heartiest varieties—even those our neighbors plant. If keeping our people alive means displaying our poor hand, then so be it. Audience dismissed."

He stalked from the room, gloved hands clenched against the onslaught of other people's worry.

"Sire, we need to talk." Hylier fell in behind him, easily keeping pace with the king's frantic stride.

"I thought I told you to speak with the city guard."

"I thought we were a bit beyond that. She recognized you."

Keplan thanked the guard who opened his chamber door, then flung himself unceremoniously into his desk chair. His boots scattered dust and dirt across his audience notes. "It's not like they're going to believe her. Not against me, against a king." The world's heart thundered in his blood, underscored by his father's fire and his mother's freezing flood.

"You're not a king, not to them, not yet, not by an arrow's shot," Hylier growled. "She's a trusted member of the city, the Silver Apron at that, and she recognizes you—a man who used to frequent a number of ill-patroned bars and, by the way, still does. They're going to listen."

"So what if they do?" Keplan snapped. "I've got guards, an army, a horned psychopath who murdered a dozen people to get me here. I don't know why you needed to discuss this."

Hylier's face lost every ounce of his usual gentleness. "You doodled a portrait of a grieving woman while she wept at your feet, you monster!"

Laughter bubbled up Keplan's throat. It was not funny and he knew it, but his body was no longer his. Now, he only had to worry about gripping the reins of his petulant tongue. He clapped a gloved hand over his mouth. "I am a monster, aren't I? But Athrolan always knew it. Domariigo certainly did."

Hylier lunged across the room, stopping just short of Keplan's shaking body, chest heaving. "I've never wished you weren't king more than I do in this moment."

"So you could strike me?"

"So I thought Athrolan had a chance." He sagged against the desk, rubbing exhausted eyes. "I'm your informant, your captain. I am not your maid to tidy the bloody mess you left in your wake."

"What do I pay you for, then?" Perhaps the buzzing in his blood was not fear but that of flies come to feast on his soul, his empathy long dead, rotting where his heart should be. The buzzing kept him from mirrors, kept him from anything that might expose the truth. *He's right, though.*

When his mouth opened again, he swore the voice was not his. Perhaps the one before had not been his, and this one was the echo of the Slummer bar boy. "Hylier, she's is not the only one grieving. I lost a friend. One of the only ones I've had. I lost someone who took me in not in spite of what I am, but because of it. Even though my sheer presence put her business in danger. Cost her patrons. Cost her life. So forgive me if I can't find a shred of mercy in my heart for someone who sheltered Mirrel's murderer. You know how I knew it was Peraan?"

"Because it's obvious, because you saw the list I left for you?"

"I only saw that when I returned. I knew because I went into that courtyard, pressed my hand into her bloodstains and lived her death until I recognized Peraan's face." Keplan staggered to the bookshelf, hand resting on the box that held the dust. *Fates, the feelings are loud today.* "Now, tell me again that I'm a monster."

Hylier had the grace to blush, though his pale skin turned every change of emotion into pinked cheeks. "I see your point. But mine still stands true. Two truths may be at once, sire. You've ended civil war. You've allied with Ban. You've planned to marry. And you've murdered. All in the name of peace. But, sire, when you're king, peace begins with you."

Keplan looked away. "Have you told anyone? Anyone about this?"

"Fates, no. I gave you his name. I gave you evidence of his intent. I burned your bloody clothes. At this point I'm almost as culpable as you."

Keplan's pale eyes flicked to Hylier's blue ones and he felt a smile flit across his face. "Monster."

Hylier heaved a sigh. "I'm meeting with Daymir this afternoon, and I'll see what others think of the accusation. If I think of something—something other than framing an innocent person or outright murdering the woman—then I'll tell you. Because, sire, neither of those are options."

"Come to me tomorrow night, then. Perhaps both of us can find a solution." Keplan looked away, listening to the door slam behind his informant. Murder was the easiest solution. The shred of himself he still recognized knew it was not an option. But at this moment he could hear nothing over the sound of a thousand thoughts and something he might have called shame.

CHAPTER FOUR

The 20th Day of Valemord, 1272
The City of Ceir Athrolan, Athrolan

"I WAS WONDERING IF I'd have to drag you down from the rooftop myself," Daymir remarked, taking in the king's windblown hair. "Your father liked them too."

Keplan rolled his eyes. "I'll have to find another hiding spot, then."

"Hylier tracked you to the slums, I'm sure he can find you again."

"Except I dole out his purse now." Keplan dropped into one of the chairs at the regent's broad desk. "What's first here?"

"An official notice of investigation from Inspector Greton, a missive from Fort Shadow, a dozen invitations to noble dinners and dances and a request for a private audience," Daymir rattled off.

"Fort Shadow?" Keplan leaned forward to get a better glimpse of the map lacquered to the top of Daymir's desk. "Which one's that?"

Daymir shook his head with a wince. "Ah, Fort Godbane, rather. Built on the site of the Athrolani camp during the siege of Fort Shadow. Old warhorses, new commands and all that."

Keplan did not answer, but something in the regent's gray eyes told him remarking on the slip would be a mistake. "Of course."

He pushed aside the invitations. "Mind looking these over? I'm not as well versed in who has influence here."

"I've been exiled for two decades, Wardyn, you think I know any better? Influence can change overnight. I'm proof of that." Daymir tugged the stack over, glancing at a few names. "I didn't even know Lord Tevon had a daughter."

"She was supposed to take the throne instead of me," Keplan muttered. "Maybe I'll ask her if she'll reconsider over dinner." He skimmed the investigator's report, then folded it into his pocket. They had yet to find the bag Keplan dropped in the gutter. *Some slum-rat probably ran off with it.* If they did find it, however, it could lead them to the dust dealer. Something told him even the man's drug-addled mind would recall a scarred face if enough coin were offered.

"News of that man — Peraan?"

"Little. I guess someone came forward having seen something, testimony scheduled in a few days." Keplan groaned. "I'd hoped to avoid starting my reign with murder."

Godbane's missive stated little else than reports of Mirikin and Banis skirmishes just across the border. They requested more grain, which Keplan denied and signed with a pang. "Is that it?"

"Audience request." Daymir handed it to him without looking up from the invitation he was drafting.

Nena'phe lui Hiral.

Even written in innocuous scribe's script, the name sent a twinge of apprehension up his spine. "It's an asai name."

"I heard they all retreated to the Northlands with their cousins," Daymir remarked. "Other than the general, I met very few. Not the friendliest, I've heard."

"Then let's hope this one's different."

He slit open the seal of the palace heraldry and leaned back to read.

> *Your Majesty King Keplan Wardyn of the Heartland and the Topin Hills*
>
> *We were honored at the response from your regent, His Highness Lord Daymir. I now humbly ask for an audience with you to discuss our prophet's news. I know when you hear her words you, too, will understand the might of the One True God's power."*

"Fates, what is this?" Keplan whispered. When Daymir glanced up, he repeated the words aloud.

Daymir did not respond. Instead, he drew a thick sheet of vellum from his desk and slid it over to the king. Then he moved to stand before the window, hands clasped before him. His eyes were distant. "This comes at an inconvenient time."

"Inconvenient?" Keplan glanced at the letter but could not bring himself to touch it. "You replied. To a letter I never saw."

"Read it. Then I will ask forgiveness."

Even through the thin silk of his gloves, the vellum irritated his fingers. With the creeping itch came images of a dozen monarchs, warlords, even the Banis emperor himself unfolding similar letters, scanning the same heretical words. Even through the dread, he found himself scoffing at the final paragraph. "'The Dhoah' Laen herself—' they think I won't know where my own mother is?"

Daymir's gaze skittered from the window to the door. "They aren't wrong, Your Majesty."

"You invited heretics into my kingdom!" he bellowed.

"Athrolan needs order, structure, especially following a civil war." Daymir straightened then, an echo of his former presence, but imposing nonetheless. "I hardly think you can call them heretics when their prophets share your visions. Your mother's visions."

"My mother's—" Keplan whirled. "One true god? She ripped the souls from the gods' chests. Only a madman calls himself a prophet, but not even I've stooped so low."

"The general and I discussed it and planned on telling you when it became relevant. After the wedding. After negotiations. How could I explain that Alea crossed the kingdom looking for you and for answers?"

Keplan snarled and, letter gripped in his clammy glove, strode from the room. Daymir's exile years before was based on an attempt at swindling. Was this more of the same? Was this just a symptom of his own particular form of insanity? Daymir's confession of fading memory had been shared in confidence. *This was the only way to unite us. Unite the city.* An'thor was not to be trusted, but if every person in his government held a different secret it was only a matter of time before one brought the whole tremulous thing crashing down.

He pounded on the general's door.

It jerked open, black sclera tinged red with alcoholic bloodshot. "What?"

Keplan's whole body shook, mind torn between his own reality and the half a dozen others rampaging through his consciousness. "Is this a bad time?"

An'thor swayed, wiping spittle and wine from his mouth a moment too late. "Wardyn. I'm beginning to think there is never a good time to see you."

Keplan did not smile. He did not have the patience for An'thor's bitterness. *But no one has seen what he has.* "I need to speak with you. When you're—" he stopped himself from implying there ever was a time the man was sober, "not busy."

An'thor shoved his door open wider but made no other move.

Keplan edged around him. The room was in disarray. Papers and letters littered the floor, and soot from the cold hearth stained the carpet in whatever manic path the general paced. He walked the same route now: hearth to window to desk to hearth.

Keplan settled on the broad window ledge. "I received a request for an audience. From someone who follows Orabon Marum of Tut Kunis."

An'thor glanced up, eyes sharpened but not surprised.

"So, you did know about the letter," Keplan noted. "And when were you thinking of informing me that fanatics were on my stoop? Or that my mother is apparently involved?"

An'thor's pacing slowed. He extended one pale hand. "May I?"

Keplan loosened his fingers, letting the vellum drop to the filthy floor.

If An'thor was bothered by the childish display, he had the fortitude not to comment. He stooped with a groan and scanned the letter.

"I find it absurd that you and Blackhouse conspired to bring these idiots to my kingdom. When did the first letter arrive?"

"A few days before the attempt on Azimir's life."

"Before Mirrel died, you mean," Keplan reminded.

"Exactly. You've not been exactly easy to find or speak with. Since the moment you wore the crown you've done nothing but avoid your duties—"

"Not the point," Keplan spat. "Why did you invite them here?"

An'thor sighed and slumped into his chair. "Honestly, I didn't. This was Daymir. Fates know why." An'thor's black eyes turned on his desk and the disarray across it. "I showed him the first letter. That's all. It was a brief discussion, mostly consisting of me scoffing at the idea of a prophet."

The fight left Keplan but the panic did not. "Why would he do this?"

"Best ask him."

Keplan looked down at his hands, not seeing the delicate fabric but the battered, stained palms beneath. "Were Tzatia's accusations against him true, then?"

"Doubtful, but the queen was scared. Too scared to see what he was actually doing or believe him. He's always been calculating but never cruel."

"And what about sane?" Keplan's words were a whisper.

An'thor stared at him. "That tastes a bit rich, coming from your mouth."

"Humor me."

An'thor shrugged. "He's old."

"Talk about rich—"

"Oh, piss off," An'thor continued. "He's not the same man he was decades ago. Honestly, though, we were never close. When I was in Athrolan before my exile, he was a child. Clever and occasionally petulant, like most children. Our time here during the Gods' War overlapped very briefly, and I was frankly distracted by your mother."

"So was he, if I recall."

An'thor grimaced. "I hardly had the same intentions. Your mother was pretty enough, but I'm not in the habit of courting monsters. Death, perhaps, but not monsters. Regardless of who wanted to tup your mother, Daymir's different. Withdrawn, maybe. I wrote it off to being alone for all those years. Is there something else I should know?"

Keplan was relieved to no longer be discussing his mother's suitors, but this was not a more comfortable turn of conversation. "I assume you remember his grandfather's last years."

"Better than most."

"He told me in confidence, in the bar in Marl Orna. It appears whatever took His Majesty King Xavier also has its claws in Blackhouse."

An'thor rubbed a pale, rough hand over his weathered face. He took a swig from his flask before sucking his teeth. "Well isn't that a fun new delight."

"Have some decency, Domariigo," Keplan muttered. "I wouldn't tell you except I'm afraid he's making choices while not...well."

"Choices including inviting this prophet's followers into Ceir Athrolan?"

"Exactly." Keplan steeled himself. "They mention my mother. Daymir said something about her visions. Last I knew she was still cloistered in the Hartland."

The general's pale hands shook as he found a large bottle under a pile of maps and took a swig. He offered it to Keplan, who shook his head. When it was stoppered again, he drew a breath. "That was the part I scoffed at. And the part Daymir proved right. Before he came here, before he slipped out of Manor Black to meet you, even, he received two visitors. Your parents. They left not long after you, it seemed. Searching for you and for answers. And, apparently, despite what the world feels like, her power hasn't waned. Whatever it is you both sense—and whatever this prophet spouts—is real."

"They're wrong, Domariigo. They have to be." Keplan dropped his head into his hands.

"Then let them come. Let them prove themselves wrong."

The floor trembled under Keplan's stiff boots. His stomach roiled at the thought. His parents had been doting, if protective. Playful, if occasionally preoccupied. Now he knew what tangled their thoughts. The idea of his mother, thin and pale, climbing the mountains between Tut Kunis and Marl Black ate at his heart. Any residual effects of dust were burned in the wake of worry. He finally met An'thor's eyes. "This is too much. How do you do it?"

"Do what?"

"Live. I'm staring down the bolt of this titanic crossbow, finding my own hand on the string more often than not. I don't know what I'm doing, other than I cannot fail. How do you do it?" he asked again. "No one survives as long as you, wins as much as you have, no one becomes a legend without some secret. How do you do it?"

"You don't want to be a legend."

"No, but my parents already made me one. How do you stomach it? I can't sleep. My body hums. My thoughts are quiet, but I can't sleep."

An'thor frowned at the wide eyes, the shaking hands. "You been drinking?"

Keplan's laugh rasped from his throat and he sank onto a bench. An'thor could not know about the dust. Far too many terrible secrets filled the palace. His entire path to the throne was littered with things best left hidden. "A bit."

"That's my secret," An'thor muttered. "But lately not even that helps."

Φ

The 24ᵗʰ of Valemord, 1272

Despite a long bath and Nehla's careful tending to her hands and head, Rih's nerves were raw. Only an hour stood between her and her wedding. She paced, still dressed in her loose dressing gown. With each turn past the door to her parlor, she caught sight of Nehla and Bimet holding some argument. Both had been dressed in their wedding finery for hours, their muted lavender and pink meant to accent the brilliant jewel tones of Rih's own attire.

It was bitterly cold, as if the Athrolani winter decided to wrap her in its arms as a sign of welcome. *Or warning.* Still, on her text trip by her balcony, she flung open the doors, letting the wind bite into her already goosefleshed skin. *Anything. I would give anything to feel something other than dread.*

Bimet's hand was almost hot against her chilled wrist. "Rih, it's time. We'll never get you into your gown if we don't start now."

She cast a pleading look at the interpreter.

"I'm sorry."

Rih glanced back. "Where's Nehla?"

"She's informing the glorious Vi-baln that you'll be ready shortly, but you needed a few more minutes to prepare yourself for the magnitude of marriage," Bimet explained, shutting the doors again.

"The magnitude of this mistake, you mean." She followed her into the dressing room.

"I told her to just wait, but she seemed to think it necessary."

"Is she his ally? Or just oblivious?" Rih dropped her gown, staring at the dress before her with nausea.

"It is hard to say." Bimet's hand was suddenly hard on hers, squeezing for a moment, then releasing to continue. "Don't trust anyone. Even here. Even when he's left. Trust no one."

"Except for you," Rih replied, trying for a smile.

Bimet did not return it, driving home the serious tone of her words. "We are all we have right now."

"I'm terrified after all of this he'll meet me at RoBal's gates in a horrific reveal, like 'blessed baniol' in tiles."

Bimet's face softened at the reference to their beloved game. "I doubt he plays well enough to hide so many moves from you. Even if he plays from the capital. Now, unless you plan on stunning the entire court with your physique, I suggest we get you dressed."

Soon layers of silk swathed her form. Her kalas was a rich plum, woven in a way that shimmered with blood red as she turned. The three wraps over it were varied from deep eggplant to the bright purple of prairie horsetail buds. Nehla reappeared in time to arrange her headdress. Black threads wove between the tiny silver links of her net, and the whole was decorated with garnets, amethysts, and feathers the color of dawn. A crimson sash cut across her waist in a fabric disembowelment.

"The piercings are a mistake," she worried.

Nehla frowned. "Why do you think that?"

"They're hardly Athrolani."

"You're hardly Athrolani," the serving woman replied, kneeling before Rih to help her into her slippers.

Rih searched Nehla's face, wondering whether the woman was just bantering or making an actual point. She so rarely spoke of anything serious, and this conversation was certainly one of the longest they had ever had.

When Rih did not respond, Nehla sat back on her heels. "You're not Athrolani. If you were there'd be no negotiation. There'd be no peace."

"I can't come here flaunting our culture."

"Why not? They have a general who has horns sprouting from his head. A boy king whose blood's hardly human. What does it matter if his bride sports a ring in her nose and wears colored silks?"

Rih wrinkled her nose. Though Bimet and Nehla were meticulous in arranging every fold and drape, it seemed as if the hour passed in a breath-span.

Mosil met her in the parlor. After glancing at her open door, he turned back. "You have conducted yourself with grace," he began. "These are not easy days, and I've been pleased by how well you navigate them. You do me honor. You do yourself honor."

She forced away the urge to respond that he had little to do with it. He was kind more often than he was cruel, and she had enemies enough. Her fingers laced with his for a moment before she stepped away. "Thank you. I've missed your counsel these past weeks, and I am sure I will miss it more when you've returned home."

He flashed a tired smile, and she wondered if the shadow Vi-baln cast over Mosil was as dark as the one over her.

Give me darts, give me a spear. Despite Nehla's reassurance and Mosil's kindness, her nerves were no better. Silks and rings felt as uncomfortable as any Athrolani attire. *Give me armor against whatever tonight brings.*

Φ

Keplan waited in the alcove, head in his hands. Writhing anxiety subsided with the coin-sized pile of dust he breathed an hour before. It did nothing for his churning gut. The throne room door stood open awaiting Rih's wedding procession, but the crowd had yet to settle. Musicians plucked a few strings, tightening others.

He glanced up as Daymir appeared in the alcove's entrance. "If you're going to wear your hair long, you could have pinned it back."

"…for fate's sake, deal with your hair!"

For a breath he pictured Firas stepping through the doors, like so many epic ballads. He would wear flowers in his beard, matching the yellow and green embroidery on his shirt. "Why don't you take my place, since you seem so ready to act without my input," he barked.

Daymir heaved a sigh. "I deserve that. You have to understand, Wardyn, I'm as out of my depth as you now. This is not my Athrolan. She's reeling. Listening to them can't hurt, and I doubt it's wise to anger zealots."

An'thor shot him a pointed look from his place just below the dais, and Keplan forced himself to his feet. "I doubt it's wise to entertain them, either."

He took up his place before the throne, the regent a step behind. A nod to the herald and the music began in earnest. Athrolan's emblem draped every wall, alternated with the gold Banis falcon on red and purple crest. A thick black carpet cut a swath through the crowd. Seemingly, the entire Athrolani court—or what remained of it—had come to witness the union. What space was left had been filled with the lesser nobles in the Banis entourage and the highest officers and wealthiest merchants.

Most had doffed their more somber mourning attire for bright colors—all save Keplan. Other than the cerulean stitching on his kosovorotka, his entire outfit was white. Even the fur trim around his hat was soft ermine.

Each member of the Banis entourage was announced, but it was all Keplan could do not to bolt past them. While he may have been the sole person in white, his future bride was a beacon of magenta.

Daymir spoke first, welcoming them to Athrolan, Keplan echoing his sentiments on behalf of the kingdom.

"We are honored to join Athrolan—a nation almost as old and mighty as our empire—in friendship, a bond symbolized by this union between Your Majesty and one of His Eminence's chosen daughters, the Kajimet Rih-elte."

The ambassador released her, ushering her up the stairs while the tablet bearing their vows was brought forward. The heavy wood bore the Athrolani wedding vows, and a piece of parchment with the Banis translation was pinned to the side.

If Keplan believed in gods—or anything at all—he would have thanked them that tradition decreed Rih make her oath first. It was harder to run when someone was already locked inside the cage they were about to share. She scanned the words, repeating them with steady hands.

Daymir turned to Keplan, tired eyes expectant.

"Today, before both our courts, I swear an oath as—" His voice cracked, dying in his throat. *It's this or war. Anything but war.* "As your king and husband. Our marriage binds our nations together in everlasting fealty and friendship, and so too it binds us, blood and bone, body and mind. I will uphold your honor and your choices, I will regard your duties with sanctity and support. May our joining be a bright point, guiding the union of our kingdoms until we both pass from this world."

Acid burned his throat at the flowery words, so many pretty turns of phrase used to describe imprisonment. He raised his hand, palm out, watching as Rih did the same. If she was as afraid as he, she did not show it. The few glimpses of her mind he caught were building clouds over the grasslands. Not empty, like the landscape seemed, but vast.

"Do you swear to uphold the vows made today?" Daymir glanced sharply at him, whispering, "Your Majesty. Gloves."

Keplan's jaw worked. Oaths were not taken with the shield of fabric. He yanked the offending garment off this left hand and pressed his green palm to hers.

Pain. The acrid stench of burning blood. Smoke as Hi-taln's rel crumbled into coals and ash. Keplan's eyes squeezed shut. Sheer panic and the burn of borrowed willpower rooted him to the throne room, kept his skin touching hers.

Battered consciousness, bright sun on baking grasses. Hands signing something before their owner glanced down and saw he was awake. *It's her.* And again, in the stables, a soldier requesting mounts with signs. There were a dozen, four dozen, people who signed at the stables, more in the city. But he knew her. He knew her bright eyes and fierce, delicate features.

"Your Majesty—" An'thor's voice was incredibly distant, his grip on the king's right wrist iron hard even across the leagues that seemed to separate Keplan from his own body.

He forced his eyes open and met hers. Whatever was written on his face, she saw. Her own gaze widened and she paled under the layers of tasteful paint. His fingers locked around hers when he felt her try to jerk away.

"I do so swear." The words were clotted lifeblood in his throat. Still, he spat them free. Keplan kissed her briefly, turning just enough to only brush the edge of her mouth.

Roaring fire, screaming filled his ears. He turned and realized it was the crowd, cheering for them, cheering for the peace their sacrifice brought.

Rih took his unresponsive arm. Tradition dictated they walk to the throne room doors and receive each guest's blessing. They walked back down the black carpet, Keplan tugging his glove back on with shaking hands. Triumphant music swelled when they flanked the doors. Despite hundreds of hands brushing him, flickering eye contact and curious, distant smiles, his mind was locked in replaying his weeks under the interrogator.

"Your Majesty, are you well?" Rih's interpreter asked.

It took him a moment to realize she was translating Rih's concern.

"Overwhelmed." He forced himself to look at her as the last few courtiers filed out, bobbing bows and curtsies. Whether the blessings took minutes or hours, he did not know. "I just—" Two signs interrupted him and he paused, waiting for the translation.

"Recognized me?"

The hall beyond was almost empty now. "Forgive me, I have to go." He took the hallway at a run, ignoring the startled questions the guards shouted after him. He saw only Hi-taln's body, bleeding into the hearthfire.

Φ

Night fell in silence. Knocks shook his door, An'thor's bitter bark and Daymir's tired coaxing did not sway him. Ballads whined through his open windows, dances picked for his wedding ball. *Who's dancing with her instead of me?*

He stared at the unstained ceiling or watched lights blaze as the city celebrated their king's marriage below. Homesickness was odd, when he could see the very place he missed from his own balcony. Did Firas light candles for fertility and peace in the windows of the Wise Hare or lead patrons in a toast for happiness? Did he grieve a shared life unlived, abandoned and mourned in the tiny attic bedroom just as his sister's had been?

Chest aching, he paced through his chambers to his study, dragging the dust box over and popping the lid open. He froze. It was empty.

His gaze skittered to his double-locked door. He never intended to use it all or have his body beg for more. He barely remembered the logic he twisted that night, hands and mind still stained with blood. None of that changed the fact that here he stood, staring into a void, forced to choose between sobriety or sanity.

Resolve steadied his movements as he ducked into his dressing room. A garish red tolstovka would draw attention from his scars and face. Another layer of powder and rouge hid them further. Plain dark breeches and a black jacket finished the look. He fumbled his plainest boots on and made for the door.

He froze. His guards were paid for their discretion, but nothing replaced loyalty. Instead, he eased open his balcony door and examined the ground below. It was not an easy climb, designed to keep the room's occupant safe, but the burn of urgency erased that of pulled muscles and twisted joints as he let himself drop.

The broad cobbled street led between the palace and the barracks toward the north gate.

A gust of wind threatened his hat's perch, and he shoved his errant hair beneath it before turning south. His steps were unsteady, body weakened from cold and too many ragged emotions.

When he stumbled into a market stall, he relished the scrape of sharp wood against his shoulder. At least the few stares were due to his behavior rather than suspicions at his true identity. In the press of celebration, he was just another drunk. Salt stung his tongue and he paused just above the steep stair down to the rear gate of the Navy compound. In withdrawal's wake, his body trembled and floundered under the waves of thoughts.

He did not realize where his boots dragged him until the stark orange glow of the Wise Hare's lantern hit his aching eyes. He stumbled and stopped. *I can't be here.* He promised Firas he would not shadow the Hare's stoop again. He crumpled into the alley where he first met Mirik's Spy Master, where his world shattered. "Firas," he called, both hoping and fearing his words would break through the ruckus of the Hare's common room. He would do almost anything to see the man again. *Anything but doom our kingdom.* But he did not want Firas to see him now, not like this, covered sweat and the trace of someone else's lips.

As if summoned by the memory of tan hands and dark blond beard, a voice cut through the foggy air from around the corner. "I'm not going to buy anything, but I'll give you a bowl of stew if you budge off our stoop."

Keplan stumbled to a halt in the corner's shadow. His former lover stood on the stair, arms crossed as he frowned at a crumpled figure.

Keplan recognized the rhuemy eyes and shuddering hands of his own dust dealer. He faltered, hands clenched.

"Don't need favors," the dealer hissed.

Firas shrugged. "Then move along."

"Where's the woman? She always let me set up on her nights."

In the low lamp light, Keplan saw Firas's hand curl into a fist. "She's dead and I don't give a shite what you think. Get."

Every ounce of Keplan's blood told him to fall at Firas's feet, beg for the charity he so willingly offered a poor stranger. *I'd give a thousand crowns to have a meal in the Hare, at the bar with you beside me.* He would give the single heavy crown of Athrolan itself if he thought he could. He watched the dealer gather his wares and shuffle a few paces down the road to a dry patch of cobbles. It took his entire will to keep his feet rooted to the ground until Firas had disappeared back inside.

"I'll buy," he offered, crossing the street.

The dealer flashed a smile. "Knew you'd enjoy it. Same amount?"

Keplan nodded, tossing the coin onto the blanket. "That should do fine."

The man's hand were incongruous with his ragged clothes and body, deft as he measured and clipped the box closed. "I'll see you again, then."

"No, you won't," Keplan muttered, wondering if it was a lie or not. He tucked the box away and made for the bars of the Center Teir. Less expensive and more welcoming than the Silver Apron, the bars in the middle of the city were large and varied. Keplan chose the loudest, seediest he could find, a three-story tavern and inn. He barely glanced at the name before finding a small private table.

"Mulled wine," he told the bartender before slumping back. A scan of the room told him this was no place to breathe dust on the tabletop, despite the vulgar banter and obvious brothel in the rear room. Instead, he distracted himself with the innocuous drunken thoughts of the other patrons.

A slight man strode in, dockhand uniform dripping. "Oi, Veska, I'll be down in a moment. Have a fireale waiting, please?"

The bartender snorted and jerked a nod. "Just wipe up your boot prints this time, Rheman, eh?"

The dockhand dashed back to the door, catching the rag tossed to him, and mopped up his tracks. Keplan watched him duck upstairs, envious. The bartender — Veska, apparently — returned a moment later, pouring hot wine into a delicate earthen goblet. Keplan slid a handful of coins across the table. "Leave the bottle, please."

The deep-red wine was thick with spices, something sweet cutting through the rich dry flavor. It made his thoughts fuzzier at the edges, but they still lingered. He turned his attention to the gossip perched on a stool, surrounded by women. *Poorer than a gutter rat but wants a patron for his bardic work. Gave his last coin to look the part.* He recalled Firas's words, that many came to Ceir Athrolan seeking fortune and never left. At the time, he thought it was because they found their fortune on her water-stained streets. He knew better now.

I'm gonna kill him. The thought was so loud, a flash in his mind and Keplan's focus flew to the hulking man across the room. He glowered at another bulkier man at the bar.

Keplan's body hummed with adrenaline, but he did not move. Instead he pressed his mind forward slightly.

If he brings back another mug of that swill claiming you can't taste the difference between gutterwrack and sail's ale, I'm gonna kill him.

Keplan relaxed. He had not realized how often people tossed idle threats until he took a life. Others, it seemed, were so distant from death that it never occurred that others had acted on those same thoughts.

Sashaying brocade and rich rose fabric dragged his attention back to the stairs. The dockhand returned, this time dressed in an elaborately embroidered sarafan, minus the usual billowing long-sleeved shift underneath. A long, wavy blond wig finished the look.

Apparently Keplan's eyes lingered too long: a breath later he no longer sat alone.

"Mind some company?"

Keplan almost refused. But there in those bright black eyes was something he sorely missed. *Compassion.* He gestured to the mulled wine. "Help yourself."

"I'm more a fireale girl, but thank you."

Sure enough, the bartender delivered the promised drink a moment later.

"You're a dockhand?" Keplan asked.

"During the day I'm Rheman, and he's a hand for the merchant docks, specifically Donas's shipping berths. But right now I'm Sha, and she's looking to spend some time with a friendly bar patron, if they've the interest."

"And the money?" Keplan hazarded, hoping it was not rude to ask. He noticed the faint lace edge of the blond wig. It was expensive, he imagined, but appreciated that she did not bother to choose one that looked more natural on her Sunamen skin.

"That's a nice bonus, yes, but I don't mind conversation first," she demurred. "And you are?"

"Lan Guardsen. I, ah…" He licked his dry lips. He could not be a bar hand from the Slummer, not with the rumors that exploded through the lower city upon the discovery of Athrolan's true heir that winter.

Her smile broadened. "You must be a merchant's son."

He grasped the small mercy. People like her were no strangers to truncated truths and altered personal history. "Indeed."

"We get a lot of men like you in this bar, looking to spend their parents' wealth," she murmured, eyes staying on his. "Merchants' sons, that is."

He hummed in response. Thoughts juddered through his mind too loudly for him to even decipher whether they were his. "Did you grow up here?" Her features were Sunamen, but she neither dressed nor spoke like one.

"In the south, border town. But my parents were both troubadours, so I picked up accents well. It makes people more at home."

"I'm not from here either," he blurted. "Well, from Athrolan. Small town in the Felds."

Sha's gaze was just shy of expectant, as if she already knew. He wondered how much of his identity she already deciphered. The hand that brushed his was calloused but warm and delicate.

He twitched but forced his hand to stay under hers.

"Is this all right?"

He nodded. "Just a bit loud in here." She did not need to know he meant his mind, not the common room.

"It gets rowdy but not out of hand. What brought you into Fussy Fat Hen?"

"The fussy what?" A smile eased onto his face, and he thought it just might be real.

She leaned forward, hair wafting perfume toward him. "The bar you're sitting in right now. It's called the Fussy Fat Hen."

He snorted. "It was close. And distracting. It's hard to celebrate a marriage when you miss someone."

"That's scribed truth, Lan." Her gaze softened further. "I've finished my drink if you'd like to come up."

He glanced at the door, then the stairs. Spending the night with Rih was unbearable, but even if he could not be with Firas, he did not want to be alone for his wedding night. "Please."

The narrow hallway was dim but clean. Sha's room was at the very end. She unlocked the door and ushered him in. The double window over the bed let moonlight stream across her thick coverlet. Soft pink light bloomed and he glanced back. Sha had lit a lamp on her dressing table. Keplan's gaze roved over the wig stand, the pallets of paint, the heavy dockhand knapsack, the heaps of rope brought back for repair. Two identities so different, yet fitting.

"How do you do this?"

Sha glanced up, gentle frown in place. "Spend time with people for money?"

"No, that makes sense. I mean, alternate? Do you forget who you are?"

"I'm both. Some days I feel more Sha and others more Rheman, but they're both me."

"It must be freeing." Everything was bright and loud and overwhelming, but in the quiet light of Sha's room, his thoughts were muffled.

"Now it is. It wasn't always, when I thought I had to choose." She drew her curtains and returned to brush a hand over Keplan's cheek. "What are you feeling?"

"Drowning," he whispered.

"Forgive the observation, but I noticed a box in your pocket, and your hands are shaking. Would this be easier if you weren't in dust-drought?"

Withdrawal. He looked down, hating his weakness. How did no one else notice? Was his court that inobservant, or was Sha just familiar with the signs? "It'll just be a moment. If you'd like some—"

"That's not my vice, but thank you," she interjected. "Would you like to tell me about who you're missing?"

Myself, more often than not. He set the dust up on her dressing table. "He's a bartender. Handsome. Roguish, I'd think. Likes to avoid serious conversation until it's dumped in his lap."

"Sounds fun-loving."

"Kinder than any I've met." Keplan leaned forward and breathed relief. It took a moment, then steadiness slipped over him.

"I usually spend the evenings as Sha, but if you'd rather, I can be Rheman tonight." Her hand lingered at the edge of her wig. Even in the grip of dust, the pity in her eyes was agony.

"Sha's fine. You're lovely either way, and I've never cared what body a lover has." He barely remembered he had only had the one lover, truly, but he doubted Sha would ask for written proof of his past experiences.

"I'm the same," she confided. Her hand found his and pulled him toward the bed. He let her unbutton his tolstovka and let his hair loose from the cap. Her hand paused at the gloves.

"It's fine," he rasped. The bed was soft when he fell back onto it, pulling her strong body after him.

"What do you like?"

His vision tunneled on her eyes and he pressed his mouth to hers once, twice. Honesty spilled from him and he blushed. "Oblivion."

Sha had enough curves to not remind him of Firas, but the faint scratch of stubble and the sweet burn of sex was enough to remind him why he was here. He buried his pain in Sha as night fell on his future. He wanted to forget, but not fully. Without those memories he would lose the reason he took the throne altogether. He would not survive forgetting. Neither would Athrolan.

CHAPTER FIVE

The 25th of Valemord, 1272
The City of Ceir Athrolan, Athrolan

RIH MOVED THE GAME piece diagonally, eyes narrowed on the tri-colored board.

Bimet countered immediately and Rih sat back, sighing. "I never lose so often. Not even against you!"

Bimet's dark brows arched and she smiled, returning the pieces to their starting position. "Sore loser, are we?"

"Hardly, I just can't focus on anything," Rih answered. Her mind was filled with the threads she wove into rebellion, with Vi-baln's vicious gaze, or her own isolation. Beyond the carnal, she had not considered all the duties that would begin the moment she became a wife. During their wedding she saw how frail he seemed — thin shoulders, thin face, peaked color. *I came here for a king and his army, not some sickly boy.*

"What is it, exactly?"

"He knows who I am. He recognized me. How can I maintain a happy marriage — or a functional one, if nothing else — when he can't even dance with me on our wedding night?"

"Or do anything else with you," Bimet remarked, shoving a finger into her closed fist crudely.

Rih grimaced. "I'd be happy if he never did that with me, honestly. But the empire is watching me. If this union fails—"

Nehla slipped into the room, holding the door ajar behind her as she bowed. "Your Highness, the Emperor's Hand is here to see you."

Cold washed over her. Now that she was married, she hoped to be done with his overseeing. "Of course."

Vi-baln swept in, scanning the room with an absent gaze. "Good morning, Your Highness. I trust you slept well."

"Well enough, if not long." She prayed he assumed it was because her husband had visited her and not that she had left the ball early and spent the night shivering in her room awaiting Keplan's arrival.

"I suppose that's to be expected." His gaze dropped to the board before her. "I didn't know you played."

She shrugged. "It's a common pastime in the barracks."

His face pinched tight. "I hope you'll give up such nonsense for your duties here, now."

"I've heard the king plays, though, and hoped to entertain him with a game." It was a blatant lie, but she would sell her own teeth to get the man to leave.

"Indeed—I played a round with him myself a few days ago. Perhaps Mosil did well in training you."

She offered a smile and asked if he wished for tea.

"I leave shortly. I came to wish you well and remind you of your loyalty to the Banis empire. Even when you enjoy the liberties of this city."

"A woman has a single mind," she replied.

He stared at her a moment, then his gaze moved to Nehla with a ferocity that made Rih gag. "You have some of the best attendants with you, chosen to support you. Trust them."

Bimet caught Rih's gaze. Apparently she had been right to distrust the other woman.

"I expect I will see you in His Eminence's palace again one day." Vi-baln offered his hand for her to kiss, sharp chin raised. "Until then."

You will. And it will be with my spear tip at your groin. She tapped her lips against his knuckles before rising to escort him to the door. "Travel well," she offered.

When he was a few steps down the hall, he turned back. "Oh, I had a question for you, Your Highness."

Chills spread over her arms at the cold calculation in his eyes. "What's that?"

"I've seen something these past few weeks, something I thought you could answer for me." He paused, then made the gesture for liberty. "Why do I keep seeing this?"

Bile built behind her clenched teeth. "I don't know what you mean."

"Of course you do. I see it between the rows of tents. I see it in the streets, even here. They sign and you answer." His dark gaze fixed hers. "Is there something I should know?"

She forced innocence onto her face, hoping he did not notice how long it took to settle over her features. "It's just a symbol of pride. It started during my last few weeks as a soldier, as things were building between us and Mirik."

"Liberty? We're hardly under their rule."

"I guess it's a sign that we'd like it to stay that way?" Dread rose. She had no idea how many of her signs he knew but refused to use.

"I see." He smiled and made the sign again, eyes never leaving hers. "Best not let the Mirikin see it, then."

"I'll be sure of it." Even when his bright silks disappeared down the hall, she did not feel safe. Panic was a prairie cat crouched in her gut, twitching its tail. She would need to write to the others, tell them the party lie. If she survived this marriage, if she survived this rebellion, the terror of the past few months might age her by decades.

Φ

The 26th Day of Valemord, 1272

"I thought I might find you up here." Azimir plopped down on the gravel beside Keplan with a dramatic sigh. His clothes were clearly from some state event, but he had loosened the neck of his vest and shirt.

"I miss the birds."

Azimir followed his gaze out to the woods beyond the city walls. "I get like that about Mirik sometimes."

"You can always go back," Keplan snapped. "I can't. This is my world now. I'm surrounded by it. The wind in the trees—it whispered or roared. It didn't howl like it does through the streets here. And I miss the creak of the Hare's sign under my bedroom window and the smell of woodsmoke and lamp oil from the docks below." He heaved a sigh of his own. "I'm surrounded by people—guards, mostly, or Domariigo and Blackhouse—but I'm so alone."

Azimir glanced over. "You could talk to your wife."

"She scares me," Keplan confessed, looping his arms around his knees. "She's been training for marriage her whole life—"

"She was a soldier before this, you know."

Keplan winced. "Of course. She told me that, I just forgot." He could barely hold onto a thought for longer than a minute. They slipped through his hands like sand, stream water sluicing from his consciousness. "How'd you know?"

"She told me. At her welcome ball."

Embarrassment flushed his cheeks. "That should have been me."

"It should have, yes. She's interesting. Smart. Something about her just," he shrugged, "makes me want to know more, I suppose."

"You should have married her then. Mirik would be at peace and we could just claim we'd be friends with your friends."

"Almost did, you know."

Keplan glanced over. "You never told me that. That you were promised."

"War happened and then that seemed bigger." He grinned. "Besides, then I'd be deprived of all the beautiful Banis serving women in her entourage. And I'm certain the emperor has more than one daughter."

Keplan grimaced. "I don't know how to be married. I don't know the first thing about it. At least war is something I know what to do with — stop it."

Azimir looked at his hands. "I know I've led a lucky life, but there are casualties with negotiations too. Both of you are sold for this." He raked his hand through his hair, driving the warm black locks into spikes.

Keplan caught sight of the line of scabs across his cousin's throat. *Mirrel wasn't the only one attacked.* "How's that?" He jerked his head at the healing wound.

Azimir shrugged, but his quick smile was gone. "Honestly harder than I thought. Pa's got guards everywhere for me and for Al, but it's hard when you don't feel safe in your own room, you know? I suppose I should be grateful someone killed the man responsible. But I'm not."

"Because you think there's more?"

Azimir frowned at him. "No. Because it doesn't do much good, does it? He's just dead. He won't learn from it. Others won't either. Whatever information you could have gotten from him is colder than he is."

"Right." Keplan stared at his hands. Every other memory and thought might be fleeting, but his hands still recalled the rending of flesh beneath them. "I'm sorry I didn't ask sooner."

"I haven't seen much of you."

"I don't have much time to myself." *And I waste it all getting dust-brained enough to survive the next day.*

"That Captain Hylier's been around a fair bit. You take to him?"

It took Keplan a moment to realize what his cousin meant by the awkward phrasing. "Fates, no. He's for women, I think, and certainly doesn't like me much. And he's not—" His throat tightened at the thought of a rough beard and laughing eyes. "No. I haven't taken to him. And I ought not to take to anyone. Marriage and all that. But, ah," he looked down, scuffing a boot, "I did see someone—a sell-love—on my wedding night."

Azimir's brows arched. "Oh. Man or woman?"

"Depends on when you ask. It's not serious. She's nice though." He longed to tell Azimir about the dust. Truthfully, he longed to tell anyone, to just have the truth out of his mouth and off his shoulders. An'thor would condone it, Daymir would condemn it. Hylier would be further disgusted—the man rarely even became drunk. *But Azimir might understand wishing to escape.* "It's just to stop me from thinking for a little while."

"I never feel like I think too much. Al always says I got Pa's head. I'm too sword-handed for much thinking."

Keplan glanced over at his cousin. He would never consider Azimir simple, but there was a straightforwardness to his speech. The way he spoke about Rih, however, made Keplan wonder if the boy had more insight than he realized. "Thank you for talking to me."

"You're family. Whatever you wear on that tangled mop, be it crown or kitchen soot."

Keplan's chest ached. He longed for the feeling to stay, the sensation of belonging for a moment. Like everything lately, it alighted for a moment, then melted into numbness.

The small palace bell chimed the half-hour. Azimir sighed. "I'm supposed to practice my economics with Al. Are you busy tomorrow evening?"

"Hardly." Keplan paused. This was official Athrolani business. It was not something he ought to share with a dignitary's son from another nation. "I've an audience with some madwoman about a prophet in the afternoon."

Azimir laughed. "Oh, I think my ma got some such letter a few weeks back. Of course, then I was almost assassinated, so she just told them to toss off until after the war with Ban was through. You think there's no truth to it?"

"I think they're a bunch of fools grasping at symbols in an attempt to suss meaning out of this pathetic existence," Keplan spat.

"You know my father was a person of faith."

"I'd argue still is, Azimir."

Azimir frowned. "How's that?"

"He worships my mother. He erected a temple to her in Mirik proper. His faith did not break or end, it simply transferred."

"I suppose you're right. 'When I looked up at her for the first time it was as if she were a star and I was drifting in the black sky.'"

Kepan raised his brows at the flowery language. "What's that from?"

"That's how he describes their first meeting."

"Proving my point." Keplan stood with a groan. "I'll see you when the audience is over with, then? Perhaps we'll have dinner together. Like before."

Azimir nodded, then glanced at the sky. "Toar, looks like snow." With a last wave, he retreated down the tower stairs.

Keplan glanced up at the soft gray clouds. It was too early for snow, but it seemed fitting, with the bite in the air. His steps dragged all the way to his chambers.

He rarely allowed even the maids in and left his parlor and study in disarray. The first empty box of dust went into the flames as soon as the fire in his study caught. A faint sweet smell rising from the cheap wood. He paused, staring at the second. His pulse was thunder, his blood storming in his limbs. He had two minutes.

Fess knocked as he was shutting the lid. "Sire, you asked to see me?"

He hid the box in his desk and called the commander in. Perhaps his nerves would hold on their own. "The door, if you please."

She nudged it shut and settled back in her easy stance. Sawdust and scuffs marred her white training clothes and sweat dampened her hair.

"I need your advice. Particularly on Dorcal."

"You know my thoughts on that, sire. Whatever you need done to keep the crown stable."

"I wanted your thoughts on him as a man, actually. Not as a commander."

"As a man, sire? I'm not sure—"

"As a person, Fess, I'm not being lewd."

Her eyes crinkled with a withheld smile and she dipped her head. "Apologies. I think he's a loyal man. And a proud one. Stubborn. I don't like him socially, but I think he did a fine job."

Keplan pinched the strong bridge of his nose. He was cornered. Watched at every turn. "Then why is he locked in his room and the general's advising me?"

She regarded him a moment, then gestured to the seat. "May I, sire?" When he nodded she settled in, leaning on her knees. "The short answer is, of course, because you put them there. I'm not sure I agree with either the commander or the general's recent methods, if I'm being quite honest."

"You're not the only one," Keplan muttered.

Her brows twitched, but she said nothing.

"He is a wealth of knowledge, but I can't have him in the city."

"Daymir was the figurehead, sire, and you allow him here."

"It was not the regent's cannonball that drove Slummer beams into my shoulder blade, Fess."

"No, I suppose not." She crossed her arms. "I'm not sure what you're aiming for here."

"I don't trust anyone. Not any of them—Dorcal, Domariigo or Blackhouse. For a whole garden of reasons, half of which are only suspicions at this juncture. Domariigo is as wrong as Dorcal, I just happened to be his project at the time. And I can hardly keep the man on house arrest for the rest of my reign. Either way a rebellion could rally around him. He was the strength of Blackhouse's side."

"Use him."

Keplan glanced up. "Use him for what?"

Her jaw worked as she thought about it. "I haven't the faintest. Keeping him as advisor or a lesser officer does not keep you safe. Or on the throne—"

"I don't care about me, I care about Athrolan."

"There're the same now, Your Majesty."

He grimaced. "We've grown stagnant. Look at Ban—they have things our philosophers haven't dreamed of."

"They built those with slave blood and labor. It's easy to dream when you're perched on the broken backs of others."

It was the first time he saw her express much beyond playful respect. "I didn't know you were political."

"Just stating a fact."

Keplan thought for a moment. "They explore. They push outward, in thought as well as land. Athrolan's borders stretch far enough—as it is, the Felds are an entity unto themselves most of the time. But there are places I've seen— on maps," he quickly lied, "—that we've never gone or learned from." He sat back, fiddling with his ostentatious quill.

"You're suggesting you send him afield? Who will keep him from starting a rebellion?"

"Proud. Loyal. That's how you described him. He didn't like it, but he took a knee before me when I asked. I'll give him a choice—explore for the Crown or stay behind bars growing fat. I think if I tell him he'll lose every connection he has with this kingdom if he strays, that will be warning enough."

"That's an awful lot of trust for someone who claims to have none."

"You think it's misplaced?"

Fess stared at him, then looked thoughtfully at the map on his desk. "Not in him, no."

"In who?"

"As your commander and a part of this military, officially, I can't say."

Keplan glanced at the door, then sat back in his seat. "If I were to ask you over ale in the city, what would your answer be? Blackhouse?"

"Daymir, though once a smart and lawful man, is a doddering fool. Your general, however, is not a man I'd invite for dinner no matter how many nasty tasks I required doing. You know ruddy five?" When Keplan shook his head, she sighed. "Tiles, then. He's a tile player, except we're the pieces.

I don't know what his goal is, and frankly, I'm beginning to wonder if he does either anymore. I think most of the time he moves us about from boredom."

"That's a studied critique."

"I believe in knowing who your allies are."

"And your enemies."

Her lips curved into a proper smile. "That's just my job."

"That's why I'm bothering with an audience from these zealous prophets. I hate their ideas, but I'd rather know what I'm facing."

"Fathoms beat all, sire," she quoted.

"You've given me much to think on, Fess. Thank you. You may go—I'm sorry to have interrupted your training."

"It's casual, among friends." She hesitated. "Your wife attends too, you know."

"I'm glad she's found something to amuse herself." Even in his own muffled ears it sounded trite and hollow.

Fess rose and bowed. "I know I prattled on about having no one to trust, sire, but I've got Athrolan's interests at heart. You can trust that."

He flashed her a smile of his own. "I know."

"You might want to have someone see to your fireplace. That smell isn't a good sign. Your brickwork might be faulty."

She slipped out the door and Keplan slumped back in his chair, staring at the fire. Her gaze had not wavered as she spoke, and he wondered if it was from sincerity or understanding.

Φ

The 27th of Valemord, 1272

Hylier met him at the garden gates an hour after the noon bells tolled. "Afternoon, sire."

Keplan grimaced. "Afternoon. Guards in place?"

"They are. Are you certain you don't want to meet in a more," he seemed to search for the best word, "traditional place for an audience? The throne room, perhaps."

Keplan shook his head. "I'm not taking this seriously."

"Exactly—"

"I mean it's not worth taking seriously. I'll toss my parents' power in their faces and be done with the matter."

"Very well, sire."

Keplan was quickly learning that his guard's use of the honorific was saved exclusively for when he disagreed with the king.

The gardens were bleak, barely clinging to the green the boasted just a few weeks before. Still, there was stark beauty to the butter-colored leaves and pale trunks. Sun lanced through the looming clouds and between the intricate marble lattice carved over the memorial for the Gods' War. It dappled the broad flagging and scattered cold sunlight across the mosaic. Keplan tilted his head, watching his shadow eclipse the delicate figures picked out in jet and pale chalcedony, coral and lapis.

A set of guards ringed the place, but otherwise the area was deserted. He slipped inside, leaving Hylier to wait by the door. He needed a moment. His chest tightened at the image of his mother, black power spilling over her bony hands, and his father, ignited by the sun. Every child thought their parents gods. He was just the only child who was not far wrong. He did not pace. Instead, he allowed the thoughts to wash over him. His body ached for distance, but this meeting necessitated sobriety.

"Your Majesty, she's here." Hylier stepped aside to allow the woman through. "Sire, this is Nena'phe lui Hiral."

The woman fell into a deep bow. "Swordbearer of the Prophet Hela. I am grateful you chose to speak with me."

Keplan eyed her. "Don't be grateful yet."

She was as tall as he and her auburn hair was cropped at the chin. At her belt hung a hand-and-half sword that explained her broad shoulders and chest. Her features remained unmoved. "Then I am grateful you deigned me the least waste of your time."

His brows rose and he turned to appraise her more fully. "Why are you here?"

"I bring the words of the One True God and the future —"

"Not that bit. That was all in your letter and Marum's. I want to know about you. The bit about why you believe those words at all."

"Ah." She turned, hands loosely clasped behind her back. He saw now the angles of her features and the faint slate tone to her skin.

Asai. At least partly.

"My father taught me so much of their history, but even he couldn't answer what would happen to a world without any of its creators. When I first heard them speak of her I was as skeptical as you. But when I first spoke with her alone, I saw reason. She delivers her prophesies alone, you know, to a single person, rarely the same one. This book is filled with the account of each of us. Together we've found the truth in her visions. And they are terrible and beautiful at once." Her face was lit with hope. "The One God is real."

"Do you know why I asked you to meet here?"

"Because those are your parents and this is a sacred place." She spoke with brazen surety that grated against him.

"No. Because I wanted to remind you what people of my blood did to the last gods that dared to walk this earth."

She stepped back, but her chin rose in defiance. "Your Majesty, that was retaliation, nothing more. They were false gods, seeking control over us."

"Doesn't your god seek the same? He's got you traipsing across the countryside doing his bidding. You know that's how my parents met—caught between the human armies of waring deities." He whirled on her, noting distantly that her eyes were not filled with fear or confusion, but pity. "Best get used to opposition, Nena'phe. You're pitching religion to a generation that saw an entire pantheon massacred. She moseyed up to their throne room and ripped the souls right from their bodies." His gaze snapped from its perusal of the tiles back to hers. "Now that I'm listening to you prattle on, I understand why she didn't have the patience to allow them to die the proper way!"

The calm in the woman's bright brown eyes did not waver. "I came to you to read scripture, not try to convince you of my own faith or prowess in debate."

"Apparently ashen skin isn't the only asai traits you acquired," Keplan quipped. "All right then, read your lady's prophesy."

She bowed, drawing out a small book bound with fine leather. Small illustrations filled some of the pages as she flipped to the center. Though her gaze rested on the page, it did not follow the words as she recited. "'The One True God will rise where the worlds meet, from death and birth, from chaos and order. His blood pools, drowning the world even as it gives it life. Though he will bear the marks of hate, he will be unable to raise its tools."

"You just studied opposites," Keplan noted, picking a loose thread of his gloves. He waved a hand for her to continue. Apprehension flashed up his body as he listened. Earnest certainty overwhelmed his mind. Full of the bite of steel and the nip of ice. Copper flooded his tongue, leaking through his clenched teeth.

Cold sunlight caught in her hair as she tucked it back to read the next lines. "His right hand will be stained bloody with wrath, and his left with the verdant green of life and mercy —"

"Enough!" Annoyance exploded into rage. "You think you can come into my city, into my home, spouting lies? You think you can stand here before the memorial to a woman who massacred the gods and tell me I ought to have a little faith 'or else?'" Blood misted from his mouth with every line. *Wrath. Stained with wrath.* The words spun in his head and clenched his palms to him, as if even through the gloves she might catch a glimpse.

Her beige brows arched and she stepped back, hand falling to her sword hilt. "Sire, it's scripture."

"Then fuck your scripture. And fuck your god." Terror thrummed through his bones. "Next he darkens my walls, I'll show you what I learned from the Godkiller herself!"

She moved back another step, lip lifting in the suggestion of a sneer. She spat on the ground between them. "May The One God grant you mercy, for his Swordbearers will not."

Keplan swayed, eyes still fixed on the bubbles of saliva dripping down the icons of his parents. He found the one thing he hated worse than war: heresy.

"Sire?" Hylier appeared in the doorway, hand resting loosely on the pommel of his sword. When Keplan did not answer, he stepped closer. "Keplan?"

Keplan's mind was a cacophony. He pushed past his guard, motioning for the others to follow him as he strode back through the gardens. Their boots clattered on the marble as they swept into the palace after him. "You," he waved at a squire posted at the door of a meeting hall, "find Domariigo. Admiral Fess too. Ask them to meet me in my study in an hour. And someone ought to inform the Mirikin Embassy I'll not be dining with my cousin tonight."

"Yes, Your Majesty, right away." When the squire disappeared, he glanced at Hylier.

The guard's eyes leveled on him. "Anything else?"

Keplan drew a shaking breath as they turned onto his corridor. "I'm afraid I'm going to need a war council."

Φ

The 29th Day of Valemord, 1272

"Evening, Dorcal."

"Evening, sire."

The neutral tone gave Keplan pause. He expected bitterness. All the fury that rent Athrolan in twain. *I've been spending too many brooding nights with Domariigo.* "I trust you've been comfortable here these past weeks."

"Comfortable enough." Raven rolled a shoulder, the motion unconscious. Isolation looked well on the former commander. His hair was still cropped at the unflattering angle of his thick jaw, but it was clean, and his clothes pressed. "I haven't been drawn to the training courts in my dotage anyway."

"May I sit?"

Raven scoffed and jerked his head at the dusty parlor. "Wherever you want. It's not like I entertain much. There a point to all of this?"

"I can hardly keep you under house arrest for the rest of my reign."

"Her Majesty — peace to her and those she loved — did. With His Highness Blackhouse."

"I'm not Tzatia." Keplan leaned forward, hoping the finality in his voice lent it strength and not a threat. "I have neither her patience nor her fears."

"Or her blood."

Keplan found a smile on his face. He never expected people to like him, and Raven's blatant distaste was refreshingly honest. Nationalism aside, he could grow to respect the man. "Why did you join the navy?"

"My parents were too poor to care after me. Mother's cousin was noble. Noble enough, at least, so I petitioned Her Majesty to let my years as a ship's hand count as page duties. Worked my way up to mariner from there."

"I asked why. Why the navy? Why not the army or going into business as a merchant and have the freedom to come and go as you wish?" Keplan could brush his mind like anyone else's, but it told as much what a person thought or claimed their reasoning to be as their actual motives did. He found, too, the knowledge came harder, jumbled, with dust in his blood.

Raven's dark eyes narrowed on Keplan for a moment, then he rose. Even in his dotage, as he called it, he was a mountain of a man. He moved to the cold hearth, broad hands grasped behind his back. Three portraits hung over the mantle. The first, of course, being of the late queen. On the right was a rendition of the former general, her bright hair a contrast against her ashen skin. *Like the Swordbearer.* His gaze roved over them before fixing on the map on the left. Hearth smoke stained the unwaxed parchment. Tiny red tick marks and Raven's surprisingly delicate handwriting marked its surface. His thick finger jabbed the blank space beyond Mirik. "This. This is why. Seas unconquered. Lands unknown. So many places Athrolan could learn of."

Keplan's smile was in earnest now. "That's what I hoped."

Raven turned back. Now curiosity warmed his reservedness. "Why is that?"

"I don't know what news trickles down through these bars."

"Most of it. Half, perhaps. I heard enough boots and hushed voices to gather we're at war or will be soon. You want me out of your hair so the only people you distrust are outside your walls, not within."

"I'd have to empty the city to do that."

"Smart man."

"First you've said of it."

"I have no doubt that you're clever beyond your years. I just doubt your ability to use that cleverness for good. So, who is it? Mirik? Ban? Yourself?"

Keplan snorted. "I've been at war with that last for the past year." He crossed his arms. "It's with a god."

Raven's full attention settled over Keplan's shoulders. The king was abruptly reminded of why, exactly, the man was revered as a commander. "Excuse me?"

"Some prophet out of the east claims there's a god coming and we all ought to be on our best behavior or he'll kill us."

Raven scoffed. "Your mother killed them."

"Exactly!" Keplan gestured wildly, relieved to finally have someone see the same sense as he. "I've been trying to explain that to everyone, and yet they seem convinced to just hear their side of things. Wouldn't have even listened to the prophet's lackey if Blackhouse hadn't invited them without my knowledge."

Raven frowned. "What does Domariigo think of it all?"

"I think he's curious. But he rarely has only a single horse in a race."

"Ridiculous claims aside, why go to war? Why not pat them on the head and send them back to their prophet?"

"The scripture—it's nonsense! And they claim—" His voice juddered to a halt and his gaze fell to his hands. "They're just wrong. There's no such thing as gods anymore."

Raven's attention moved from the king's face to the gloved palms and back. "Didn't like what they said? I've never claimed to like deities. People having power they shouldn't. Go to war with them if you want but—and I say this from experience—you'd better be certain they're wrong. There are things in this world we might never understand fully."

Keplan seized the change in subject like a lifeline. "That's why I'm here. You joined the navy to explore. We both know there are places and people and things we've never encountered before. If Athrolan is going to survive this new world and all its changes, she'll have to change too." He laughed at Raven's scowl. "She'll have to regain her power, her might. Think of it as a new set of armor, a new sword." He paused. "A new ship. For both of you."

Raven's thick lips twisted in what might have been intended as a smile. "I'm listening."

"Sail beyond the edges of that map, beyond where we've gone before. Map coastlines, document people and places and food. Write a thousand logs on what you find. You come back too soon or come back with an army, you're dead. But I figure exile on the high sea is better than a barred room for a person like you. I can give you time—"

Raven leaned through the bars as if already buffeted by an ocean wind. "When can I leave?"

Φ

The 30th Day of Valemord, 1272

Bitter air buffeted the glass. The sullen gray sky glowered above, close and watchful. Rih sat at the edge of her bed watching the clouds. The sky was so different here. Mercurial and full of so many shades of gray and blue and green and gold. The Banis sky was uniform in its vastness. When red and purple storms rolled across the expanse, her patrol would see them coming hours ahead. Sometimes it still was not enough warning to find shelter in the huge prairie, but they had warning.

Howling wind only now seemed to settle. Rih trusted it as little as she trusted the new court and palace around her. At least in Ban, she knew why she should not believe any of the various nobles and dignitaries.

"Will you go to your training this evening?" Bimet looked up from her place by the window, making sure to face toward Rih. Her hands were occupied with mending a leather pauldron for herself. It was not often they were alone together anymore, but Nehla had requested the afternoon free to visit family in the city.

"I thought I might. I'm used to my time being filled with lessons or training. It's a relief to relax, but I'm at a loss as to what to do most of the time."

"We could explore the city."

Rih cast a horrified glance outside. "Perhaps when we're not at risk of becoming icicles. Besides," she gnawed on one lip, "it doesn't sound safe."

"Safe?"

"A man was murdered just before we arrived—a man important enough to spur a woman to appeal to the king himself. His Majesty may be new to the throne, and perhaps unconventional, but everything seems more precarious than I was led to believe."

Rih paced to her dressing table, laid with the dozens of face paints from her wedding. She had not used them since the ball. Dark bottles of scented oil filled one drawer and she poured a few drops into her hand. Of all the many things she missed of home, the cold weather had her longing for the steam of the bathhouses.

She massaged the oil into her scalp as she turned back to Bimet. "I wouldn't mind meeting Nehla's family—a silk weaver."

Bimet's eyes narrowed and she set aside her work for a moment. "I'm not sure if that's wise, considering."

"She hasn't done anything—other than visit with Vibaln privately."

"She's his niece, you know. It's why she's so flippant around him. Doesn't have to worry about discipline."

Rih's brows rose. The feeling of being watched had not waned much since the entourage departed. Perhaps Nehla was why. She was humorous and quick, and Rih wished to make her a friend. *But friends don't inform their uncles of your every misstep.* "I didn't know."

"There's hardly a moment away from her—which I'm sure she orchestrates. Hopefully she's close enough with this cousin or sister or whatever she is to visit more often than during the celebrations."

"Such as they were," Rih retorted. "Even still, perhaps I'll go with her one day, meet this family." A Banis silk shop would be a balm on her heart. Her private network had no hierarchy, but her developing friendships with Athrolan should be with nobles, not textile merchants and naval commanders.

Bimet brushed Rih's hand to get her attention. "There's someone knocking."

Rih glanced at the door. Perhaps she could ask the steward to outfit the room with some way to get her attention. The thick wood did not lend itself to renovations, however. As exhausted as she was, her mind begged for something to occupy her. Something other than worry. She changed to a warmer wrap and settled herself on the tall couch in her parlor. "Let them in."

The young man from the ball wavered in the doorway. He flashed a smile and waved an awkward hand. His bow, however, was to an equal. "Afternoon, Princess Rih-elte. I thought you might be needing a visitor, busy as His Majesty is this evening."

She let herself smile in return, wondering at the best way to ask who, exactly, he was. "Then I'm happy to see you. Would you like tea?"

"I wanted to offer to tour you about Athrolan, since I came a lot as a child. But it seems the howling has teeth as well. It'll snow soon, no doubt."

"Another time, perhaps." Rih seized her chance. "What brings you to Ceir Athrolan?"

His broad smile faltered when Bimet finished her translation. "You have no idea who I am, do you?"

Rih felt the flush of embarrassment on her cheeks and looked away for a moment, hoping her dark skin hid the sudden pink. "I've met more strangers in the past two days than in all my years before now combined. My lady Nehla has been indispensable, but I'm afraid she wasn't with us when we first met, and I missed you at the wedding ball."

"It was a long day, I'm sure. I'm not surprised you slipped out early." He gestured to the couch across from them as the Athrolani tea arrived. "May I?" When she nodded, he sat and made himself busy pouring tea. When he had taken a sip, he inclined his head to her. "I'm Azimir A'hane, son of Kemmer A'hane, Military Commissioner of Mirik —"

"And acting Hetmir," Rih finished with him. *And the boy I was supposed to marry to stop his mother's war.* Then he was not Athrolani at all, but Mirikin.

Rih gripped Bimet's wrist even as the other woman brought her weapon to ready. As much as her instincts screamed that they were enemies, his open face was kind and honest. "We ordered that tea, and he's already drunk it. Mirik would be foolish to use their second son as an assassin."

Azimir's dark eyes were wide and fixed on the blade aimed at his gut. "I'm not the most tactful when it comes to these things. My father's the ambassador. I'm just a friendly fool." Hand raised, he leaned back in the couch. "By all means, order your own drinks. I doubt you enjoy Athrolani bitterroot as it is."

His crooked smile was contagious, and after a moment Rih motioned for the woman at the door to request their own tea. "So if you're not here to kill me, what do you want?"

"Politics are funny. My mother wages war against your father, yet leagues away from any bloodshed, we can sit across a —" he peered at the dark, decorated wood of the table between them, " — Berrin captain's table and drink tea."

"And yet, thousands of soldiers still die." She let her teeth add a bite to her smile, to her words. "I was supposed to marry you, you know."

He looked down, mumbling something.

"I know. Considering, I imagine Keplan's more agreeable," Bimet translated.

Rih rolled her eyes but was saved from replying by the arrival of a heavy clay dish of Banis tea. She stirred it absently before pouring the thick liquid into her mug. Their only commonality, as far as she was concerned, was war. It did not bode well for conversation. "Your mother just set sail for our shores, I am told."

"And your father just redirected most of his cavalry and foot soldiers to the beaches."

"He's not my father," she corrected without thinking.

His brows rose. "Forgive me, I just assumed —"

"By blood, I suppose," she explained, brown hands flashing in impatience. "But he never raised me, never acknowledged me. Perhaps this is why I was originally offered to you. Which, I was told, was an insult."

"There's no need to apologize—"

"I wasn't." She lifted her chin, forcing pride she often lacked into her gaze.

He regarded her with narrowed eyes for a moment. Then his smile widened. "No, I don't imagine you would. You remind me of my mother. Clever. Uncompromising. You weren't the insult in the negotiation. Most of Mirik still remembers starving as my grandfather bled her treasury dry in the gods' names. Living in warrens of derelict buildings and eating rotted food sounds a bit like slavery, don't you think?"

She paused in stirring her tea. Under the friendly youth in his face, she caught a glimpse of the woman steering her battleships west. "I think I'd know more about slavery than you might, ambassador's son."

"Probably." His gaze did not waver nor his expression change. After a moment he pointed to the dish between them. "Might I try some of your tea? I've never acquired a taste for the bitter Athrolani stuff."

She finally returned his smile in earnest and poured him a cup. "So, I assume the wedding brought you to Athrolan, to answer my question."

"And the coronation. My father's a bit preoccupied with my cousin. It was all I could do to keep my father from screaming at Kep to change his mind. At least it made the whole thing more interesting."

"I thought Athrolan just avoided civil war. Now I hear of wildfire politics and murders in the streets."

"I wouldn't say avoided. Stopped before it gripped much more than the capital is more accurate." He peered at her. "Was Ban that much safer?"

She shrugged. "I was a soldier, so safety was relative. But the city itself, and others like it, were peaceful in many ways. Peaceful but terrified."

"I've always taken better to battle than politics."

"Do you not agree that negotiations will always be better than war?" she countered. Her tea cooled, almost forgotten on the table in favor of playful verbal sparring.

"Not in all cases—Mirik's war with Ban is a noble one. We're sacrificing some of our own lives so that some of your people are saved."

"That's a poetic way of looking at it," Rih agreed. "Wars take many lives, though. Negotiations only cost one."

"One? I would think none," Azimir said, eyes narrowed in thought. He took a sip and his eyes brightened at the flavor.

"The price of a kingdom's safety is one person's life. Instead of sacrificing the lives of hundreds in a war against Athrolan, I'm just sacrificing mine."

"Perhaps it's just a choice who we sacrifice for peace—the common folk or the aristocracy." He sat back, expression abruptly wistful. "Nothing an ambassador's son would understand, eh?"

"I see your point. Though I will never agree that their suffering is the same."

"Hardly. You've given me a bit to think on." Azimir finished his tea and poured another. "So, what do you think of Athrolan?"

"It's confusing. Disorganized. In RoBal even our leisure time is marked with fear that something we did will have upset the baniol, or fates forbid, His Divine Eminence. And everything is tidy, organized. Traffic in the streets moves smoothly, people keeping to the proper sides. Here it's inefficient. Chaotic, even." She steeled herself. "His Majesty's guards storm from rooms, the general has been drunk every time we speak. The king disregards the protocol of the ball—did you know I studied for weeks to learn that dance?"

Azimir broke into laughter. "I've seen Kep dance with one person only and it was certainly not at a ball. You ought to be counting your luckcharms—he'd have stepped on your foot, likely as not."

Rih sighed dramatically. "I could have been studying something interesting and useful!"

"Well, I appreciated your tutelage." Azimir's shoulders still shook with laughter. "I imagine we'll both need entertainment in the coming months."

Rih's mood sobered. She did have something interesting and useful to occupy her. "I imagine with weather as harsh as this there is little to do."

"Plenty to do around fires—reading, if you're inclined. I struggle being still so I spend much of my time in the training courts."

"I've been training with Admiral Fess and some of her colleagues," Rih confessed. "I'm not certain they appreciate my presence, but they act welcoming enough."

Azimir leaned forward, happily pouring another mug for himself. "Do you know atlatl, then? And those long polearms?"

"Glaives and prairie stars. I'm learning some grappling from another woman there. But I'm surprised at how free my days are."

"Well my offer to show you the city stands." Azimir glanced out the window and his face brightened. "Snow! Mirik doesn't get much of it, island winds sweep it clear."

Rih stared at the snow. It drifted, frozen milkgrass seeds in legion, and settled on every roof and rampart. "It's beautiful."

His smile echoed hers. "I know. Most loathe it, and it mucks up the roads for wagons and mail. Still, there's something freeing about giving up responsibility for a day."

"I expected it to be ugly."

"Snow?"

"Ceir Athrolan. And it's not pretty, not in the way Ban is, with is richness and elaborate details. But it's elegant in a way." She watched the streets fill with snow, ground into wet gray hummocks where wagon wheels churned through. "Perhaps not all of it."

Azimir's chin jerked as he snorted. "Lately I hardly recognize her. I can't imagine what An'thor thinks of how much everything has changed since he first arrived."

Rih's gaze moved from Bimet's hands to the city and back, trying to take everything in. After a moment she frowned, pointing at the dark smudge on the horizon. "Is that more snow?"

Azimir followed her gesture, smile fading. "No. That's the smoke. They're burning the fields, trying to keep blight from spreading."

Half of the gate in the wall eased open, permitting a train of harvest wagons. What should have been overflowing beds were barely stacked past the sideboards. Even the wagoneers looked exhausted.

"I suppose that's one task for the cold months," Rih noted, pulling her wrap closer against the cold. "Try to keep everyone from starving."

Φ

The 31st Day of Valemord, 1272
The Tundra of the Northlands

"At least it's not as bleak as it was last time," Alea offered.

Arman stared at her, incredulous, until his horse stumbled over an icy crag. "Less bleak? Fates, it's a small wonder half the Nenev are monstrous if this is their good day."

Alea chuckled and nudged her mount faster. "We're almost there, if this map's correct."

"I see nothing. And this place is flatter than the sky. Not sure I entirely trust those people either. Didn't tell us the woman had gone at first."

"I think they were protecting her. Last few of our kind, former citadel and so forth. Like Vielrona." Alea glanced up at the clear gray above them. Even at night the light never truly died. "I'll know it when I see it."

Arman hummed noncommittally. It was unlikely they would find her up here. Just another trail to follow. *Why would she even drive them this way?* A glance at Alea told him her face was still set in certainty. It was more than he had seen in weeks.

"There!" Alea's rough voice cut through his musing. One of her water-wrinkled fingers pointed ahead and to the east. A massive iron mile marker jutted, rusty, from the barren hill. She smiled. "We're here."

"There's nothing."

"Look down." She gestured to the base of the hill beyond. A round iron door was set in the earth, ruts from mighty machines softened by several decades of scrubgrass and frost. She pulled up just beside it and dismounted. Her hands tested it, turning it one way, then another, head tilted as if waiting for it to impart some secret. After a few more tries she shook her head. "I don't know the code."

"It's iron, right?"

"Yes. Only thing that survives the seasons up here."

Arman swung himself down and rested a hand on the metal. The sputtering power he could barely access was gone.

Rather, the human part of him had burned so much, it was a charred layer barely separating him from his power. Withered conduits between himself and his power trembled and charred as he taxed them too far. Metal was earth. Heat bubbled from his throat. He groaned at the effort. Rust flaked from the surface as it heated, glowing from within. One hand, claws sprouting from the blackened tips of his fingers, made a dragging motion. The hill shuddered. Grasses under his boots wilted and turned black. The skin around his mouth paled to white and cracked over the angry flesh below. Gears squealed beneath the earth. A thud, a thunk, and the door opened.

Alea's cold-tinged lips curled and she handed him his reins. "Perhaps I should have brought you the first time."

He laughed, the sound echoing oddly down the tunnel before them. "I doubt I would have been good company." He dipped his hand into the gutter along the wall digging at the thin residue of fat. It sputtered and ignited.

"Who goes?" The shout echoed from far ahead, made loud by the iron confines.

"An old friend of the Wanderer, riding from Lymorda," Alea answered.

Arman wondered if they could smell the salt from the other end, feel the creeping, unseasonable frost curling down the entrance. Silence, then a second row of flame flickered into being. Arman peered up, blinking at the brightness. A figure limped closer, metal clacking with every other step. The man stopped when he was just a few paces away, leaning on his iron cane. "Dhoah' Lyne'alea. Never thought I'd see you again."

Alea tilted her head, watery eyes peering at the faded burgundy hair and ashen skin. "You're General Aneral's friend."

"Albi'giran. Yes. We never met properly—"

"You fought for us. That's enough," Alea whispered. Were those tears or just the ocean flooding her skin?

"Why don't you come in and rest. We have little in the way of comfort, but if you rode from Berr I doubt you'll snub it," he explained. His chuckle was the rasp of dry grass.

"Old friends are comfort enough," Arman answered. They fell into step behind the asai warrior.

Silence reigned as they walked. A second door opened the same way as the first, though this with a twist of Albi'giran's hand. The tunnel terminated at the base of a circular courtyard. Three stories of rooms circled it, with a dome of bare iron bars making up the open ceiling. Arman glimpsed a crag of rock ringing the opening on the surface. They'd passed a few random clusters of boulders on their journey. How many had hidden the grated ceilings of Nenev houses?

"They're covered with ice blocks in winter, save for the smoke-hole. If you're wondering how we keep winter out."

Arman hummed in response. It felt good to be surrounded by stone and metal and feel the heat of fire beneath his feet. His attention returned to the conversation to hear Alea answering some question.

"It's been months, actually. A bit of a foxhunt across the wilderness, at least for the latter half of it."

"I can't imagine what brings you this far north."

"We're just passing through, I think."

"On your way to where?" His gray-laced brows curled in. "There's nothing north of this. At least, nothing more than ruins and ice. The world's spire is pretty, surely, but you're in the wrong season for malostrii."

"We didn't come for the sky-lights. Just a woman." Alea glanced at the bank of stalls as they stabled their mounts. All but four were empty. "Where is everyone?"

The asai did not meet her eyes. "I'll put some tea and food on. Second floor, third door on the right." He disappeared from view.

Arman leaned on the stall door, running a soothing hand over his horse's neck. He checked over her hooves and sniffed the water in the bucket on her door before joining Alea in the courtyard. She waited for him on a tight grate suspended on chains. She smiled and pulled back a long lever. After a moment gears engaged and they lurched upwards. Arman laughed, watching the ground inch away from under their boots. "I like the Nenev, I think."

She snorted. "Their structures are about the only thing I care to see again."

"We'll have our answers soon, love."

"I don't know," she answered as the platform shuddered to a halt at the second story. "I have more questions now. I want to know the nature of Keplan's—" her voice broke on their son's name, "of his power. Most of me just wants to see him again, power be tossed. I'd sell our last breath to have our answer be here."

Arman followed her into the room Albi'giran had indicated, dumping their bags in an undignified heap. "And if it's not?"

"Then we'll keep looking. Somewhere there's an answer. And if I have to sail to the Gods' Island itself, to Le'yne again, then so be it."

He reached out for her hand, wincing at the clammy chill. "We," he corrected. "This time you won't go alone."

Her brief smile was wan but sincere.

Downstairs, a small, warm room waited, door propped open in welcome. Albi'giran limped to the fireplace, tray of dried meat and kelp in his free hand. "So. What's brought you here?"

Alea seemed transfixed by the fire, so Arman guided her to a seat before answering. "We're looking for an old woman. She had others with her, supporters, of a kind."

"Just a woman? A friend or enemy?"

"Family," Alea interjected, voice breaking through ice on its way from her throat. "Of a kind."

The asai's features showed no surprise. Simply vague interest.

No wonder they're called the Stonefaced, Arman realized. *Calm in the face of the Dhoah' Laen, in the face of her desperate search for the last of her people.*

"You're looking for a book. Not a woman." He jabbed at the coals with the iron tip of his cane.

Alea shook her head. "I've seen her, she keeps talking of blood. Screaming."

"I'm sure. It's all she ever said."

"She was here?" Arman's focus sharpened on the man. They had been quick to trust him, but his flat affect now tightened his nerves. *What do you know?* He took a tentative sip of the tea, winced, and took a larger gulp. "Where did she go? Is she dead?"

"I'd know if she were dead," Alea snapped. The air chilled and the man glanced between them.

"She's not dead, no. She acquired some," he hesitated, glancing at the narrow dim hall outside his open door, "believers."

"Orabon Marum." Alea's hand skimmed the pocket that held their map.

His copper eyes blinked and he reached for another slice of cured bear. "More than him now. Many more. Some from Berr, but some from here as well. They focus not on our past but, like my people, our future. They've heard her teachings, her visions, and have taken them to heart. She speaks of One God who will raise us from this in-between state."

Arman's skin crawled. Alea's visions echoed those words. When she slipped into sleep or away from consciousness, her mouth never ceased moving, whispering whatever messages she heard within. Beside him, Alea's eyes were screwed shut, tears leaking from their corners. "In-between?"

"While you were holed up in your cabin in the forest, this world's been dying. Crops won't grow as fast. Blight strikes harder. Summer here is shorter, colder. I haven't seen the snow geese in four years. Even the ice bears are starving. Perhaps we see it better, up here in the dark north, where even the smallest change would threaten our existence. Something is strangling the world. And they believe he — this One God — will save us."

"God's blood is strangling the world,'" Alea paraphrased.

Albi'giran's face tightened a fraction. "When they arrived I assumed the same as most would — she was a madwomen and they fools. But then I recognized the words. Most of her more coherent babbling matched the histories my people kept. The few of us who remained settled here for a time but then pushed farther north. They felt they had to cast off the shackles of the old ways for hope at a new beginning. So they left our tomes. And the few of us who hindered travel. Suffice to say, I've had plenty of time to read."

Arman felt a flash of pity for the man. Living in the forest had been lonely, surely, but he had Alea and Keplan. Locked in a world of ice and broken machines seemed a terrible fate.

Alea's tearstained face was luminous in the dark. "You said I was looking for a book. You mean your people's history?"

"I mean a book referenced there. It's the history of all of us. You, Earth Shakers, gods, the lot of us."

Her eyes dimmed at his tone. "It's not here, is it?"

"We don't know where it is."

"Neneviir," Arman realized. "It's where you found the Laen Crown. If it's anywhere, it'll be there."

Alea shuddered, face paling further. "I would truly rather not. I've been before and once was more than enough."

"But surely—"

"Where are they headed now?" Alea interrupted him.

Albi'giran's jaw worked and he glared at the fire. "They're marching on Athrolan."

"Keplan's there." Frantic energy lit Alea's features now, looking more alert than she had been in days.

Dread lit Arman's veins, searing his arteries. The food in his hand heated, bear lard dripping down the cracked back of his hand. "Marching?"

"In the name of the One God, they fear if we don't all bow before him then he won't come at all and the world will fall to ruin. So they ride to every city between here and the Banis jungles and see that they have no choice."

"Arman, if Kep's caught in this—" Alea protested.

"Then we had best have all the answers." He reached for her hand, but her fingers were fisted. "No matter where they are. Or what they might be."

Φ

The night air whipped between the bare bars overhead. The low ceiling in the room behind her kept the smoke low, stinging her eyes. Arman had not seemed to notice. Instead, he crouched over the table still holding their barely touched food, making tick marks on the map. She could not stomach planning another journey to Neneviir. It did not matter that Albi'giran claimed it was all but deserted. Neneviir was where she had broken. Cracks from the massacre in Cehn were furthered by pain, by solitude. *And another ally lost faith in me.* If Arman realized how much of herself she left there, his face showed nothing.

Not even the howling wind was loud enough. The screaming never stopped. Each time she closed her eyes to sleep it was there, wavering with the same breath. It hitched when the throat was slit, gurgled over cooling blood. Still it went on. The head in her lap wore a mask of myriad faces, flickering from one to the next once death fell. It was Arman, Ahren, Narier, Bren, that poor man she could not save, the woman who cleaned the manor, the children she helped raise.

Half the time she had no name to pin on the face, but they were familiar as her own blood for the moment they lay there, staring up at her with accusing, puzzled eyes. Their blood pulsed through her hands, entered her flesh and roared through her power. She reached into their chests and parted ribs, parted the wall of souls, ripped the Laen's power open, ripped lungs and hearts open. Then it was Keplan, thin face scarred in a strange pattern. His eyes rolled, pupils blown. The blood spurting from him was brilliant copper, as copper as the gods' had been.

"Is there anything I can do?" Albi'giran's low voice tempered those still muttering in her mind.

She shook her head, glancing back. The smoldering coals of the hearthfire backlit him. Inside, Arman traced some trail Alea's eyes hardened on the asai. "I don't want our path to lead to Neneviir. I know I swore I'd go anywhere for him but," she looked up at the blackness beyond the open roof, "doesn't mean it will be easy."

"Neneviir fell. During the Gods' War, An'thoriend gathered who he could, rallied enough of a force to help. It fractured them, seeing you, I think. Some held faith in the gods or you, others lost it entirely."

"And what about Edrodene?"

"Dead. Years ago. He ruled for a while, clinging to order as they do. There was a bit of a revolt and afterward not much was left of the city. Not enough worth saving." The wind moaned.

"Revolt? Last I heard Athrolan suffers from something similar."

"I heard the same." His copper eyes turned to hers. "You said your son was in their capital? Kap something?"

She nodded. "Keplan. His name is Keplan Wardyn and he's seventeen."

Albi'giran's face softened, the most expression she had seen since they arrived. "I have a daughter, just twenty at the beginning of the month."

"Where is she now?"

"She left with the prophet. Like many of the others her age, they did not know a world with gods in it."

Alea shivered at the thought. "How could you let her go?"

"How could I not? The most I can do is love her and listen. You protect them for too long, the greatest danger becomes themselves."

"I'm realizing that." Alea frowned at him. "Even so, they're fanatics."

"I don't know." His eyes were fixed on the sky. "Read the book and then tell me they're wrong."

CHAPTER SIX

The 32nd Day of Valemord, 1272
The City of Ceir Athrolan, Athrolan

KEPLAN RAN THE LEATHER over the knife again. The library was deserted at dawn. The sharp scent of rich parchment filled the air, bolstered with oil. The leather sank against the steel with a gentle swish. War.

It was all he had been avoiding since he left the Hartland. Perhaps, though, he had not been avoiding it, but rather running from it as it dogged him across the continent. Now it slavered at his sanity and his city. *Swish.* War. It was the only thought in his mind. There was something poetic about it— the only reason he was still in Athrolan, the only reason he married Rih, and the only reason he was still alive was to stop war.

And here I am, starting one over faith. His gaze dropped to his hands, grease-stained and gripping the skin around the blade. *"His right hand will be red with wrath, and his left verdant green of mercy."*

Whatever terrible mistake his parents had made in creating him had come home to roost. It was mighty enough to creep into a madwoman's thoughts, poisoning her mind with lies.

If he feared Athrolan would fall with a pauper king, now he had to see if it could survive a heretic.

An'thor's rasp was grit underfoot. "We need to talk."

"The counsel is in an hour. I'd like to be alone until then."

"Then why aren't you locked in your rooms as usual?"

Keplan gestured to the shelves around him. "Look at these. How many books do you think sit on these shelves?"

"Hundreds. Thousands, perhaps. And in various languages."

"And yet, not a one contains a whisper of what I am. I see so much and understand so little. Now I'm speaking in contradictions too."

"You called a war counsel." The general's hands were too steady for sobriety, but his voice shook with frustration.

"Because we're at war."

"What did you do?"

"I don't think she liked my tone," Keplan whispered. Stillness washed over him, buoyed by a hundred fragments of thoughts rolling off the city. "People have gone to war for less."

An'thor shook his head. "I've been in countless wars, Wardyn. Even started some myself. None of them have been worth it, but this is absurd. And you're sending Dorcal away? Do you wish us to crumble?"

"Dorcal is where I need him to be. We're desiccated. A thousand books and not one written in the last seventeen years. We can barely keep our aqueducts from bursting or running dry. Our crops wither in the field or molder after harvest. We need more. We need to stretch our legs, learn from others. I'll stay here and hold whatever this is at bay. He can bring back hope."

"You trust him?"

"Fates, no," Keplan scoffed, twisting the blade in his hand to send spots of light dancing over the stone walls. "But I don't trust you or Blackhouse either."

"I got you on this cursed throne—"

"That makes me like you less."

"What did she say to you?" An'thor hissed. "You sound as mad as her."

"She read her prophesies. About the god. This woman has been having the same visions I have—earth cracking open, empires rising, falling and blood. Always blood. But she's got it wrong. I think she sees me, watching the same events unfold and mistook me for a piece of it."

"Aren't you? Parents such as yours, you can hardly be irrelevant."

Keplan shook his head. "In the visions something's killing the world. She thinks I'm here to save it."

An'thor's chin rose, his eyes narrowing on the king. "What are you here for, then?"

Keplan flexed his hands, setting aside the knife. "I don't think I'm supposed to be. Whatever my parents were meant to do, it didn't involve me. I interrupted it, broke it somehow. Strangled it. I just have to keep Athrolan whole until something can come along and stop it—stop me."

"Visions. How much of this is because of dust?"

Keplan reared back. "What?"

"I'm not oblivious, boy. You might not be on it now, but you have been. Pacing, chewing on your lips. Your eyes are blacker than mine half the time. You can't focus on anything, or it's all you can think of, just fixating. I'm not for dust, personally, but I've known plenty who are."

"Domariigo, I swear, if you tell," Keplan breathed.

"I'm not telling anyone. It'd be—what was your phrase?—rich coming from a man who hasn't been sober in a decade. I'm not judging you. I don't care enough. But I do care about Athrolan."

"Then give me your firearm."

An'thor's hand dropped to the weapon at his belt. "Why?"

"Because there's something at our door. It's ravaging our fields and laying waste to our people. How many murders have been reported in the past year? We're desperate, frantic. The sky is closing in around us and we can all feel it. Whether it's because of the prophet's lies or mine, I don't know, but I'm going to need everything we have. I promised Ban your knowledge, but I think it's fair I get first choice."

"We can discuss what machines and technology you need after we determine if war is wise."

"I've already decided, General. I'm king here," he leveled his wide eyes on the Nenev, "or have you forgotten that?"

The shelves behind him rattled. Dust drifted from the beams overhead. An'thor's black eyes followed the movement, tracing a phantom trail across the ceiling and down to the window. The glass rattled.

"I told you, Domariigo: something's knocking."

Φ

Roast meat and biscuits cooled on the table. Keplan fiddled with his food as Fess argued with An'thor; it had been going on for the past four minutes and he had long since lost interest.

"I just don't see the sense in arguing with them! Let them erect their temples, let them proselytize on our corners. What harm does it do?"

"Harm?" Fess asked. "They've threatened war if we don't. What happens when this prophet's new scripture decrees her more powerful than His Majesty? What happens when her visions show Athrolan bequeathing half her treasury to their cause? It's a slippery slope, and we're well down it already."

"How is that any different from our alliance with Ban? We married slave traders for peace, I don't see how heretics are any different."

Keplan's frayed patience snapped. "I married them!" he roared. "Not you, Domariigo. And none of you heard what I did, none of you had to stomach that prophet's lies. I've done nothing but avoid war since I ascended, so when I say heresy is worth fighting, I expect you to put down your biscuits and go to war!"

Fess stared at him, her brown eyes wary. "Of course, sire. While General Domariigo seems concerned, I think we all agree this is a threat. And even you, sire, admit it's one we haven't faced before. Perhaps if you tell us what she said we'd be able to ascertain how best to approach them. Do you even know when they'll attack?"

Keplan shook his head. "Has anyone seen Blackhouse? He had first correspondence with them. And," his voice faltered, "he was the last person to speak with my mother."

"The Dhoah' Laen?" an officer asked. "I thought they were gone — hidden in some mountain somewhere."

"The Hartland, actually. And so did I." The king put aside his food and leaned on the table.

"What else did she say? The soldier, that is."

"They call themselves Swordbearers. There's this creature coming, and its existence is smothering the world. That much I can agree on. I've seen it too. But they're wrong. It's not a god. It's a mistake. One my parents made, I think. She said we'd best hope the One True God has mercy on us." He looked up at Fess, then An'thor. "Because their Swordbearers wouldn't."

An'thor's head sank to his pale, ragged hands. "Toss it all."

"I don't think we need to waste any more time discussing whether we should fight them. War's already been declared."

"We don't have the troops. We don't have the grain. We don't have the money," he countered.

"Ban does."

Keplan turned at the new voice. Rih and her translator stood in the doorway to the counsel hall. His wife's hands moved again.

"Forgive me for inviting myself, but I only just learned there was a counsel."

An'thor opened his mouth, but Fess interrupted him. "Her Highness Rih-elte is a valuable asset, sire. We train together and I've already learned much."

Keplan waved for a page to produce a chair. He did not want to think of Ban or his marriage, but if she was willing to find a solution, he welcomed her. *I just can't look her in the eye.* "Of course. I apologize for not thinking to invite you."

"How many do they number? Where are they based?" An'thor asked. "Do we even know their allies?"

"Mirik hasn't allied with them," Keplan noted. "Azimir claimed they ignored the letter due to their focus on Ban," he glanced at Rih, "begging your pardon."

A single black brow rose. "It's hardly your fault our nations attack each other," she noted.

"I can hardly beg either of you for support in this, though, when your people are already at war."

"What's one more war?" she quipped.

An'thor's dark gaze bounced between the two of them, narrowing further. "His Majesty has a good point, Your Highness—"

"His Eminence styles himself a god, general," Rih interrupted. "If you think he would tolerate another deity in his empire, you don't know Ban well at all. He is not what one would call tolerant. It's why we win every war we've ever fought."

"I can't ask for help in this, not after we already argued over the wheat we were promised months ago."

"That's negotiations," Fess explained. "Everyone attempts to bring their own costs down."

"You hardly did, offering up our dear general's mind for picking."

An'thor's pale lips thinned and he sat back. "I'm hardly willing to give over that information to Athrolan, let alone a foreign megalomaniac."

Keplan turned on him. "What happened to caring about Athrolan? Or was that just pretty talk this morning?"

An'thor shot him a glare. "If you understood the magnitude of what my people created, you would realize why I can't trust it to humans."

"Then why don't we agree: I'll trust that you'll only give us the technology our pathetic human minds can handle, and you'll trust that what Nena'phe told me is worth going to war over."

Fess cleared her throat. "Let's reach out to other nations to ask what they have heard and their reactions. I'll send scouting ships along the coast to determine the reach of these Swordbearers, if you permit me, of course, sire."

Her deference was pointed in the wake of An'thor's insubordination. Keplan nodded. "Granted. Please see that Dorcal departs tomorrow as well. An escort until he's out of our waters should do, but I trust you'll know best."

"Consider it done."

"Rih," he switched to Banis, "would you write to your friends or cousins in RoBal? Ask if they've heard of these people. Informally if you can."

She nodded, making a note on a wax tablet before her.

"Colonels, send missives to each of your holdings and your neighboring nobles. If they have any force worth fighting, someone will have seen it already."

The officers rose, bowing. Conversation hummed in the hallway beyond as they filed out.

"And you, General," Keplan continued, when just he and Fess were alone with the man. "Give me schematics for your weapon or the weapon itself by the end of this meeting or I'll order bars on your door just as I did with Dorcal."

Fess glanced between them. "Sire, I don't know if that's necessary."

"You can't see what I do when I close my eyes. What lies before us if we succumb to fanatics. We will need every asset moving forward."

An'thor slumped in his chair, knocking back his drink. It smelled of mildew and honey. "I don't agree with this. Any of it."

"Your concern has been noted."

The general unclipped his revolver from its holster and placed the weapon on the table with a *thunk*. His hand did not move from the oiled leather and polished bone. "I've used this a handful of times. Most was in defense of your mother and her people. It's a responsibility. When you take up a weapon like this you must be ready to kill, because unlike blades, bullets can't be blocked."

"Is that how you became general after the war?"

An'thor did not respond, only rose, leaving his weapon on the table, and made for the door. Above bells tolled, echoing balefully from snow-dusted white towers. Riders burst from the stables, their white and turquoise uniforms covered with blood-red cloaks. By week's end, news of war would reach every corner of Athrolan.

Φ

The 34th Day of Valemord, 1272

Raven jerked the door open, blinking against the sudden light from the hall. "Yes?"

An'thor swayed in the doorway, peering up at him. "Your arrest is lifted."

"I know. I leave tomorrow." Raven faltered, realizing the man was not announcing it. "Is this your attempt at amends?"

"Fuck if I know. I'm too drunk to sleep and too tired to fight. You have a minute?"

Raven preferred to sleep. The hours before a journey were meant to be spent in solitude. He opened the door wider and sighed. "A minute."

An'thor lurched into the dark study, slumping into Raven's chair without further invitation. "I think you got the better end of the gamble here."

"I was under house arrest for a month. I've lost my titles. Lost my queen."

"We both lost her, Raven," An'thor muttered. "Everyone lost Tzatia. Eras too. Yet you're leaving their memories here."

"You left Claimiirn. It's hardly different."

"Claimiirn was in ruins."

"Arguably, so is Athrolan." Raven crossed his arms over his bare chest. "I thought you were too tired to fight."

An'thor stared at his hands, sullen. "Do you have any —
"

"No. You're not drinking my best liquor like it's brook water. His Majesty gave me a choice — house arrest for the rest of my days or go explore. I wouldn't say it was much of a choice, frankly."

"I suppose you have no ties here, no children, no wife. Just duty."

Raven winced. "There was a child. Once." He rarely spoke of it. Rarely held it in his waking mind.

An'thor looked away. "You never told me."

"Eras hardly told me, either," Raven excused. "I'd make a gutterwash father. I'd have tried, but…" He trailed off and shrugged. An'thor would have made just a mess of parenthood, he was sure, but perhaps half of the man's personality was built upon a father's grief.

"I think I tried, with Mel'iend. Failed him, in the end. But I tried."

"Did he survive the war?"

An'thor looked away and Raven knew to press the issue no further. "When are you due back?"

"When I've found something worth reporting, I suppose."

"Until nothing looks familiar," the general whispered. "Wardyn asked for my revolver."

Raven's gaze dropped to An'thor's belt. Sure enough, a dark splotch marked where the weapon usually hung. His concern flared. "And you gave it to him?"

"I wouldn't say it was much of a choice," An'thor repeated. "What do you think he expects you to find out there?"

"He said we were stagnant. We needed to progress."

"First that, then asking for Nenev machines? It bodes ill."

"Does it?" Raven shrugged. "He's not wrong. But I think there's more. Whatever it is he sees in that mind of his, whether it's real or not, I think he wants it explained."

"You think you'll find the answers?"

Raven sighed, looking down at his packed bags. "Doesn't matter if I do or don't. Athrolan has no place for me. You either, I'd wager. He's changing the face of her. I'm not saying he won't do the kingdom good, I just refuse to believe a human throne should be sat by," he raked a hand through his hair, "by that."

"But Eras was fine."

"Eras never sat the throne, and she was half human."

"So is Keplan," An'thor reminded him.

Raven clenched his teeth, mind flickering back to the colorless, luminous gaze of his king. "You've clearly never looked His Majesty in the eyes. Leastwise, not while sober."

An'thor seemed to debate a response, then shook his head. "I know he's what's best. For the same reasons you think he's a mistake. He knows so much, I have to believe he'll see us through this chaos. But I wonder how much of it is his own making."

"How much is yours, though?"

An'thor met his eyes, expression unreadable. "Tell me about the last time you saw her. Alive. Well."

Raven sighed. He did not have to ask which her An'thor meant. "It was just before she named the new fort in memory of Fort Shadow. She invited me to tea."

By the time the Nenev left, dawn brightened the skyline. Raven scrubbed a hand over his exhausted eyes. His chests were already packed, his uniform — conspicuously lacking his commander's badge — pressed and waiting on the armor stand. He brushed a hand over Eras's portrait and spared a nod to his queen before lifting the map down. It rolled easily and he tucked it into a waterproof pouch in his writing kit. It left a pale spot on the soot-stained wall above the mantle.

"Sir Dorcal!" A woman's voice cut through the quiet study.

"Mariner Jorn?" He looked up to see his first mate in the doorway, burly arms crossed over the bright Athrolani naval uniform. Her wicked grin widened. "See you slept as well as I did."

"Keep chattering and I'll give you night's watch," he snapped. Her smile tugged an answering one from him, however, and he shouldered his bags. "It's been a while since I went farther than a diplomat's run," he mused, pausing at the top of the steep stairs down the naval docks. The city was awash with brilliant white, filth masked by snow, and cold enough that the Slummer stench had yet to permeate. He would even miss that.

The docks were quiet, lacquered wood thunking against the canvas padding in the thick air. Three boats awaited them, prepared to sail, but only one held all they might need for a voyage.

"I see His Majesty provided us an escort in the chance we decide to turn back to port."

Jorn bounced on the balls of her feet. "He hardly knows us at all, it seems. I could smell the salt in my dreams last night."

"Hardly slept," Raven answered before adjusting his bag on his shoulder. He glanced at the palace, then out at the fog-shrouded horizon. Curiosity uncurled in his gut.

Φ

The 36th Day of Valemord, 1272
The Village of Jai, Ban

Jani propped his head on his crossed arms as he peered over the wall. "Anything to do this morning?"

"Nothing I know about yet," Reka responded in Banis.

He grinned. "That's how it often is in this busy house. Come hunting with me?"

She grinned, vaulting over the wall he leaned on and into the garden behind their rel. "Love nothing more."

It was easy to fall into the familiar truncated speech. Ikel spoke Banis better than Jani spoke Border or Trade. Reka spoke enough Banis not to be a concern for the town guards, apparently.

She crept back inside through the rear ladder. Her hammock hung across the narrow hall from the children's, and the last thing she wanted to do was wake them. The quiet hours of morning were precious. She grabbed her bow and the oiled leather hood that kept her head and shoulders dry. By the time she had slipped through the kitchen, grabbed a handful of pressed meat and nut mix, and emerged, Jani already waited in the street.

"You survived," he noted with a nod to the still quiet house. "Took me years to figure out how to get out without waking them."

"Tools of the trade," she joked, falling into stride beside him.

The town was beginning to stir, but just barely. With the rains came gray mornings and the urge to stay inside and weave. Jani whistled up to the guard on duty, tossing a string of beads up.

Reka glanced at him curiously.

"Bribe. Not allowed out during war, but a fair few of us can't survive on rations. I've picked up a few private guard jobs, but nothing big enough to pay for all of us to eat. Can't with the scheduled shifts."

Reka shook her head. "They ought to pay you for your time. Athrolan military does. Extra if you're an officer."

Jani shook his head as they ducked through the small door set in the gate. "We get all our own needs met—food, clothes, housing if we need. It's just our families that suffer. Incentive not to have one," he explained.

Reka grimaced. Ban had so many more resources than Athrolan, though much of it was gleaned on the back of slavery and rarely seen by anyone below the nobles and dignitaries. Athrolan had her own host of issues with corruption and nationalism. *I can't say which I'd choose if I had to.* Sometimes there was a benefit to belonging nowhere.

Rich yellow grasses stretched between copses of broad-branched trees, brilliant green wedged at their roots as they prepared to push new growth. Each step dampened Reka's boots. Hot smells of baking wheat were replaced by the damp earth and rain on the exposed juts of brown stone. Above, the slate-colored sky warned of a wet afternoon. Trails wove between the tender stalks, and it was along one of these they walked. They did not speak, Jani pointing occasionally to where a snare hid in the grass or a print sank particularly deep into the damp earth.

The first string of snares was camouflaged in the dense mat of dead grasses at the roots of the waving green stalks. Jani knelt, checking that the loop was still open. Reka scanned the rise ahead while he adjusted the supports.

"It's unnerving," she murmured. Even with the distant rumble of thunder and the wind, she did not trust her voice not to carry.

He sat back, following her gaze. After a second he nodded. "Most don't last long out here, if they weren't raised on it. So open, makes you feel too small."

Reka hummed. "Anyone could be watching us and we'd never know. Makes me feel like we're being stalked."

"Half of Ban feels like that. Even in the city." Jani rose with a sigh, moving to the next loop.

Reka eyed him. Ikel had yet to speak to her privately, and while Reka was happy to relax, she could not shake the shadow hanging over her visit. "Is that what Ikel meant in her letter? About something brewing?"

Jani paused, fingers cradling the hemp string. This one had been nibbled through and the soil below was stained with flecks of dried blood. "What did she tell you?"

Panic flashed in Reka's veins. Had Ikel told him, even? When she found her way, it was with little guidance, save for her first meeting with the merchant's guard. She chose a neutral phrase. "That Ban was changing."

He did not answer, moving from empty snare to empty snare. Then, among the prairie grass, there was a flutter of frantic movement. He crouched, following the line for another few paces before he found the trapped creature. It was a hare, fat with the wet season's abundance.

Jani crouched and grabbed it by the tethered foot. With practiced efficiency he snapped its neck and loosened the snare. He sat for a moment, staring at the cooling body. Finally he cleared his throat. "This is an insidious country. Always watched, always measured, and always, always, left wanting. It started with the women. A woman, really. Many have carried the idea and even acted upon it, but we'd only hear about it at the end, when they were executed. This time it was different." He flashed a smile as the sky rumbled a prelude to the storm.

"There was nothing to hear," Reka realized. "The word—it's just a typical sign. One half your empire uses."

"Half is a bit optimistic, but yes. You can't just see the sign or hear a word and know its second meaning, the life it lives when prayed and spoken and signed with hope. There's a network, hardly any of it written, but each of us who carries the spark of liberty also carries a piece of the revolution in their bones. My sister brought word first. She's a—"

"The soldier." Reka knelt beside him, pressing forward. "It's reached the military? That's where a rebellion goes to die."

"You just left Athrolan, you know that's not true. It's not where they die if they're born there. We've a general—I don't know her name or her rank or even where she is or how old.

I just know that she began this, and with our help — and yours too, I hope — she will win it."

Thunder clapped above them, and rain began in earnest. Jani laughed and tucked the hare into his bag. "There's an outcropping ahead, we'll wait out the worst of it."

Reka nodded, ducking her head to keep the rain from her eyes as they broke into a jog. A boulder topped the next rise, one piece broken and creating a makeshift angled roof. They wedged themselves inside and Jani dropped to a crouch. "Should bag another three hares — the snares on the southern loop are the farthest from the road and often catch something."

"I'll see if those gazelle are still by the lake on our way back," Reka agreed. She did not know how she felt about revolution. Athrolan's attempt at civil war was ugly and clumsy. War was not the Border way. Even with their bands dissolved and absorbed into other cultures as empires spread, she adhered to her moral rule of single combat wherever she could. Thoughtful lines on Jani's calm face told her the discussion of revolution was over the for the time being, but leaving it dangling felt a bit like the hare, tugging on a string as it waited for death.

"Jani, about what you said —"

His fingers were hard on her bicep and he pointed. The grasses waved, the movement almost masked by the wind. Except this angled southwest.

Rih eased herself farther into the rock's cleft, timing her motion with the gusts of wind. The line of horses bore no riders, only the tips of their ears and heads bobbing above the tall grasses in the swale. Still, movement before and after them told her they were flanked by people. "Banis?" she mouthed.

Jani's head shook once and he pointed at her. "Mirikin. Horses."

She glanced back out. Sure enough, the few sets of ears and manes were long and loose, not the upright elegance of riahs. *Toar, what are they doing this far south?* She knew, of course, that the war brought them here, but she had not realized how far Kemmer pressed.

Thankfully the shelter barely fit the two of them, and was of no use to the dozen or so riders. The march moved on through the rain and disappeared to the west.

Jani drew a slow breath. His face was pale and Reka saw the flutter of a pounding pulse in his throat. "I didn't know they were so close."

Reka shook her head. "Neither did I. You going to tell the guards?"

"I'll warn them, but they can't make an official report when we're not allowed outside the village walls. Or permitted to let anyone in." He fiddled with the end of his braid. "I can't keep leaving, not if they're that close. It's only a matter of time before I either get caught or they follow me back. We're on few enough maps that we've been ignored so far, but it won't last."

"Let's finish your snares and head home then," she offered.

Using curtains of rain as cover, they kept to the gullies. It was a death wish to follow streambeds during the wet season, but the steep banks had enough vegetation to hide most of their movement. Reka's heart raced with every particularly active hummock of grass or grouse that took to the sky with their passing. More than once she glanced over her shoulder, expecting to see a line of Mirikin riders bearing down.

The rest of Jani's snares were empty, save one that clearly had been cut with a knife. He grimaced and untied the string, shortening the tether to make a new loop.

"I think your friends there might have taken our supper."

Reka winced. "Not my friends."

The gazelle had gone from the gully just beyond the town, startled by all the traffic in the last few hours. Reka followed Jani back across the deserted prairie and through the gates without comment.

Their house was awake and bustling when they returned. Kas sat at one of the tiers chopping roots while her younger brother attempted to mend his doll's sandal.

"Any luck?" Ikel asked, looking up with a smile.

"Some." Jani retrieved the hare from his bag and brought it over to the basin by the door to clean. He glanced at their children. "Saw some former friends of your cousin while sheltering from the rain."

Ikel paled and her gaze moved from him to Reka and back. "I'm glad you made such good time, then."

Reka sighed. She was not sure she agreed with keeping everything from the children. Innocence was only noticed by its absence and was something she had no interest in preserving. "There were only a few, but I didn't expect them."

Jani hung the hare's feet up to dry to be sold for hunting cats or dogs. Ikel lapsed into quiet, stirring the spices toasting in the broad skillet.

"I spoke with your cousin today," Jani commented, tugging the hare's skin free in one smooth motion. "About my sister."

Ikel did not look up, but her every movement was sharp, its normalcy rehearsed. "Oh? And what did you think, Reka?"

Reka stared at the fire. She may not have agreed with armies or battles, but crouched under red rock as the patrol passed, she had apparently made her choice. "I think she and I would get along. And you're right—I'm ready for the ruak."

Φ

The 38th Day of Valemord, 1272
The City of Ceir Athrolan, Athrolan

Rih drew back, free arm pointed, guiding her sight to the target. She breathed once, twice, then let fly. Her room was stifling. Even her own skin felt too close, too tight. Each throw she hoped would settle her nerves enough to prevent her bones from quaking. Training with the commander and her friends was a diversion, but she rarely let herself sink into practice like she used to. She longed for the training halls in RoBal where she would throw until she settled in a thoughtless trance.

Ragged skin edged her nails from picking in her idle moments. She was not sure whether the insurmountable issues rising before her were real or just shadows cast by other, larger problems. Conversation took weeks when she was so far from any of her allies, and since the failure of Bet, she had not risked anything beyond suggesting movements of her trusted people to safer locations until it was time.

She jogged across the training court to collect her darts. When she turned back she saw Azimir leaning on the doorframe, dressed in training gear.

"Morning, Your Highness," he greeted.

She raised a hand. Knowing the training courts were deserted, she'd offered Bimet the morning off. She returned to the bench, looking through her plain wrap. She missed the pockets and pouches of soldiers' clothes, where she could keep a tablet and stylus at all times.

When she glanced up at a loss, he smiled. "I'll ask yes or no questions. I just finished training. Are you busy?"

She shook her head.

"Would you like to go into the city? It's warmer today."

She smiled and nodded, placing her weapon back in its case and bundling its darts together.

He crouched to catch her eye again. "I'm going to clean up and change into something more suitable. Should I meet you and Bimet at your rooms in an hour?"

Again, she nodded.

He sprang up and made for the door, waving cheerfully.

She waited to ring for Bimet until her bath was done, but even after weeks of practice she could not manage all her piercings and nets with the same ease.

By the time her translator arrived, Rih had draped a wrap over her head and shoulders. Bimet flashed a smile. "Where are we off to, Your Highness?"

"Azimir offered to show me the city," Rih explained before handing her the tray of rings that matched her dark blue outfit. "It's warmer today, he said."

Bimet threaded the wire through Rih's ears and nose, twirling the metal until the onyx and sapphire beads were centered. "You've spent a lot of time with Master A'hane," Bimet noted, surveying her handiwork. "More than with your husband."

Rih scowled, stepping back from Bimet's preening. "He knows where I live. He can visit at any time. I wouldn't want to spend time with the woman who brought me to the interrogators either."

"Of course. But people talk."

"You and Nehla are with us, and surely there will be guards. We're hardly alone. If he doesn't want to see me, His Majesty can suffer the rumors." She raised her head, surveying her reflection in the broad mirror. Her nerves did not show in her expression, thankfully. It was not true, and she knew it. The bravado was false, and whatever repercussions came would fall on her head more than Athrolan's king. *I just want to see the city!*

Nehla arrived a moment later, dressed for the cold city and bearing her usual bright smile. "Morning! I met Master A'hane at the door. He says we're going into the city?"

Rih nodded. "I thought we could also visit your family, if we have time. I wanted to see their silks."

Rih led them through her rooms and out the door where the young man waited with two guards dressed in Mirikin green.

"I don't suppose we should even try a pretense, with half the court following after us," he joked. "My father's been absurd since the attempt."

"I thought you said it was directed at one of Keplan's supporters in the city."

He winced, lively face sobering for a moment. "There was another. On me. On those of us who helped Keplan when he was first in the city, 'fore we knew what he was."

Fear was sharp in her gut. "I'm beginning to think the ordered evil of RoBal is preferable to this mess. I suppose that's what His Eminence bargains on." She stopped as two Banis guards appeared, realizing how bitter, how traitorous her words sounded.

Azimir did not seem to notice, face brightening at Bimet's presence. "I hoped you might join us, Lady Bimet." He bowed to Rih. "As much as I enjoy a challenge, your dialect of Banis is not one I can learn over one excursion."

Rih laughed. "It's not a dialect, which might make it easier. But not that easy."

"It's another language?" he asked, falling in beside her. His guards took up the rear. "Surely it's based in Banis."

"I wouldn't know, really, what Banis sounds like—I know the shapes your mouth makes to speak it, but signing is a different language altogether. The gestures are not in the same order as the words when someone speaks, just as sentences in Trade are structured differently than those in

Banis. Signs are different too, in that we put the most important part first, and there are fewer fiddly words that get in the way."

Azimir frowned. "So, like me, you know two languages."

"Yes, but unlike you, here, I am one of the only people who speaks my first language."

He looked down, then back up. "You must be lonely."

The understanding in his eyes sent an ache through her chest. "Truthfully, I have always been, even in Ban. Even in the army. Even surrounded by my sisters who bled for me and for whom I would gladly bleed, I was alone."

His smile was fleeting. "I imagine there are many who feel that way. Your errant husband, for one."

She ducked her head to hide the flush in her cheeks. "He's surrounded by an entourage whose sole purpose is to keep him occupied. I'm sure he's simply busy."

The palace doors opened before them, permitting a biting wind that ushered them into the cold courtyard. Rih shivered, blinking in the bright sunlight.

"You all right?" Azimir asked.

She nodded and tugged her short Athrolani cloak tighter. The deep blue wool had been a gift from Keplan, apparently. Her layers did much to protect her from the worst of the chill, but the wind was insistent. "Just adjusting!"

He strode onto Tzama, heading toward the largest of the roads leading down toward the harbor. "I think you'd have more to talk about if either of you gave it a chance. Though I knew him before he ever ascended the throne, so perhaps I view him differently."

Rih frowned. "But he was always heir."

"Officially, yes, his mother's child was named as heir to the Athrolani throne, but he did not know who his mother was, who she had been to Athrolan, at least, nor that he was heir. He arrived on the back of a fuzzy draft pony and worked for his bed and board in the slums. He lived there longer than he's been crowned, actually." He paused, expression tense. "It's his story, though. Not mine to tell."

He gestured to the frost-covered city before them. "I've got little to do this afternoon, so I am yours to command. Would you like food? What would you like to see?"

"Nehla's cousin owns a silk shop. Perhaps we could go there?"

Azimir turned to Nehla, asking a series of questions Rih did not try to follow. Instead, she took in the view. Cracks in the stone were stained black from decades exposed to the ocean's moisture. It lent depth to the otherwise uniform white. The gray wood of every lamppost bore a coat of frost. Curls of it decorated the southern windows, sheltered from the brunt of the ocean wind.

Now women's fan-shaped embroidered headdresses were replaced with pointed wool felt edged with fur, most with flaps over the ears. Men, too, donned thick fur caps.

Azimir waved to get her attention. "Lady Nehla says it's in the Guildhall courts. Fairly safe there, and we'd cross a fair bit of the city, if you're not well sick of me yet."

Bimet began to protest, but Rih refused to look at her hands. "That sounds lovely."

They set out, Azimir waving exuberantly at the first large state building they passed. "The second-largest city guardhouse, Your Highness. The largest is by the docks, of course, but I prefer the Thorns—the guards from here." He grinned. "They know the best Slummer bars."

They continued, his tirade interrupted only when he spotted something new to explain. It was clear much of the nuance and detail of Azimir's tour were lost in Bimet's efforts to keep up with his rapid words.

While verbose, Azimir seemed harmless, and they were surrounded by her own guards. Rih let herself relax. Recalling the depth in his gaze as they spoke of war, she amended that thought. *Friendly. Not harmless.* Stalls and open store counters lined the main street, scents of cooking meat and sweet bread wafting out on steam and smoke. Her stomach uncurled in interest, and Azimir glanced over.

"Hungry?" Bimet translated, craning to catch Rih's eye.

"Is there anything you can't eat?" he asked.

There was no need to translate Rih's headshake, and after dodging a few larger wagons, Azimir returned from a small tavern bearing a covered woven tray.

"Best in the city," he insisted. Thick dark sauce covered thin strips of shaved, raw mutton. Curling green leaves topped the affair, their sharp scent accenting the heat of the sauce.

Her eyes narrowed with skepticism, half teasing, half serious. To her relief, it was rich and delicious. He laughed as she reached for another before following him farther down the tiers.

The food was gone by the time Azimir stopped outside a broad storefront. "After you, Your Highness."

Rih slipped through the door, eyes fluttering shut. Raw silk. The acrid smell of dye. Warm sandalwood. Tears pricked the edges of her eyes. *Home.*

A woman appeared from the back, mouth moving rapidly in a language Rih did not know. It seemed to bear the wide-mouthed words of Trade, but she knew too few words to pick any out. Some form of lizard decorated her left jawline.

She reached to embrace Nehla, who stepped back quickly and gestured to Rih. "May I introduce Kajimet Rih-elte of RoBal."

The woman paled and dropped into a curtsey. "Forgive me, You Highness—"

"It's nothing," Rih promised. "I just came to look about and give you and Nehla a chance to visit. Please go about your business."

The woman's face brightened and her hands flew into motion. "Mobeka. I'm honored you would grace our humble shop. And it's lovely to see our signs again," she confided, "I've worried I'll forget it from disuse. My father was Deaf too."

Rih grinned, heart thundering with melancholy and comfort at once. "I'm happy to see them too. And to see familiar colors. I didn't know you were Banis, though," she equivocated, eyes lingering on the tattoo. "I haven't seen art like your lizard before. Is it common in Athrolan?"

Mobeka's head flung back in laugher. "Oh, fate's trail, no. I grew up a day's hike from Jai—how I met my husband. My father was Banis, surely, but my mother was Border. Their tradition is to get a tattoo. Salamanders because I'm a child of two worlds. Three now, if you count Athrolan." She pushed her hair away again. "Forgive me, again. I'll let you browse, if you please."

Azimir had already become distracted with a high-collared vest in a blood red. Taking the opportunity to have a moment to herself, Rih stepped away. She slipped down an aisle of massive silk bolts. Several were undyed, but many more bore the brilliant crimson and purples and cerulean of RoBal. One was embroidered like Athrolani brocade but picked out in distinctly Banis colors. Another set of silks beside it were more subdued.

Her attention lingered on a pale-yellow wool cap with a Banis net stitched overtop. The bright white threads were dotted with gold topaz and pearls. Beaded fringe hung from the front like a wealthy woman's kokoshnik.

Nehla's cousin appeared from the other end of the aisle. "Do you see something you like?"

Rih gestured to the hat. "Do you make these in lavender?"

"I would be honored to create something bespoke for Your Highness." Her bright smile faded and she angled her back to the door before confiding, "My brother is a baniol."

"That must bring you honor," Rih replied, uncertain.

The weaver rolled her eyes, hand quickly signing, "Liberty."

Rih's nerves flamed. "Does he know, your brother?"

"Yes. He's an ally. He's been fighting for us for months. Quietly, of course, but he admires you." Mobeka's eyes flicked to something behind them, and Rih whirled.

Azimir leaned against one of the textile racks, watching her curiously.

Now panic flooded her limbs. *Don't react.*

"Your signs," he remarked, mimicking a few. "They're beautiful. I might not learn it in an afternoon, but would it be hard to teach?"

"It's a language, same as any, I suppose."

"I'm good at languages. Perhaps you could teach me."

"I'd love to learn as well," Nehla agreed, emerging with a folded bolt of black cloth over one arm. "What's that one again? I remember Vi-baln asking after it."

"Just a farewell. A sign of solidarity," Rih answered quickly, looking away at her rebellion's calling card as Mobeka translated. The memory of teaching the women in the Purple Throne weighed on her. The wound of losing them was raw, still. "It was lovely to see a small piece of home, but we ought to let Mistress Mobeka have her shop back."

"I'll send my runner with some samples for you to look over," Mobeka offered. When Rih frowned, she smiled, reminding her, "For the cap you admired."

Rih tried a grin of her own, but her nerves were too frayed for it to feel sincere.

Once their goodbyes were said, they emerged again, onto the street. Azimir was as boisterous as before, leading them down to docks. The Guildhalls were beautiful, the elaborate marble filigree edging their rooves containing hints at the trades represented within. Rih's gaze was caught by the new red stripe trimming the Athrolani sigils over each gate and aqueduct. *War.* "What is Mirik's opinion of Athrolan's new war?"

Azimir shrugged. "I don't think my father cares for it. But the whole thing is complex. More complex than we realized. What about yourself?"

"I wasn't invited to the counsel."

Azimir shook his head. "You're a soldier."

She grinned. "I arrived anyway. Suggested His Majesty request aide from Ban. We've enough troops. I doubt he'll consider it, though."

"I don't see why," Azimir scoffed. "If he's concerned enough to wage war on this religion, he should be able to put aside his fears. Send you, in the least."

"Me?" Rih rolled her eyes. "They'd as soon listen to me as an inbred colt. Actually, they'd listen to the colt first, I'd imagine."

Azimir stepped under an awning of the Berrin Trade Guild. A long counter connected the kitchens within to the street. He tossed a couple coins on the counter and ordered before turning back to her. "You're practically queen here."

Rih let that settle in her mind. *Queen.* She doubted Keplan considered her such, or that anyone else did. She wielded about as much clout as any of the lesser noble ladies. "I think you're optimistic."

"You said you went to the war counsel without invitation," the Hetmir's son noted, pressing a hot mug into her hands. At her cautious sniff, he laughed. "It's Berrin *ucal.*"

She took a sip, letting the hot, bitter flavor wash over her tongue. Setting the mug on the counter so she could sign, she responded, "It's good. But I still think you're wrong."

"Maybe." He shrugged. "They didn't tell you to leave, did they?"

"No." She frowned. "They listened."

"You interrupted an Athrolani war counsel and they considered your thoughts. You're closer to queen than me, at least. Perhaps Keplan would consider taking Banis help if you were the one to ask for it." He knocked back a tiny glass of steaming yellow liquor before nursing his own mug of ucal.

When they had finished their drinks, Azimir's face lit up. "We've got guards enough—care to see the Thread?"

Bimet's weapon hand flexed. "Your Highness, it's late. The Emperor's Hand—"

"I'm being diplomatic," Rih interjected. "I need to see the city, we have guards with us, and alienating His Majesty's cousin is a poor idea. They're not at war with one another and Athrolan refuses to be."

"You're not Athrolani," Bimet countered in sign. "I'm just thinking of your safety. You mean too much to take so many risks."

Rih took a moment, hand reaching for Bimet. She needed friends. As much as Azimir was witty and kind, Bimet was her solace. The only woman she could trust. *A reminder of why I'm here.* "Perhaps another time, Azimir. There's another audience tomorrow, and I'd like to study the notes from the last one."

He shrugged and easily turned around. "I'll walk you back to the palace then. My father will be wanting me home for dinner—I swear he'd follow me about himself out of worry if he didn't have duties to attend."

It was a long walk, and the air grew colder. By the time they arrived at the palace courtyard, even Azimir's enthusiasm had slackened.

"Thank you for your company. I fear I may be overwhelming at times. Keplan barely listened the first time I dragged him through the markets and warehouses."

"I enjoyed myself, actually." Exhaustion weighed on her, but she had enjoyed the glimpse of her new home. "I'm just a bit tired and find homesickness is as debilitating as any other illness. I hope to see you again."

"You surely will." He turned, waving as he walked backward. "Good evening, Your Highness!"

Nehla watched him go, eyes appreciative. "Begging your pardon, Your Highness, but I understand why you danced with him."

"He's barely a man—sixteen, I think," Rih argued. Her chest was tight. If the Hetmir had stayed her hand, Rih would have been married to Azimir. She had as much interest in his body as she did in Keplan's, but Azimir's face held nothing of his cousin's mercurial calculation.

"You think his mother set him up for this?" Bimet asked.

Rih scoffed, sweeping into the faint warmth of the drafty palace. "I have no doubt. But is it because I'm His Eminence's daughter, or because we both plan to overthrow him?"

Φ

The 39th Day of Valemord, 1272

The heavy metal projectiles clattered on Keplan's desk. He watched them roll about before gathering them into his hand and lining them upright on the lacquered wood. Schematics in thin, cheap notebooks replaced the audience records and missives of a king's usual study.

He still did not understand what provided the force, and as much as he wished for An'thor's help, he knew his general's temper was far too short to press his luck just yet.

Keplan raked his hand through his hair. With a mechanism of death arrayed before him, his thoughts refused to quiet. He slumped into his chair, eyeing the box on his desk. *I can't keep doing this.* The thought was fleeting, but unless he was mistaken, it was his own.

A servingman appeared at his door. "Your Majesty, Captain Hylier is here to see you. Said you asked for him."

"Show him in, thank you, Gorden."

The captain paused in the doorway. "Am I interrupting?"

Keplan grunted. "How've you been? I haven't seen you lately."

"You sent me away, last I recall." Hylier shook his head. "Been busy."

He pointed to the chair across the desk from the king, and Keplan nodded. "Have you learned anything?"

"I have." Hylier's eyes fixed on the disassembled weapon on Keplan's desk. "Is that what I think it is?"

"I demanded it. The last war Athrolan fought against the gods, she had my parents in her armory. I don't. I don't even know where they are, Hylier." He looked up, noting the captain's usually bright and energetic face was drawn. "What is it?"

The captain shook his head. "I haven't found everything I wanted to. They might have simply let it go if it weren't for Greton spurring the cursed thing on. Our only saving grace is they haven't found his pack."

Keplan lifted a shoulder, suddenly unable to meet the man's eyes. "Did you look under the aqueducts in the Slummer?"

Hylier sighed. "I didn't. I don't know why they would. They put a call out, of course, but nothing specific. That where you left it?"

"Should still be there, unless urchins got to it. But the wine he carried is gone. Tasted like arse anyway."

"I'll see what I can do. It gives us a tiny step above them, though I don't know what I'll do with it yet." He rubbed a hand over his tired face. "There's something else, something I've been keeping from you—not out of malice, but until I knew more, knew for certain. And I didn't know, not until today."

"What is it?"

"I found something the night Mirrel died. It's how I knew to look for her and for Azimir. When I agreed to work for you—in both capacities—I assumed it would complement my work for Daymir. In the very least, it wouldn't interfere."

"What're you aiming for here?"

Hylier's pale brows furrowed. "I'm getting to it. I've worked for Daymir for a long time. And my family before me. He's not always been a kind man, or charitable, but he's never cruel. Never killed. But it seems I have, in advertently, been working for opposing sides."

Keplan's head tilted. His thoughts were tangled. He wished, fleetingly, that he had breathed dust before this meeting. It would make him calmer but perhaps hinder his ability to suss out what his captain possibly meant. "You implying he was more than just a figurehead?"

"I don't know. I found a list and a letter in Peraan's desk. It contained a name—the final name on the list."

"Mirrel's?"

Hylier's voice lost the edge it had borne since learning Keplan had killed. Instead it was weary and full of regret. "I owe you an apology, Keplan. I saw two names on that list and I was forced to choose."

Anger flashed through Keplan's chest, followed by fear and despair. *Mirrel might have lived.* Perhaps Peraan would still have attacked, perhaps he would still have harmed her, harmed the inn, but she would be alive. He forced sense through the emotional miasma. "What's that to do with Blackhouse?"

"The letter with the name — it was signed by Dam Ornsen."

"I don't know that name."

"Few do. It's Daymir's. Like you, most nobles have lay-names, aliases for business that might tarnish or confuse their standing in court. He hasn't used it for business in years — I'd know. We read every letter that passed over Manor Black's threshold."

"But you missed this one?"

"I was hardly the only one on duty. Perhaps someone didn't understand the significance. But I can't suss out what his reasoning would be."

"Daymir has no interest in the throne," Keplan insisted.

"You were screaming at him not so long ago. Inviting zealots into your city."

"I hardly trust him with state affairs, but not because he's malicious. His sense is just misplaced. I can't see how sending Mirrel to her death behooves him. What's left of his mind might be a warren, but it's a fairly honest one."

"I know." Hylier sighed. "I think good men do bad things in the name of what's right. You've done the same. But it doesn't seem to be the case here."

Keplan ignored the vague compliment. "Who else knows about the letter?"

"No one." He bated, fiddling with the badge on his breast. "Someone. One person. Someone who does work like mine." He glanced up. "Not captain's work."

"I followed," Keplan assured. "A spy."

"She works for Mirik, and I assume she was there to protect Azimir."

Keplan snorted. "Spymaster Elang. We've met. I don't care for her."

Hylier smiled. "She's better off duty."

Keplan made a face. "I'd rather not carry that image. What about the name—Dom what?"

"Dam Ornsen."

"I don't know if Reka knows whose name it is. Few did. Daymir rarely used it, honestly."

Keplan's eyes narrowed. "It's his name, but perhaps someone borrowed it."

Hylier leaned forward, eyes narrowed in thought. "If there's someone pretending to be your regent—even in disguise—we've got a larger issue than blaming someone for murder."

CHAPTER SEVEN

The 40th Day of Valemord, 1272
The City of Neneviir

FROST CLUNG TO IRON. Rust dripped bloody stains on the ice. Alea's boots ground against the packed snow as she edged down the street. Last she entered Neneviir it was by steam engine. She pulled her cloak higher around her neck, though she was not truly cold. Her bones did not recognize cold.

"Up here," Arman called. "There's a main road." Even against the wind his voice sounded too loud.

She did not answer, just trudged farther into the city. Here, stone formed the buildings' frames. Ice walls had long since crumbled, weakened with each summer's perpetual days.

Much of the city still teetered atop itself, buildings piled high on permafrost. Like most cities they'd seen, its grandeur was an echo, an underpinning long tattered and faded.

Arman waited at a crossroad, cloak open, sweat dripping down his face. A bead clung to the cracked skin around his mouth. "I think it's up this way. With machines and technology, you'd think they would have designed their streets in squares."

"It's a wheel. Spokes," Alea ground out, one arm lifting in the direction of the palace. Bitter salt water pooled under her tongue. "Hub."

He watched her face for a moment, then followed her gesture with his gaze. "Right. I suppose this will lead right there, then."

I would rather it didn't. Alea followed the swirling heat of his wake as they continued. Already the days were shorter, the sun never reaching near its zenith, even at midday. She was grateful to the faint green curtains that lit the sky each evening. They kept her awake, grounded from all but the darkest of her dreams. With every league farther north, the sky-lights grew brighter, and her thoughts grew more sickening.

"Fates."

She glanced up at Arman's breathed awe. The massive blocks of the palace's dome echoed Athrolan's. Most were still intact, save for the crest of the structure, blown out from within. Towering ridges ran down the curve from the opening where the ice had melted and solidified again. "It wasn't like that before. Something happened."

"Albi'giran said there was a revolt. Perhaps it collapsed then."

Alea shrugged, pushing past him and into the courtyard. The bank of oversized carriage houses for the steam engines stretched from the edge of the palace. All but one had collapsed, the stone scorched and buried in decades of snow. She wondered absently what had happened to the boy who helped her, the boy sent to his death by his own uncle. Tearing herself away from the tangled path of memories, she lurched up the broad stairs. Hoare frost covered most of the rooms, protected from the clawing fingers of the wind or the brief warmth of summer.

The iron doors to the great hall, however, stood open. Snow piled at their foot, drifting like ghosts as the air breathed down the gaping hole in the ceiling.

"Where do we even start?" Arman wondered aloud. "Down here?"

Alea shuddered, dragging her eyes from the yawning door to the prison's entrance. "I doubt it." Truth was, though, the palace was huge, and catacombs were as good a place to hide ugly truths as any. *I never saw the book in the treasury. Though I wasn't looking.*

Arman trotted down the stairs, even the thick soles of his boots slipping on the ice-covered steps. Alea stayed at the foot of the stairs. Every thud of her laboring heart sent droplets misting from her skin, her gasps ice crystals in the air. War followed so quickly on the heels of what she experienced in Neneviir's dungeon and, like so many things, those memories were mostly locked behind iron gates in her mind. But now, with their setting before her, they were too vivid to ignore.

Bren had asked, in passing, if anything had been taken from her. Whether he meant physically or mentally, she was not sure. Of course not, she had replied. What she really meant, though, was how could they not?

Little snow had drifted in through the barred windows, and the interrogation room was untouched. Arman stepped in, lip curled as he winced at the chair and bloodstains. "Places like this make me wonder if the world's worth saving at all. Whose blood do you think it is?"

She spared a single glance for the room where her fingers were ripped out of place, her nose broken, her spirit crushed and hidden behind the mask of a captain named Lenna Grayhill. In many ways she had never removed it. "Some of it's mine."

"Yours? You said you—" His voice faltered into silence. By the time he saw her just before the battle, her bruises were almost faded and the darkness behind her eyes could have been due to any number of wartime horrors.

Rows of cells led deeper under the palace, faint, snow-filtered light creeping through the windows. He paused beside one, bars rent open. Bones littered the floor. Alea crouched, wrinkled fingertips brushing the dome of a horned skull.

"You did this."

She nodded. "Mel'iend arrived just afterward. I couldn't wait. They realized who I was." She wondered at his unreadable stare, what new uncomfortable thoughts drifted through his fevered head.

"I can't believe An'thor sent you into this alone. Makes me trust him less. Though I'm not certain I trusted him since childhood." He looked away.

"He didn't know. Didn't send me, really. I sent myself. Besides, time makes monsters of most heroes." She glanced down at the body. "Even us."

"Especially us." His whisper rasped through the quiet. "Let's keep looking."

She slipped from her prison cell and led the way deeper into the palace's knotted gut. She remembered bolting up the stairs, turning a corner and finding another stairway. She followed the memory, faltering to a halt when a beam twice as thick as her own body barred the way. "I thought this was the way."

"I'm sure there's another," Arman murmured, fingers burning on the sallow skin of her wrist. "Here, a hall beside it. Let's just go around." To the left, thick iron bulkheads lay open, the metal scorched and dimpled. Pipes crowded the ceiling, leading from somewhere farther in. Arman fell in behind her again, but even so, the air was warmer, if only from its stillness. Their steps hissed in heaps piled at the edge of the corridor. "Snow?" she asked.

"Ash," he answered. He turned, scanning the iron plates lining the hall. "Something burned."

Alea turned to look back the way they came, instinct flaring ice across her cheeks. Her boot caught on something in the lee of a pipe's large elbow. She knelt, brushing ash and dust away. Seared sinew mummified over delicate scorched phalanges. Fire, then isolated bitter cold petrified what was left of their body. Alea's eyes picked out another and another, tucked in corners and behind columns of reaching ductwork. "Not something," she whispered. "Someone. Many of them."

"Accident or the revolt?"

Alea did not answer, just continued, each step carefully chosen. After another dozen bulkheads, the hall ended. A cavern yawned ahead, plummeting into a crevasse and reaching up to the lattice of iron that made the foundation of some room far above. Rent metal curved outward, bent by fury and fire. Perhaps it was the throne room's floor. Gears, each the height of a house, filled the space. Some stood vertical, others overlaid one another like interlocking flagging.

If a guardrail ever bordered the platform they now stood upon, it was long rusted or ripped away. Rent metal jutted from each side of the cleft, whatever structure it held blasted to pieces below. More fragments pierced the walls.

"What is this?" Arman's whisper bounced from the walls, skipping downward.

"When I first arrived, the ground hummed. I think this is why. Perhaps this is where they drew the metal to make their steam engines, their lattice, their revolvers. Pipes lay along the roads, too—channeling hot air to the central houses."

"It must have broken. Or overheated." He pointed. "There are boulders wedged in some of the gears."

"Sabotage."

"Something this thorough seems closer to suicide." Arman brushed a hand along the ice-covered wall. Rivulets trickled from the wake of his touch. "We ought to turn back. None of this looks stable — at least not for me. You said it was upstairs?"

Alea followed his gesture. Far above, rising from the iron lattice, was a chimney. Tangled pipes clustered at its entrance. "If we could get there, I imagine some of those pipes lead —"

Grinding metal interrupted her musing. Arman's sweat misted in the air, his clenched fist hardening in plated stone. A ladder below them ripped from its moorings, rising to hover before them. Alea placed a tentative boot on the bottom rung. Arman leaped on beside, one arm looped behind her. Before she could protest further, the ladder lurched upward. Stone crumbled from the walls as they passed, Arman's green eyes squeezed shut with the effort. They flew out, over the abyss, and rose incrementally, until the chimney swallowed them. The cavern shrank into a tiny square beneath their boots.

Hearths passed, their metal grates flashing glimpses of the rooms beyond. More bodies. Bedrooms. Manufacturing halls. Their journey into the bowels of the palace must have delved deeper than Alea realized. Mel'iend's comment that the Nenev built up and not down, seemed ill-founded.

"Stop!" The metal ladder clattered against the side and Alea grabbed at the pipes, panting. "I think I saw it. Storage of some sort."

When Arman turned to her, pale marble plates scabbed his face. The flesh between glowed sickly yellow. Her own power curled out, unbidden. As much as he was her guard, her partner, her companion for this journey and so many before this, he was also a stranger. A touch of his fingers softened the bars of the hearth enough to wrench them free.

It was wide enough to crawl through, but not by much. Alea pushed herself into the square vent, sloughing skin snagging as she wedged herself past the metal grate. She tumbled into the room and lay, panting on the floor for a moment. Black coagulated blood oozed from the torn flesh of her shoulder where the rusted metal peeled it back. Already, the ragged edge grayed, vitality fading with her every shallow breath.

Arman slipped through behind her, body flickering with translucence. He crouched beside her, smoldering fingers hovering over her scrape. "Are you all right?"

"It's just my body," she muttered. And it was. Every day her mind seemed more connected to the power drenching the world and less tethered to its physical cage of meat and bone. She glanced around. "We found it. I remember the smell of the dust."

"Creosote. I think I would have liked this place when it still churned."

She staggered to her feet and took stock. What was left of the finery of a dozen fallen nations had faded, picked over as much as the bones of the bodies below. Alea scanned the chests and shelves, searching for anything that resembled a book or scroll. *Fates, I'd settle for child's scrawl on a tutor's wax tablet.* Arman wandered in the other direction, his steps fading between the stacked furniture. Sealed treaties were shoved beside Athrolani royal lineages. The Kovasit, the Tzoan, the Xain. Somewhere in those pages lay the dead end of An'thor's line, crushed in Claimiirn. What bloodline would rise now that Tzatia had died?

She turned a corner and froze. A blanket draped over a shelf, stretched on a rope in a lean-to. Ragged furs and straw-stuffed pillows piled beneath. That is where she found the shrine.

The images were simple, strange in their style but unmistakable. They were scrawled across the raw wood of the back of a wardrobe. A woman, sooty hair and smoky power radiating from her. Beside her stood another, drawn in chalk and rust.

"Arman," she whispered, as much a recognition as a call.

She knelt on the cold furs of the makeshift bed. Parchment, weathered into spidersilk fragility, disintegrated beneath her knees.

A moment later Arman emerged from around the corner. "Found a handful of weapons, a map of a continent I'm not sure exists, and enough foreign coin to buy a Sunamen oasis two centuries ago. No book, though." When she did not answer, he settled beside her. "It's a shrine, as if someone worshiped you. Us."

Mel'iend. "I'm not something to be worshiped," she protested. "Not even you, with your sacrifice and burning hope."

Arman peered at the wall. "Someone survived the revolt. Someone who saw the mural in Lymorda."

"Or the book." Alea pointed to a fragment of parchment illustrated with a white hand set aflame. Even if they gathered all the pieces, their salt water and scorch would destroy every fragment. "Why is it each victory we have is overwhelmed by defeat?"

"There's more." Arman pointed to the wall, where another image was hidden by the tattered blanket. He lifted the corner.

Above the two figures stood a third, larger and drawn in sharp, violent strokes. He was painted in blood.

"Have you thought about what this means? We keep seeking answers, and all we find is this—icons of us created from priceless tiles and child's chalk. And our son. You were the one who poured over texts before the war, who learned the nature of yourself and our enemies. Tell me this doesn't mean what I think it does."

"Copper power, red blood. Bright brown. The gods." She drew a shuddering breath, the truth weighing on her heart, on her mind. She did not want to believe it either. Her damp fingers hovered over the marks. Corrosion flowed in her fingers' wake, rust knotting the art until it was unrecognizable. "We found our answer in Elanasa. I just refused to see it."

"He's what you saw, what the Laen predicted, then. What these people worship." Arman sat back on his heels. "Do you think An'thor had anything to do with this?"

Alea shook her head. "This is hope. He lost his decades ago—before we ever met him, I think." Her heart ached, every flick of its watery valves sending flashes of electricity through her chest. "It's how he recognized me."

Arman opened his mouth to argue, perhaps, or reassure, but whatever words he thought died, left to atrophy with his tongue. Even now, it wasn't hope that drove them. It was desperation, duty. Love, perhaps. But not hope. "What's next?"

"I don't even know where to look. If he's the blood the prophet means, then why are my dreams so violent? Why is the world dying?"

"What you saw in the Laen book, you said it was more powerful, more beautiful than we could ever be. Perhaps we're just missing one piece, one step we were meant to complete."

"It's not because of him," she snapped. *It can't be.*

Arman's eyes were exhausted, but the reassurance on his face was sincere. "I know. It's not our son's blood that poisons the world." He reached out, as if to brush a lank strand from her face but stopped, hand dropping back to his lap. "We'll figure out our next step in the morning. Though with this light it's anyone's guess when dawn comes."

She flashed a smile, seawater trickling from between pearlescent teeth. As sheltered as the treasury was, she could not bear to sleep beneath her own shrine, no matter how rudimentary. Instead, she borrowed the blankets and pillow and found a few cloaks hung on forms. Half the winding corridors were blocked, but there was no reason to hurry.

A massive iron bar had crashed from the throne room ceiling, protecting the dais from the worst of the weather. Snow drifted at the sides, and Alea cleared a space for their stolen comfort.

"I think I can get some of this straw to light, if you'd like a fire," Arman offered, kicking at the long moldered hay on the floor. "I can't feel the cold."

Alea shrugged, tucked in the fur, eyes fixed on the sky through the gash in the roof. Iron dug into her shoulder as she tucked herself against the stairs. Cold gnawed her bones, dragged at her heart and feet and hands. She did not really mind. "Malonostrii."

Arman frowned, following her gaze. Faint pink and blue curtains drifted across the clear black sky, sending rainbow glimmers through what little ice was still translucent. "You came here just before the war."

"You knew that." Her mind flickered with every terrible dream of blood, every beautiful memory of Keplan.

"I'm just marveling. You rode here all on your own."

"I had help. An'thor. His cousin—no, nephew." She forced the words past the ice in her throat. "I think he's the one who made the shrine."

Fabric rustled and then Arman was beside her, radiated heat rippling the air but never breaching the dense film of cold on her skin. "I've spent so many years protecting you.

Somewhere along the way I forgot you didn't need me to. Maybe I never knew." The smoke and stone in him shook his voice, or perhaps it was regret.

"There are a lot of things we both forgot. But mostly it's been each other."

"I'm so sorry, Alea. I'm sorry I never saw you through all my worrying. I've built up this image of who and what you are and I realize now, I was wrong." The straw beneath him smoked. "Fates, I would have loved to see you, see who you were, under all of it."

"Naked. Years ago I told someone that no one had ever seen me naked — my true self bared." She could not meet his eyes, only stare at the marbled white and charred cracks in his face. It was too late for a marriage, too late for a legendary love story.

His fingers found hers. The brush of hard, dry skin sent lightning crackling over her clammy hand. The sullen olive of his irises flamed to emerald, to gold. Black writhed up her flesh. *Warmth.* Her gaze rose to his and ice crystalized in her bones.

Their lips met. Lightning exploded from her flesh, crackling over him, through them both. Arman shuddered under her, but a smile curled his lips on hers.

Like he walked through air, as smoke, echoes of every event they ever lived fluttered between their briefly shared mind. Seawater and crackling ozone overlaid the stench of damp campfires, of burning bone. They shared so much, so little. Everything. Nothing. Death and life and pain.

Clawed hands, barely corporeal, gripped her tangled gray hair, her sloughing skin, and tugged her over him, onto him. Ice melted and froze again. Iron rusted. Far below, massive engines ignited, gears shuddered into waking with Arman's fire before the stone and steel crumbled to ash with her ferocity.

When consciousness, what was left of it, returned to her, they lay in ruins. Overhead the sky flamed with emerald, with azure.

Smoke drifted along the stones, coated in black ice. Cracks juddered across the slick surface, forming and retreating in rhythm, in breath. Hay and crushed Nenev bodies burned in every corner. Arman glanced down at his hands. They were nothing more than twisting smoke, blackened stone dust locked in Alea's ice. "Alea?"

Ice crackled again, louder. Brontide shook the building. Electricity flickered across the floor, concentrating where they lay. Dark water curled around each fork of lightning, coagulating until something barely human crouched on the floor.

Arman smiled, fingers materializing from the writhing smoke long enough to brush stringy black hair from rotted skin. "You're beautiful."

She stared down at herself, at the creature reflected in ice. Whatever form she had was mercurial now, at best. "I didn't want to believe it before. But I understand. The gods' blood I shed is killing us all. Us. Our lives. Whatever I severed, whatever connection you and I opened all those years ago, it's infected."

"Battle triage," he whispered. "Just to keep something alive until it can be properly healed."

"Every image we're together. The three of us. Our little family with mighty power. Maybe we'll find the final part of this mystery when we return to him." Her form melted, skin decaying until she was nothing more than black water trickling toward the door.

Arman's own bones and muscle fading into smoke, following her south. "We were meant to repair the world, return our power to the earth."

Her voice was snapping ice, groaning iron. "Instead we birthed a god."

Φ

The 43rd Day of Valemord, 1272
The City of Ceir Athrolan, Athrolan

Dense clouds hung low over the city. The night's dusting of snow was already packed into sullen gray ruts from wagons and hooves and boots. Keplan stomped on a particularly large chunk, wincing when he discovered it was frozen. Thankfully, his guards said nothing. The vermillion and green draping the Mirikin ambassador's manor was bright against the pale stone and frosty street. Keplan waited at the front door for the footman to announce him. This was hardly an official visit, but kings could scarcely barge in and rap on a man's study door.

"Right this way, Your Majesty."

Keplan waved for his guards to wait in the parlor and trudged upstairs. "Barrackborn?"

Bren jerked the door open. The shadows hanging from the bags under his eyes were darker than Keplan imagined possible. "You came."

"You asked." Keplan stepped in, taking a seat by the window without invitation.

"We'll be heading home soon, before the seas get worse. I thought we ought to talk beforehand. As allies, but as family, too." Bren poured a glass of wine for himself, gesturing with the bottle. "Care for some? We've got some charcuterie left, but it's old."

"It's not my taste." Truthfully his fingers trembled. He wished that like An'thor, like Brentemir, he could soothe his nerves with something so easily accepted. Instead, his peace was found in dark corners and a prostitute's pity.

"Kem's secretary sent me a letter—the one you received as well. About the priests."

Keplan pretended to gag. "They're a lot of fools. Will you respond?"

"I did this morning." Brentemir looked away.

"Thank fates." He peered at the scant offering of a cornucopia on the table between his chair and Brentemir's before choosing a thin slice of dry cheese. Fighting the priests was easier if his allies agreed with him—even if they warred with each other.

Brentemir moved from his desk to the window, looking down at Keplan with an expression unreadable behind his reservedness. Outside the still, foggy air settled lower over the city.

"I wanted to talk to you about something myself, actually."

"I assumed. You haven't seen us outside of state business since you were crowned."

"I've seen Azi. Besides, I'm busy kinging and all." He grimaced at the dry food but continued to nibble. "What happened the night he was attacked?"

"I thought I was going to die of fear. I saw my baby boy with a sword to his throat. Haven't quite recovered from it, though it appears he has."

Keplan grunted. Azimir had a new depth behind his eyes. Whether it was from fear or enlightenment he could never guess, but apparently it was something the boy's own father failed to recognize. "And the assassin—she was killed?"

"One of our swords took her—your captain helped, or tried to. I honestly can't recall much beyond the look in Azi's eyes. You'll understand when you have children. Why do you ask?"

"There's an ongoing investigation into the death of the man who ordered the assassinations. I'm trying to determine who might still be active and whether whoever murdered him was acting politically."

"As opposed to?"

Keplan met the ambassador's eyes. "Vengeance. Azimir was not the only one attacked. There were others on their list, and still more who simply disappeared. Most connected with my ascension, however superficially. But risking war by attacking a visiting ambassador's family is further than I expected. Surely your Spy Master knows something."

Bren glanced up, surprise widening his tired gray eyes. "I didn't realize you knew each other. She's out of the country. Traveling."

"Working for Kemmer, you mean." Keplan sighed. "Surely my people have their own avenues. I was just hoping you knew something."

"My family was attacked on foreign ground. I've tripled my guard, we're leaving Athrolan, and my son is safe," Bren reiterated. "This is not my country. Beyond that I couldn't give a shit what happens."

"I wish I could say the same." Keplan rose in a fluid motion and snatched the wine from the table. It smelled like overripe fruit. "So why did you ask me here? Besides my jovial company."

"You're married now."

Keplan poured some into the empty goblet and knocked it back. The sticky taste would distract him enough for the moment. He leaned on the polished desk. "I'd like to forget that fact."

Brentemir raised his brows. "You made your bed and now you've got to sleep in it—both of you. Azimir mentioned you've barely spoken to her. Have you thought about heirs?"

Keplan twisted the goblet slowly, watching the dark drink coat the thin glass. He had not. "I'm seventeen."

"If you're old enough to sit on the throne, you're old enough to father a child. If you're bedding people—regardless of what sits in their breeches—you'd best be prepared to accept the various consequences, one of which is children. And when you're king, the kingdom expects heirs. Tzatia only had you and look what happened."

"That was hardly the same situation."

"I know it's complicated. Your parents aren't here, and I wanted to let you know it wasn't easy with Kemmer and I—"

"I'm not forcing my friend to bear the children I can't!" Keplan made for the door. "This is a horrific conversation, one I'd rather not have."

"I don't see the Earth Shaker about to have it with you, so I'll have to suffice!"

Keplan whirled. "My father's not here because he and my mother are halfway across the tundra trying to save this pathetic excuse for a world. Again!"

Bren sat back, eyes alight with sudden desperation. "You heard from them?"

Keplan snorted, grateful to have the ambassador off the topic of procreation. "Fates, no. It's all just rumors. Daymir did. And those fanatics. And their prophet, and seemingly everyone but us." His chest ached with homesickness. It was easy to say he longed to return to the Hare. But he missed the forest and simplicity of woodcraft and hunting.

The room fell silent. Below, the guards burst into laughter at some jest. Gongs sounded the call for dinner in the neighboring Berrin ambassador's manor. Bren scrubbed a hand through his gray hair. The gesture was so akin to Azimir's, it made Keplan stare for a moment.

"I miss them too." Bren sighed. "I'm sorry for this, Keplan. For all of it."

The fight left Keplan. He was tired of fighting—fighting religion, fighting Domariigo, fighting Hylier. *Mostly just fighting myself.* He barely remembered how to converse without vitriol. "If I weren't the only one who could fix it, I'd think it was a mistake," Keplan confessed.

"I remember that feeling. The power in it. The dread." Brentemir met his gaze. "The lie. There is always someone who can do it better, wiser. Look at Kemmer. I don't agree with half her choices but Mirik's military is so much stronger under her than it ever was under me."

"I'm the only one with my parents' blood," the king reminded. "I don't think there's someone else suited. I'd drain my treasury to find them if I thought there were."

The glass rattled in the study window. Their guards fell silent below.

Bren glanced up, frowning. "Wind?"

Keplan shook his head, striding to the window. "Trees are still." It was dusk, but in the sliver of the market he could see at the end of the street, dozens of people had stopped, peering about in confusion. Beneath them, the floor quivered. Cracking stone echoed across the city. *Is Dorcal back?* Keplan pushed aside the fearful first thought. His breath misted the glass as he pressed against it, peering down into the city proper. Water burst from the single aqueduct arching over the walls from the southern hills. Curtains of water obscured half the noble district. The cobblestones disappeared under churning floodwaters.

Dread sank in Keplan's gut. "What is this?"

Bren's frown had not changed. "It happens from time to time. One of the lesser ducts will freeze and weaken, and the stone cracks under the pressure. Your father helped fix one years ago."

"That's not a lesser aqueduct." Keplan peered toward the harbor. Another geyser exploded into the air from the warehouse district, another in the Slummer, in the Silver Apron. "It's all of them."

Fire bloomed, following the slick brown streaks of spilled lamp oil. A moment later the harbor itself ignited. Keplan's guard burst into the room. "Sire—!"

"I can see it, Noren."

The guard gaped, glancing between the two men standing at the window, hands clasped behind their backs as the world seemingly ended outside. Keplan ignored whatever faltering warning or concern his guard babbled behind him. Thousands of thoughts bombarded the king's mind. Fear, his own and his people's. Through them all came one, ferocious and bitter and burning: *wrath.*

Φ

The 44th Day of Valemord, 1272

"Why don't you pick up a hobby?" Bimet asked. "Most queens and noble wives have projects—hopefully charitable, but we can't win every battle."

Rih rolled her eyes, staring out the window for a moment before answering. The streets were still filled with water, though the worst leaks had been repaired during the night. *I never thought the infrastructure would be what I missed most about Ban.* She turned back to her interpreter. "I don't miss being busy—hooves of Faco-il, I'm planning a rebellion against the largest empire in the known world, it's not like I'm bored."

Bimet's dark eyes crinkled in a laugh. "I meant something that soothes you, or delights you, or feeds your heart. You've been training and corresponding when you can, but unless I don't know you very well, I didn't think planning a war fed your heart."

Rih smirked. "Hardly. Though it certainly makes new friends, which I wouldn't have predicted."

"Eh, bloodshed, blood bonds, where's the difference?" Bimet joked. "Have you had a chance to look over the materials from Mobeka?"

Rih shook her head, glancing at the delicate wooden box that held textile samples. "I'm just wistful, which makes me restless. I miss the green and the air and the smell of the baking clay and sunburnt grass."

"You could garden."

Rih laughed in earnest. "I'm on the second story of a drafty building and I haven't touched earth in almost a week."

Bimet shrugged. "I suppose. I'd hardly know how to help either. I kill most things I touch—plant-wise, of course."

"Of course." The princess drew the box toward her and thumbed through the silks and wool. As much as she was drawn to the soft blues and purples, she felt uncomfortable in those colors, as if they no longer complemented her changing image. Her fingers paused on a particularly rich moss green. In Ban it was a color permitted only to the emperor himself. "Maybe I'll choose more reds and pinks to try to brighten this dismal weather."

Nehla burst through the door, already speaking. Rih turned away, wishing the woman would remember how difficult understanding her was normally, let alone when rushed and unable to see half her words.

After a moment Bimet turned to the princess. "Lady Nehla says there's another war council starting in half an hour."

Rih scowled. "I know we arrived at the last one uninvited, but you would think they would invite me out of courtesy alone."

Nehla grinned, this time turning so Rih could read her lips. "They did. I met the king's guard—Hyland something—in the hall. He said to pass the invitation to you from the king himself."

Warmth bloomed in Rih's chest. *I'm invited.* She rushed to her wardrobe, digging through the colored silks. She did not bother with a net or changing her onyx rings to match the peach tone of her nicer wrap. War did not require fashion.

Bimet appeared before her, eyes narrowed on the doorway behind them. "This is not what I meant when I suggested you find a hobby."

Rih frowned. "I'm invited and have little else to do."

"Boredom is no reason to go playing in someone else's war!" Her signs were furtive and sharp, hidden from Nehla by Rih's body.

"This war is as much mine now, and if I intend on borrowing my husband's army, I'll need his trust that I can use it properly. Besides, no harm can come from simply learning what they have to say." She turned, effectively ending the conversation.

Once again, the war council was held in one of the smaller council halls. Judging by the slight warmth emanating from the doorway, they had already started arguing. As much as she hated the imperial rule, she had to admit it was easier to get things done there, than it was with Athrolan's endless debates. *Perhaps that says more about the debaters than iron rules.*

The king was slumped in a chair, colorless eyes unfocused and hands shaking. The food on the table was meager, mostly dried meats. They had not had bread in weeks.

The general's eyes narrowed on Rih as she took her seat.

"Your Highness," he greeted. "I didn't expect you to join us. There's little enough to concern you here."

She felt her brow arch. "Unless more has been decided in the interim, General—which I highly doubt—I imagine there's plenty to discuss."

Keplan glanced between them, gaze absent. "We were just remarking on how this would be a good time to attack, given the weakness of the city. Most of our navy is busy containing the fires in the harbor, and our army has another week of repairs before the masons can properly fix the ducts."

"Have you considered switching to fired clay? RoBal uses pipes for much of their water system, and even under the high heat and pressure from our springs, they rarely break."

Keplan's attention sharpened. "Fewer seams make for fewer weak points?"

"Indeed. I can see if there's a Banis potter in the city who might know more."

Something that almost looked like a smile flitted across his face. "That would be helpful. Consulate, when the head of the Masonry Guild returns, both you and she must reach out to the Kajimet."

The general launched into recounting everything he gleaned from his missives to other cities, most of which had either not heard from the prophet or had seen nothing since the first letter. Rih flipped through her notes from the previous meeting, making tick marks by a few points. *If they boast an army large enough to attack the capital, then where are they hiding them?*

"Honestly, sire, we have little enough proof that they even have an army."

"They threatened the second largest kingdom in the known world. That'd be a whale of a bluff." Fess crossed her arms, leaning back in her chair in a manner far too casual for the king's presence. Keplan did not seem to notice.

Rih waited for the commander to finish the rest of her acerbic rant at the general before raising a hand for attention. "General Domariigo, have you considered that an army of believers may not look like a traditional military? The largest of your cities have indeed heard of this prophet and seen some of her followers. But you simply asked if they had seen Swordbearers. The best invasion isn't one you don't notice, it's one you ignore."

He glared but seemed unable or unwilling to give her a counter-argument.

Keplan's drink spilled as he attempted to drain the last of it. He winced, mopping blood-colored liquor from his embroidered shirt. It already bore old stains. "I'm honestly tempted to ignore it anyway. I can't be worrying about how to fight them off when I can't feed my people and half our harbor is aflame."

That's exactly what they want.

"You could accept Her Highness's offer of troops."

Rih stared at Bimet, wondering if the woman had mistranslated Fess's suggestion.

"You think Mirik would turn a cheek to their enemy's army arriving within jumping distance of their capital? There was no official argument when we allied with the empire, but I fear Banis troops would be a league too far."

The general scoffed. "They value our trade too much. Besides, you're family and Bren won't risk you." He grabbed the last piece of meat, gnawing on it with disinterest.

"Bren isn't Hetmir, and from what I've seen Kemmer is far from gutless," the king argued. "Their family was already attacked on our cobbles."

Rih watched Bimet's hands, her mind bouncing between the opposing verbal volleys. "For the sake of safety, Your

Majesty, let's assume they do have an army. The only way to weaken Athrolan further is to separate you from the throne. If you go to Ban to beg for soldiers, the Swordbearers will surely attack."

Keplan frowned, leaning forward. "You just offered aide, now you say it's a poor choice? I don't want to go to Ban. The place disgusts me, but I fear it's the only way to protect my people from this prophet's insanity."

Rih drew a breath and summoned her strength. "Stay in your city. Tend to your people's food, their water. Extinguish these fires. I will go to Ban in your stead and ask my people for aide."

She could not be certain, but she swore the conversation died. Azimir might be idealistic, but he knew Athrolan better than she. She could ask for troops and get a better view of the Banis army for her own machinations.

"You've been married less than a month and you already seek to return home?" the general snapped.

Acting as an ambassador was hardly returning home, but Rih let him have his concerns. Instead, she simply sat back. "I think it's a sound suggestion, but I'm sure you'll have to debate the matter."

Colonel Hamacad rose from the end of the table. "Sire, how do you think that would look, sending your wife to do your bidding? Begging pardon, Your Highness."

Keplan sighed, rubbing a gloved hand over his exhausted face. "I'll think it over. Let's turn our focus to determining where the prophet's strength lies. No matter which troops we use, we'll need a strategy."

Rih glanced at Bimet. The translator's eyes were wide, and it took her a moment to catch up to the others' new arguments.

"I'm sorry," Rih signed to her. "I know you disagree."

"Disagreeing isn't up to me," she answered, but her hands were stiff with forced formality. "But I'm glad you know my reservations." She turned sharply, and Rih felt a puff of air brush her cheek as the door swung open.

Fess paused, the council watching the king's personal guard stride up to Keplan's chair. Hylier bent, whispering something in the man's ear before straightening.

Keplan's face paled and he smacked his hand on the table top. "Something urgent has come up. You have your orders, and for now, I want everyone's focus on bolstering the city or tracking down evidence of this prophet's forces. Dismissed." He hurried from the room, his guard on his heels looking ill.

Φ

Bimet stepped into Rih's study, knocking one of the weights off the bookcase by the door to get her attention. "This came for you. If that's all for the evening, I'll be in my room. Nehla is here finishing some mending if you need anything."

"That'll be all. Have a good night." Rih leaned over her desk to take the scroll. It was plain, with a colorless seal. She cracked the wax and slid the scroll onto a stand to read it better.

> *My dear friend,*
> *I hope this finds you well. It was such a delight to see you during your journey to Ceir Athrolan. I know you asked after our mutual sisters-in-arms, and I've finally had a moment to myself.*

Rih's heart thundered into wakefulness. After the endless drama of Athrolan's court and seemingly useless debates, her mind begged for something new.

Osak is doing well, though I'm sure she misses home, being on the coast. Of course Sefer, who's there too, with the 17th Arc, loves being so close to the ocean.

Neither were names Rih recognized. *It's a code!* She drew another paper toward her and began to write. Each name received a dot of colored ink. Blue for best suited for being stationed on the coast, red for on the Athrolani border, and emerald for the capital. Figuring out how best to make use of this would take time, but if nothing else, she had a list of allies. Her eye caught the title of one of the two male names on the list of a dozen. *Powerful allies.*

Her blood pounded with anticipation. She had Bimet, she had Majilah Ag. But this was more. This was the beginnings of a network. She dug a map from her desk next, weighing it with the scroll stand and her discarded wrap. Two marks by the coast. Another four along the Hartland. Five in the capital. And one in a little town just shy of the Athrolani border.

For now, she needed them safe, scattered across the empire so they might spread the word to everyone they could. Her finger paused on the name of an ally far in the south. They were within a few days' march of the edge of the Valen territory. *It's time to write to Majilah Ag.* So much had happened since meeting with the Queen of the Vales, but it could be said her entire course was set by that single handshake in the dark Stytown brothel.

When she glanced up again, Nehla stood in the doorway.

Rih flinched. Her instinct screamed to shove the map and list into her drawers before the other woman could see a single line. *But that would only draw suspicion.* Instead, she shuffled the pages together, as if done with some mundane task. The edges of the parchment trembled with her shaking hands. When she had set it aside, facedown, she looked up expectantly.

It was then that she saw Nehla's rigid body. Her eyes were wide with forced calm and her shoulders were at least a finger-space higher than her usual easy stance. Her jaw bunched, making it almost impossible for Rih to read her lips. "His Majesty Keplan Wardyn."

"What about him?" Rih gave an exaggerated confused look.

"His Majesty is here to see you, Your Highness."

Cold sank over Rih's body. It was late, well past evening. Her hands formed the few signs Nehla knew. "Get Bimet."

She extinguished her lamp and swept from the room to answer the door herself. The gangly figure of the king loomed in the dim hallway. Bile flooded Rih's throat.

"May I?" One gloved hand gestured to her parlor.

She opened the door wider, eyes meeting Bimet's as the interpreter appeared from the servants' stairs.

Bimet glanced from the king to her princess before signing. "What does he want?"

Rih shook her head. There was only one reason a man visited his wife's chambers after dark. Her mind flashed to the box in her chest. Nothing would protect enduring the next few hours. Ki-elte's teas, however, would make them easier. "Would you order tea?" she asked Bimet, words almost lost in a pharyngeal stutter. Would her interpreter stay for the duration, witness to Rih's undoing, or would he request she leave, condemning them to miscommunication? She did not know what to wish for.

Bimet's hand pressed hers and she flinched. "Rih, he asked how your day was."

Rih forced herself to look at the man. "It was uneventful, save for the council."

"Did I interrupt you?"

She followed his gesture to her fist clenched around her pen, hard enough to bleed ink over the lines of her palm. Perhaps that was why her hands seemed unable to sign. She let it fall into her lap, broken. "I was just writing to family. Telling them about the city."

"Have you been able to visit it much?"

"Master A'hane toured us about."

Keplan's head tilted. "Azimir? My cousin?"

Fear flashed up her spine. Would he question their visits, as others had? Would it anger him? "Yes. He visits occasionally to discuss the events between our nations. I think he hopes to forge peace in the future, despite tension now."

The king looked down at his gloved hands. "I didn't know he had an interest in that."

"He seems to just wish everyone would get on well."

"I've been thinking of the same." His jaw clenched, shoulders hunched. She had not realized how tall he was, despite his slender build.

Hot water arrived with an array of teas. Bimet excused herself and returned with a small silk sachet from Rih's ornate box. They were quiet as Keplan poured himself a mug and Rih took a long sip. It scalded her throat, but numbness quickly followed. Her hands and feet tingled.

"Your alliance is appreciated, if a surprise," she began. "Given the circumstances."

His face twitched as if he felt her gaze on his scars. "So you know."

There was an honesty in his terrifying eyes. She recalled his slight smile earlier that day. Perhaps he wanted honesty in return. "I recognized you when I arrived. Could have sworn you wanted Ban to burn."

"I did. A large part of me still does. I would pay dearly, time was I'd die, even, to watch your empire fall to ruin."

"But not anymore?"

Keplan twisted the mug slowly, watching the dark drink coat the clay. "We're married, aren't we?"

She was a league away from her body, it seemed, whether from panic or her drink, she did not know or care.

"I thought I'd hate you. And most of me does, but you still burst into my war council, you still offer help." He surged to his feet.

She flinched, adrenaline, even distant, exploded through her chest.

His thin brows curled together, and for the first time his frigid eyes settled on hers. Seeing. The muscles in one cheek flickered, lamplight gleaming off the scar below. He paled further, gloved hands rising, as if encountering a prairie cat. "Fates. I didn't think—" He looked between the two of them and backed toward the door. "You're going to RoBal for me. You leave in four days."

Rih watched the door close, watched Bimet slide the bolt closed. One hand dragged over her face. Rih's body was aflame, as if every fragment of control, of peace, was burned from her nerves by the flash of colorless irises. Terror that she had displeased him drowned any relief at his absence. "What—" She stopped, shaking, fiddled with the ink on her skirt, and then tried again. "Why did he leave?"

Bimet shook her head. "I don't know. I couldn't know, but I could guess." She crouched before Rih, movements slow, careful not to touch the other woman. "It almost seemed as if he realized what you thought, that he had a moment of empathy, perhaps."

"How could he not have known? A man doesn't appear at his wife's door just before midnight without intending to—" She pushed the woman out of the way and rushed to the privy. Even the acrid taste and stench of vomit did not erase her fear. When her stomach was empty, she still felt no safer, no less afraid.

When she sat back, Bimet's hand appeared holding a damp, warm cloth. She did not sign or attempt to voice anything. Instead, she dabbed at Rih's cheeks, washing away tears and vomit. Another cloth dried her face before the interpreter lifted her off the tiled floor and into her bedroom. A blanket settled over Rih's shoulders, and a mug warmed her palms. *Kava. For trauma.*

Wind eddied and she glanced from the swirling pink depths of the tea to see Bimet had cracked open the door to the balcony. The bedroom door was shut and a heavy chair was pushed against it. Bimet caught Rih's glance from it to her and back.

Her smile was faint but full of feeling. She poured herself a mug of tea and settled at the end of Rih's bed. "I learned signs long before I was sent to become a noble interpreter. It was all I wanted to do. To travel, to speak with people, help them connect. And I was good. My first teacher was one of the scribes in the merchant quarter, a friend of my father's and the only man in his family who voiced. He was a kind man and a good teacher. He was the one who brought me to Vibaln's attention. He knew my skills were good enough to earn a place in the Hand's entourage. Neither of us knew the price. Naïve. The Emperor's Hand makes sure everyone in his service knows who owns them. My first night in his court I learned he owned my body. I still don't know if this career, the one I wanted more than anything, was worth it."

Rih's heart ached for her, but fear thrummed too loud to let her reach out a hand. She forced her hands into stilted motion. "We're going home. You'll have to see him again."

Bimet must have seen the compassion in her eyes because she smiled, a broader one now. "It was long ago, and I've made my peace."

Bimet leaned against the post of the bed, gaze lost out the window. Rih's nerves still screamed, but there was a spark, deep at the base of her heart. She let it gutter and burn, let her mind wander between dissociation and relief. Outside night deepened, a cosmic burial shroud over her gasping breath.

CHAPTER EIGHT

The 45th Day of Valemord, 1272
The City of Ceir Athrolan, Athrolan

MILDEW BLOOMED IN THE garden. The acrid stench of burning lamp oil clung to the damp stone. Mud squelched under Keplan's leather boots. Beside him, Hylier's strides were almost silent.

"You're quiet this morning."

Keplan shrugged. "I have a lot to think about."

"I thought you avoided such things."

"Usually." Keplan turned his face to the dawn light, seeking the phantom of its warmth. Even on a clear day, cold seemed to seep from the very ground. "I suppose today's problems are ones I feel I can actually solve."

Hylier snorted. "If you have insight into how we're going to solve the issue of Greton's letter, by all means, share."

"He's just asking for an audience with my administration." Keplan shrugged, clasping his hands behind him. It was cold enough to warrant a hat and coat, and for once he was grateful traditional Athrolani style had a penchant for fur.

"An inspector can act on his own. He doesn't need you or His Highness Daymir to arrest anyone. Unless, of course, he's arresting you."

"I doubt he'd arrest me. Accuse, surely, but in what country could a common man march up and dismantle the throne?"

"Arguably, that's what you did."

Keplan glowered. "I don't have time for that nonsense."

"I thought you said you could solve it."

"That wasn't what I meant. I saw Rih last night."

Hylier stared, blue eyes scanning the king's frame as if searching for evidence of how their evening was spent. "And?"

Keplan turned toward the memorials, ducking under a broken arbor. Even here damage from the burst aqueducts was rampant. "In four days she rides to RoBal to ask for troops on my behalf. What she says or does isn't my concern. But she's going. I think I startled her, though."

"Begging your pardon, Your Majesty, but you're a startling fellow on the best of days."

"And on the worst of them?" Keplan asked wryly.

"Ah, I decline to answer, sire." He cleared his throat. "Speaking of troops, have you spoken to Daymir at all? I noticed he was absent from the war councils."

"I don't trust him."

"You can't wage war without the regent's approval."

"I invited him to the first, he didn't come. His servant said he was ill. I didn't bother telling him about the second. You saw him more often than most while he was exiled. You know his mind is not what it once was."

"He deserves kindness, not exclusion," Hylier argued. Pity and sorrow tinged his voice and Keplan was reminded that the guard's family had served Daymir's for longer than the man had been in exile. "Your family served him from before?"

"My mother's father, Currow, was his steward. He saw the entire house crumble. I was just a boy at the time."

Keplan glanced at the captain. The man was so youthful, it was hard to remember he was at least a decade older than the king. "It must be difficult to see him suffer this way. Reduced to an echo of who he was supposed to be."

"It is. Almost a mockery."

"I'm sorry for my part in it. I don't see another path, and I didn't then, either, but I'm sorry it's this way."

Hylier sighed, lifting his chin a bit. "I'm not the one owed an apology, and you're too young for regrets yet, Wardyn."

Keplan scoffed. "It's not the years you've ridden, but the leagues, I think." They lapsed into silence. The city below was a cacophony of wrenching metal and shouts from bucket brigades as fires began and were extinguished. Somewhere on the docks Fess organized lines of leather bladders to contain the worst of the spilled oil. He wished the city did not look like the chaos and filth of his own mind.

"I found Peraan's bag." Hylier's voice was barely above a murmur, so faint Keplan wondered if it was the wind.

He let the man think over his next words without interruption.

"I looked through it, enough to see it was his. Missing his usual bottle of wine. The parchment is mostly destroyed, but there's a waxed writing kit that might have survived. A signet ring, too. One from Daymir's family that was auctioned off when he was exiled."

They rounded a bend and drew up outside the entrance to the memorials. Ahead, someone was shouting.

"Where is it now?"

"My room in the city. I wrapped it in an old cloak. The sooner we deal with it the better. I dislike being so entangled in this."

"For someone who has such distaste for this work, you're incredibly good at it," Keplan noted.

"Same could be said of you."

"Ruling?"

"I wouldn't go that far." Hylier's tone would have been teasing, were it not for the truth in it. "Influencing people."

"Most of that is wrangling my parents' myths into sense."

"You didn't see them when they were building those myths, though. They weren't people to be wrangled."

"How?" The cry cut through their musing.

Keplan glanced at the memorials. "Grieving?"

Hylier's eyes narrowed. "It's been months since anyone noble died." He loosened his sword in his scabbard and paced up the stairs. "Stay behind me, sire. Just in case."

Keplan did not argue, falling in a few steps behind. Something thumped against stone in the center of the raised lawn.

"How could this happen?"

They crept along the paved walk in the Circuit of Honor. The Xain mausoleum stood in the center, just beside the older, weathered pink granite of the Tzoan.

A crack echoed from between the white marble columns.

Grief flooded Keplan's body. The ache of longing, of regret and burning shame crashed through his senses. He pushed past Hylier.

The mausoleum was dark. There was too little lamp oil for the living to waste it on the dead. The scorched stone table stood empty in the center, ringed by a dozen vaults. All but one was filled. One day Daymir's burnt remains would be sealed behind it. For now, though, he crouched on the floor beside his aunt's grave, sobbing.

"Blackhouse."

The man glanced up, parchment cheeks raw from tears. "Why do you all keep calling me that?"

Frustration crashed into pity in a mental maelstrom. Few things kept him grounded when his own mind spun. *And I'm not about to shove dust up an old man's nostril.* He folded himself onto the floor a few paces from the regent. "This cold weather really sets the bones aching, eh?"

Daymir did not answer, but he watched the king warily.

A moment later Hylier knelt beside his friend. "I know my knees are never pleased in winter."

"You're Dill—Currow's grandson. You look older."

Hylier nodded. "It's been a while indeed. I thought we could visit, maybe over tea?"

Daymir was still fixated by Keplan. "And him, I know his face."

Keplan drew a card from Hylier's deck and tried for vague calmness. "You knew my parents. Hy—ah, Dill—and I have been working together."

Daymir seemed to remember where he was, if not when, and fresh tears leaked from the creases around his fogged eyes. His voice was a distant groan. "Tzatia. Why did no one tell me she passed? No one even fetched me for the funeral. I'm not even across the city. I can't believe I'm king."

Even Hylier seemed uncertain of what to say. "Why don't you come inside? There's so much to discuss. Her memory deserves a bright fire and hot food."

Daymir's hand brushed the inscription on his aunt's vault, gnarled fingers picking out the tiny intricacies that had long since weathered from the older graves. "I never said goodbye. Last we spoke it was a ball, I think, when..." He stopped, looking back up to Keplan. "Did your mother send you?"

He shook his head, at a loss. "She's traveling. Let's get you warm."

Hylier rose, offering the regent an arm to haul himself upright. Together they left the mausoleum, Keplan a step behind. He was an intruder on this moment, witness to vulnerability that should have been sacred, reserved only for family. For those who loved the man. He glanced back at the dark, deserted monument. How soon would it be before Daymir joined them?

They skirted the gardens, entering the palace from a small rear door by the southeast tower. Keplan flagged down a squire as they made their way toward the regent's rooms. "Hot tea, please, and a small lunch—some of that roasted duck, perhaps. To High Highness the Regent's parlor."

"We're clear out of the duck, sire," the squire apologized, ducking her head in a bow. "Our meat and cold storage are low, what with no bread. We could bring some pickled fish."

"Fine, whatever there is, then," he answered, watching her disappear into the servants' hall. *No bread.* His stomach growled in protest. How was the Hare faring, with so little to serve?

"Wardyn."

He glanced ahead, to where Hylier waited by Daymir's open door. The king jogged to catch up. "I ordered something for him."

He glanced into the room from the doorway. The old man sat by the window now. The cold sun glinted off the white stone and shone on pale naked trees.

Daymir's gaze settled somewhere far distant. "I always loved snow, even in exile. It made us equal. At least everyone would be caught in the same storm, unable to leave. No visitors. Sometimes, your mind's the best friend you have when you're left be, left gone to seed."

Keplan knew that feeling well, caught between realities, never certain which one everyone else experienced. "We've ordered you some lunch. Would you like us to leave?"

"I'm surprised you made it up the road in this. Slippery, with fresh fallen—though your parents did. Last they visited." He frowned. "Are they still here?"

Keplan shook his head. "No. They aren't. They went on."

Daymir hummed in response, eyes lidding while his head lolled with exhaustion.

Hylier opened his mouth to speak, but Keplan shook his head. When they left and the heavy wood separated them from Daymir's gentle mutters, the captain turned to him.

"It's as if he sees all of his past and present at once. You were there and so was your mother."

"Seeing moments simultaneously," Keplan reiterated. "Small wonder his mind's lost. I know seeing so much frays mine."

Hylier looked at the king, expression unreadable. "Is that why you didn't you tell him he was in Athrolan? Or that he can go where he pleases? Most people argue with him when he gets confused."

"No sense in it." Keplan trudged down the hall. "Wherever he is, he wants to stay there. He wants to be left alone. There, at least, he isn't mad."

"Sire, the matter we spoke of," Hylier reminded him.

Keplan winced. His nerves were aflame from dealing with Daymir. The amount of himself he saw in the older man terrified him. No matter what glimpses of time he saw, like Daymir, the future was unknowable. Of all the briars in his palm, Greton and his murder investigation were the most irritating. "Have you found anything more about the network?"

Hylier glanced down the hall. "Perhaps elsewhere—"

"It's a legitimate question. No one knows where all these names originated or what anyone would gain from simply removing the people who helped me. Some of them, surely, but not all. All we've got is a piss-stained bag, a man I'm glad is dead, and the alias of a man who, more often than not, doesn't even recall my name." Frustration was a caldera, echoing the mighty seething deep down in his mind.

"I've learned all of that while acting as your guard," Hylier spat. "It's not my issue that you've decided to start a war over disliking someone's faith—"

"Blasphemy!" Keplan roared. His thoughts ignited with panic. "They preach this sickening image composed of contradictions. I'm not some all-knowing creature, and if anyone ought to be worried about wrath, it should be them!"

Hylier stepped back, eyes wide. "Sire, I only meant your actions may have been reactive and could have benefited from more time and thought."

Embarrassment slapped his cheeks. The same concerns overhung most of his conversations lately. "Then you sit the throne! Go ahead," he snarled, ripping the signet ring from his hand. It clattered across the flagging. "Take it, take all of it. Take my fate-cursed life while you're at it and save us all some trouble!"

His captain turned on his heel without another word. The palace guards at the end of the hall pretended not to see, and Keplan wondered whether it was out of disdain or pity. The king crumpled to the floor. He backed into an alcove, relishing the bite of cold tile on the back of his head. He ripped the gloves from his hands and pressed them to the slush-splattered floor. His sanity may have been slipping, but even so, he did not miss the allusions in the prophet's scripture. *Green hand, red hand. Sees all, understands none.* He wished he thought to call after Hylier, apologize, offer to help with the puzzle of who needed his allies in the city removed. Loneliness yawned in his chest, and even the fading effects of dust did nothing to help. His allies in the palace were dwindling too, and he had only himself to blame.

Φ

Hylier strode into the city, boots tromping the path to the narrow apartment tucked between the old inn and a milliner's workshop. The window was dark. Cobwebs were strung between the doorknob and the wood of the door. He had a fraction of the connections Reka did, and half of hers were probably to inform on Athrolan herself. *Or on Ambassador Barrackborn's sister.*

He understood better why she left Brentemir's service. It appeared Azirik's lineage had a penchant for perfection and mercurial temperament. *Or outright illness.* Hylier was almost convinced being a monarch required a certain mental instability. Perhaps it was simply because the unintended casualties were so much greater when madness sat the throne. His steps slowed. Reka was Mirik's Spy Master. She had a network ten times his own. Maybe it was time they shared more than just a bed and bitter conversation.

As much as he disliked the pauper-king, he had made a vow — to Daymir, to Athrolan, and to Keplan himself. *And it's not as if I'm untarnished.* He kept a murder victim's bag in his room, hidden from the city inspectors. He helped cover up the crime. And plotted to blame it on someone else. The most he could do was find out Peraan's motives and make sure whoever took the axe-blow was as guilty as the king himself.

He found his way to a Slummer bar, close enough to the docks to have a variety of clientele. He sank into the seat facing the door, leg crooked outward in a welcoming gesture. Once his drink was ordered, he fished a bag of tiles from his pocket. It was a game that required opposition, and with the new alliance, there were more Banis in the city than ever. Hylier could think of one country, at least, who would benefit from both Athrolani instability and the death of the Mirikin Hetmir's son.

"Looking for a partner?"

His brows rose. Of all the people he expected to see, Lady Nehla was not one. Asking what brought her there, however, might lead her to ask him the same. "You play?"

She smiled, flipping her wrap aside and dropping gracefully into the opposite seat. "Well enough. Buy me a drink?"

"I thought Banis didn't drink."

"Most don't." Her eyes leveled on him. "But I've traveled enough to pick up all manner of things from every map corner."

Warning shot up his spine. Until that moment he swore the Banis princess's handmaiden was charming on her best day, vacuous on her worst. The fire in her eyes now, however, told him he was sorely mistaken. "I enjoy tales of travel," he replied, cautious. "I would love to hear some of yours."

Her head tilted, her dark eyes regarding him a moment. "Perhaps you can tell me some Athrolani gossip in return."

He slid the bag of tiles to her. "What's your drink of choice?"

Φ

The 47th Day of Valemord, 1272

Sha's ceiling was draped with gold silks and delicate netting. After a moment Keplan realized they were tied in the same knots as the fishing nets heaped on the floor during his last visit. These, though, were ties of soft cotton. "Your room is beautiful," he whispered.

She propped herself up on one lean arm. Her wig had been discarded at some point earlier, and her shorn dark hair curled at wild angles. "It's hardly much, but I like it."

"It's yours." He frowned. "Wholly yours. I haven't had a room that was just mine since I left home. My life doesn't even feel like mine."

Her dark eyes softened with empathy. "I've been lucky in that. But I know many—common and noble alike—who feel the same. Most of us are trapped by our fear and our circumstance."

His finger traced the faint curves of her chest and narrow hips. "I think I feel trapped by myself. The choices I've made. They didn't seem like choices, like there were other options when I made them." He swallowed past a sudden lump in his throat. "Recently I realized I've been trapping others too. And that's the bit that nags me."

Sha's gaze flicked to the box on her dressing table, the pale green dust scattered on the smooth surface. "Is that what you're trying to forget? Or is it these?" Her thumb smoothed the pocket of his cheek as if it could wipe the scar from his skin.

"It's just..." He shook his head. Tears erupted and he ducked his head. "Fates, I don't even know anymore! There's just so much pain! Pain I've felt and witnessed, pain I've caused. Sometimes it all feels the same."

"Pain is all the same. Joy too. It's what we do with it that changes us. Believe it or not, as carefree as I am, this life isn't easy. Folks are confused by me, whether they're looking at Sha or Rheman. I don't fit into expectations. Most ignore it, but a few don't." Her fingers tightened around his. "That's why we need friends. Lovers. Family, blood or otherwise."

A frown strained his exhausted face. "Can I tell you something?"

She waited, expectant.

"I'm married. It wasn't what I wanted, but I chose it because I thought it would make things better. The whole thing terrified me. I only just realized she's terrified too."

Sha sat up, drawing his head into her lap. Her fingers combed tangles from his long hair. "In this world marriage is a livelihood. And not just our lives rest on its success, but our families or, if it's political, those of thousands." When he cocked his head, she continued. "The soldiers who die when negotiations fall through. The couriers and clerks and ambassadors who must find excuses for what happened or whose families starve when they can no longer do their job because of war. And, of course," her pointed gaze flicked up to his, "the woman abused because she did not please her husband."

His stomach twisted. Rih's terror when he appeared at her door settled in his mind. Perhaps, if dust hadn't burned away empathy with the errant thoughts, he would have understood the origin of her fear sooner. He was so wrapped up in how painful his own life was, the drama of his journey, his conception, that he failed to see the strength it took to face him. *She's a better king than I.*

"Where do you go when you kick up dust?" Sha asked.

"Kick up dust?"

"That drifting of the thoughts, the spinning without care."

His raised his brows. "I thought you didn't breathe it."

"I don't anymore. It never did much for me. Few things get their claws in me. Some people find it easy, others don't."

He shook his head. "I don't know. Inside, I suppose."

"Sometimes that's the scariest." Sha's head tilted. "Would you like to tell me about your marriage?"

He stared at his bare hands for a breath. "I imagine disinterest is better than cruelty, but these marks and my face make it difficult. Make me difficult." The weight of Firas's rejection settled over his shoulders, his lover's face when he realized what trouble their bar boy brought to the inn. "I'm a difficult man. I wish I weren't."

"You said you didn't have a choice."

"Of course I did. But I wasn't ready for it. I didn't have someone to train me, I didn't have my whole life to prepare."

"Perhaps she had a choice too." Sha sat up straighter, extricating her folded legs from under him. "It's my turn to ask if I can tell you something."

"Whatever you wish."

"Someone's been asking around. An inspector. A good one. Asking after a boy, one with a habit for dust." Her dark eyes flicked to his, steady and full of honesty. "Says he murdered a man."

His thoughts were spinning again. There was no way Sha did not know who he was. It was written under every line she spoke. "That could be anyone."

"Could be."

"Why are you telling me?"

"Because the man who was murdered deserved everything he got and more. I've lived in the shadows of this city for years and many here are those I count among my friends, people I would do anything for. And he took one of them from us."

"Mirrel."

Sorrow tugged at Sha's smile. "I'm just thinking if someone is asking for Lan Guardsen, perhaps it's time he takes a trip. Until this wind changes."

Only I will remain. He straightened and looked about for his shirt. "Surely you have somewhere else to be, instead of me just wasting your time with chatter."

"You've paid for my time. It's up to you how you spend it." She took his hand, pausing his retreat. "Why don't you just rest here."

He settled on the bed, the covers soft against his skin, Sha's large calloused hands working knots from his shoulders. The scent of ale and cooking food drifted from below. Outside, the city sounds were muffled.

"The window, would you mind?"

Sha padded soundlessly across her room and swung opened the casement, letting the night air eddy its news through the room. It carried an infant's furious, hungry wail to the corner by the door. It scattered male laughter by their tray of food, swirling there for a moment before it brought the thoughts to where he sprawled on the bed. It seared him, the hunger, the fear, the hope, but he closed his eyes and bathed in his tiny corner of peace.

Φ

The 10th Day of Glasmord, 1272
The City of RoBal, Ban

Noon sun lanced through the building clouds, beams tracking across the prairie like a guard's search lamp. Despite her lack of sleep, humming energy filled Rih. Her eyes picked out familiar hills, dipping swales that marked her journey home. Threatening rain necessitated keeping the cover raised on her wagon, but she leaned out the front as if able to spur the horses faster simply with the force of her own anticipation. Two dozen Athrolani guards augmented her own retinue, and while they kept to themselves for the first days, now fires, food, and the occasional bedroll were shared each evening. Rih even noted Curiel among the paler faces.

RoBal towered in the distance, and Rih's pulse quickened as the mound grew on the horizon. Even under the slate clouds, it loomed an angry red. Already her skin was invigorated by the absence of salt and raw wind. Glinting spears ahead heralded their waiting imperial escort.

Burning joined the thrumming excitement in her limbs. *Anger.* She had longed for home, for the rich flavors and layers of color, even as she detested the inequality and hatred upon which the entire system was built. Still, it was home.

Damp wind picked up, ushering them forward. A glance at Bimet told her they had already been heralded. Sure enough, their escort fell in around them at the next rise.

Adrenaline spiked again at the red armbands. Surreptitious signs passed between a few of her own retinue and the Banis soldiers. It gave her pause. *I thought Bimet was my only ally in Athrolan.* The interpreter's face was unmoved, dark eyes fixed on the stacks of houses ahead. Did she know how far — and close — their movement reached?

"Are you looking forward to being home?" Rih asked Nehla. She knew Bimet's feelings mirrored her own in their ambivalence.

"I am. Letters from family say much has changed. It's been a long time since war waged here, beyond the usual imperial expansion. Undoubtedly fashions have changed, too." Nehla flashed a smile. Her bright eyes were fixed on the road ahead, her perpetual giddiness tempered only by the fatigue of travel. "I can't wait to add new wraps and jewels to bring back to Athrolan."

"I wonder how many Athrolani trends made their way back already."

"Depends on how many you wear while we're here," Nehla countered. "You're a king's wife, you'll set trends faster than most."

Rih laughed. She had only just mastered the basic traditional attire. Learning something new with each season was more daunting than any rebellion.

The road widened, the packed earth giving way to bricks as the scattered huts and shacks closed in along the riverbanks and roadside. Wooden grating and narrow walls ran along the road to keep guests from witnessing the worst of the poverty that crowded outside the walls, caught between clawing free and pressing in.

One of the Athrolani guards rode up, raising the face of her helm to flash Rih a smile. "You promised to teach me that atlatl, and I've heard your training courts are rivaled only by the emperor's gardens."

Rih's mouth curled. "I'd love to, though I fear once you get a taste of proper tea and fruit it might be impossible to pry you from your rooms."

"I want to taste it all! I was on guard duty the night they brought out that candied stuff, it was gone by the time Jaik took over for me. Hardly blame them."

Rih laughed. "You'll have more than enough to try here, as long as you stay close to our wing. If we've a spare moment I'll gladly show you the courts—I've only used those in the barracks and the Purple Throne, but I've been told those in the palace are stunning."

"Purple Throne? That sounds more like a brothel than a place to train," Curiel joked.

"Essentially. It's where I was trained for marriage," Rih explained. Her gaze wandered past her friend to the building tucked against the palace. "It's there, if you have any interest in such things."

Curiel shook her head. "My evenings are occupied by La-naket lately. Your pretty Banis horses aren't the only thing he can ride—"

Rih rolled her eyes. She might have enjoyed a clever, vulgar joke as much as anyone, but the image Curiel's words evoked was one she would rather not see. "As long as our afternoon is free, then, come find me."

The wagon lurched onto the brick-laid main road and Rih glanced forward. As a soldier, she rode through the smaller military gates of RoBal countless times. Today they entered through the massive front gates.

Steeply sloped double walls ringed the city. Though rain washed much of the surface filth away, black blood and brown fluids still streaked the baked clay, draining from the bodies pinned along the top. Most were accused of theft or treason. Rih suppressed a shudder. She wondered how many were innocent. How many had been members of her rebellion. *Did any confess under the interrogators' blades?* Or were they simply dragged through the streets to die atop the heights?

Even the cold, damp air was rank with refuse. Here, the pervasive scent of fruit and clay veered closer to rot and muck. Opulence was a glimmer of dawn far ahead, over the teetering rooftops and haze of the Rises and Stytown. Steam drifted from vents set into the wall, exhaust from the massive churning spring that provided the force for opening and closing the double gates. For now, however, they stood open.

Bimet nudged her. "The herald says we meet with the Hand of the Emperor tomorrow, midmorning. It's an official audience. He received our message only yesterday."

Rih shifted in her seat. She hoped for more time to acclimate, but at least Vi-baln would be as off-guard as she. This may have been her home, but she had never been here as a dignitary. It was a wholly different city when arriving as a guest. The winding streets were crowded as ever, but there was an edge—even without hearing their shouts, Rih caught new lines of tension on faces. Eyes once pinched with exhaustion were now narrowed in anger. Defiance.

Higher, among the sprawling manors, new bars blocked doors, and extra guards paced walls that once only boasted draping vines. Heady lilies and gardenias scented the air, kept damp from other steam vents and water forced through pipes, weaving through the city until cool enough not to scorch the roots.

They drew up in the courtyard, their military escort traded for a diplomatic one. Guards were ushered into smaller guest accommodations, while the officers and Rih's personal attendants fell in behind the princess herself.

Mosil appeared at her elbow as she descended. His smile was tired but true, and his hand on her arm was gentle. "It's good to see you again, cousin."

She flashed a smile. "I did not expect to see you so soon."

His grin widened. "I had a feeling I might. Come, let's get you settled. I'm sure you could use a proper bed and good food. Tell me," he asked, guiding her up the palace stairs and into the dignitaries' wing, "have the Athrolani cooks learned how to make proper buttered tea yet?"

After the inefficiency and rough accommodations of Ceir Athrolan, Rih relaxed into the lush hospitality of home. Everywhere screens were flung open to welcome the fertile breeze, and every question or need was met with gracious acquiescence.

Her travel clothes were whisked away, replaced with new finery once she had visited the sprawling women's baths. When she retreated to her room just before dusk, however, it was empty, save for Nehla. Bimet had left a note explaining she had gone to visit family but would return that night.

Rih collapsed onto her bed with a sigh. Aches she had not realized she had were erased by hot, sulfurous water and the strong hands of a trained masseuse. She glanced up when Nehla settled in a chair by the window.

After a moment her hands rose in awkward signs. "Would you like some tea?"

Rih's heart leapt. "You're learning?"

"Mobeka has been teaching me during our visits. I've always wanted to learn, but my focus was on the politics of fashion. Politics in general."

"Politics of fashion?" The term reminded Rih of Ki-elte and their discussion of clothing as a communication. Perhaps she would find a moment to see her friend.

"It's like anything with culture or meaning behind it. What someone chooses to wear means as much as what they say—it's how they intend to be seen. Before they ever open their mouths—or raise their hands," she amended.

Some words were out of order, but the whole of her meaning was easy to decipher—easier than trying to read the animated woman's lips, at least. "I'm surprised you haven't practiced with either Bimet or me before now."

Nehla's excitement withdrew again. "I don't think Bimet likes me. I know she doesn't, truthfully. I've spent my life studying people and the connections they make with one another. What influences them. I don't trust her, honestly."

Rih sat back. She was not used to having a large group of friends. Even her training group as a child was now scattered among a handful of different positions and assignments; their time together rarely overlapped. *But outright distrust on both sides is unusual, and for the same reasons—connections.* "What influences Bimet, to your mind?"

Nehla's shoulders lifted in a sigh. "Fear."

Rih scanned Nehla's outfit again, more carefully. The woman was always meticulously styled, and now she knew why. Still, every ring bore a jewel, and nothing could be mistaken for a red band. With the false public meaning behind her sign, Rih could not easily ask if Nehla knew or supported the rebellion. "It must be nice to learn from your cousin. Does she get news from home? You said much had changed."

"I've learned a lot from her. She said to tell you that whatever you need, all you need to do is ask and she'll provide—" The ground trembled and Rih turned to see a weight resting on the ground by the door. The chain attached to it cranked it upward again and she rose before her visitor was forced to knock again.

Curiel waited in the hall, easy smile in place. The loose sleeves of her tolstovka were rolled up, and someone had found a plain cotton wrap to protect her shoulders and head from the rain.

She jerked her thumb down the hall, brows curled in a question.

Rih nodded, ducking back into her room to quickly change. As much as she wanted to stay and learn exactly how much Nehla knew, this was neither the time nor place. Too many ears and eyes were fixed on them, and without fluency, Rih worried how much nuance might be lost.

She set out with Curiel alone. In the press and chaos of the city it did not matter that the colonel did not know Banis or how to sign. They took turns pointing at interesting or colorful sights. Though Curiel might have been little more than a stranger, Rih was delighted to see the other woman enjoyed overhanging ivy and took joy in the curtains of drying silk hanging from a hundred lines overhead when they cut through the servants' wing.

Nerves sang up her back when Curiel gripped her arm. She pointed to where an armored figure jogged toward them, waving one hand. They crossed the cobbled walk and Rih caught sight of the tattoo on the woman's shaved scalp.

"Il-fald!"

"Rih!" The woman was barely done signing before Rih locked her arms around her teacher. They stood that way for a moment before she stepped back. "This is Curiel. She's a colonel of Athrolan. I promised to teach her the atlatl, and we found we had some time before the press of dignitary duties descended."

"I don't envy you," Il-fald joked. "Either duty, frankly. If she's as slow a learner as you, you might be sun-weathered as clay before she masters it."

Rih rolled her eyes. "I've been training when I can," she promised. "How are you? How goes the war?"

"Banis hooves are many and swift," she answered, "though Mirik's forces continue to harry our coastline. It's the skirmishes that bite us most. How is Athrolan?" Her dark eyes flitted to Curiel, then back to Rih. "And your studies?"

"Athrolan is cold and wet. My studies have been difficult, though I have more time than I'd prefer, there are few study partners. And now there's war."

"We heard something was brewing — something about a mad king?"

Rih snorted. "My husband is mad, yes, but I'm not certain this war is entirely his own doing."

Il-fald turned, seemingly hearing a call to join her companions. "I've got a missive to deliver, but I need to speak with you." She drew Rih close again, pressing their brows together for a moment before stepping back to sign. "I've got a message from an old friend. In the south."

Majilah Ag. "I'll call on you before I leave." Rih reached out to squeeze her hand once before her former teacher was lost to the crowd. She led Curiel to the palace training courts, but her mind whirled a thousand leagues a second. RoBal was a hulking thing, dark and bloody. It was lush and violent and layered in beauty and complexity. But still, her heart soared. *Home.*

CHAPTER NINE

The 10th Day of Glasmord, 1272
The City of Ceir Athrolan, Athrolan

MIDDAY BELLS TOLLED AGAIN. Keplan jogged from the throne room, waving a dismissive hand as the herald reminded him of his afternoon obligations. He spent the last weeks wallowing, drowning in the despair of a failing city, failing crop, failing leadership.

When he reached the greenhouse, Fess already waited for him. Her greeting was tired, and her smile did not meet her eyes. "Afternoon, sire."

"Fess," he answered. "Domariigo should be here soon."

A bright ray of light flooded her face for a second and she winced. "Remind me again why we're meeting here instead of your study or the audience chamber. Or anywhere else, frankly."

"I was going to ask the same thing," An'thor remarked, appearing on the path from the greenhouse's other entrance.

"That's where we always meet. I need new perspectives. Outside is doom and snow and chaos, and I need to be reminded more exists than that." He took a seat at one of the small tables tucked into a cluster of broad-leaved plants. He guessed they were the same as those that decorated the ballroom for the Banis welcoming celebrations.

Fess tugged a faded kerchief from her breast pocket and wiped her nose. "Seems I'm allergic to something in here, so grab your inspiration and let's make this brief."

"I wanted to speak to both of you outside a war council. They all have opinions and many are good, but I can't think with that many voices rattling around."

"I don't think anyone can," Fess muttered. "I've reports—official and unofficial. And Dorcal's most recent letter."

"Begin there."

She flipped through her officer's log, finding the relevant page and scanning her notes. "He's along the Northland coast. Says if the weather holds, he'll make near Neneviir soon. He's got another dozen message birds. One of his sailors dabbles in art and included several illustrations of the creatures they've encountered."

Keplan smiled. "I'd like to see those when you have a moment."

She made a note and continued. "Next, we've extinguished the fires and most of the spills are contained, though all the water brought down from the hills before the burst is contaminated."

"We have more?"

"We're well into winter. There will be some, but most is locked in ice in the hills. We usually rely on our cisterns until snowmelt."

Keplan looked down. Snowmelt was months away. "Rations. I'll see if we can ship some from the rivers to the east and west, but it will take a year to build another aqueduct from either." He rubbed the bridge of his nose. "Anyone outside the city is to use snow. If there's not enough snowfall, we'll send soldiers into the towns to rig rain collection."

"Our ships use seawater for tea sometimes," she realized. "Boil it and collect the steam the way you would distill wraith. It's not perfect, but it works well enough. If we can find something to burn other than lamp oil or each other, we might be able to create fresh water from the ocean for other uses."

Other uses. "Bathwater will have to be drawn up from the harbor — where it's cleanest, of course."

"You know what happens to your skin, bathing in seawater?" Fess reminded him.

"You know what happens to a city when they begin to run out of water?" An'thor snapped back.

"Enough. I'll speak to the commissioners about how best to implement these ideas. Surely they'll have more, too." Keplan sighed, wishing he had tea. At least his drug habit gave him energy. "You mentioned other reports? Unofficial ones?"

Fess closed her book. "I have a friend who accompanied Her Highness Rih-elte to Ban with the Athrolani guard. They arrived in the city yesterday, if they kept up their pace. But she noticed something — rumors, only — on their journey. They stopped in a few towns briefly, and she said there was something under the surface."

"How so?"

An'thor leaned forward, his black eyes lit with curiosity. "Physical or cultural?"

"Not certain. She just noticed certain people among the Banis retinue speaking with individuals in town. They were signing —"

"Half of them are Deaf," Keplan excused. "Probably just looking for others who know their language."

"It's less than half," Fess corrected, "and they weren't just signing. It seems like something more. She said it looks like a network. A community, in the least."

"I fail to see how that involves me."

"You allied with them. Their business is yours."

"Can you ask her to look further into it?"

"I can. Is there something in particular?"

"No, but when she returns, I'd like to speak with her. There's someone else who might have another piece to the puzzle." He did not know what Hylier gleaned that he kept to himself, but if someone knew more, it would be him. "And speaking of unofficial channels, I've a concern of my own. About the investigation into Peraan's murder."

Fess's brows rose. "They certainly seem to think it's related to your allies. Though honestly, I'd imagine Mirik would be as likely. The man called for the assassination of the Hetmir's son. His known Athrolani victims were just common folk from the slums."

Keplan winced. *Mirrel wasn't "just" anything!* "I imagine his reach was farther than we realized, Fess. A friend in the slums informed me they're looking for an addict, someone who was avenging one of their own. Seems like it might have more to do with class than politics."

"Class is politics, Wardyn." An'thor picked at the peeling lacquer on the table.

"There's hunger out there, and filthy water, and a religious war on the horizon. Vigilantes are part of the bargain," Fess argued. "The most you can do is help the investigation and let the rest of it fall by the wayside. We've got far bigger leviathans to spear here."

"I suppose." Keplan's nerves were raw. He hoped for incredulity or answers as useful as her suggestions about the tainted water. Nonchalance was a surprise.

She sneezed, blinking watering eyes. "If that's all you need of me, sire, I'm going to go before my eyes are raisins."

"Apologies, dismissed." He watched her go before turning back to An'thor.

The general rose with a groan, lurching over to examine a colorful flower that resembled large bobbing genitalia. "Where do these even grow?" he muttered before turning back to the king. "So, rumor has it Peraan's murderer is a mad young man with ties to the Slummer. If that's the case, where were you the night he got his throat ripped out?"

Keplan rolled his eyes. He hoped the warrior's eyes were too bloodshot to pick out the pulse thundering in his throat. "Look at me. From what I recall he was a big man. You think I have the strength to fight, let alone kill him?" An'thor's expression was unwavering, and Keplan threw in a shrug. "I wouldn't have minded being the one and have no doubt he deserved death, but it wasn't me."

"If you insist."

"If my path to the throne is drenched in blood, Domariigo, I'm not the one who should be blamed for it."

An'thor seemed to give up the path of questioning and crossed his arms. "You want to sling blame or listen to my report?"

"Do you have one?"

An'thor heaved a sigh. "If I'd known placing your arse on the throne would be akin to raising a petulant adolescent monster, I'd have let Dorcal sack the place."

"I am a petulant adolescent monster, Domariigo," Keplan flashed a grin with all his father's teeth. "Anyway, where are our fanatics now?"

"Gone. Disappeared. Most we can find is tracks and cold campfires. They move fast, for an army."

Keplan's racing blood chilled. "Army? How many?"

"The group sighted to the southeast was two hundred. More if they aren't the same as those seen camping in Claimiirn. Another from Bodian province was seen just before they disappeared into the Ru'un Felds. Estimated close to a hundred. All moving north."

"We're the capital," Keplan argued. "We can handle a few hundred."

"We're a glorified city with poisoned water, no food, and a child for a king," An'thor snapped, whirling on the boy. Every shred of his drunken apathy evaporated.

"What do you suggest, then?"

"Pull whatever you have to out of your arse, pray your wife does your begging for you, and cut whatever ties you still have to the Slummer. You're a king, not a barkeep's bed-buck." He stalked back down the greenhouse path.

Keplan looked down, picking a loose thread from the dingy cotton of his gloves. He did not like the general. Nor did he care if the man liked him at all in return. But he did not want him as an enemy. *He might be a drunk, might be a sorry remnant of a warrior, but you don't live so long without influence and power.* If An'thor was willing to murder people to get Keplan crowned, he did not doubt the violent lengths he would stretch to remove him if he saw fit.

The winter sun sank lower, disappearing from the glass panes overhead. He straightened and traipsed through the palace. Despite his usual scheduled audience times, the throne room was conspicuously empty. Interest in Banis relations had kept his audiences full weeks before, but the current chaos in the city and barren storehouses had people clamoring at Guild Houses and robbing neighbors instead of petitioning the king. Perhaps they realized the latter did little good.

Even Hylier had yet to appear. An'thor would be holed up with the Captain of the City Guard discussing enforced gate checks against the Swordbearers.

Keplan wandered farther into the palace warren until he stood before what had once been the royal wing. He ducked under the heavy velvet curtains, still colored mourning black and covered in dust. Beyond, the double doors stood shut and barred. *To think, an entire wing of a palace squirreled away like a secret.* Keplan lifted one of the lamps. Its wick was still damp with oil, but the tinderbox no longer hung from the lamp hook. He let the curtain fall shut behind him, darkness settling over him.

The silver inlays on the door glimmered. A shove, and they groaned open. Rolled carpets were stacked over the white and gray flagging. High-backed chairs and long couches stood in one corner, shrouded in sheets like the queen herself had been. Cobwebs draped every corner. Dust softened each surface.

A parlor waited beyond, and a study. The few bits of brocade cushions and embroidered curtains he glimpsed were picked out in lavenders and blues, accented with the royal turquoise.

Keplan had yet to make any part of his chambers his own. He may not have arrived in Athrolan with anything, but neither had he acquired anything he cared enough about to display. *My only connection is Moly, and I hardly ever ride anymore.* He had not even seen her in weeks. Guilt panged in his chest.

His city crumbled around his ignorant ears, and the most he could do was succumb to dust in his empty rooms. Energy flared through his veins. First he yanked the curtains back, dust motes exploding from the heavy fabric. Next came the sheets. The ornate carved wood was perhaps a bit outdated, but he never cared for trends. He paced from room to room, uncovering an entire life of a woman he had never met.

Hairbrushes waited by her mirror. Gowns hung in her dressing room. No face paints were laid out, however, and every washbasin and faucet was dusty. It was closer to a shrine than a home. He did not test the bedroom door. Even for him, some places were sacred.

Dozens of books lined the shelves of her study. Histories and the expected lineages were dotted with a few philosophical texts and folders of old letters. He pulled a sheet from the wall behind the sprawling desk and stood face-to-face with his own mother.

Even caught in canvas, her eyes froze him. It was worlds away from the portrait Brentemir showed him in the Hare. Instead of a tender, laughing moment around a fire, it was a formal portrait, akin to those of monarchs. Cascades of black fabric and embroidery made up her sarafan and delicate silver veils hung below the towering silver spines of her kokoshnik. Beside her stood the Earth Shaker, garbed in brilliant golds and white, coiled whip at his hip. Gilding and pearlescent paint freckled his forearms and face.

Keplan sank back against her desk, shaking. Homesickness overwhelmed him. Their faces were so familiar, if younger. Dressed in finery, heads raised with pride at their blood, at their power, they were a vision of the life he never had. Knowledge he was only now cobbling together. He would give it all up in a heartbeat for some semblance of home.

"No wonder you ran," he whispered. "You might not have known what awaited me here, but fates, you still knew better." Parchment crunched beneath him and he looked down. Notes. Plans. Ideas for a future she was desperately trying to wrench from the failing kingdom. *Inspiration.* He wove back through the rooms, emerging from the hall, blinking in the bright light.

"Sire, are you well?" The steward hovered in the hall, frowning. "One of the maids said you were looking for something in those chambers."

"I'm fine, Valadai, thank you." He glanced at the doors, shut behind him. "It's time those rooms were cleaned. And I would like more desks brought in. And notebooks." He raked a hand through his hair. "Please."

He pictured war machine schematics across each surface. Designs of distillation systems to create water for his people on others. If Athrolan would survive, her path would not be forged between the naked walls of his study.

Φ

The 11ᵗʰ Day of Glasmord, 1272

Muscles Rih forgot she had ached in ways she did not recall they could. Sun cast patterns of light across the ceiling through the carved wood window screen. Nehla was gone. Instead, Bimet sat by the windows looking out. Rain saturated the colors, transforming blues and red into sky and blood.

Rih stretched, popping joints back into place that had been subluxated by travel. Donning a robe over her bare skin, she padded across the room to sit at the other bench beside the window. "How was your family?"

Bimet glanced over long enough to read the signs, then her gaze roved back to the city spilling below. Purple shadows clung to the puffiness beneath her eyes. "I missed them. My brother won't be called to the military. He's younger, wants to be an officer, but his request was denied again."

"Is it political?" Rih asked. "Because of your position with me? The rebellion?" Bimet was all she had sometimes, it seemed, but if she had to leave for family, Rih would never question it.

"It's complicated, Rih." Bimet's shoulders heaved in a sigh. "He's younger and has an incredibly good heart, but you know the rules. He works as a guard at the main gates for now, and can only request thrice. They wanted to discuss the rebellion—"

"Did they know about us, about you helping me?"

"No, and they won't. He won't stand a chance of being promoted if he's connected to it."

"He could be an ally," Rih suggested. "We need them."

"He's a boy and I won't hear of him destroying his future." She rose. "I told Nehla to see her own family today. She'll be back in time for the audience, but not before."

"Did you speak to her at all?"

Bimet frowned. "What would I have to say?"

Rih shrugged. "We just had a nice evening. I'm trying to create stronger friendships, even without the rebellion." Rih stopped, suddenly uncertain. "Are you all right?"

"I'm fine." The signs were sharp, and Bimet's face lined with stress. "Being here, seeing family, it's hard, you know."

"I do. I'm sorry I brought you here, but I'm grateful for your support. Truly."

Sorrow and frustration flitted over the interpreter's face. "I sent a request for someone else to help you dress. I may not like her, but Nehla knows far more about the intricacies of fashion. Hopefully they send someone equally skilled." Her smile was tired and insincere.

"I'm sure. I'm going to the bathhouse, if you'd like to come."

"I've already been. I didn't sleep much last night."

Rih paused by the door. "Is there anything I can do?"

"No, but thank you."

Rih's thoughts churned as she gathered her clothes and slipped down to the bathhouse several stories below. Being home was strange. Her time in Athrolan barely amounted to a month but seemed like eternity. It was almost worth dealing with looming imperial eyes to avoid the disorganization and isolation of her husband's kingdom. *Husband. King's wife.* She tugged her robe closer about her shoulders. Those words still felt as foreign as Trade to her.

Damp heat rolled from the double doors to the women's baths as they opened for her. After the raw ocean air this was ecstasy. Golden glass globes hung from chains, casting everything in a rich warm light. She doffed her robes and slipped into the dark steam room. A fired clay grate made up the floor, and water roiled beneath, billowing steam into the small room on its way to the baths themselves. Bottles of scented oils lined a shelf by the door, and she hesitated before choosing something floral over her usual sandalwood.

She started with her arms. Usually one could hire a masseuse for such work, but after years on the road, she enjoyed the opportunity to take stock of her own body. Now it was as much an exercise in remembering the flesh under her hands was, in fact, hers. The line across her calf from an arrow graze. A gnarled circle on her knee where she fell onto scorched ground when along a fire line. Countless nicks and scratches over her forearms from spear combat.

Her head rocked back onto the leather padded seat and she let her eyes lid. Aromatic wood and jasmine combined in a heady scent that relaxed her iron grip on her thoughts as much as the heat and oil coaxed knots from her muscles.

Air wafted over her skin and she cracked one eye to watch the two women who entered. One was broad and heavy, walking with the deliberate grace of a dancer. The other had her same straight black brows but was a good two handspans taller. Rih was too relaxed to greet them or try to bother with conversation.

"It's been such a week—I've had two performances a night for three days. I wouldn't think anyone from the western jungle would be interested in our art, but the ambassador enjoys it apparently."

"Nothing wrong with being in favor."

"Except my feet might never be the same."

Rih only caught a few words as they continued and was almost drifting off when she glimpsed one of the women's hands move incongruously with her words. "I've heard the general herself plans on coming to the city soon."

Rih kept her eyes almost shut, hoping they looked closed in the dark room.

"So she's a diplomat?"

"I think it's the Valen queen."

"You think she'd risk inciting a rebellion while our countries are finally in peace talks?"

Their innocuous spoken conversation continued, but Rih could not tear her attention from their hands. It took all her will not to leap up and confess that she was the leader, to please tell her everything they knew. They thought her sleeping. They thought her voiced. For now, she would feign ignorance. Their rebellion's strength lay in its anonymity.

"I heard a speaker will be at my meeting tonight, we'll have some orders surely. As it is, half of us are in place already."

The door opened and both women's hands fell into stillness. A third woman entered, and Rih made a show of opening her eyes fully and stretching. Nodding to the others, she slipped out before anyone could try to speak to her.

She wiped sweat and dirt from her skin with the excess oil and dipped into the hot tiled pool. Even a plunge in the cool water afterward barely registered among her whirling thoughts. These rumors were new. Her pride twinged at the thought of Majilah Ag receiving credit for the cause, but for now, it behooved them. The fact that she was negotiating with Ban came as a surprise, but perhaps it made perfect sense — no one enjoyed fighting two different wars, and the easiest way into a city was with an invitation.

A letter awaited her when she returned to her room. Ilfald's handwriting was messy, her words almost hurried.

> *R,*
>
> *I've sorely missed you, but my duties are greater than ever, and I fear I won't see you before you're gone again. If your journey back to Athrolan takes you past Jai, I'm sure our dear friend will find you, for she's visiting as well.*
>
> *May your horse's hooves be swift and your spear strike true.*

> *All of my love and hope rides with you.*
> *-I*

Rih's heart sank. Seeing Il-fald was a bright point in her time here. Her finger brushed over the final line of the letter. She wondered which ally her teacher meant, and despite her heartache, a tiny thrill of hope thrummed through her. A thought percolated through the fear and excitement, settling to add steel to her strength. *I'll be home again soon, with spears and hooves and fury.*

Φ

Other than her yearly visits as one of the emperor's wards, Rih had rarely seen the man. It took a moment, then, for her to realize the man dressed in swaths of emerald silk beside Vi-baln was His Eminence himself.

She dropped to her knees, eyes sliding anywhere but his face. Dizziness flooded her head and she clenched her teeth to keep terror and breakfast spilling across his silk slippers. He inspected his nails, filed short, save for the longest, which was lacquered in a deep red. Perhaps it was her own blood that dyed it, taken the moment she crossed the border. Did that cause her light-headedness now?

"Welcome home, Rih-elte."

"I'm grateful you took the time to meet with me. It's been lovely to see familiar walls again."

Vi-baln leaned forward from his seat, a step beneath the emperor's. "We did not expect to see your bright face so soon after parting."

Bright face. It belied the anonymity she was reassured of in the baths. Were her own allies the only ones who did not know who she was? Or were Vi-baln's words prophylactic? "I'm honored you both chose to receive me, Your Glory, and at such short notice. Indeed I, too, did not foresee returning so soon, even if just as a favor to my beloved, His Majesty the King of Athrolan." She wondered if her face betrayed how stiff the endearment felt in her fingers.

"I am curious of that, of course, but I'm more curious about the current state of our new allies."

The emperor was perusing a fruit tray, seemingly unaware of her presence.

Rih settled back on her heels, glancing to make sure Bimet was prepared for a longwinded translation. Did she distract them with Athrolan's instability or focus their gaze wholly elsewhere? *How can I convince them fighting a budding religion is even worthwhile?* "Living in Athrolan has been quite an adjustment, and they are so different from us that I urge you to consider these have been issues for decades, and I simply haven't seen them. Their governing is one of debate — pedantic more often than not. Currently they struggle to feed their people, and some accident destroyed an aqueduct shortly before I departed. It's since been repaired, but I've heard there are concerns about filling a cistern." She added a shrug to her feigned uncertainty in the off chance the emperor was watching her and not Bimet.

"I see," Vi-baln answered. "I assume you're here to beg for more grain than we've already sent?"

"To my knowledge those shipments have been sealed away, protected from the blight and in storage until next spring when they can be sowed. I'm here about the war."

The Emperor's Hand's brow arched, and Rih quickly looked back to Bimet, crouched at their feet, to catch his response. "War?"

She seized Keplan's line, tossed aside in the dismissive clamor of common sense. "His Majesty sent me to ask for support against Mirik."

"They would never go to war. Family ties, history, and so forth."

"The Hetmir's son was attacked in Ceir Athrolan — by an Athrolani assassin. They are leaving within the month. Now His Majesty has closed his doors to the prophets, and all his attention is on preventing heresy and keeping his people fed."

Vi-baln rolled his eyes. "Prophets? The nonsense from Kut Tunis, you mean."

"With his eyes elsewhere, he fears Mirik will move against them because of their war with us." It was not a lie, but surely Keplan had not intended her to spout his wandering fears to the Emperor of Ban. Rih paused long enough for his mind to run wild but not enough for him to formulate an opinion of his own yet.

The emperor seemed unmoved by her suggestion. "I am surprised His Majesty sent you in his stead. It bodes poorly for Athrolan's stability that he could not risk visiting our beautiful gardens himself."

"It was only because of your considerate tutelage. You had me trained in diplomacy as well as all other traits so important to marriage. He did ask I send his deepest regrets that he would not see RoBal's beauty again. Athrolan would be grateful for both the show of unity against this annoyance and the aide so they might extend their army to their other cities in preparation for whatever the prophet's Swordbearers bring."

"Again?"

She risked a glance at the Emperor's Hand. Vi-baln ducked his chin, whispering something to the emperor.

One black brow arched. The emperor inspected a particularly plump plum, lips pursed with skepticism, then took a bite.

"And what do you think?"

Rih stared at him, blinking. Warning seared her spine straighter. The emperor was dangerous, incredibly so. But Rih recognized the teeth in the man's smile. Her thoughts did not matter. Her body, her mind, did not matter. *So why is he asking me?* "The prophets are an annoyance, a mosquito bite, but it threatens to become necrotic if let fester. I imagine having soldiers in the Athrolani capital is a position of power in regard to Mirik. False deities undermine authority, both your own and his, as a child of the Dhoah' Laen. Athrolan's army is large, but spread thin and underfed. I think it shows a united force against these heretics and Mirik both by sending two hundred spears to the capital." She hardened her nerves, shoulders stiff. "It's what I would do, were I in your place."

Vi-baln rocked back, nostrils flaring. "An entire baniol?"

The sting of danger skittered up her arms. This was a duel. Words, sharper than steel and far more subtle, cut through the swaddling fabric of pretense and manners. She locked eyes with the man, spreading her hands in deference before demurring, "I'm certain His Eminence will find a suitable solution."

The emperor did not speak for a minute, then his left brow twitched. A serving man bowed out and began issuing rapid orders in the hall. Gooseflesh rippled over Rih's arms. Sheer power was often tremulous at best. But here, surrounded by the might, the systemic terror that you might be next, it seemed impervious. "They will ride out with you in two days."

Rih bowed, pressing her brow to the cold stone. "His Majesty will be delighted when I tell him Athrolan and Ban continue to have a long and fruitful friendship."

The emperor leaned back in dismissal. Food was whisked away, and Bimet shuffled on her knees until she was suitably far enough from the dais to respectfully stand. Rih followed suit, both of them backing from the room. Exhaustion warred with adrenaline and her limbs trembled. Only when the massive double doors were shut again and they were out of sight of the four guards did Rih allow herself to slump against the wall.

"That was too bold, Rih!" Bimet's fingers shook as she signed.

"They listened, didn't they?"

"At what cost? The entire city might know who you are."

Rih shook her head. "I don't think they do. Suspect, perhaps, but nothing more than their usual distrust of everything. It's how they stay safe."

Movement drew her attention to the end of the hall. Mosil approached, hand raised in greeting. When he was closer, Rih saw his smile was tight and his eyes deeply shadowed. "Your Highness, I'd be honored if you joined me in the gardens."

"Excuse me?"

His gaze flicked between her interpreter and the audience room doors. "Surely you won't begrudge a cousin the news from afar. Besides, His Eminence would despair to know a guest was left to their own devices."

Rih did not need Bimet to translate the meaning of those heavy words. *I'm not to be left unattended.* She smiled. The emperor had secrets. The massive emerald mound of the palace was built on them. *And they fear I'll find them.* "I'd be delighted."

"Perhaps your attendant would like time to see family."

Bimet frowned, mouth opening to protest before Rih dismissed her concern. "I'll be fine for the afternoon. I look forward to playing tiles later, though."

Bimet nodded and, with a last distrustful look at the ambassador, disappeared.

Mosil's face relaxed a fraction and he gestured to a long narrow hall angling to the rear of the palace. His signing had improved, though his health was seemingly the price. "It's good to see you."

"And you. Are you sure you can afford the diversion of conversation? Things seem quite busy."

His expression darkened. "RoBal always rides at the forefront." It was an old saying, one that used to speak to progress.

The hall cut right as they rounded to the rear of the palace. Mosil did not speak again until they stepped through double doors and onto a long, covered walk. The outer halls of each palace floor were broad, open balconies, each decorated with a different set of colors accented by flowers and rich foliage.

Here, the building's face was no longer tiered, but a sheer wall dozens of stories in height. Thousands of blossoming plants covered its surface, tucked into nooks and hanging pots, many just perched atop one another without a root to be seen. A single ramp led down into a sea of green below. Rih's stomach lurched. The blood gardens were half the size of the city itself. "This is incredible. The water they must require—"

"RoBal is the city of springs," Mosil reminded her.

"The six fountains of the city called Seven Springs." It was a common joke, built on the fact that only six were accounted for, the final one long since dried up.

"This is where the seventh went," he confided. "His Eminence allows it to be used for these gardens alone."

Allows. As if the man had any control over the life flowing from the earth. He was better at bloodletting than nurture. An image flashed through her mind—springs, bubbling from the earth, thick and clotted with blood. She shuddered.

"Each section is tended by a devoted gardener who is lucky enough to live in the palace below. Last winter the palace was decorated with imperial purple and some blue as well."

She scanned the planted wall. It was awash with crimson blooms. "Red for war?"

"Or wrath."

She frowned. "His Majesty said something similar. What does it mean?"

"You didn't read the prophet's scripture?"

"No one did, save His Majesty." The ramp was steep but carved with intricate designs for traction. Above the clouds billowed and grew, darkening from dove to slate.

"I was hoping to get your opinion on it, actually."

"Mine? That's the second time my opinion has been asked by those who don't often seek it."

He had the grace to blush. "His Eminence learns as much from what we openly tell him as what he gleans from his thousand insidious avenues." He flashed a smile, gesturing to the lush world engulfing them. "Here, at least, I can hope the very leaves don't boast ears. I'd like to show you His Eminence's world of miniature."

It was only then that she recognized a wheat ear and a falcon's talon were carved into the stone beneath their sandals. "Tiles. The ramp is decorated in tiles."

"It's his favorite game," Mosil signed.

"Is he any good?"

Mosil's lips twitched and his shoulder tensed. "There is no one better. How else would he still be emperor?"

Rih laughed. Though bitter and weak under stress, she had forgotten her cousin was a master of two-sided answers.

A faint summer breeze drifted from the north, and he raised his nose. "I could visit here every day until I die and I'd still not recognize every scent and bloom. That sweetness, it could be any number of a hundred flowers."

Every word seemed to bear unnatural weight. The emperor was an overarching shadow, but not something oft discussed. It was too dangerous. Ban was hardly a place of faith beyond that in their own emperor. If Mosil thought the prophet's words bore consideration, there was more to it than she realized. "What does the prophesy claim?"

Mosil did not answer. Were it not for the set of his jaw, she would have thought he had not seen the signs. Heat grew the farther down they walked. The massive boughs cradled the brief sun from that morning, holding it between their reaching branches as rain approached. Clamor from the city streets and the bustle of the palace faded with each step, replaced by the chatter of birds and the burble of fountains.

The ambassador gazed at the whiskered fish in a pool along the path. "The One True God will rise where the worlds meet, from death and birth, from chaos and order. His blood pools, drowning the world even as it gives it life. Though he will bear the marks of hate, he will be unable to raise its tools. His right hand will be stained bloody with wrath, and his left with the verdant green of life and mercy. Thrice he will die and..."

Rih's blood chilled and she turned away. Moss blanketed the forest floor, a living carpet of a thousand different greens. One mound, at the base of a winding curling tree, boasted tiny white blossoms. She remembered the king's palm, naked and green, pressed to hers. "Not many are pardoned, but they number in the dozens, at least in RoBal," she began. "Many have both tattoos. And those scars."

He fixed her with a stare, his eyes lit with something previously hidden. "So you recognize your husband in the words."

"He's the child of the Dhoah' Laen. His blood carries Earth Shaker power. I'd be a fool not to wonder how it manifests in him. He's not well, though. If he is a god, then he is a mad one. What god doesn't seek worship?"

"And the other line—where two worlds meet. Ban, Athrolan?"

"Perhaps. Our cities are the opposite. Even in their design: RoBal is built up, Ceir Athrolan dug down, both in tiers. Perhaps one would fit around the other."

"They chose to push the cityfolk beneath them, while we just climbed over ours. Wouldn't you agree? And what of the drowning in blood?"

The nerves that sang of danger while she knelt at the emperor's feet piped again, but this time the tone was different. Athrolan's king was scarred and broken at the interrogators hands, perhaps misused by others with power. Still, he could scarcely wield divine power. "I'm not a priestess—I can't interpret scripture."

Mosil gestured deeper into the forest. "The path is this way." Massive boles closed in about them, blocking the fading light and the faint misting rain. Beyond, tucked between the towering boles, was an entire forest in miniature. Rivulets were tiny rivers, gnarled pines and birches and a dozen trees she did not recognize were bent over rocks and curled from tiny cliffs. "How does one make this — are they very young?"

"On the contrary," Mosil answered, "they are very old. His Eminence acquired a Berrin gardener some years ago — during the Gods' War, I believe. She has tended this grove ever since. Each one is formed in a pleasing shape, both artistic and natural. Even the fountain water itself is altered with salts and minerals specific to these trees' needs."

"I think Ceir Athrolan has one like this in the conservatory."

Mosil smiled. "I saw the conservatory during negotiations. It's quaint."

Rih snorted at the gentle condescension. "I'd argue it's a place of restraint rather than," she gestured to the surrounding vibrance, "abundance. Though this is beautiful."

Mosil nodded. "It reminds me of government. Both require decades of planning, pruning, a tiny metaphor for the surrounding world. One is a garden tended, and the other is a king debating the lives of his people or his enemies. A balance between mercy and wrath in itself." He paused, body motionless, save for his hands. "You may not be a priestess, but I've heard you are a general."

Her heart faltered. The forest seemed to spin around her. *No.*

Mosil's gaze pinned her into stillness. "Hi-alan spoke to me when we heard you were returning. She told me the truth. You allied with His Majesty so one day you could bring his army here. You allied with a god," he hesitated, eyes full of fear, of hope, and just a shadow of pride, "in the name of liberty."

She faltered, fear and hope colliding with the shuddering of her own heart. Bimet would insist trusting anyone was dangerous, but Mosil was a far cry safer than Keplan—he understood the grinding attrition of spirit from living under the emperor's eye. Instead of a denial, she simply asked, "And what do you think, cousin?"

"These past few months I've spent more time with Ki-elte. With Hi-alan. You may not need my help; in fact, surely you've planned everything without it, but His Eminence trusts me. Many trust me." His eyes did not leave hers, but he knelt, palms pressed to the gravel path. When he straightened, his eyes glistened. "I say: if His Eminence hoped to reap peace, then he should have sowed seeds, not bones."

Φ

The 14ᵗʰ Day of Glasmord, 1272
The City of Ceir Athrolan, Athrolan

Peace drained from Keplan the moment he opened his bedroom door. "Barrackborn."

"Keplan." Brentemir grabbed him by the shoulders. "What, by Toar, were you're thinking?"

Keplan pried himself away. The touch was cloying. His longing for parents, for approval, for someone to take the weight, did not extend to Azimir's father. *My uncle*, he reminded himself. "What do you want?"

"I want an explanation. Bringing Banis troops here? To our doorstep? I feel like I hardly know you."

"You barely knew me before now!" he retorted. "I've got more than enough people dropping the Dhoah' Laen's duties on my shoulders. I don't need you dropping her personality on me as well. You don't know who I am and, fates, I doubt you'd like me if you did."

"Cut the melodrama," Brentemir muttered. "It was your father's gimmick, and one often accompanied by murder and fire."

Keplan resisted the urge to confess murder often accompanied his, as well. Hylier knew, and that was already too much. The echoes of Peraan's throat snapped through his head. He did not trust himself. The thoughts may never had stayed long, but they only came when his blood sang with dust. They weren't his, he didn't think. But they came from somewhere inside. *Only I will remain.* He shuddered. "I needed their help. I'm not a soldier like you, like my parents were. I'm not a warrior. If this prophesy gets out, we'll have something far more terrifying at our door, and I can't face it alone."

"The Swordbearers." Bren looked away, and this time, Keplan caught the truth behind his shame.

"You couldn't have. You accepted them?"

"Keplan, you can't possibly believe it's a lie. Just listen to the words."

"You inherited your father's thrall? Their god is nothing more than a misunderstanding, but in their hands it becomes a weapon. I can feel the terror. The despair. Tastes like Ban. All of them crying into the abyss and praying for an answer."

Brentemir frowned. "Doesn't matter how hard you pretend, Keplan, your blood doesn't lie. Your father tried that too."

Keplan flung his hands up. "It doesn't matter how true their words might sound, I won't have myself deified! I'm going to war, regardless of your tiny island nation."

Brentemir staggered back. "Keplan, our navy's gone and you brought our enemies within two days of our shores."

"And you brought heretics to ours! I'm not your spy on Ban, I'm not your meek nephew, and I'm surely not your sister. I am king here, despite being gutterwash at it. Believe what you want about me, but it won't change the fact that you're wrong."

He staggered from the room, energy leaving his body in a rush. He locked the bedroom door, ignoring the ambassador's pounding knocks. Keplan's knees cracked on the tiles and he retched. He sought peace with the same dogged ferocity as the emperor sought control. *I've seen his face in dreams and my own stared back.* Nerves danced up his skin, as if his entire skin might leap from his flesh and go dancing down Palace Way.

The knocking had ceased, and when he jerked the door open, it was to an empty study. He needed calm. Peace. Silence. He scrambled through his rooms, checking every box, the top of each shelf. It was gone.

His pulse fluttered, tattered and weak in his arteries. He slumped against his desk and froze. *Of course.* That morning he had slipped it into his trunk for safekeeping when the maid cleaned. Two minutes later the chaos and tang of blood sank beneath the surface again. His body burned with too much energy, and he took off to the training courts.

Three broken arrows and an hour later, his cousin appeared in the doorway. "General Domariigo said you'd be in here."

Keplan barely glanced back as Azimir stepped into the training hall. His cousin's voice buzzed under his skull, both exciting and infuriating at once. "What'd you want? Train?"

Azimir frowned. "I wasn't planning on it, but if you'd like." He moved to the rack of practice swords, testing a few before choosing a falchion.

Keplan watched him, wondering what he measured in each. He mimicked the motions, frowning at one, then rolling his eyes at the next. He finally chose a long, narrow blade.

"Rapier?" Azimir asked, brows arched.

"It's red," Keplan explained, tapping the crimson leather binding the hilt, then wiggling the fingers of his bare right hand. "We match."

Azimir did not answer and instead paced to the center of the training hall. "Pa told me what you said. What he said. I didn't know, but I should have. My grandfather did the same."

Keplan rolled his eyes. "Those gods are gone. And I'm well sick of your father's obsession with my bloodline. With the gods."

"I read it, Keplan. They might be wrong about how much power you wield, but we both agree that description fits you more than a little."

Keplan's body ignited. "She's mistaken—"

"The world is dying. Half the continent is at war. I don't know how you interpret the world drowning, but it seems pretty clear to me. Mirik may have once worshiped, but it isn't faith anymore when you know they're real. Feels more like dread."

Keplan's nerves froze. Was he simply the figurehead of a larger, darker disease? Perhaps whatever rooted in his chest had metastasized farther than Athrolan. Keplan looped his sword in a clumsy circle. The general's voice was a high-pitched whine in the back of his mind telling him that's not how one used a rapier. "I'm just forced to tidy all the messes that were made before me," he snapped.

"Maybe you weren't meant to do both," Azimir suggested. "Maybe inheriting the throne was just the machinations of a scared queen and an elitist general."

Keplan looked down at his hands. "I wish that were true. But I saw what their civil war did to the city. I think I'm the only one who can clean up this chaos."

"People have been tidying up after your parents for decades. After our grandfather. I think we've managed fine, for lowly humans." Azimir shrugged. "I understand you're upset. I hate change—"

"Change?" Anger and something deeper flashed through him, bitter on his tongue. "I'm married to the bitch who imprisoned me, my city is dying, and one of my friends was murdered! By a traitor!"

Azimir winced. He still had not raised his sword, though his stance was ready. "She hardly imprisoned you, Keplan."

"Can you hear her thoughts?" he bellowed. "Can you hear the confession that burst into my head the moment she set eyes on me? *'The foreign spy.'* She knew me somehow. I remember about three painful minutes of the entire march to RoBal, but a piece of it, a piece, is the woman I swore vows to. You think she's the only one terrified in this?" He swung.

His blade clattered against Azimir's as the younger man blocked, wordlessly.

"It's not just memories from Ban or what they did to me. I hear them all, all the time. Feel the pain, of all of it. The only bit I yearn for is the oblivion at the end, but death doesn't even want me. I wish Peraan took me instead of her. I see his face. Mirrel's face."

"Is that why no one's been charged? Do you think he deserved it?" Azimir's voice trailed to a murmur. Each counter was easy, graceful. One arm still tucked casually at his belt for balance.

"And even though he's dead they still won't let me rest. They're hunting his killer, and I wish they'd leave me be. And even though I took this throne, part of me prays they'll find out the truth and accuse me just so I could give up the crown." He was yammering, but the thoughts rushed faster, a deep current under the muffled stillness of his forebrain.

"Accuse..." Azimir shook his head. "Toar, Keplan, you talk like you're the one who killed him."

Keplan's teeth rattled shut, blood welling where his raw cheek caught against incisors. *Are those from you, too, Da? Along with the thoughts?* "I just mean the responsibility."

But Azimir's dark eyes said he knew the truth. His wrist flicked and he stepped easily inside Keplan's guard. The rapier thudded to the sawdusted floor. "You're not right, Lan. Whatever is going on, whatever makes you like this, you need to stop."

Keplan lunged, fist tightening at the last moment. At least he was halfway decent with his hands.

"Keplan!" Azimir's forearms were up, blocking a moment too late.

Mirrel's blood. The interrogator. Bone, or perhaps teeth, crunched under Keplan's knuckles and he suppressed a burble of laughter. Azimir punched his cheek, but even through the haze of dust and pain and despair, Keplan knew his cousin held back. He did not want him to hold back. He wanted to feel everything. And nothing. He dove, toppling them both to the floor. A boot or knee thudded into his gut. Bile welled in his throat, but he had not eaten enough to vomit. Azimir's short hair knotted in his fingers, and he slammed Azimir's head against the flagging.

Firas's tears, burning his shoulder. Peraan's smug face. His hand on Peraan's throat pressing, squeezing, digging —

Pain slammed into the side of Keplan's head. White flashed across his vision and he fell back. His hands were sticky. His vision cleared to show bloodstained sawdust. His cousin rasped on the floor. "Azi—"

"You need help, Keplan." Azimir's voice was hoarse, and a livid bruise already formed on his throat and over one eye. He staggered up, panting. He spat blood on the flagging, but his expression was not contempt. It was not even anger. His mouth was already swollen and bloody. "I'm sorry those things happened. To Mirrel. To you. I'm sorry Firas doesn't love you anymore. But you can't hurt people because of it. You can't hurt me or Rih or Athrolan just because your heart won't stop screaming."

Keplan could not watch his cousin leave. He could barely hear through the panic, through the buzzing. He slumped down, face to the cooling, sticky blood, and closed his eyes.

Φ

Azimir sank onto one of the benches lining the dark hall. Pain throbbed in his head and throat, but his heart hurt worse. He debated telling An'thor or even Fess. But he did not want someone who only knew Keplan as a bitter, foulmouthed man. Last year Keplan replaced the general as his idol. It was his chance at something close to his father's relationship with Alea. At least, that's what he had thought. He wound down the halls, pausing at Rih's door. If she were back, he might rush to her. *She already knows he's been a right arse.*

If he returned home his father would ask, and Azimir certainly did not need idealism and old values. Before he could think better of it, his feet were stomping the path to the Slummer. The high-collared jerkin hid what he imagined was an ugly purple line around his neck, and a handful of water at the courtyard fountain removed most of the blood from his chin. He doubted anyone would care about a blackened eye.

The roads seemed somehow narrower, and he noticed several empty storefronts. The Wise Hare's lanterns cast the street in gold and faint music drifted from within. He stepped in and found the seat at the end of the bar where Keplan had always sat.

A Banis boy was minding the tables and shot him a nod before ducking into the kitchen. Moments later Firas emerged. If ever there was a man haggard enough to look dead on his feet, it was Firas.

Toar. Azimir grimaced. This might have been a poor idea. The bartender stepped up to where Azimir sat, barely spared him a glance. "What'll it be?"

The words slurred, and Azimir looked down. "Just an ale please, Firas."

Recognition flickered across Firas's bloodshot eyes. "Fates, Azi. Didn't recognize you with all the…" He gestured to the boy's face. Without looking he poured a mug and slid it over. "What happened?"

"I was actually hoping you'd have a minute to talk."

Firas's face closed, his beard and mustache meeting as his mouth thinned. "If it's about a certain pauper king, I have nothing to say on the matter."

Azimir took a long, slow sip. "I'm begging here, Firas. Please."

Firas's jaw tightened and he stalked wordlessly away.

This was a mistake. Still, Azimir stayed. There was nowhere better to be, and what little he knew about battle injuries, he ought not to sleep with his head pounding so.

Despite Firas's words and Azimir's refusal of dinner, the boy brought a plate of stew. It tasted of ash. The music was faint, and by morning he could not have named the tunes if his life depended on remembering. An hour later, when the stool beside him was vacated for a final time, he rose with a groan and went to the privy. It was still dark, too dark to see more than the contrast of his skin against the void of the privy depths. His lower back ached. *I'm probably pissing blood.*

"You have a handspan of minutes here," Firas growled across the courtyard as Azimir's swollen fingers messed with the buttons of his trousers. He emerged.

The pain on Firas's face was familiar, and though his eyes were green, the loneliness in them could have made them the king's. "You and I were never close enough for you to come wandering in asking advice on how to tup."

"I don't need advice on—yes, it's about him." Azimir rubbed his face with one hand, hissing as pain sparked through his bruises.

"You never said what happened." Firas passed him the mug he had left inside.

"Keplan. Keplan happened."

"What?" Incredulity laced the words. "He's not a violent man."

"Then you know him less than I thought."

"I just mean...his whole reason for taking the throne was for peace. It's hard to marry that man—" His voice broke on the words. He cleared his throat and tried again. "It's hard to picture that man beating someone senseless. Let alone his own cousin."

"He wants peace, surely, but he can't find any himself. There's something wrong with him, something different. I can't speak with Rih-elte about it, or my father. She'd argue there was never any good in him, and my father would say there was never any evil—"

Firas's snort cut the words. "He's human. For a man descended from ancient titanic power, he's as perfect, perfectly human, as folks are born."

"I'm afraid you and I are the only ones who see it. Especially once this prophesy is loosed upon the world. He needs help but I'm not the one to do it."

"I surely can't. I think it'd do more harm, actually, to see me, to hear how I felt, how I still feel."

Azimir glanced up, startled. "I'm sorry."

"For?"

"I guess I didn't think you had feelings for him. Not anymore, at least. Thought he was a casual dalliance."

"I did too." Firas's whisper cut through the soft summer air. "Fates, I really wish he had been. And sometimes, I wish I'd never met him. Maybe then Mirrel—" He slumped and let out a racking sigh, too exhausted to be a proper sob. "But there are days, more than I'd care to admit, where I think it was worth it. Not her dying, but meeting him. Might have been worth this fucking empty chasm in my chest."

Does he know about Peraan? "Firas, about Mirrel and the man who did it."

Firas snarled, "That bastard, if I found whoever killed him, I'd be so grateful I'd kiss him full on the mouth."

Azimir frowned at his drink. "I think you already have." In the following silence he did not dare look up. "Keplan is a violent man. A tortured one—in his mind I mean, not just the scars. He's killed. Almost did again, with me, tonight. But even I don't think he's evil."

Firas's face was unreadable. His eyes fixed on the city wall towering behind the Hare. "You saying what I think you are? About Peraan? And Keplan? Where he went that night, after Mirrel—?"

"Yes. I am. And I assume that fact will die in this courtyard."

"Seems to be a lot of that." Firas regarded his own ale, then finished it in several slow sips. He placed the mug on the stoop and laced his fingers before speaking. "So why come here? Why, really?"

Azimir scuffed his boots against the stair. It was times like this that he really felt the years between him and most of the men he knew. "What does it look like when someone breathes dust?"

Firas's exhausted body tightened and he turned to look at Azimir. "No. You don't mean that. He can't have, he wouldn't have, why in the name of every dead god..." He trailed off. "'This won't make you forget.'"

Azimir frowned. "What's that?"

"A conversation he and I had. I told him that, ah, sharing intimate time together, if you will, wouldn't make him forget what happened, though he disagreed. I guess in my absence he found something that would." He heaved a sigh. "Azi, if he's breathing dust, I don't know what'll help. I've never, myself, but we're in the Slummer. Folks here have more reasons to forget than most. Once that shite's in your body you...you're not the same." He rose and paced to the privy, then back.

"Firas, I'm sorry, I just don't know who else to turn to."

"I'm trying to keep this inn floating in this putrid sea of bad news. And you've just told me our king is as good as dead."

"He's not dead. I know dust won't kill me, even if my ma said it would—"

"I don't mean physically. The man on the throne isn't the man who stepped up to it. He's not the man who promised to raise Athrolan from stagnation. And he surely isn't the man I—" He growled, kicking the frame of the wagon in the corner. "You should go."

"You think he can get better?"

Firas's eyes were fathomless depths. "It would take a god mightier than we've seen."

Azimir's veins echoed with the blood he shared with Keplan, with the woman who killed the gods his father once worshiped. "If anyone can it's him."

"I pray you're right," Firas shrugged, backlit by the oily lantern at the rear door, "but you and I both know there's no one to listen anymore.

CHAPTER TEN

The 16th Day of Glasmord, 1272
The Icelock, Northern Ilmar Ocean

THE WOOD CREAKED AGAINST the press of icy water, and Raven glanced up. He took pride in his ship working like a single being and, no matter how far from home they may be, he expected the best of his sailors.

Jorn poked her head in. "Thought you might still be up. Midnight shift change."

He rose from his desk with a groan and followed her outside. Sailors shot salutes as he stepped onto the deck. He was respected but rarely liked. Most on board had never been past Athrolani waters and none had been this far north. Storms struck quickly and lasted days before dissipating as swiftly as they had arisen. He tightened his jerkin's hood and stopped beside the fore-shipmen at the helm. "How does she sail?"

"The evening went well, sir. Smooth. We averaged nine knots. Temperature still falls—even with the sun it's past freezing, and the days are ever shorter. We passed more ice an hour ago and should pass Neneviir within the week. Sooner if we unfurled more sail."

Raven eyed the water surrounding them. The depths were black, eerie compared to the gray-green of the waves near Ceir Athrolan. "Not with the ice. We have the moon only for another hour. I'm ordering the bolts and reinforcements to be checked again. I'd hate to discover the hard way that we were unready for ice." He turned to the herald waiting on the decks. "Mek, signal for them to ready the ice-breaks."

As the boy ran up to do his bidding, the former commander watched the ships behind them. He had to admit they made an impressive sight. Once he commanded forty-six runners—fully armed vessels that were smaller than the traditional battleships under Admiral Nellon. Raven's fleet of one was newly outfitted with chevrons of iron-plated hardwood on their bows. The precaution against the massive blocks of ice in the northern-most waters had been raised to keep speed. With temperatures dropping and ice sighted, Raven listened to the tingling instinct that always served him well. The ice-breaks would hopefully not be tested.

The fleet had hugged the land for the first half of the journey, but upon signs of camps on the tundra he had ordered to push into the open ocean. Bergs and other unknown dangers kept the trade routes to the west or by land. While they were unlikely to meet any other vessels, it also meant Fess was sailing with only the most rudimentary maps. Much of their knowledge of the pole had been gleaned from the legends of the Ageless and Claimiirn histories. "Keep pace, Kusen, and wake me if anything changes. Anything on the horizon that isn't ice or water—wake me." He glanced at Jorn. "A word?"

They moved back into his study, weighing a map between them. Black dots marked their progress across the sparsely detailed area through which they sailed. The ship trembled as the ice-break lowered. Raven lifted his mug to keep it from spilling.

The officer leaned against the desk. "We have just over thirty leagues before we reached the pole. What lies between here and there worries me. We'll round the headland tomorrow, if the weather holds."

"That's a gamble this time of year." His gaze slipped back south to the night-shrouded horizon they left weeks before. "Makes me wonder if this was an elaborate execution, sending us in winter. Weather's been worse than ever."

"You think it's him?" Jorn's words were low, but superstition did not tinge her dark eyes. "Or is the world just dying around us?"

"Let's just focus on the headland, eh?"

Jorn's chair creaked as she leaned back, eyes narrowed on him. "You've destroyed men, faced fire and flood in the battle at Claimiirn. You guarded his parents north and turned cannons on your own home to uphold your values. I haven't agreed with you often lately, but I'd never call you a coward."

"I don't stand for creatures thinking they're better than us. I don't think monsters have a place in ruling us. Helping us, surely, but handing down decrees? Forcing us into worship at the foot of a throne meant for one of our own?" He shook his head. "And he arrives, poor and mad and battered and ascends to where she sat."

"I know he's not human by blood, but I can't think of a single person who isn't poor and mad and battered. Noble and commoner alike." Raven ran a finger up the coast they paralleled. He paused at the blank space past the pole. The cartographer had not even bothered to draw little waves. *This is why I became a sailor.*

"You're terrified of him."

"I hate him."

"Same thing, Dorcal." Jorn hunched over her illustrations, glancing up each time ice broke on the bow.

Raven added a few lines to his log, though there was less to say with each passing day. He reread every note they had made for the journey, guttering lantern shedding jumping light on the paper. Nerves set Raven's gut writhing. He paced to the windows to peer at the void beyond. "I've grown soft, sitting state in the city," he confided.

The ship's floor muttered as she crossed the distance between them, hand resting on his for a breath. She did not speak.

Raven looked down at her hand gripping his limp fingers. Fatigue weighed his slumped shoulders. His heart hammered, hollow. He turned, twisting his hand to grasp hers. It had been years since he lay with a woman he didn't have to pay.

"I'm not gonna pretend to be her," she warned.

"I'm not gonna ask you to. I'm not asking anything, if you don't want."

She shrugged, smile tired but sincere. "I think we could both stand to get our minds off tomorrow."

A disused laugh rasped from his throat as he followed her into the bed chamber and shut the door behind. Waves hissed along the lacquered wood as he pulled off his stained coat. He slid a hesitant hand under the waist of her shirt. Her tanned skin and Athrolani dark hair were unfamiliar to his calloused touch, but only the dark, secret part of his heart still cried for Eras's ashen complexion and pale orange hair. The *Endurance* glided, lonely, through black waters.

Φ

The 19th Day of Glasmord, 1272
The Eastern Banis Prairie

Rih took a long sip of tea. The rich flavors that erred on the side of decadence in the cloying heat of Banis summer were comforting in the winter rains. Like the empire itself, every flavor was bright, intense, and fleeting.

They were still days from Athrolan, their progress slowed by the two hundred soldiers marching alongside them. Rih grinned wolfishly. *My army.* It was not strictly true, but for now she could pretend and call it practice.

Oily tea spilled over her lap as the wagon lurched to a halt. *Of all the hoof-trod roads!* Setting the mug aside, she scrambled to peer through the waterproofed carriage cover. The entire train had stopped, horses pawing the road as their riders shifted in their saddles.

"What is it?"

Bimet turned to the driver to relay the princess's question. He shrugged, gesturing at the road ahead and muttering something.

"Says a group of riders blocks the way."

Fear sparked in Rih's chest. "Give me a moment." She grabbed a wrap to hide the fresh greasy stain across her clothes and freed a spear from the rank before jumping down. "Bimet, with me, please."

She strode to the front of the line, edging between snorting horses and uneasy soldiers. Sure enough, twelve riders stretched across the road. Red and orange knots decorated their armor. *Vales.* Despite the Banis spears lowered in their direction, none of their weapons were held at the ready. Rih steeled herself. She did not know most of the soldiers behind her or whether they supported or even knew of her rebellion. Her eyes narrowed on the lead rider. Their features were shadowed, but the masses of black braids spilled from under the heavy leather helm. They dismounted and approached, hands empty and extended.

"I am Kajimet Rih-elte and wife of the Athrolani king, His Majesty Keplan of the Hartland."

The sharp lips curled. "I hardly recognized you, swaddled in silks there."

"Majilah Ag?"

The arms opened farther and she closed the distance between them to clasp Rih's hand, her other clapping the woman on the back. The Valen queen tugged her helm off. "I'm sure you have a long way to ride, but perhaps we could journey together for a stretch."

Rih could not help the bright smile on her face. "I'd be happy to. Why don't you come to my carriage?"

The Valen guards ranged about the royal carriage, watching with wary curiosity as their queen ascended. When Rih joined her a moment later, she caught Nehla's wide-eyed gaze.

"You're friends with the Valen queen?" she signed.

Rih's smile grew tense. Between their brief visit and the close quarters in the carriage, she had not found time to continue their conversation from the Banis capital. Now seemed like a poor time to test the woman's loyalty, however. "It's odd the friends one makes, I suppose."

Majilah Ag scanned both of Rih's attendants. "Would you mind giving us a bit of privacy?"

Nehla glanced at Bimet, then back at Rih before wordlessly retreating to the carriage the attendants shared. Bimet made to followed and a moment later the army swayed back into motion. The queen drew a small notebook from her belt and set about writing.

There are too many curious ears to risk speech. Besides, this way there will be no misunderstandings. You may trust your women, but I don't.

Rih scanned the words as she poured them tea and found a case of dried fruit. She pulled the book toward her.

What brings you this far from home? I've heard you're treating with the emperor. It's unexpected.

Majilah Ag grinned.

We'll never get as far as swearing anything, you have my word on that. It just brokers peace while we get into position. I'm here to investigate a new potential ally — unofficially, for now.

For Vale or our shared interest?

Majilah Ag sipped her tea and chose a dried kiwi.

Your rebellion.

Excitement bloomed in Rih.

And who might that be?

Mirik. There is a woman who joined your cause, according to our informant. She has ties to the island, and there's even rumor she might be a member of their former spy network. Regardless, we plan on meeting with her soon.

Rih hesitated, then moved to answer. Bimet's council focused on secrecy above all else, but more often it seemed to veer toward inaction.

It's something I've considered myself. But not because of any Spy Master.

When Majilah Ag's delicate brow arched in question, Rih continued.

Because of the Hetmir's younger son.

Majilah Ag's eyes widened, lapsing into speech with her surprise. "You're direct. I hadn't realized she had a second child."

He's scarcely out of boyhood — seventeen at most. We were supposed to marry before the war began. Instead, we've become something like friends. He's clever, I think, though he doesn't let on often.

Does he share your bed?

Rih's cheeks flamed and she smoothed her skirts with a firm head shake. No one would share her bed as long as she had any say in the matter.

"Good. It always complicates things."

The queen sat back, eyes distant for a moment while she finished her tea. When her attention returned to Rih, her expression was guarded.

Perhaps I will discuss things with this supposed spy, and you work on the boy. Our meeting is another week away, but we ride fast. I hoped to write you afterward, but considering the circumstances, I decided to delay our journey and meet you in person.

Circumstances?

Perhaps you don't get news, far as you are from home, but things are changing. Armies moving. Every day brings a new patrol or baniol that's redirected. I'd be curious to know your allies in the officers' ranks, for I imagine there's a pattern.

She produced a battered map, marked with movements of various troops. A second paper detailed which baniols or officers were known. Rih's heart dropped. Her every ally was marching north. Despite what her eavesdropping gleaned, many were no longer in place.

How old is this information?

Our most recent report was the day before yesterday, via messenger bird.

Were they avoiding Mirikin ambush? Or did they know? How many people saw the letter delivered before she left Ceir Athrolan? Her thoughts hesitated on Nehla. Keplan had appeared before she could hide the information and her attention had been wholly occupied with terror. She glanced up at Majilah Ag, desperate for direction, for advice. The queen's gaze was grave and reserved. It held no answers.

We need to get into the city. We don't stand a chance if all our allies are outside the walls. You get in regularly despite being an imperial enemy.

Smuggling in twelve Valen warriors in a city where women are inconsequential is far different from hiding hundreds of soldiers. And it will take hundreds.

Rih drew a slow, steady breath.

We have one ally in the palace. My cousin, Mosil, the ambassador to the east. While at war with Mirik many of his duties overlap with the ambassador to Athrolan.

A man? They are quick-tempered and bullheaded.

Contempt settled on the queen's features.

Many might be, in Ban and Vale both, and I understand your hesitancy. I understand your fear. But please know that they are not all evil. They do not all seek to crush us beneath their sandals. We need allies and he is one.

Majilah Ag's lips twisted in scorn and she sat back. "You'll deal with him, then. Ban is built on the bones of a thousand queens, and her rivers still stink of their blood."

I will. And our every movement must be perfect. We'll need a new strategy, one from outside the Banis walls. The Golden Three cities will be the only other threat if we lay our tiles right.

I can handle them easily, though it will draw spears from the assault on the capital.

We'll make up for it. I hoped the war with Mirik would be a distraction. Instead, paranoia is at every corner.

I've lost three allies in as many weeks, not counting Il-fald."

Rih's vision tunneled. "What?"

Majilah Ag's face fell. She did not need to know the signs for the woman's name to recognize grief. "Forgive me, I thought you knew."

"I just saw her. How? When?"

"The twelfth. She was supposed to meet with my man in Stytown. Never showed. He called on her the next morning and found her dead in her bunk. Tongue and hands were cut off."

Rih rushed to the side of the carriage and pushed aside the fabric to vomit onto the muddy road. She lost sisters-in-arms before. She lost her mother. She lost her entire sense of self when she became Keplan's wife. *But none of those were my fault.*

A strong hand rested on her shoulder, long thumb tracing circles. She sat back, accepting the napkin from the Valen queen with a nod of thanks. Dabbing her mouth, she returned to her seat.

We need to act quickly. The longer we wait, the more they'll discover.

The queen nodded in agreement, lapsing back into speech. "I'll be in the capital in a few weeks for negotiations. And again, to sign our official alliance at the end of the year."

Anxiety flooded Rih's body, distant and tingling in the wake of numb grief. That was too soon. Only a general could marshal enough soldiers to besiege a city the size of RoBal in a month and a half. They needed an advantage. A large one. She was certain the answer lay in the grinding gears of the Athrolani general's mind and the weapon he relinquished to Keplan. That was a puzzle for when she returned.

There's much to plan, but we'll be in contact. Keep me apprised of your informant and the woman from Mirik.

Majilah Ag smiled, hand grasping Rih's tightly. She did not have to say anything. Her dark eyes shone with understanding and a dozen sorrows of her own. She rose, steadying herself on the arching supports. "We'd best be off."

She swung onto her mount's back from the swaying carriage, movements effortless. Saluting, she motioned for her guards to fall in about her. "May your horse's hooves be swift and your spear strike true."

The riders wheeled north, aiming for some point concealed by the undulating, stormy horizon. Even in the damp, dust trailed behind as the wagon train inched north. Something burst in Rih's heart, hot with fury and warm with hope. Perhaps wrath's bloody red did not belong solely to one heretical god.

Φ

The 21st Day of Glasmord, 1272
The City of Ceir Athrolan

Wind buffeted the riders, bringing biting hail and roiling thoughts. Keplan shuddered, wishing fashion dictated swaddling cloaks and not crisp wool coats. If he pulled his fur hat any lower it would obscure the road before him. *Perhaps that'd be a boon.*

The slippery stones were no place for a fine mount, even ridden by a king. Instead, he convinced the stable hands to groom and tack up Moly. His boots may have hung below her belly, but her swaying gait and fuzzy ears, pricked forward, were a balm to his raw psyche.

"Your Majesty!"

Keplan glanced to the left, hand raised and false smile affixed to his mouth.

"When will we have water again?"

His body chilled further. "Commander Fess and I've plans for the warehouses beyond. If we outfit them with a distillation system, they'll be —"

"Brief, boy." An'thor growled from behind him, eyes scanning the crowd with distrust.

Keplan turned back to the woman. He saw now her clothes were filthy, her cheeks sunken. "I'm working on it, miss."

"Sire!"

An'thor spurred his charger on, shoving Keplan ahead before he could try to answer another query.

"Questions don't hurt, Domariigo," he hissed to his general.

"One or two, no, but you stand there and it becomes an audience. One on their territory. I've seen riots start from less. And I've never seen a king more deserving of a riot."

"Toss off, old man," he muttered. They rounded the bend and emerged on the broad cobblestones of the docks. Keplan recoiled, his shifted weight bringing Moly to a halt before An'thor's horse collided with her. *I do deserve a riot.*

Fess had insisted he inspect the city himself, probably more for the appearance of caring than wanting his opinion. Still, his heart sank. Despite the driving hail, the stench of burnt lacquered wood clung to the streets. The harbor was clogged with battered ships, their burnt husks jutting from the gnawing waves like bodies after battle.

"Over here, sire!" Fess balanced on a beam between two of the worst warehouses, waving. The one closest to the harbor had all but collapsed into the water, two merchant docks crushed beneath it. The timbers of the other were black with mildew and rot.

Keplan dismounted beside them, looping Moly's reins around a tie-off. "These are the two you meant?"

"Nay, two behind them. I'm trying to figure out a way to destroy the rest of these without making a worse mess."

"This whole place is a mess," Keplan noted, voice low.

She caught the words, flashing a humorless smile. "Welcome to monarchy, sire. If you'll follow me?" She led him into the next bank of warehouses, the two commissioners trailing after.

"Used to make gutterwrack in here. Figured we could pump in seawater to boil it up. Use the equipment we've got." She offered the king a flask.

"No, thank you."

"It's water, sire. Munson over there rigged a small version, just to test. Wouldn't call the water good, but it's drinkable."

Keplan took a hesitant sip. His mouth seemed drier for it, and he still caught the faint acrid taste of lamp oil. Still, his stomach rumbled for more. He took a second taste before handing it back. "Your description was optimistic, Fess."

She laughed, the sound loud in the damp, empty building. "We could stand a bit of hope this winter. Might be all that gets us through, begging your pardon."

He waved away the words. They were honest. He needed that. "How soon? Are the pumps to the cistern repaired?"

The commissioner grimaced, looking over from his low conversation with the man Fess called Munson. "Pumps are fine, one just needed a new wheel. It's the cistern that's the issue now. Cracked sometime last week. Think it was the freeze, sire."

Keplan rubbed a hand over his tired face. "Fates. Can you fix it?"

"It's built into the city's foundations. Dug into the stone. We could line it, I suppose, but we'd have to drain what's left in there."

"Where's an Earth Shaker when you need one?" Keplan whispered. If the commissioner heard, he gave no sign. Clearing his throat, he turned back to the commander. "How many barrels are still useable?"

"For water? Enough, but we'll have to hire wagoneers to transport them up to the higher districts."

"Then hire them." Keplan sighed, exasperated. "I don't care what you do, frankly, or who you have to pay or how much. Get this done."

"Right away, sire." Her playful face was stony. "But may I ask where the money will come from?"

"Fess," An'thor barked. "Not now."

Apprehension weaseled into his blood. He knew the treasury was low. He knew little money was coming in, save for their small allotment from Ban. Though small, Berr was a rich nation, and generous. *But I can't go begging on every stoop.* If he could not raise Athrolan from poverty on his own, then the kingdom would never maintain itself, he feared. Guilt stacked like the unread fiscal reports from his treasurer. Money seemed useless in the face of starvation and thirst. *Until suddenly, it isn't.*

It was as if his every resolution and strength were washed from under him with the flood, eroded like the very stone they stood on. In his mind he saw Ceir Athrolan plummet into a chasm, ocean rushing after the crumbling white towers until nothing was left, save maelstrom and flecks of blue foam. "Consulate?"

The man turned, the sallow light from the dim winter sun glinting on his wan face. "Yes, sire?"

"You said it was cracked. Part of the city's foundation. How deep do those cracks run?"

The commissioner glanced at Munson, at Fess, and to An'thor's boots. "Hard to say, Your Majesty. But deep. They're small yet. And the city is strong. It'll hold for a time."

"But not forever."

The consulate did not speak, but Keplan already knew the answer. He strode from the warehouse. "Anything you need, Fess," he called over his shoulder. "I mean it."

An'thor strode after him, eyes uneasy. "Wardyn, we can't just keep throwing good plans after bad."

"Arguably, the bad ones weren't mine."

"Arguably, you are a bad plan incarnate."

"Agreed." Keplan mounted up, patting Moly's neck. Coarse white hairs dusted his jacket, but he did not care. All that occupied his thoughts was the city collapsing beneath the weight of his misuse and the perfect peace of dust.

They broke into a trot, Keplan's head high. Perhaps their progress would give the illusion of a solution. The streets were full of clamor. Storefronts once boasting the best ale in the house now barked their untainted water, thrice the price of any old-aged wraith. Keplan longed for quiet. Even taverns no longer baked bread. Instead, only the mellow scent of rice drifted over the Berrin section of the market. His heart twinged at the memory of weaving through the market stalls with Azimir. Guilt slipped from his numb fingers, however. *They made their choice.*

"Sire."

Keplan ignored An'thor's low voice. He was tired of the hypocritical judgement tossed from the black eyes. If the city had no faith in him, it was little wonder, with his general sowing bitter words like blight-bitten seeds. He was tired of the breath in his lungs.

"Keplan!" An'thor snarled, "The market!"

An edge to the general's voice cut through Keplan's reverie. The world was suddenly bright and loud before his blown pupils. The crowd was moving, but not in its usual random veins, like an exposed capillary bed. Figures approached from the Slummer. From the docks. From outside the gates. He slowed, scanning the crowd, wondering where they all aimed.

Me. "An'thor—"

"Wrath!" The scream went up from the street corner as he passed. A woman threw back her hood, exposing her cropped hair. It was Nena'phe. And she was dressed as a Mirikin merchant.

Panic exploded in him, and he whirled, yanking Moly's head about. When he called for his general, his voice was a shriek. "Domariigo!"

"Ride, you idiot!"

Moly leapt over the stones, stocky body barreling past the press of people as more and more doffed hoods and hats. Keplan caught the glint of steel.

An'thor's charger broke ahead, cleaving a path.

The half-hearted designs on Keplan's worktable would do nothing to protect them. The war they planned for was here. And Rih would never arrive in time.

Blood spurted across his face. Moly slowed, her whinny a scream over the shouted scripture. She shuddered and sank beneath him, dragging him to the cobbles, one thin leg pinned beneath her heaving flank. It occurred to the king that the hundreds of faces turned toward him in anger were not only

Mirikin, but Berrin, Banis, a scattering of other Nenev. And just as many were Athrolani.

The heat in him was no longer panic. It was fury. He was familiar with madness, the kind that piled in the corners of an isolated mind, wriggled in when he was not looking. This was different. It was churning, burning and brittle, bright and almost akin to laughter. He ripped himself free of his decorated saddle, yanking the fur hat from his head, hair coming loose as he did.

"Wardyn!" Domariigo fought to turn back, horse's hooves crushing toes and toppling any who attempted to flee. His hand dropped to the empty holster on his hip and his purple lips knotted in a curse.

In the periphery soldiers clattered onto the walls, helms glinting on rooftops around him. His tendons creaked with their crossbow strings as they drew back and held. An'thor raised his hand to hold fire, at least until the king was out of range. Fanatics' faith bled into his mind, igniting it with fervor. He no longer knew whether his certainty was theirs or his own. Perhaps it did not matter. Perhaps they were the same.

The heretics did not notice the approaching guards or did not heed. Would they pardon the city if he begged? Like him, these people cared for nothing. Nothing beyond their god. The monstrous man rocking at the back of his mind grinned, daring him. Mirth bubbled with spittle from between Keplan's bared teeth. He would give them what they asked for.

"You!" he shouted, gesturing to the asai Swordbearer's ardent face. Beside her a Nenev warrior dropped into a guard stance, pale visage a beacon. The din subsided. Keplan's arms shook with as much adrenaline as dust-drought. Their faith was a heavy ache pressing down on his lungs and fluttering heart.

The crowd eased back a few paces and he staggered toward them.

"You don't even bear a weapon," the Nenev hissed, voice more surprised than scornful. His wiry arms were bare, despite the clawing wind.

"Just the marks of hate." Keplan winked.

"Excuse me?"

Keplan let his gaze rove over the devotees until they settled back on the asai woman. "Read it to me, Nena'phe lui Hiral, Swordbearer of the Seer of Lymorda. You arrived at my door with an army fit for war because I do not worship your god. The least you can do is remind me why."

"You've denied the Truth before."

"Read it!" he roared.

Her voice shook, rattling low over the cobbles toward him. "'Thrice born, the One True God will rise where the worlds meet, from death and birth, from chaos and order. His blood pools, drowning the world even as it gives it life. Though he will bear the marks of hate, he will be unable to raise its tools. His right hand —'"

"That part, yes," he interrupted. He eased the glove from his right hand, praying every Athrolani spyglass trained on him would crack and fog. He fell back into the archaic speech of their doctrines, his blasphemy a mirror of their scripture. "His right hand will be stained bloody with wrath."

He raised the claret palm.

"Blasphemer," Nena'phe whispered, face pinched in defiance.

Keplan went on, yanking his other glove free. "And his left with the verdant green of life and mercy. He will know all, hear all, but listen to none. He will wreak havoc from the sky if you rob him! You've robbed me of peace!" Spittle flew from his mouth, mania flashing through every artery with their every flickering fearful thought. His gaze jumped from one to the next. Terror shimmered over the crowd as the hail returned in earnest.

Keplan's right hand rose, fingers held in the signal to his archers. "You want to spread the truth? Truth is, I am your one god. And I am no longer merciful."

His hand dropped.

Arrows exploded into the ground around him, punctuating his rising laughter. Thrills chased up his spine as he dashed through the deadly rain. Bodies churned around him as panic swept the crowd. An elbow cracked into his cheek. It was joy to just to feel the power. *To feel at all.* For once, the bloody sweet scent was not in his imagination. It was real and fresh and full of hope.

A body collided with him and they crashed to the cobbles. The Nenev warrior staggered back, ghostly hands cupping something silver. A mechanical thunderclap exploded between them.

Heat and cold flashed through Keplan's chest. He chuckled, scrambling upright as the man lowered the weapon. The revolver must have malfunctioned.

"No!" An'thor's voice boomed across the square, and he plunged toward them. His eyes were fixed not on Keplan, but the Nenev boy.

Keplan tried to reach for the general's horse as they clattered past. His hand refused to obey. He glanced down. Blood soaked his left sleeve. *My hand.* Thoughts tumbled out of order now, even the traces of dust unable to keep his mind racing. Cold spread through his shoulder, his arm, and sauntered across the left side of his chest. A glance showed him gnarled flesh and black pulsing blood. *Oh.*

A child stumbled into him screaming, and another spray of blood cascaded over him. This time it was hers. Cold stone rushed to meet him.

The End of Mercy

CHAPTER ELEVEN

The 23rd Day of Glasmord, 1272
The Athrolani Coast

RIH'S EYES NARROWED ON the figure approaching from the east. He was riding hard, and poorly. Clods and froth flew behind them as he crested the hill.

Azimir tumbled from his horse, breath heaving. Old bruises colored his eyes and throat. Thin red lines marred his broad cheekbone where it had scraped across something hard. "Your Highness," he gasped, dropping to one knee, swaying at her feet.

Dread chilled her body. "What happened? Are you hurt?"

"Athrolan's occupied. Fanatics. No water." He glanced down at himself. "It's not from battle, mostly. Blood is."

She signaled for them to make camp, drawing Azimir up the stairs into her carriage. She pressed him into one of the seats and set about making tea. He did not speak, head hanging low from his hunched shoulders.

It was only when steaming mugs sat before all three of them that she asked the question again.

"My father accepted the One God's scripture. Before you left, but I didn't know. He left three days ago. I was meant to as well, but I couldn't. Not the way he left things with Keplan. Hardly be a surprise if we had gone to war."

"Mirik and Athrolan?"

He nodded, taking a deep sip of tea. His eyes lidded for a moment, then he shook himself alert. "The Swordbearers came from Mirik. Merchant ships. Two days ago, they attacked. Keplan was riding in the street, trying to give Athrolan water. Just chaos." He shuddered.

"You said it was occupied?"

"They took over, guarding every street. Only way to be allowed out is to accept the One True God and swear fealty."

"Is that how you escaped?"

Azimir's dry lips cracked as he laughed. "I pretended to be their ally—told them I was there on behalf of my father to convince my dear cousin. Said I was going to beg you to consider negotiation just to get you in the walls."

"Why would they negotiate with me?"

"You're his wife, everything falls to you until the heir arrives."

"Heir?" Rih's stomach flipped. "How was he killed? The riot?"

"He's not dead yet, but his doctor says could be any day. Hasn't woken." Azimir's throat bobbed as he swallowed hard. "Shot by a revolver—the Ageless weapon. One of the Swordbearers carried it."

"Athrolan has thousands of people—surely they could organize and overthrow just by sheer numbers."

"It's a bit tricky."

"Planning a rebellion isn't easy but it's surely possible!" she scoffed.

His eyes settled on her, head tilting ever so slightly as if to observe a new angle of her. "Surely, yes. But many are accepting the God. It's easier."

"How can they, after watching their king fall?"

"That's the tricky bit," Azimir elaborated. "Keplan was shot because he revealed himself. Stripped his coat and gloves off in the market and proclaimed he was their One God." The memory of a smile ghosted across his face. "Fairly incredible, really."

"He couldn't be serious," she wondered.

"I don't know. He hated the prophet, her words, hated everything they stood for. Most men would ridicule such prophesies. His loathing was that of a man faced with truth. Not falsehood."

Rih stared at her own hands, wondering if she looked upon them long enough, they would be stained too. "I heard the words in Ban. My cousin told me them. And I, too, was skeptical." Her gaze moved to his.

"But?"

"'In battle we must imagine the worst our enemy could do and plan accordingly.' It's indeed bizarre that I may have married a god, the spawn of two mighty inhuman creatures. But not unlikely."

"Minata Kaz." His smile had life this time. "I'm familiar with her teaching. Read through *Joy in Death* for the second time last summer. You must observe your opponent like a lover, imagining what their body is capable of so you might answer it. Just with a sword instead of ardor."

Rih rolled her eyes. She appreciated the warrior's expertise but had never cared for the sexual metaphors pervading her prose. "I prefer *Waking Blood*."

"Bit heavy on theory in that one for my tastes. I learn so much from her accounts alone." He ducked his head, then glanced back up. "Funny, sitting here, bruised and half dead joking about dead strategists."

"We'll need her. Once I'm in the city, how do you plan on getting the baniol in to attack?"

Azimir eyed her warily. "Attack? I assumed you'd actually negotiate."

Her brow arched. "My new home is under attack and my husband very well dead. I'm a soldier. I don't negotiate."

He sat back, raking a hand through his matted hair. "What do you need from me?"

"To be rested. You'll have to be our ticket inside those walls. But how to get the soldiers in without being seen?"

"They know you traveled with a retinue."

"Not over two hundred," she countered. I could add a dozen maybe, but any more and they'll question it." She stared at the floor, listening to the horses chomp on their hay just outside. "Wagons."

"They'll search them."

"Then we put just enough on top that it's believable."

Azimir started nodding, leaning forward with eagerness. "Leave anyone who isn't battle-tried behind. Dress a soldier in their stead."

"That's another fifteen."

He swayed in his seat, blinking rapidly. "Do you have water?"

She fished a flagon out and handed it to him.

Half was gone by the time he set it down and wiped his mouth. "Toar, my mind can hardly focus on anything but thirst."

"There's none?"

"Rations. Tight ones. Didn't dare bring any on my ride." He gestured vaguely in the direction of the city. "Anyway, tuck a good four under the canvas in the tent wagons, I'd wager."

"Go rest, Azi," she insisted. "I'll wake you if I need something, but you're no good dead."

He sighed but obeyed, almost falling when he tried to bow and back up at the same time. He paused halfway down the carriage steps. "I hadn't seen it. Battle. Fought, surely, and seen violence. But not battle." For once his head was low, barely meeting her eyes. "You were right when you said I didn't know it."

She watched him go, heart heavy. Azimir was likeable enough, even if she did not trust him. If only the world were kind enough for no one to experience battle. She drew a deep breath, then another, drawing strength into her blood with every billow of her lungs.

When she left her carriage, her resolve was steel. Bimet jogged after her, shouting her signed orders to the gathered troops. "Toss the tents! Dump everything! We can fit enough of you in the wagons to sneak in. The rest will await orders just outside the walls." She jabbed a finger at the camp cook. "Anyone who's more likely to die than kill, stay back, trade with a soldier."

The wagon train writhed with movement. Chests and pans littered the slush-covered roadside. A young squire stripped, trading his gear to a Banis soldier barely a year older. She wrapped her spear in a rag before tethering the Athrolani flag to its end.

Rih whirled, eyes settling on the baniol himself. "And someone find me armor."

Φ

The City of Ceir Athrolan, Athrolan

An'thor slumped in the chair. Blood splattered the floor. Moans drifted from the long infirmary hall outside. The room was dark, empty save for the guard by the door. And the body in the bed, he supposed. Already so much of Keplan's life had fled.

The king's head lolled on the pillow, cracked lips parted. An'thor did not know who dragged the boy from the fray. He recalled only racing after the medics as they flopped Keplan's limp form onto a stretcher. Digging twisted metal from shreds of thin muscle took hours. Now a thick bandage wrapped Keplan's left shoulder and chest. Already the center tinged pink.

"You have a minute?" Fess was silhouetted in the doorway, voice low so as not to disturb the dying.

"Come in."

"What I have to say, he doesn't need to hear."

An'thor watched the carefully folded sheet over the king's sunken chest. If he focused hard, he could see ribs faintly rising. Spiderwebbed veins inched up his exposed skin as life drained from his body. "I don't think he can hear much."

"Last thing to go, and you know it. Don't doom a man not already dead. I'll be in the hall."

An'thor straightened with a groan, nodding to the guard before following the commander. "Been a week now."

"Been four days," she corrected. Biting teeth replaced her gentleness. Her eyes were tired, her face shadowed and pale. "I received a bird from Lady Gella. She'll be here once the roads clear. A week, maybe less."

"The heir? You said he wasn't dead yet."

Fess's hand smacked into the wall beside the general's head. "I don't need to tell you what happens if we wait for him to be cold and withered before calling heirs in. I'm not making your mistakes. We'll speak with Her Grace."

"What about Daymir? I haven't left the infirmary, but I assume someone updated him?"

"He could not recall who Keplan was. Will arrive soon. Until then we have the Kajimet."

"She's hardly useful. The king's wife. A princess. Little more." He leaned on the wall, scratching at the base of one horn. He would have to grind it down soon. The cap was slipping. *Everything's slipping.* "There's still hope. His mother was unconscious for weeks when she bound the worlds—"

"He was shot by some fanatic, not ripping souls from gods."

"Mel'iend is a fool, not a fanatic!"

Fess stepped back, brows arching. Her thick arms crossed over her chest. "So. I was right. You knew that man. That why you went chasing after him, screaming, and left attending your king to the city folk? Some dockhand in a dress dragged him from the chaos."

An'thor shook his head. "I knew him once. My nephew. Thought he was dead."

"It would appear not. Would he listen to you?"

"We ended things poorly. Barrackborn's son has better luck with those zealots than I do, if he ever returns."

"Four days, Domariigo. Give them another three. Regardless, when this is over, whether His Majesty breathes or not, we'll have a mess on our hands. He can't just claim divinity and then sweep it under the nearest rug."

"So you saw that."

"He stood in the city square half naked and proclaimed he was God. Half the city saw it. Coupled with his bloodline, that proclamation is the reason the Swordbearers have been able to subdue us all so easily. We believe him."

An'thor stared at her. "We."

Fess lifted a shoulder in an exhausted shadow of a shrug. "Either he's a madman, or he's right. I know which I'd prefer."

An'thor glowered at her. "I've always known he wasn't human."

"Elitist. I didn't have to meet his parents to know they weren't monarchy material. Sure, they saved us, but humans are meant to rule themselves. It's why the gods rebelled against their creators in the first place—they didn't want to be subjugated. I'd think you'd remember that. All the stories say you were there when the war broke out."

"Only for part of it," he muttered. "Look at this world. Look at your own country. You don't need to have lived half as long as I have to realize you people can't govern yourselves."

Her dark brows arched. "I've always felt the worst rulers are those who think they're better than others. I'm sure our dear Kajimet would agree, having lived under an imperial gaze."

"Not better, as in worth, simply—"

"Keep the rest of those thoughts to yourself. I'm tired of bigotry."

An'thor snarled, but his argument died in his throat when he saw a healer and doctor slipping into Keplan's room. "I'd better see what that's about."

"An'thor."

He turned back to the commander. "Fess."

"Dorcal might have looked away from your myriad indiscretions, but I won't. I won't go to war with you. I won't cow to your archaic ideals. I'd advise you not to even try."

There was nothing he could say that would not sound bitter or childish. He retreated to his vigil over the pauper king. Neither healer nor doctor spoke was they unwrapped the bandages, but their expressions were reserved. The sweet tang of blood and rot hung heavy in the close air.

"He's hardly breathing," An'thor noted.

"He's resting. We gave him something to help with the pain."

"He should have been weaned off that shite a day ago. It's too much."

Neither answered him, and he settled back in his seat as they finished rebandaging the ugly wound. Dread was a deep ache in An'thor's bones. He was so desperate to leave this world in good hands, tended the way it ought to be. If not the Laen, then her offspring. And now that very boy threatened to drift from the world as modestly as he came.

Hold on, you miserable bastard.

Φ

The 24th Day of Glasmord, 1272

It was odd to see the Athrolani gates shut at noon. The wagons drew up at the towering walls, Rih peering up at where guards should stand, far above. The ramparts were deserted.

Azimir cupped his hands about his mouth and shouted something. No response came. Smoke drifted overhead, but it did not smell of cooking and warmth. Azimir was raising his hands to call a second time when the gatehouse door slammed open. A pale man blocked the narrow doorway.

Fresh, cheap embroidery emblazoned his dirty shirt with some sigil: a black ring centered on two overlapping handprints. His mouth moved too rapidly for her to decipher which language he used, but both Azimir and Bimet seemed to understand.

"This man's one of the Swordbearers. Says he and his partner will speak with you and Master A'hane alone. The wagons can stay outside."

"We've had a long journey, and I'm eager to put this bloodshed behind us. But please, my people need rest." She looked pointedly at the green palm on his clothes. "Prove you're as interested in upholding the One God's mercy as you are his wrath."

The man shifted, tongue probing the livid void where a tooth sat not long before. His black eyes examined the wagons and riders. Even Rih's carriage had been stripped of its covering. "Fine. But we meet in the market. Neutral ground."

"Agreed."

He eyed her, then Azimir, before retreating. No sooner did the door shut than the whole gate trembled and one-half wrenched open. Azimir nudged his horse forward, glancing back at her once he was through. At Rih's nod, her carriage followed. Every corner was guarded by a pair of Swordbearers. Those Athrolani who moved about the streets did so with furtive steps and a downcast gaze. She did not need to hear to know the city was silent. Hidden by the driver's seat, her hand clenched, white-knuckled, on her atlatl's grip.

Her driver halted at the market. Weapons and viscera littered the streets and bodies piled in the market square. Her teeth clenched. Few belonged to soldiers. Most were children, crushed under panicked, fleeing feet. Scorch marks splashed the pale stone.

Beside her, Bimet's hands moved. "How can they let this go on?"

Rih did not answer. She never understood Athrolan more than she did now. Immobilizing fear was familiar. The Nenev was in conversation with a muscled woman wearing the handprint emblem. The hard lines of the female Swordbearer's muscles did not relax while the pale man fiddled with something. Rih's stare dropped to the holster at his hip. It was empty.

Warning shot up her arms.

Azimir's fingers tightened on his reins.

An arrow burst through the meat of her thigh. Panic was fire in her gut. She tumbled from the carriage, landing in an unsteady crouch.

Hooves pawed above her, and she ducked under the animal's belly. Azimir yanked his mount about, mouth wide in a yell. Another roll brought her to the back of her carriage. Soldiers erupted from her wagons. Bimet appeared at the stairs, belly to the carriage floor. She thrust a fistful of darts at the Kajimet with a nod. Her free hand ripped a delicately curved blade from a sheath under her skirts.

Soldiers erupted from under piled tent poles and supplies. A spear bounced across the cobblestones a hand's breadth from the Nenev man. He whirled, gesturing wildly for his allies to close the gate.

Swordbearers spilled from side streets. A wagoneer whipped his team forward, wedging his wagon in the closing gate. Wood cracked. *Hold,* Rih begged. *Just long enough for the second baniol!* The road beyond the walls was dusty but deserted.

Rih bolted into a deserted stall. She eased backward, wincing as a jug tumbled from a broken shelf and shattered across her face. Spoiled wine stung her eyes and she blinked, wiping a shaking arm across her face. *What are you doing, Rih?* she asked herself. *Cowering?*

Her free hand fingered the wound in her leg. The arrow had passed clear through, leaving two dripping punctures. Tugging her wrap from the armor hidden beneath, she swiped at it with a dart point. The silk ripped easily. It was a scant bandage but would slow the blood. She yanked the quiver over her shoulder and eased weight onto her leg. The pain brought a smile to her face. War. She bathed in the adrenaline. *Finally, something I'm good at.*

A shadow fell across her. The Nenev man loomed in the doorway, strange weapon raised. Rih tucked her shoulder and lunged into his gut. They fell back into the stall, crashing through cheap wood. She tugged her arm free from under him and brought her atlatl around. Blood spurted as the metal spur on the weighted end collided with the side of his head. The blow raced up her arm with a satisfying hum. He stilled beneath her.

Rih dipped her head to the row of whistles on her shoulder. Two short breaths on the smaller one rallied a handful of Banis to her. She pointed toward the docks, then the wealthy upper tier. The officers broke apart, calling for their patrols to strike deeper into the city.

The female Swordbearer bounded across the market toward the trapped wagon, massive sword wheeling. Rih's first tossed dart skittered wide, spinning away from her quarry. The second bounced off the woman's heavy armor. Rih spat in frustration. She had always been better with a spear. She ripped another dart from her quiver but didn't nock it.

Townsfolk leapt from their houses armed with clubs and kitchen knives. She broke into a run, pushing toward where Azimir leaned against a building. She fell against the wall beside him, flashing a bright smile. She jerked her head at the gate. The wagon's sides splintered, the one axle shattering under the weight of the door.

Azimir followed her gaze, pupils huge from excitement or fear. A shaking hand clasped hers tightly. Their fingers laced, sticky with blood. "Gatehouse."

Together they broke into a sprint. Rih's pulse matched her racing stride. Another twenty paces. Another ten. Two. Then she was bolting up the gatehouse stairs, Azimir a step behind. A small clay ball, barely the size of a head, tumbled from above. It rolled, smoking, on the cobbles between them and the gatehouse. A blast knocked them to the ground. Light and heat exploded across her face, tightening her skin. Blinking, she shoved herself upright. The storefronts nearest her were leveled. Another ball rolled across the street. Grabbing Azimir's arm, she dragged them into the shelter of the gatehouse.

Three fanatics crowded in the room, blocking the mechanism and lever. Dodging the first spear thrust, she jabbed the Swordbearer with her dart. His arm cracked beneath her whipping atlatl. She whirled in time to see Azimir kick one Swordbearer down the stairs. The third raised his hands and knelt, murmuring. She shoved him at the mechanism and brandished another dart.

No translation was needed. He dragged the lever up and the walls shook and the gate crept back open.

Azimir jerked his head at the open door, grin feral. "Hear hooves! Go!"

She pushed past him, almost tripping down the stairs. Sure enough, the market swarmed with Banis riders. Spears cut ribbons from the sea air. She grabbed the reins of a bucking Athrolani horse and jerked the spear from its flank before dragging herself into the saddle.

Wind buffeted her as An'thor rushed past, followed by Curiel and all her swords. A baniol wheeled, the Swordbearer's flag trampled into the stone. She punched her weapon in the air, looping it overhead. Allies fell in about her as more and more fanatics were driven into the streets, chased from buildings, cornered in the square.

Beside the broken remains of her carriage, the Nenev man staggered upright. Rih drove her horse forward until her borrowed spear tip rested at the man's throat. A bloody knot marked where she had knocked one horn from his skull. He raised his empty hands, shouting something over his shoulder. Weapons lowered. Blows stilled.

An'thor trotted up beside her, black eyes narrowed. He spat a couple of words; then, realizing she could not understand, looked about for Bimet.

Victory and surprise and joy burned through her. Guards arrived to take the surviving Swordbearers. Every face she recognized was thinner than before and looked as tired as she felt.

After a moment Bimet appeared, limping but otherwise whole. "They'll handle them from here, Kajimet."

Rih fell back with several officers. The courtyard was deserted, most of the guards in the streets. She bent over the fountain after relinquishing her reins. The water sloshed, pinking with blood, light dancing on the lamp oil at the surface.

When she straightened, Azimir swayed beside her, new wounds over his old bruises. He bared bloody teeth in a grin. "Minata Kaz at the fall of Yeth." Their brows pressed together for a breath, then he pulled back, leaving a streak of his sweat and someone else's blood.

Her vision tunneled when she shifted her weight and pain shot down her leg. The world was abruptly real again.

"Infirmary." Azimir waved toward the rear of the palace and looped an arm under hers.

I never realized how long these halls were, she mentally growled. One did not count steps until each one drove fire into her thigh.

There were no beds, not even for the king's wife. Instead, Azimir settled her on a bench in a room off to the side. He unwrapped the matted silk from her flesh and paled. Blood trickled down her leg, puddling on the flagging. Her right arm twitched in reflexive memory of throwing darts.

A healer appeared a moment later and set to work. Bimet slumped on the bench beside Rih, and Azimir leaned against the wall. Rih winced as the wound was cleaned and inflamed flesh was stitched closed.

The healer sat back and bowed, relaying something to Bimet. "She thanks you for bringing the Banis healing kits."

Rih smiled. Banis medicine was prized in the east. Skill in war naturally led to skills in medicine. "I'm glad they can help."

Azimir shook his head when she asked if he was hurt. "Not badly. Most is from before."

"The riot?"

"Kep and I argued."

She stared at the purple ringing his throat. It looked like far more than an argument. "When?"

"Just before. He lost his temper with me. Blamed me for the priests. Can't really fault him there." He looked away at the shadowed bed in the corner of the room.

Cold filled her when she followed his gaze. The bed was not empty.

Keplan's body was sunken, atrophied. His dry skin like pale rawhide. The flickering pulse in the lacework purple veins across his skin was the only sign of vitality. Stinking bloody bandages piled in the corner, forgotten in the chaos of battle.

Air moved and she turned back to the door.

The general loomed in the doorway, bloody and stinking of alcohol as much as gore. His glare fixed on her. "What was that?"

A trace of her fury still burned. "I saved the city, sir."

Azimir pushed off the wall, gaze bouncing between them in frustration. "General, we did what we had to. I told you I was bringing her back, her troops too."

"You can't just storm the city without telling us!"

Rih's temper snapped. "You didn't want my soldiers, but you needed them. You didn't want my help, but you needed it. And now you're furious that once again a human is cleverer than you! Forgive me for undermining your authority, General," she twisted her fingers, adding mockery to the word, "but someone must do your job if you won't. Might as well be me."

"My job?" he retaliated, lip curling, white hand jerking toward Keplan's motionless form. "Your job is to wait for that mad creature to fu —"

"Enough!" Azimir shoved between them. "This isn't the place to debate who failed Athrolan. Argue who's better at saving this piss-ridden excuse for a kingdom in the privy for all I care, but don't do it here."

"His Majesty shouldn't be —" An'thor wheedled.

"Out! Both of you!" Azimir glared at the general. "I'm the only family he's got. If anyone's going sit at his bedside, it'll be me."

Rih staggered upright. The boy was right, and she was exhausted. She longed for a bath, even in the polluted brackish water Athrolan had to offer. Bimet helped her from the room, both watching as An'thor disappeared down the hall.

One corner of the translator's mouth lifted. "Well done, General. Tomorrow RoBal."

Rih offered an exhausted smile. "Perhaps the day after."

Φ

The 25th Day of Glasmord, 1272

Azimir burst into wakefulness. His back ached from sleeping on the bench outside Keplan's door. He shook feeling back into one leg, searching for the source of the shouts that woke him.

"We need help, now!"

He shouldered open the door to the king's infirmary room. His gut clenched at the sight before him. Keplan convulsed, sheets tangled around his emaciated limbs. His pale eyes rolled back, and froth spilled over his blue lips. "What's wrong?"

"I meant a healer, not a boy!" the doctor snarled.

Another healer burst in, eyes wide. She gripped the king's limbs, glancing from the doctor to Azimir. "What's he doing in here?"

"Getting in the way," the man growled, before pressing fingers to Keplan's pulse points. "He's slipping."

Azimir watched them rip sheets and clothes from the lanky, frail body. *No.* His body quaked watching his cousin, his friend spasm into death.

"What did you do?" the healer snarled at the doctor, streaking fluid across her brow as she pushed her hair away.

"Nothing! We lowered the peaceleaf, hoping he might rally, but he's been comatose for days."

"Peaceleaf?" Azimir whispered, heart thudding to a halt.

"For pain." The healer attempted to still Keplan's spasm. Frustration hissed from her as the newly tied bandage dislodged.

"It's made of dust, isn't it?" Azimir's gaze was fixed on his cousin. Cold nausea wormed in his throat. He could not break the confidence of Keplan's snarled implications, but neither could he watch him die.

She rolled her eyes. "Same plant. Hardly the same thing, though."

"But if someone breathed dust, peaceleaf would have less effect, right?"

"This isn't the scholar's debate hall," the doctor ground out. "Unless you have something useful—"

"How much?" the woman interrupted. Her eyes were bitter and steady on Azimir's.

"I don't know. But often. Daily at least."

"He's falling from it. Dust drought." She fumbled in her apron and drew out a gleaming glass tube equipped with a needle and plunger. "You, hold him."

Azimir gripped his cousin's arm, pressing it into stillness against the mattress. "What in Toar's name—"

"Banis medicine is better than ours." The needle slid into Keplan's vein, blood blooming in the clear liquid for a second before she depressed the plunger. The seizing slowed. Color returned to his face. Lines of agony smoothed slightly. He still seemed unresponsive. But alive.

"You. Outside. Now," the healer snapped, ripping her gloves off and dumping them in the bin beside Keplan's door.

Azimir slunk outside after her. Her tone was, for all the world, his mother's. And he was just as chagrined when she turned the weight of her anger on him. "I'm sorry."

"For what?"

He shrugged. "I just think you're expecting an apology."

"Only if you know what you did." She raked a hand through her short black hair. "You could have killed him."

"I wasn't the one who took away the medicine for pain—"

"He fell into dust drought when we weaned him from peaceleaf. We wouldn't have if you'd been honest with us."

Azimir glared. "Honest? In case you didn't notice, he's the Athrolani king. You think he needs rumors like that drifting around?"

"We're doctors. We don't spread rumors," she countered. "And if you hadn't been there, he may well have died."

"You're welcome," Azimir snapped.

"Shut it."

Azimir stepped back. It was not often someone blatantly ignored his perceived rank. Hetmir's son had weight, and Dhoah' Laen's nephew had more. "I'm sorry," he repeated, looking away. "I should have been more honest."

"Is there anything else we ought to know?"

"Not that I know of."

"By the end of this he'll be sober, if he lives. You think he'll stay that way?"

Azimir sighed. "I can hardly guess. I can imagine why he started in the first place, but I don't know."

"Who else knows?"

"No one." *Firas.* "That I'm aware of, at least."

"We'll keep it that way."

"Will he be all right?"

She glanced at the closed door. "Hard to say. Our first priority now is weaning him from the drugs. He can't heal until then, really. His body doesn't know what to do with its resources. But we'll do all we can." She paused, then looked back at him. "It does good, you visiting. He doesn't strike me as someone with many friends. But if he has any, this is where they need to be. We're tending his body, but if he doesn't have a will, there's nothing we can do."

Azimir nodded. "I'll see if anyone else wants to sit with him."

The doctor's hand was warm on his arm. "You're a good man. He gets through this, he'll have you to thank."

Azimir watched her go. If Keplan lived, he wondered what they might say to one another. *Last we spoke his hand was at my throat.*

Φ

Death was different this time. It was silence. It was blackness. It was oblivion. Keplan welcomed it. There was no difference now between his own face and the hideous reflection. Waxy flesh stretched in a grin, sallow cast yellowing.

A voice, thunderous, broke through. "I brought you peace. I'll survive and wrest it from the world. We're a god. Deny all you like, but that prophet spoke true. They'll bow before us, lathe filth from our feet and there will be peace."

"You didn't bring peace. Not to Athrolan. Not to me. Firas did," Keplan bit back.

It was not just Firas that had brought him peace, but the man he allowed himself to be in Firas's arms. A man who hoped. Who laughed. Who saw beauty in the rainbows of oil on the Slummer puddles. He whirled on the mirror. It was just a pane between who he was and who he could be, though he lost sight of who was which. It cracked beneath his fist. "Fuck you," he growled.

The reflection lunged, winding through the cracks in the glass until his almost physical form manifested before Keplan's own. He looked real except at the very corners of Keplan's vision. Hard hands slid over his body, the touch hovering somewhere between lust and loathing. Cracked lips crashed into his, blood and spit mingling until he no longer smelled the rot.

He tasted of dirt and ash. Maybe they both did.

The voice rang in his head now. "Think of how glorious we'd be together, your body, my mind, your monster, my madness tearing violence from the world." Fingers gripped his nape, fumbled at his groin. "Together we'd birth a new pantheon. One deserving of their worship."

Too many days had passed since someone touched him, all of him, even his excuse for a soul. He tilted his chin, mouth parting, and accepted his reflection's cold tongue.

CHAPTER TWELVE

The 28th Day of Glasmord, 1272
The Icelock, Northern Ilmar Ocean

THE WIND HOWLED ACROSS the ice with bitter teeth. Raven stared at the coast, eyes narrowed against the onslaught. *There*. A flash of orange and black against the blue-gray of the snow-blown landscape.

"You see that?"

"See what, sir?"

Raven glanced down at the map without answering. The ink was still wet, the pen strokes lacking details that would come with decades of forays. "Where the fates are we?"

"West of the Ageless city by several leagues, sir. More than that I don't know. Haven't named it yet, thought you might want to."

"Places like this already have names, Jorn." Raven squinted at the paper and then back up to the landscape. "There's something out there."

"Ice bears?"

Shudders ghosted over Raven's shoulders like a lover's taunt. "Haven't yet met a bear that makes the hairs stand on end like this."

"Haven't been to my neck of the world then, sir," she joked, following him from the cabin. A breeze eddied, tugging at his poorly cut hair, snapping lines, almost playful.

He paced along the rail, glancing from his first mate to the men in the rigging. Who would shout it first?

"My ma went out one night to put the sheep in and came face-to-face with a big sow, teeth the size of Metters' —"

"Commander! Wind's a-changing!"

"I know." The affirmation was too quiet for them to hear, but it didn't matter. The breeze billowed, mutters rising into moans through the storm's snapping teeth.

The cold brass of his spyglass bit his fingers. He focused on the massive ice outcropping. Chunks skittered down the surface to splash into the frigid ocean, but there was no judging their exact size. Through the clear blue ice, however, he caught another bloom of light. *Firelight.* He raised his nose, sampling the air whipping about their furled sails. *Stone. Salt. Soot. Decay.*

Above, stars glittered in the cold, cloudless sky. So, not a storm, then. "Hold course!"

Even under the thick wool of his naval coat, hairs stood upright along his arms. He lifted his nose and frowned.

"What is it?"

"We're in the open ocean."

"Aye, and?"

"So why does it smell like low tide?" Dread churned in his gut. The gods were dead, he knew that. He stood on the ramparts of Ceir Athrolan when the world shuddered with their passing. *But those who killed them, they're still here.* His gaze never wavered from the pulsing, flickering glow. "To starboard!" he called.

"Sir, that will bring us within—"

"The Northlands aren't Athrolan. His Majesty won't give a bloody tup how close we come to land. Starboard!"

"Dorcal, it could just be a hunting outpost. Berrin whalers wrecked far afield." The muscles in Jorn's jaw clenched as she attempted to be the voice of reason.

"I doubt Berrin would wreck, even this far north." Raven tugged on another cloak and wrapped gloves over his weather-beaten hands. Something tugged at his chest, like excitement, but underscored with the certainty of dread. "To explore and record, eh, Jorn?"

"Sir?"

"I'm going ashore." He paused and glanced back at Jorn. "And if you mention Metters' crotch again, I'll personally fasten you to the bow and use you as an ice-break."

She cackled and pulled her own cloak tighter. "I'll get the boat."

Waves hissed against the skiff's sides as he rowed, each pull sending a twinge of pain through his right shoulder. Instead of slacking, as he might have done a month ago in the cushioned apathy of his life in the city, he leaned in, let curiosity slip into his belly.

Jorn, perched in aft, scanned the sheer side of the berg, picking out breaking waves that spoke of hazards below. "When His Majesty bundled us off to freeze to death, I don't think this is what he had in mind."

"I think it's exactly this. There's only so much mapping one can do. Last letter we got said he liked your sketches."

"It's not an island. Just a massive berg," she murmured, ignoring the rest of his words. "There's a pull-off ahead."

He slowed and brought the boat alongside the berg, keeping her steady as Jorn slammed a mooring into the ice. Sharp excitement burned in her eyes, belying her skeptical words. One hand loosened his sword in its sheath, damp and salt sticking the steel. She led the way, picks thudding as she hauled herself hand over hand up the undulating face. Raven followed, watching each hold and footing for danger. Breath escaped his mouth in a groan as he rolled over the berg's lip. Fire waited for them.

Flames devoured the wet pile of broken bones. Hanks of dried flesh shuddered under the inferno's might. It was built like a campfire, banked and tended. But campfires were not made the height of the tall commander. Raven's eyes picked out the monstrous curved tusks, the pile of hairy skin stretched over half of a rib cage.

"Fates." Raven's instincts screamed to return to the ship, skitter down the ice, maybe dive into the ocean. Anything but stay. Wind spun around the ice, but where he crouched the air was still. Any snowflake was swept from the ground, bare ice left gleaming under the midmorning stars. Sparks puffed from the fire as bones settled. A shadow loomed from the flames, tibia, humerus, the wing of a scapula that once, perhaps, belonged to a man, ground into articulation.

Raven scrambled backwards, catching himself on the lip of the ice cliff. His breath puffed from between layers of his scarf, freezing a moment later across the mouth of his scarf. Jorn's gasps were eaten by the swirling snow squall.

Blackened skin unrolled across jerked flesh, hunched shoulders straightening into a predator's crouch. Jaundiced eyes blinked and a long ashen nail flicked locks of flame from their face. "Evening, Commander."

"Arrowlash?"

The body unfolded, creosote tumbling from his clothes as he stepped from the fire. The musk of burnt hair and bone wafted across the frigid ice.

"It's just sir now," Raven whispered, though it did not matter. The creature could destroy him whether he were a peasant or a king.

"Demoted. Interesting. And so far north." The voice was rocks cracking in winter's grip. Arman's head tilted slow, entirely reptilian. "Have a seat, kettle's just boiled."

Other than the shelter crafted from some creature's corpse, the camp suffered an utter lack of equipment. Raven recalled passes through the Orn de Galin littered with bones, crags lost to time and haunted by titans. Titans that once were men. "What are you doing?"

The jittering scream of metal against stone set Raven's nerves afire. Arman was laughing. "The usual—looking for allies. Artifacts. World ending. We've been on the road for months now."

We? "Dhoah' Lyne'alea's with you?"

The laugh came again, low. He gestured to the ice beneath him. "You didn't notice? These flames are hotter than any campfire, any inferno lit by war machines. Why hasn't the ice melted, Dorcal?"

Raven found his stomach threatening to revolt. The terror dragged from his bones was the promise in Keplan's eyes brought to fruition. "Dhoah'?" He hoped he forced enough reverence into his voice, but at Jorn's glance, he knew the words sounded closer to horror.

Water trickled across the iceberg, winding between invisible faults in surface, blue and reeking of salt. Droplets congealed, trembling as sullen sparks lit them from within, a rotted tree with lightning boughs. Streaks of black seaweed, of mildew writhed upwards. Fish-pale eyes rolled to focus on him, unmoved, disinterested. Water puddled from her pale, bloated lips, skin slipping from putrefied muscle as she spoke. "How lovely of you to drop by, Raven. What brings you to the skull of the world?"

"Explore," he croaked. Clearing the fear from his throat, he tried again. "We were sent to expand Athrolan's maps. Learn from other places, other people. Found a lot of odd creatures, sea monsters." He gnawed one thick lip. "Didn't think we'd find you."

"No, I imagine not. World's tidier when legends stay quiet."

"Last we all heard you were in the Hartland. Where Keplan left you."

Lightning crackled louder, larger, and her vacant eyes sharpened with interest. "Our son? You've seen him?"

Raven glanced between the two of them. Had she always been taller than he? How could they not know? "Yes, I—"

"Of course, he sent us here. He's king." Jorn's words were out before Raven could stop her. He did not like the creatures before him. He did not trust them, but the one thing he understood was wishing your child was safe. A king was never safe.

"King?" Arman's voice was an avalanche in the mountains.

"His Majesty Keplan of the Hartland and the Topin Hills, king of Athrolan, ascended the throne two months ago. Athrolan was locked in civil war, you might have missed that. Up here. He ended it, in a fashion."

"You don't put him on a throne," she keened. "You don't put something that precious, that beautiful and cut it down, bloody and whimpering to fit on a tidy human throne with a tidy human crown." Alea's voice thundered from every crystal of snow, every droplet of sea air.

Clear blue water bled from cracks rent in centuries-old ice.

"Lyne'alea," Raven protested.

Bones still piled in the flames shuddered and crumbled into white ash, drifting, eddying until they, too, formed pieces of the Earth Shaker's body.

"Dorcal!" Jorn called, voice pitched to carry to him alone.

The iceberg cracked. Raven pitched forward, gloved hands unable to find purchase on the gleaming surface. He scrambled, spiked boots gripping for a moment, then slipping as water trickled past. His hands were drenched, already numbing. Something splashed into the black water below, but he could not crane his neck far enough to see if it was Jorn.

"Milady!" he begged. Tears froze in his stubble. The fluid in his body writhed, agony ripping in his veins as his blood halted, then inched backward, upward. His vision hazed red with puppeteered blood. "Dhoah', I beg you, please!"

The ice inches from his face cracked, reformed into a terrible face with lidless electric eyes. "Why?"

"I didn't want him on the throne. I've never trusted your kind. I wanted human, Xain blood on the Athrolani throne. It was An'thoriend who engineered Keplan's reign." The cowardice tasted like bile on Raven's tongue. Frostbite's black fronds eased up his grasping hands. "Mercy, please."

The storm stilled. Silence pressed on his ears after the slavering wind. "Mercy," the snow hummed. "We gave all of ours to our son."

The iceberg bucked, launching him into the ocean. Aching cold enveloped him. He sank, clawing off his cloak and scarf. Raven had been commander of Athrolan's navy for four decades. Before then, he had been a soldier, running rigging and mending lines. His thick, frostbitten fingers ripped at the buckles of his boots. But before anyone became an Athrolani sailor, they had to dive to the deepest point off the cliffs and bring back a single piece of the hundreds of shipwrecked vessels. Raven clenched his teeth against his final breath bubbling from his body. That air was his ticket to the surface.

Another tug, another kick, and his feet were free. Muscles protested and his chest screamed as he shoved his way to the surface. Waves shoved salt into his gasping mouth. He coughed, choked, then checked the stars. The sky was black, but once more his blood beat forward, not back, and his lungs billowed with air, not ocean.

"Raven!" Jorn's voice was shrill, faint in the dark, but then came the slap of paddles and the groan of weathered wood. Her nose bled, though whether it was from Alea's administrations or her tumble off the berg, he could not guess.

She leaned away, counterbalancing his leaden body as he dragged himself into the skiff. The moment he was he huddled in the bow, she thrust them toward the safety and warmth of their ship.

Jorn shuddered, lips paled by her effort not to vomit. "I understand it now."

Raven raked a hand though his sodden hair. "Understand what?"

"Why you're terrified of Keplan. That blood, that power, on an Athrolani throne? With a Banis army behind him?" She lost her battle and emptied her stomach into the waves.

"They weren't like that, not even in war. Then they were mighty, horrifying, but I knew why folk worshiped them." His gaze followed the roiled stain in the clouds above as the two creatures traveled south. "I ought to warn Athrolan."

"But you won't."

"There's no warning loud enough to prepare them," he whispered. "Our eyes are now fixed north, fixed ahead of us, to lands we've yet to see." He wondered if she heard the shatter of his heart breaking to allow him to speak the next words. "Athrolan has made her choice."

Φ

29th Day of Glasmord, 1272
The City of Ceir Athrolan, Athrolan

The palace was already in mourning, it seemed. Rih drifted through the halls, sometimes with Bimet in tow, but more often alone. She had yet to return to her husband's bedside but did not care whether rumors flew. *I saved their hoof-kicked city. That should be enough.* Neither had she seen An'thor, which was a blessing, save for the fact that she did not trust him. Without her careful gaze, she had no idea what he might do.

Now, however, she dragged her feet toward the infirmary. It was not required of her, but each afternoon she sat vigil, as much to relieve Azimir of the duty as to keep up appearances. With every passing day he seemed more distant, his body more a husk than a living, vital thing.

Rih faced the door to his private room. Illness made her uncomfortable. In the military it was met with death, if one was not deemed useful in another field. But with Athrolan so precarious, even she could not weather the rumors that would arise were she to avoid her husband's bedside.

Her spirits lifted when the guards opened the door and she found Azimir napping in the chair at Keplan's head.

He straightened, wiping his mouth and blinking himself alert. "Ah, Rih. Forgive me, I must have dozed off."

"It's nothing," she offered, belatedly realizing he did not understand. She pointed at the king's still form questioningly.

"I don't know. It seems as if he doesn't have the will," Azimir confessed. "Can't blame him, really."

The sentiment took Rih by surprise, and she found she did not have a response. She had endured as much as he, perhaps, though systemic attrition was different from sudden torture, she knew. Both left lasting marks, physical and otherwise. It was easy to look at a king upon a throne and presume him lucky. In many ways he was, but a cage, however gilded, was nonetheless a cage.

"If you'd like me to stay, I can ask the guard to call for a translator. But if you'd like to be alone, I'd understand. I've been here since dawn anyway."

Rih's brow arched. No one—not even Athrolan's own general—had taken their vigil duties as seriously as the young man before her. *They're family,* she reminded herself. As much as she wanted to speak with him, she was tired of being at the mercy of Bimet's schedule, even if it made conversation easier. She mimed writing and added a quizzical expression.

His face broke into a smile and he fished a notebook from his belt purse. "Da always told me to keep a log—habit left over from his soldier days, I think—but I rarely find a use, other than to give something else for the cutpurses to grab. Would you prefer I write, or is reading my lips easier?"

She mimed the writing motion again and took his offered notebook and pen.

> *Lip reading takes much effort, and I often must piece the meaning together based on half the words at most. Writing is nice, for me. It's scary, being dependent on a translator. I can't argue with her or fight. I'm so used to a single step outside meaning death or pain or punishment.*

"You're hardly dependent," he voiced.
She scoffed, hastily adding:

> *Aren't I? Hardly anyone here speaks Banis. Fewer know my signs. Not that the two are related, but surely your Deaf people have their own signs.*

He looked down, cheeks flushing with a rare blush before reaching for the log.

> *I wouldn't know. You're the first I've met. I'm not sure whether it's because fewer of our people are Deaf or that we support them less. Do you wish you could argue with Bimet?*

She stared at him, wondering how different her life would have been were she born to Mirik. His question was friendly, if probing.

> *If she was mad, she could mistranslate — either from simple frustration and confusion or actual malice. And I would never know. She tells me something wrong in negotiations, it means death.*

Azimir read her words, pen poised to respond while he ordered his thoughts.

> *What if others knew your signs? Knew Banis. What if they learned? I'd gladly translate for you.*

> *I taught women before, in RoBal, so they might —*

She stopped, heart pounding, hand traitorously close to writing the truth. Minata Kaz's words bloomed in her heart. *"A war is begun by making enemies, but it is won by making allies."* Azimir watched her. Open. Honest. Mirikin. *Not yet.*

So they might have more agency. Men enough know the signs, of course. One in ten Banis are like I am, but it's still fewer. And it cannot be eavesdropped upon. Not as easily.

"That's noble. As much as we tout wanting to free your people, I don't know the first thing about slavery. What it's like." He jerked a thumb at the king, comatose, beside them. "Kep knows Banis."

Rih faltered.

I know. I remember. From before. He was unconscious for most of the ride to RoBal, but the little he did speak was recognizable.

Azimir tilted his head. His bushy brows curled together. Rih was abruptly reminded that he was seventeen. A privileged seventeen. "What happened?"

That's his story.

"No, I mean, it is, and I know as much as he's willing to tell me." He caught himself speaking aloud and extended his hand for the book, taking care with his next words.

I want to know yours.

It would be a lot to write, and she noted as much.

I'm a fast reader. And I'm picking up some of your signs. If you want to try both.

I wasn't always Kajimet.

"What's that one?"

Princess, in your language, but not exactly. Emperor's line, or chosen or favored. Before that I was a soldier, a scout in my arc. I idolized my training master — she was the leader of my troop for the first five years."

"How old were you when you began?" Sure enough, his broad, tan hands curled in a few signs. They were out of order and some wholly nonsense, but his earnest frown warmed her heart.

She corrected him, then held up the appropriate fingers. "Fourteen? That's young. What about before that?"

We die young.

She sank back in the chair for a moment. How did she tell him of the summer heat in the Purple Throne? Or the imperial concubines' quarters? The cloying silk curtains and perfume that separated the mothers and their work from the children? Of the press of people and parties so loud, even her ears could pick up the vibrations? Food so fine each plate cost more than what was allotted a soldier for a year? And how could she explain to this sweet man — boy, sometimes — that she missed it? Despair welled in her, aching fire, heavy with sun and wind. She let out a sob.

Azimir's calloused fingers were on hers, and he ducked his head so she might see his face through her tears. His dun hands squeezed her brown ones. "I'm sorry."

She shook her head. Ban was homogenous in the way that a stew was — occasionally spicy or sparks of unique flavor, but nothing lasting. She had never been homesick before, even traveling hundreds of leagues. Or felt so homeless. Ban was never so jarring. She wiped her cheek and wrote again.

> *I've never missed it before. Never expected to. But I realize now I may have missed home for a long time. Even before Athrolan. Even when I was there.*

"I love Athrolan but I miss home too. Nothing's the same as I remember it."

> *What do you miss? You visit often, does so much change for you?*

> *It's something that follows me. I miss my father. He's not the man I remember him being.*

> *Then I'm sorry too.*

His smile was sad, and he neither spoke nor wrote any more, but his hand stayed on hers.

It was almost evening when Bimet arrived to ask if they wanted dinner.

"I'll be staying here," Azimir explained. "But thank you."

"I'm tired, I think I'll go for the evening, if you don't mind eating alone."

"I'm not alone." He smiled, patting Keplan's hand. "He's not much of a talker lately, but he rarely was before."

Rih rose and followed Bimet to the door. "Thank you for the conversation. As always, I enjoyed it."

"Any time you wish to talk — well," he hastily corrected himself, "communicate?"

"Talk is fine," Rih signed with a laugh. "It's just a different language is all, same as Trade and Banis. Thankfully you know the latter."

"Then, any time you wish to talk, I'll be here. Have a good evening, Kajimet."

"And you, Azi."

Bimet eyed her as they returned to her rooms. It was only when the door was shut carefully behind them that she launched into questions. "He's the son of your enemy and cousin to your husband. A husband who lies dying."

"He's not dead yet, Bimet," Rih protested, "and it's just conversation. Friendly. As interesting as you are, I'd rather not be beholden to you for all my social activities."

"Beholden?" Bimet's face hardened. "I'm merely advising you to be careful. That was the son of the Hetmir in there, and I don't care what you think, the look in his eyes is far from friendly!"

"I think I have more instinct in me than you, having fought for my life more times than I can recall. He means no harm."

"Harm's not what I was implying, Kajimet," Bimet retorted, signs sharp as blows. "That boy wants you spread on silk for him, and anyone can see it."

Rih stepped back, horrified. She recognized predatory advances easily, it was the only way to survive the Banis court. Azimir had never made her skin crawl or her stomach revolt. He was a friend, as good as Nehla. *He touched my hand. Held it. The city was under attack and his family dying, and the first place he rode was to me.* To her, it was the camaraderie of battle. The bond forged in pain and quenched in blood spilt for a shared cause.

"Sex aside, you need to be careful who you confide in anyway, Rih." Bimet's hands were gentle now, soothing, and her frown eased into concern. "I know you were hoping for more from Nehla, but neither she nor Master A'hane care for our sisters like you do. Like I do."

"I think Nehla is just young and curious," Rih protested. "I didn't want to share this with you when we were in RoBal, since you were so worn by being there, but I did speak with her. She's learning my signs."

Bimet paled. "You know she's niece to the Hand."

"I am daughter to the emperor himself."

Bemit shook her head. "Do you know, when we were in RoBal, she met with him every day."

Rih's stomach clenched. Is that what Nehla had meant when they spoke? Was is not the offer of support as she hoped, but instead a warning from a neutral party or even the enemy themselves?

"You always say I am your caution," Bimet explained, kneeling before Rih. Like Azimir, she took Rih's hands, one thumb circling the webbing of her thumb before continuing. "I want you safe. I want you whole. I want you to keep your position here, in case all else fails."

"If all fails, Bimet, then I will be dragged back to RoBal by the Hand himself, I don't doubt, then raped, beaten, and strung up on the walls." Bemit flinched at her description. "I know the risks, Bimet, and I choose this path anyway. I'll do what I must here, then we'll go west. And take our home back."

"And what about everything here? Have you thought that far ahead?"

Rih rolled her eyes. "There's no point setting down roots here. The grasslands are our home, not these cloying forests and cliffs hemming us in, pinching us between sea and mountain and stone."

"But what if they weren't," Bemit hazarded. The gentle expression on her face looked closer to pity now, and Rih's stomach dropped.

"What do you mean?"

"What if this does have to be our home? If the rebellion falters. It could take a decade to wrest power from the Emerald throne. You are here, even if your heart isn't. I'm here. Your dozen sisters and guards are here too. And while we may be your allies — your most dedicated allies —"

"And friends?"

"And friends," Bimet continued, "we're aware dying here, of age, is as likely as being killed in a bloody revolution."

Rih paced to her windows, shaking with fury and something else, something called forth by her tears earlier. Her breath misted the glass, melting the faint whorls of frost from the evening. The blue night loomed outside. Horses crowded the street below as a dignitary arrived. Rih peered closer. She recognized the livery from her studies with Mosil but could not recall which house it belonged to.

Bimet stepped up beside her, one hand ghosting comfort over her shoulder. "I think that's Lady Gella. They said the Xain heirs were being called forth again as Keplan fades."

Rih realized what emotion weighed on her all afternoon. *Longing.* Longing for freedom, for friendship, and, in the dark part of her mind, for the man in the infirmary to die. "I feel such guilt." The signs were small, a whisper.

"For wishing him gone?" Bimet met her eyes knowingly. "Do you think they'll let you stay if your husband is dead?"

Rih turned away. Her words to Azimir burned in her mind. Arguing with Bimet was dangerous, even as close as they were. Here she was a political prisoner in the guise of a wife. A new fear emerged in her chest. With a new monarch and negotiations to revisit, she was not afraid they would send her home. *I'm afraid they won't let me leave.*

Φ

The 30th Day of Glasmord, 1272

Firas scraped his hair into order again, cursing his decision to cut it short. With his hat doffed, there was no way to hide the wild angle from being pressed under felt and fur for the long walk from the Slummer.

He had been to the palace once before with Mirrel to petition that, despite their youth, they were fit to inherit the inn without anything left in trust.

At the time he had marveled at the striking marble and towering dome. Perhaps it was experience, or perhaps the years had truly been unkind to the building, but he was no longer impressed.

He peered down the hall to the left. A wall of glass stretched at the end, showing towering plants and brilliant blooms. He could not smell the blooms from where he stood, but he could pretend.

"Master Smythesen?"

He whirled, swallowed hard, then nodded. "Aye. Firas Smythesen. Master A'hane wished to speak with me, I believe."

"Indeed." The old man scanned Firas's appearance again before gesturing down another, narrower hall radiating from the entry. "This way. He will receive you in the infirmary."

Dread was sour beer in his gut, and with every step it threatened to overflow his mind as much as his mouth. He could think of one reason, one reason only, that Azimir would summon him to the palace. To the infirmary. The mourning bells had not rung, but surely, they would soon. At least for now he was almost numb.

Azimir met him at the base of the stairs leading down to the infirmary wing. He looked exhausted, thin, like all of them, but not grief-stricken. "Morning, Master Smythesen."

"And you, Master A'hane."

"I'll take him from here, Corporal. Thank you."

When the guard had gone, Azimir gripped the barkeep in a tight embrace. "Thank you for coming."

Firas stepped away, eyes narrowed. "I'm still not exactly sure why you asked for me. You obviously know how to traipse into the Hare at all hours when you need advice." He could not summon any malice to his voice, which was fine. He realized, once the words were out, that he felt none.

Azimir did not answer but set off down the hall. One side held supply rooms, the other private chambers for the wealthy and ailing. At the last door, Azimir nodded to the two guards. "He's with me."

"No one whom General Domariigo himself doesn't permit, Master."

"I'll be there the whole time." When they did not step aside, he sighed. "Captain Hylier and I both know this man."

"Captain Hylier is on assignment elsewhere."

"Bind my hands, if you must." The words were out before Firas thought better of them, but he forced himself not to waver. "Please. For His Majesty."

The female guard seemed to consider the merit of his suggestion but finally stepped aside. "Whatever, just be quick, Azi."

Azimir winked at her and opened the door. "You're a perfect snowdrop, Halfe, thank you."

She rolled her eyes and shut the door behind them.

Firas took in the curtains, the open window, the dry, dusty chamber pot in the corner, and the folded cloth pads for wounds or waste. Anything to avoid looking at the man in the bed. He sniffed, staring at the blanket-covered feet. "I don't know if I can do this."

"You don't have to do anything. I just thought you'd want—"

"I do, it's just… This is hard. After Mirrel, I…" His voice teetered into a whisper and he closed his eyes.

"I'll wait by the window."

Firas sat on the edge of the chair beside the bed. Rough palms scrubbed at the thighs of his breeches. He sucked air in through his teeth and glanced from the motionless shape on the bed to Azimir. The boy was absorbed in a modern scroll that looked like a primer.

He reached out a shaking hand and his weathered fingers laced with Keplan's limp ones. Breath rushed from his lungs when he finally looked at the king's face. "Fates."

Keplan looked both decades older and younger. Frown lines had formed but smile lines faded. His bruise-purple lips were lax and Firas realized that, when awake, Keplan's mouth always held the promise of a smile or a sneer. When he spoke, his voice was a whine. "Hey, Lan. It's good to see you."

He cleared his throat and tried again. "I miss you. I miss when we weren't strangers. When we'd spend the evenings dancing and talking, when you'd come to me in the dark unable to sleep. You always fell asleep by the third line of whatever story I chose to tell you. I've never felt more powerful than when I could bring you peace. I know you're troubled. I know you've been tortured, and not just in Ban. I know you've fallen back on dust and I can imagine why. But please hear me, if you can understand my words or my intent, listen. I know you said not to walk this road, but every day since you left, I realized I already had. Athrolan needs you. I need—"

His voice cracked and his eyes squeezed shut. "I'm so sorry. I'm sorry it came to this. I'm sorry. If I could go back,

I'd ask you more, I'd pay more attention, enough that you'd tell me about your foolish plan to take the throne. Maybe then you'd be awake and in the Hare and maybe you'd have woken with Mirrel that morning and—" His other hand fisted in his lap and he squeezed his eyes shut against the wave of grief and fear pummeling his breast. "Neither of us were ready for it. Now that I am, it's too late." The words choked out in a dry sob. "I just can't lose you too."

The bells rang and he jumped. "Guess I ought to be going."

"When you're ready," Azimir answered. The boy's cheeks glistened.

Firas gripped Keplan's unresponsive hand tighter, so tight he hoped he left bruises on both their fingers. "You might be the man who brought peace to Athrolan, but I hope, even for a moment, that I brought peace to you, too."

He was halfway down the infirmary hall when Azimir caught up to him. "Thank you."

Firas turned, anger flaring at this interruption to his private world crumbling. "For what?"

"I don't know if he can hear us, but if anyone's voice could reach him, it'd be yours."

"I wasn't lying." His voice was a rattle over the mountains of his emotion. "I can't handle losing him too."

"None of us can."

"Don't act like your life's mine, boy," he snapped. "The man in there is my light. Bright enough to shed hope on my corner of the Slummer."

Azimir fell silent and stared at their boots, bright and polished, dusty and worn. "I'll let you know when you can visit again."

Firas shook his head. "Next time I hear from you it'll be either because he's awake or he's—" He shook his head. "I suppose I'll know the second one. Rung from the towers and all that."

"I'll find you." Azimir promised.

Firas left without another word. In so many ways it was as if Keplan was already dead. As if he died the night he fled the Hare. What did it matter to Firas if he lived? He was already king. He would always be king. And Firas was history in the biography of Athrolan's most controversial king. *Fates, I wish I was more than a footnote.*

Φ

The 34th Day of Glasmord, 1272
The Village of Jai, Ban

Music pressed on Reka's ears, and smoke hung heavy in the air, stinging her eyes and pinking her rain-raw cheeks. This is what she missed of Athrolan, of Mirik: the weight of people around her, the invisibility of a crowd.

"There's the honored guest!"

Except this party was for her. She cringed at the attention, but stood nonetheless, taking the offered drink and bowing. Banis rarely drank liquor, but tradition dictated every guest buy a drink for the ruakek. Reka was already a bit tired of the grass-wine. It was bitter, tasted mostly of earth, and—as far as she could tell—contained no alcohol whatsoever. Somehow, despite war and death, or perhaps because of it, Ikel had managed to convince the matet to let them commandeer his hall for the gathering.

"I'm happy you let her do this for you," Jani confided. His eyes were bright and warm in the firelight.

Reka laughed. "We both know she'd do it regardless. Any excuse for a celebration."

"If you said no—"

"Oh, it's grand," Reka brushed away the concern. "I'm just happy to feel home around us."

"Have you given any thought to if you'll go to the capital or stay here?"

Reka looked down. "I'm wondering whether I should write to Hetmir A'hane."

His brows arched. "I thought you were for our cause."

"I am, wholly. That's why I think I should. She's a smart woman, and she'll see plain as I have that fighting half the Banis army is better than fighting the whole."

The door banged open, caught by the buffeting wind, and in blew a handful of Banis soldiers and a gust of rain. Most fell into conversation with family, but one caught Reka's eye. His long hair was tied back in a series of bunches, and dark freckles dusted his light brown cheeks. Warmth fluttered in her belly. "What do you know of him?"

Jani followed her gaze. "He's young for his position. My sister said he was an ally, but I've yet to find time to speak to him. Why do you ask? Thinking of following when they go?"

"Thinking of following him to bed, is all."

Jani's brows twitched upward and he followed her gaze to the officer's long, lean legs. "You're not one to settle, eh?"

"Never have been. Doubt the ruak will change that."

"I guess it's silly hoping."

"You want me to stay?" She stared at him, incredulous. "Whyever is that?"

"Because I love my wife more dearly than the stars, and you are a balm to her homesick heart."

"That's poetic."

"It's true. She lights up when she speaks of you, and for the week before you arrived there was no making sense of her, she was so excited. Banis families are so large, with cousins considered siblings and further relations named cousins. It's something I didn't appreciate until she arrived, alone in all the world, her only family scattered like seed."

"I'll stay as long as I can," Reka offered. It was all she had ever offered, but it was the first time she wanted to mean it. She always donned titles and names and faces like a noble donned finery—and discarded them just as easily. None had ever been hers, save for Reka and the scars on her face. But even those belonged more to the person she had been—Border warrior. Spy Master. Surrogate.

"I'm told you will choose a new name."

"I'll keep Reka—it's my skera. My base name. Bone name. The rest of it, I'm not sure." She rubbed her nose, the tattered butterfly tattoo more scar than colored wing. "It's rude to ask, you know."

"I didn't, forgive me."

She grinned. "I don't take offense, just thought you ought to know. Ikel doesn't speak often of our culture?"

"Occasionally, when one of us does something odd to the other. I know lots of the small cultural things. But of the big ceremonies I know nothing. Even weddings."

Reka laughed. "Because we don't have them. The ruak is the only time we really gathered in large groups, and the same ceremony is used for all things because transition is the same—whether for birth, death, childbearing, or a new role. Something old is passing and something new has arrived."

"I look forward to seeing it, then. Ban is progressive with our medicine and war machines and infrastructure. But we are not a culture of ritual."

"It's almost moonrise, are you ready?" Ikel's voice was soft behind her, and Reka nodded. They left, sent with a chorus of goodbyes and well wishes. Reka laughed and shut the door behind them.

Outside the wind rustled in the grasses. Behind the hall stretched a reaching acacia tree and beneath it was a plain fur. By the stripes, Reka guessed it was a gazelle. She stripped and settled onto the fur, legs crossed, hands resting on her knees. The wind sang.

Ikel's face grew shadowed. "Do you ever wonder if they're all truly dead? The gods, I mean. We thought the Laen were all but gone for decades before the Dhoah' herself arose. I miss the prayers, but it seems odd to pray to nothing."

"I always felt prayers were more for us than for them. So rarely were they answered, save for the ruak. And even then, I'd wager a fair few were just theatrics of the ritemaster." She was not accustomed to being celebrated. Not like this. Bren surely doted on her, even long after both his children were born. But like his relationships with all the women in his life, he adored her without truly knowing her at all.

Ikel knelt before her, pulling a thick, sharp needle and a tiny pot of ink from her sash. Blacker than night, Border tattoo ink was made with the ashes of the first Border campfire. Reka suspected this might be from this morning's hearth.

"Who are you?" Ikel asked, her tone focused.

"I am Monareka Elang."

"Why are you here?"

"Because that name and this face no longer sing truth."

"You wish to undergo the ruak?"

Reka nodded, marveling at how much her hands shook.

"Say it, Rek," Ikel murmured gently.

"I wish to undergo the ruak."

"Do you yet know who you will become?"

"I do not, but none who are born ever do."

Her cousin lifted the needle and pressed it into Reka's skin, dipped it in ink, then pressed again. The pinpricks spread over the bridge of her nose, claret blood and crimson ink mingling as her flame-winged butterfly turned wine and burgundy. New curls tapped their way over her cheeks, and delicate feathered antennae unfurled along the arch of her brows. It could have been a minute or an hour later when her cousin sat back. Another pot appeared, this one filled with pale ashes.

Her brows burned as they arched in surprise. Holy ash was hard to find in the wake of the gods' death.

"Eyes closed, fawn." The diminutive name was a balm to her raw identity.

She closed them, relishing in the sharp sensation as ashes and oil were rubbed into her open wound, softening the stark color of the ink. Ikel's hands left her, and the gentle throb of a small drum began.

"We call the lifeblood of the world, we call the spirits who make us, who end us, who guide our arrows. This one has stripped herself before you, asking for guidance. Remind her of her name, of her purpose."

The rain began in earnest, and energy and joy sparked in her veins in the wake of pain and adrenaline. The pain was sweet, scalding her mind until her memory and body were sanitized. She would bear her past like any carefully researched history, but the trauma, the exhaustion, the weight would be left here. *Who am I?* The drum grew louder.

"Who are you?" Ikel asked, wary.

"I am the child of the earth, soothed in the waters of creation, lit with the fires of chaos, gestated in the blood of birth. My bones are stone and my life is light." Across the back of her eyelid, images flickered—Azimir, Alleanthus, Brentemir, Keplan. Male faces, upturned, asked guidance. And a woman, someone she had not seen but knew, knew in her heart, reached out. Smiled.

"Who are you?" Demanding, now disbelieving. "Are you Monareka Elang?"

"No," she whispered. Her painted cheeks were damp, but it did not matter. The symbols were burned into her spirit, into her soul, the core that never changed. Like the landscape, her mind and her body were cut with scars, ridged from collisions, and gouged by flood. But if one looked, the echoes of long-worn mountains were still there, found in the undulating plain. "No. She is my blood, my strength, my endurance. But I am not she."

"Who are you?" This time it was inquisitive, gentle. Welcoming.

"I am Rekajat Monre." Drumming ceased. Her eyes opened. The rain splattered on the roof, filling the air with freshness. Her hair hung loose, long without its binding braids. Her chest was light. Her mind clear.

The space was empty, save for her cousin, silhouetted by the moonlight flickering through the clouds. "I'm honored to greet you."

Ajat released her hold on the bar and shook the tension from her arms. "I'm honored to be here and call you cousin."

"When you are ready." Ikel pressed a kiss to Ajat's forehead, and the reborn woman realized she was not the only one who wept.

She walked naked to the bathhouse, washed with tepid water. She caught her hair up in several thicker braids, the streak of white a braid unto itself now, stark and proud. She twisted them close to her scalp. The side she shaved until the fresh skin gleamed pink and new. Only then did she risk a glance in the mirror at her new face. The scars were livid with the flush of injury, and her butterfly's black wings now spread down, framing her nose and up just under her brows and through.

"Hello."

There were new clothes, altered from her spare traveling set, silk and linen added to the sleeveless leather. It showed more skin but also more muscle. It, like the pale streak in her hair, was proud, she decided.

Once her sandals were laced, she left the bathhouse and returned to the hall. By the soft scent in the air and the fading rain, it was nearly midnight.

Ikel waited in the open doorway and grinned at the sight of her cousin. She gripped Ajat's hand and tugged her inside, holding her arm aloft. "This is my cousin, Rekajat Monre!"

The gathered Banis cheered. They did not need to know the details of the ritual or its weight. All they needed to know was that this was a moment to celebrate. Music began and food appeared, followed by juice and tea.

The freckled man from before grinned and wove through the gathered people.

"I'm told I have you Border women to thank for such a fun party."

"Mostly Ikel," Reka insisted. "I'm just the excuse. It's a rite of passage, of sorts. Been on the road a while."

"So what brought you back home?" A tall young man leaned in, face bright in the light of the fire. Ikel glanced between the two and excused herself.

Reka knew most of the faces, if not their names, but this man was new. "You know how time and life cycle," she lied,

"I found myself missing home and family more than I wished to ply my trade. When there's more longing than contentment, it's time."

"And what was your trade again? Jani said you were a tutor, but I've never seen a tutor with shoulders as broad as yours."

Reka's smile was genuine now. Commitment aside, she always enjoyed a good flirt. "Combat tutor. For the children of merchants and lesser nobles. You part of the riding that came last week?"

"What gave it away?"

"Your face."

He put a hand to his faintly freckled cheek in mock embarrassment. "Is there dung on it? Travel-dust?"

"It's new to me," she answered, nudging his sandal with hers. She took a sip. Someone had found a Banis fiddle. "You can call me Ajat."

"Then you can call me Sefer." His hand pressed something cold and hard into her palm. "Lifted this from a Mirikin patrol. Thought you'd appreciate it more than most here."

She glanced down. It was a flask, dented and battered but still full. Unscrewing the top, she sniffed carefully. "Wraith," she noted. "Not my usual, but I'm honored by the gift."

"I'm just happy you took it off my hands. Tell me, do you like dancing?"

Excitement surged stronger than any drug, and she threw herself into the music. Hands brushed over her shoulders, admiring her skin as if new. Often, they belonged to Sefer. Many hours later, though, when she tottered to bed, it was alone, and the sky was not yet light.

Φ

The 35th Day of Glasmord, 1272
The City of Ceir Athrolan

Keplan lay in the grassland, relishing silence. The rocky outcroppings were Athrolani, but the wheat brushing his palms was Banis. Screaming energy from dust no longer coursed through him, but neither did he need it. He floated.

Smoke drifted through the grasses like incense through a censer. He reached out to twist the curl of smoke around his red finger. No matter how much he pleaded with his body, his left shoulder did no more than twitch, limp mold-green hand flopping at the end.

His reflection lounged beside him, one hand trailing through Keplan's hair, humming. The notes slipped past his hearing before he could hear them properly and left him only with the knowledge that music was playing, but not which tune. There was no time here, Keplan realized. So, there could be no music.

His reflection leaned closer, brushing a kiss over the corner of Keplan's mouth. "I want to show you something."

Keplan pushed himself upright, blinking as the dim pink sun hit his eyes. Sunset was continuous here, he realized, but somehow every moment it differed, an unending display of raw, bruised sky.

"There. See?"

Keplan squinted into the sun. A mound rose, earth shuddering as it redistributed itself. It twitched, writhed, until dust settled into a perfect replica of RoBal. No, it was RoBal, as much as they were both Keplan and the grasses under his feet were real. They were not somewhere else, but everywhere and everywhen, always and never. His chest clenched. Opposites.

His reflection flicked its fingers and the earth shuddered again. The walls exploded outward, fire and rubble raining. Geysers burst from the ground, freed after centuries of domesticity. Its mouth opened and out whispered all the screams from the city, close enough so Keplan felt the breath on his neck. When the screaming had finally petered out, the reflection's mouth snapped shut and he smiled. "I made that for you."

Keplan stared at the distant ruins. If he still had a pulse it would be pounding. He could not deny the spectacle had been cathartic. "For me?"

"I wanted to show you what was possible together. What I could do for you if you let me."

"That doesn't look like peace."

His reflection scoffed. "Of course it is."

"People died."

"People die. That's what they do," it snapped. "They'll always burst forth, shining, wither bleating into darkness, and die. It's not war. It's peace — for you and for every Banis slave. Just think." His hand trailed up Keplan's bare thigh, prickling like a spider's legs.

"This is where they end. I end." His thoughts were a jumble, not from the insistent brush of fingers, but the voices.

Voices? He heard them, drifting from somewhere just past the horizon. Infrequent, unintelligible.

But these were words he knew.

"We call the lifeblood of the world, spirit who makes us, who ends us, who guides our arrows. Stripped, remember your name, your purpose."

Their legs were tangled, and his reflection's hand combed through his unwashed hair. **Let me go.** *Revulsion shuddered through him and he pushed away. "Let go."*

The reflection rose, towering over him, stinking breath hot and needful. "I won't stop until God's Blood touches every corner of this world —"

"I don't care if my existence is what's killing the world. This isn't how it ends. This isn't how it's fixed. I made this mess. I'm going to fix it." The reflection's skin glittered as if constructed of

countless shattered flecks of glass. Its face flickered between a hundred expressions, some scared, others not.

Keplan lunged, grinding his fist into the sandpaper skin, then again and again, pounding until nothing but glass dust and blood covered the barren earth below him. He blinked and he was in darkness again, alone.

"You think I'm just broken glass?" The voice leapt from his own throat, but it was not his. "I'm inside of you, I'm the burn in your veins, the lust in your groin."

"So be it." Keplan's fingers wrapped around his own throat. His jaw ground, and he refused to close his eyes. He sputtered and the touch of a free hand, invisible but rough, clawed against the grip on his throat. Keplan's green palm twitched with the memory of a fist.

"Mercy! You're the merciful one!" The voice roared in his skull.

His vision flickered as they both fought for air. Thoughts scattered before the battering ram of his resolve. "No. I'm the human one." His chapped lips cracked over his clenched teeth as he grinned. "You're the monster. I'm the madness. Someday I'll be the mercy, but it's not today. You were right. One of us will die. And only I will remain."

His vision flickered. Roaring flames softened to a distant hum. The voices blended into one, the lilting plea of a bartender, then it too faded to a whisper winding around his mind. Keplan smiled and fell into blackness.

Φ

Firas stumbled downstairs, one hand scrubbing wakefulness onto his face. No good news arrived before noon in the Slummer. A second knock, louder, came and he jerked the door open. On his stoop in the dim dawn light stood Azimir, hand raised to knock again.

Firas caught the descending fist with his cupped hand. "Master A'hane."

Shadows underscored the boy's bloodshot eyes, but his face broke into an exhausted smile. "Master Smythesen."

Hope ignited in his gut at the expression. "Is he—"

Overhead a bell tolled, then another. The towers shook, but it was not with a death knell. Firas sank onto the stoop, tears trickling through the shaking fingers over his eyes. "He's awake."

"Yes. At midnight."

"Thank you." Firas shuddered.

"Toar can take all the doctors in the world. You saved Athrolan's king." The younger man nodded once, stepping backward off the steps. "You know what he said, just as he awoke?"

Firas shook his head.

"'You brought me peace.'"

"Tell him…" He fell quiet. Emotions rampaged between his ribs. "Tell him nothing. Please, if he doesn't remember, don't tell him. Athrolan needs his love, his focus, and as much as I do, too, I'm grateful just to know he still breathes. It's enough knowing we're under the same city lamps, even if he's looking down at them and I'm looking up."

CHAPTER THIRTEEN

The 36th Day of Glasmord, 1272
The City of Ceir Athrolan, Athrolan

DAWN CREPT ACROSS THE stone ceiling. Keplan blinked again. Taking stock, he noted his muscles ached from disuse. Screaming or smoke had burned his throat. But pain meant he was alive. An empty chair sat beside him, and a depression on the comforter marked where someone had leaned their hand while holding his. Thoughts scattered as he tore through his mind, searching for the other him, the reflection with too many teeth. There was nothing.

"Kep?" A blurry tan shape by the window stirred, and Azimir's voice came again. "You awake?"

He groaned, throat too raw for proper speech.

"Water?" His cousin poured a mug and pressed it gently to the king's lips, tilting it just enough to drink.

It was cold and tasted stale but not oily. *Are the distillers working then?* Memories of when he first woke were jumbled, doctors excitedly remarking, prodding, Azimir bolting for the door, laughing.

"How do you feel?" Azimir asked when the now-empty glass was set once more beside the bed.

"Throat, body hurts." He tried to push himself farther up on his pillows, but his left arm did not move. Cold weaseled through his chest. Still, he waved his cousin's aid away and managed to sit up on his own. "My arm—what happened?"

Azimir sighed and looked down. "How much do you remember?"

I remember fire and crushing the throat of who I used to be. He doubted Azimir needed to hear that. "Little. Smoke. Priests. An'thor shouting something. Pain. Lots."

Azimir rolled his eyes. "I had to toss General Domariigo from this room—arguing in front of a dying man, can you imagine?" He winced but seemed pleased. "Sorry. Not dying, apparently."

"It's fine. I wasn't sure there, for a while."

"Neither were we." Azimir frowned at the blanket where Keplan's green hand lay until his eyes were less glassy.

"What was he arguing about?"

"With Rih. This city's been a mess since—well you remember that, surely."

"I do. The water and ship and crops—any news?"

"I'm sure your commissioners and officers will have reports," Azimir reassured. "But I don't think you need to be worrying about it just yet."

Keplan sank back against the pillows. He was already exhausted. Apparently, however long he had been unconscious had not counted as sleep. "Why are you still here? I thought you and your father left."

"He did. I didn't." Azimir looked down.

"Why?" His face and neck bore no bruises, but Keplan's hands remembered his cousin's flesh under his fingers. Pain throbbed, and the clear feeling in his veins told him it had been days since he last breathed dust. "Especially after what I—"

"I don't want to talk about that," Azimir interrupted. "I know why you were angry, and why you were scared, and why you lost control."

"What do you mean?"

"You were ill." His dark eyes flicked up to Keplan's. "You went through dust-drought here. They didn't realize, weren't treating you properly."

They can't know. "Dust-drought kills people," Keplan protested, forcing a scoff into his exhausted voice. "I was probably just fevered."

"It almost killed you and would have done if I hadn't explained what was wrong to the nurse."

"I never said I was breathing dust—"

"I'm not arguing, Keplan. I'm telling you I understand. That they're going to help."

Whatever shone in Azimir's eyes looked far too much like empathy for Keplan's comfort. "Tell me about the battle then. After I went down. An'thor rallied the troops?"

"No, actually. An'thor was useless—more interested in having some bloodbath reunion with the Swordbearer who shot you—"

"Right. The Nenev. They know each other?"

"I guess. At any rate they were chasing each other through the city, the guards were at a loss, couldn't get to you or fire on the market without hitting townsfolk or their own. They must have been here for a day or two before, I think. They crawled from the buildings like cockroaches. Started tossing these clay balls, which exploded with fire. Someone finally pulled you free and delivered you to the guards. Then An'thor called a retreat."

"You left the city to their mercy?"

"An'thor did. They didn't kill many afterward. Most casualties were from the panic, honestly."

"I remember a child, and her blood —"

"Be better if you didn't," Azimir suggested, voice low.

"How many dead?"

"A couple hundred. Half as many Swordbearers. They patrolled the streets, hauling people from their homes and demanding fealty to their god."

To me. Keplan's gut heaved and he tossed over just in time to vomit across the flagging. It was dotted with black flecks like soil, and tasted of his reflection's tongue. When he was upright again and had wiped his mouth, he asked, "It's not still like that out there, is it?"

Azimir's face darkened. "I ought to call for them. They're going to want to see you properly alert before they dismiss Lady Gella."

"Poor woman keeps being dragged here for nothing. I'm surprised they weren't all clustered about my feet casting dice and taking wagers." Keplan snorted. "Would you ring for the healers? I want to wash before they all traipse in here."

Azimir leaned around the door, murmuring to the guards outside. When he returned, Keplan asked, "Have you seen Hylier?"

"No. No one has. His fellow guards claim he's still on assignment."

"I'll see what I can find out. There were many favors I asked of him that were not official."

Azimir waggled his brows suggestively and Keplan rolled his eyes.

"Fates, not that. He'd sooner slap me than tup, I'd imagine."

Azimir seemed locked in a brief mental debate but then rose without saying anything more. "I'll talk to the healer and have a maid fetch some loose clothes. Easier with the arm."

The arm. Keplan glanced down at it, at the flaccid green palm. "Right."

Azimir wavered in the doorway a moment longer. "I imagine part of you still wishes for oblivion. And perhaps regrets waking at all. But for what it's worth, I'm glad you're here."

Keplan could not meet his cousin's gaze. He was right, but Keplan made his choice—in the dusty fields of everywhere, everywhen, he chose to live, at least for a little while longer.

Half an hour later Keplan was struggling to put a shirt on. He was half in, tugging at his unyielding arm when the doctor arrived. He looked as if he could use a rest as long as Keplan's.

"Your Majesty." He perched on the chair as he moved Keplan's limp arm. "Injured arm first is easier."

Keplan winced as it was raised. Pain knotted deep in his shoulder. "If I can feel it, why can't I use it?"

"The bullet tore the ligaments and nerves. More superficial ones were missed. If you regain use it will be limited and will take a fair amount of work on your part. One of our healers will visit you daily to help you if you'd like, sire."

Keplan nodded, belly cold. He had so little attachment to his body, his limbs, after his ordeal in RoBal. He stared at the arm; it did not even seem like his anymore. "How long will I stay here? I'm certain there are tasks that need my attention."

The doctor peered outside, as if something might crawl in through the window. "Another few days, then bedrest in your own chambers. You may discuss more with a healer after that."

"Your Majesty, Doctor Kessel?" The guard peered in, glancing between them. "General Domariigo is here with Lady Gella and Master A'hane."

The doctor finished up and bowed himself out while Keplan tried to sit straighter. At least he was properly dressed from the waist up and, as far as he could tell, no longer smelled like the death he so narrowly avoided.

"Wardyn, good to see you didn't leave us." Domariigo's thin pale lips stretched in a smile and the scent of alcohol wafted in with him.

"You'll have to try harder to be rid of me next time," he joked, though neither the woman hovering in the doorway nor Azimir smiled.

Keplan looked over at the woman. "It's good to finally meet you, Lady Gella. I'm surprised you arrived so quickly."

"I'm overjoyed to see you've awoken, sire." She was younger than he expected, and he realized his words about her to Azimir were unfounded. She stood with a back of stone, eyes flashing with enough bite to cow An'thor, in the very least.

"Only because you've no interest in the throne," An'thor muttered.

Her gray glare narrowed on him, but she said nothing in response. "Roads were busy for this time of year—everyone fleeing the war in Ban."

"I'm certain you'd like to be returning home to family, but there are a few matters to tidy before we do so—I'm grateful for your patience."

"It's nothing, Your Majesty."

Realizing she had yet to sit, he gestured to the chair at his bedside. An'thor had already deposited himself by the window, and Azimir seemed content to hover by the door.

"First, I'd like a report on the city, please. Is Fess joining us?"

The general glanced at Azimir accusingly. "I thought you were going to update him."

"It's hardly my job, General."

"If you stopped snapping at each other it could have been done by now," Gella noted.

Keplan's smile broadened. He liked her.

"Commander Fess is at the navy barracks with most of her people and will be until there is safe passage across the city to us."

"Safe passage." Keplan glanced between them. "The Swordbearers won? Where is Rih-elte? She should have arrived home by now —" He frowned. "What day is it?"

"The 36th of Glasmord, sire," Gella offered. "And your wife is indeed safely home. I'm sure she will come visit you as soon as she may."

Keplan waved the sentiment away, remembering his actions before she left, the terror in her eyes, and the steel. He hardly blamed Rih for avoiding him. "She failed to bring troops?"

"Rih saved us, much as she could." Azimir's face broke into a playful grin. He relayed his harrowing journey west to find Rih and their hurried plan to enter the city. "The surprise alone gave the Athrolani army enough advantage to reclaim parts of city—the Noble District, the docks, and naval yards. Keplan—she's magnificent, truly. Fighting beside her was an honor. You're lucky, both as a man and as a king to have her by your side."

An'thor heaved a dramatic sigh. "If you're done spilling seed over it all, A'hane?"

Keplan stared at the general. "Domariigo, you'd do well to mind your tongue, and if you're too drunk to do so, perhaps we could meet another time. If I recall, saving the city from invaders is actually your job, not my wife's."

Gella ducked her head, but the corners of her mouth twitched.

An'thor's black glare inched over Keplan's face and shoulders as if searching for the panicked uncertain boy from a few weeks before.

Don't worry, Domariigo, he's still in here. He's just a bit annoyed. "So, will someone tell me what condition the city is in, please?"

"Least half of it belongs to the Swordbearers still. It started as just the Slummer and Merchant Tier. The swath between them was contested for days, but it's mostly theirs too now.

"So we've the Noble District and the Silver Apron? And some warehouses?"

"Yes, sire," the general bit out.

"And we have you. And Commander Fess. And surely armies coming from the nearest cities. And two Banis baniols awaiting your wife's command." Gella's voice was quiet but demanded attention.

Keplan's skin crawled at the fact that he was first on that list. "So what are we going to do?"

"You're going to sit in here and get better, because we can't risk the throne again. I'll discuss the logistics of routing them out with my officers."

"Perhaps I'm missing something," Keplan interjected, "but why don't you just attack? For fates' sake, this is our city and our people will work with us."

"That's the issue currently, sire," Gella replied, looking up. "They moved door-to-door hauling people out and demanding they swear fealty to the One God or risk death. Claiming the crops, the water, everything was due to following a false god."

"It was under duress—"

"Kep, they believe it." Azimir's face was lined with anguish. "Even in districts they don't control I see red gloves cropping up everywhere. Enough people believe it that those who don't are terrified their neighbors will attack them even if the Swordbearers themselves are held accountable."

The ground trembled, just enough to rattle the panes in the window. Keplan frowned at the glass. "Is that—"

"Earthquakes. Been happening since the battle. Hoped once you woke it'd—"

Keplan's glare stopped Azimir's next words. "And our other cities?"

"Most fare well enough. All the lords have called upon their militias as well as their personal armies to bolster our troops there."

"Right." Keplan cleared his throat with a wince. "Then the next order of business is to deal with the inheritance of the throne so our dear lady can be on her way."

"I doubt the Mirikin boy needs to be here for this," An'thor drawled. "Though I'm sure were he to have a say, he'd advocate dismantling the throne entirely."

Azimir straightened with a snort. "Of course not—peacefully dismantling an existing monarchy in a country of this size would take the work of thousands and at least a few years. Learn your history, General." He shot a wink at Keplan and disappeared.

Silence settled in the corners of the room and under Gella and An'thor's watch, Keplan felt as if he were a child who had misbehaved — or perhaps, more accurately, been injured by doing something ill-planned. "May I ask why Blackhouse isn't the heir? Considering he's regent for another few months. Even if he's got no memory of it."

"His Highness Blackhouse, while regent, was stripped of his titles. His reinstatement at court did not, in fact, reinstate his line of succession. And due to both his concerns and yours, I thought it wise to keep it that way."

Keplan's gut twisted. He suspected An'thor had something to do with that choice in particular. *Don't tell me I have to produce a blood heir. Don't do that to us.* He was already reconsidering Brentemir's offer of advice on surrogacy. "While I know you have duties and a life beyond your lineage, Lady Gella, I hope you'll consider the stability you would lend were something to happen to me again."

"That's a lot of words to say 'please,'" she noted, but it was with a faint smile. "There is still one step between me and the throne — which I knew was a point of debate, which is why I'm here at all, instead of a letter or spokeswoman."

"Rih's not with child. We haven't even —"

She held up her graceful hand. "Begging your pardon, sire, but that's neither what I'm referring to nor any of my business. I'm referring to Her Highness Rih-elte herself."

"She's not queen," An'thor barked.

"Forgive me, General." Her eyes snapped to the man. "But as much as you tout your love for this kingdom and worship the very earth Her Majesty Tzatia walked, you are not Athrolani. I don't care to know how you spent your entire youth, but I am willing to wager it was not studying our court affairs and laws. I did. Every noble did. And Athrolan has no designation between a consort and a queen or king. Surely, we bestow 'Highness' and refrain from the official title until they, too, are crowned upon their partner's passing, but, fate forbid, were something to befall our dear king here, she would become queen. Unless, of course, you write an objection to the traditional line of succession, and it is voted upon by both House of Nobles and House of Guilds."

Something released between Keplan's shoulder blades. Muscles he had not known were tight uncurled a fraction. "There are a hundred better uses of our time. Thank you, Lady Gella. I think, in light of her actions, she has proven her loyalty and her skill. It appears Rih-elte is making a habit of saving Athrolan."

An'thor shoved from his seat and stalked to the door. "As you say, we're busy. If we're through here, I'll be on my way."

"Dismissed," Keplan retorted. When the door slammed, he turned back to the lady. "Thank you. For your counsel. And your candid speech to the general." He frowned. "No offense, but why are you really here? Might not have been as inspiring, but nevertheless, that was nothing a proxy couldn't have said."

Her gentle smile was gone. "Sire, there is a matter I wanted to discuss with you. My cousin is dead. His father died several years after your parents went south." Her bright eyes held his. "Someone is picking off the line of succession and making it look like accidents. I'm not certain whether they kneel to you or to His Highness Blackhouse, or to another altogether, but you need to be on guard."

He stared at her, fitting her words into the pieces of news he caught in the market or from the Hare's patrons. "There were several deaths surrounding the queen's demise as well."

Gella winced. "That was ugly business."

"Indeed. And so is this." He leaned forward, hissing at the pain in his shoulder and disused muscles. "How long can you stay?"

She laid her hands in her lap, fingers held perhaps to hide their shaking. "As long as you need me, sire, you know that."

"Your words are another piece to something I'm already pursuing. Your testimony, should we act, would be invaluable."

"You have me until then. Roads are rough this time of year anyway, and I fear my return to Vale through Ban would be ill-timed."

A distant longing, concern deeper than he had felt, stabbed his chest. "You have children?"

"One, a daughter. She is with my husband."

"You worry for her."

"A parent always worries for their child," she answered. "I can write up details for your investigation, if you'd like."

"Please, when you have a moment. If that's all, you may go. I imagine you have much to tend to, now that you're staying."

She rose and curtsied, low and genuine. "All reigns are perilous, sire. It just depends on how honest we are about it." Her gaze dropped to his green hand. "You have my faith."

Φ

The 40th Day of Glasmord, 1272

Keplan was finally able to walk, though it was only around his chambers. He took full advantage, pacing from his study to door and back. On his third circuit of the day, a knock sounded.

"Yes?" he called from the parlor, easing toward the door.

"It's Captain Hylier, Your Majesty."

Surprise warred with distrust. It had been weeks since they last spoke. Whatever kept the unofficial spy from the king was either treason or danger. "Come in."

The captain entered. His face was thinner and his stance slumped. "Do you have a moment?"

Keplan gestured broadly to the room. "I'm a captive audience, sadly."

"I won't take up too much time," he offered, flashing a smile. "Azimir said he'd be by this afternoon."

"No, please, stay as long as you wish. If I have to sit through one more retelling of something ridiculous he or Al did as boys, I might go properly mad. I think he's trying to keep my spirits up."

Hylier nodded in agreement but did not sit down. "I just came from the south. I hope you'll forgive my absence."

"Honestly, I was unconscious for over half of it."

"I heard. I'm glad to see you're doing better."

"Are you?" The hard words escaped before Keplan could think better of them. He winced and gestured to a chair. "That was uncalled for. I'm sorry. Seems the only thing this arm can do is hurt and it wears on me. Though I suppose I've always been snippy."

The blond captain flashed a grin. "Perhaps. You got my note?"

"I did, though it said precious little. Will you tell me why you were gone? And sit down, I'm tired of looking up at you.

Your letter said assignment, though I don't know which you meant."

"I met with Nehla."

"Rih-elte's handmaiden?"

"Just before I left, yes. We traded stories. Her experience in politics makes her as…observant as I am, but about nobles.

"What'd you tell her in return?"

Hylier held his gaze. "That you preferred men, which is why you didn't force yourself on your wife."

"I didn't force myself on her because I could never hurt someone like that, not because I prefer men — which I don't."

Hylier raised a hand. "I was teasing, sire. I just told her gossip from the city, rumors most knew — the water, the priests, so forth. Enough to get Banis news. I could have told her more and gotten more in return, but I don't trust her enough yet."

"What did she say?"

"There's something brewing in Ban. Something big. She's heard of three baniols being rerouted — more I'm sure by now. Officers are juggled like scarves at a fair. Someone is moving pawns, putting trusted people in certain places, removing the distrusted."

"Curiel — the colonel from the army — said something similar."

"I know her, yes. What would she know of Ban?"

"I sent her with Rih-elte's retinue. She mentioned to Admiral Fess, who trains with her, that there was something going on. Does it have to do with Athrolan?"

"I doubt it." Hylier shrugged. "Ban is huge, and to think we're a threat is a bit narcissistic. I do know, though, that war is a good cover for rebellion. And her words got me thinking."

"Of rebelling?"

Hylier's smile was almost back to his usual joking grin. "I'm too comfortable with the purse and my rooms to rebel, sire, and perhaps I've grown used to your acid. Whatever that says about me."

Keplan chuckled and rubbed his shoulder, trying to ease a knot of scar tissue from whatever nerve it seemed to be strangling. "So, rebellion."

"It was more the strategic removal and movement of people. That list of Peraan's contained names that make no sense. If he were getting those names from elsewhere — somewhere he trusted, like His Highness Blackhouse — then he would not question them."

"Even if they made no sense?"

"I met him more than you. He was an ass, puffed up and proud, but not much of a strategist. He left much of that to others, and what he did execute was clumsy at best."

"So this is not his making."

"No, but I still refuse to believe it. I thought of something else — Nehla said she was not sure if the odd movement of their military units was to protect the emperor," Hylier began.

"Or threaten him," Keplan finished. "That list — it was just murders, yes?"

"Yes, and many had yet to be committed. Someone saw to it that he didn't finish the job."

"You're welcome," Keplan quipped. He stared at his red hand. "If we take Peraan's goals out of the puzzle, perhaps the pieces will finally fit. What do all those names have in common?"

Hylier tugged his travel-stained copy of the list from his purse, smoothing it as if somehow the wrinkles hindered his ability to think. "Azimir and Mirrel were your allies. I don't know about one — he was killed in the Swordbearer's attack, I heard."

Keplan peered at the name in question. "You know who he was?"

"Patron of the Hare, I heard, but that's half the Slummer."

"There are noble names on that list. Lesser Athrolani ones."

"Aye, but most are distant relatives to the queen — people I assumed threatened Daymir's claim to the throne. Most are still alive, save for Duke Jaytian."

"And Tzavanir of Ceir Pardelan. He was just in the city before I was crowned." Keplan's stomach dropped. "Hylier, I spoke to Lady Gella earlier this week. She expressed concerns that someone was murdering the line of succession — her cousin and their parents in particular — and making the deaths look accidental. All these people threatened my claim too. Whether because they were heirs or they were a reason to give up the throne."

The guard's face paled. "Whoever was pulling Peraan's strings was trying to help you."

"Killing Mirrel was no favor."

"Maybe not in your eyes, but in theirs." He heaved a sigh. "Perhaps we ought to warn the other heirs while they're in the city."

"How do we explain how we know? And we don't know, honestly. Suspicions are hardly cause for action. If they were, I'd have been imprisoned for murder months ago."

Hylier nodded and sat back. "I'll look into this — and think about expressing your thoughts to Greton, even if it's just under the guise of a passing concern."

"Indeed." Keplan's eyes narrowed on the list. "If this person is clever, and it's safe to assume they are, then Peraan was not their only puppet. Will you look into other notable deaths? See if there's a pattern?"

"Pattern?"

"Manner of death. Time. Who they knew. Where it took place. Was anything missing?" Keplan shrugged, the gesture uneven with his weakened left shoulder. One hand rose to rub a circle on his temple. The voices were different since he awoke, but no less loud. "If I didn't already have a headache this would give me one."

"Keplan, I—" He stopped and corrected himself. "Sire. I owe you an apology. I failed you."

"You're making me nervous," Keplan confessed.

Hylier's words and stance were the most formal he had ever acted toward the king, though he had never been disrespectful. "I saw you every day. It was right before my eyes—the changing moods, the energy—fates, I followed you to the Slummer more than once. But it took your cousin being beaten senseless for us to realize there was anything wrong. We were so convinced you had a proper reason to be vile, that you were simply beyond humanity, that we let you fall so far. It doesn't excuse what you did, the people you—" He drew a breath. "Even if we all agree they deserved it. But I'd be an arse if I didn't acknowledge my part in it."

Embarrassment warmed Keplan's face. "What are you on about?"

"The dust. I heard about what happened—the fight, the priests, so forth. No matter who you are, palaces talk. And I missed it. Holding onto morals too hard sometimes makes me miss the point, I think."

Keplan held a hand up. "I hated you for it, but you were the voice of shame in my head. Shame I needed. I'm going to need allies in the coming months. But I'm going to need friends. You've been a good one, even if I didn't appreciate it at the time. I'd like to make you head of my personal guard. If you're interested."

Hylier's brows rose and he slipped into familiar formality. "That's usually reserved for nobles, sire. A gallant in the least."

"The throne is usually reserved for the same. I think you'll find I've no taste for traditional monarchy." He turned. "Think on it, will you?"

"I don't have to," he answered, taking a knee. "I'd be honored. I assume our unofficial roles will stay?"

"Yes, as before. But your comings and goings will be less questioned. You might have to find other, less recognizable faces to do some of your smaller errands."

"I already have had to."

"And I trust you'll help keep me free of the stuff. At least until this is all over."

"I will." Hylier returned to his seat and leaned on his knees, expression thoughtful. "There's something coming, isn't there? Something dark. Did you see it, wherever you went when you were ill?"

"I saw a lot. Not all of it true, but all of it possible. Often the future looks so like the past it's hard to disentangle them. No wonder we err often. But there is one thing, I could smell it on the wind. I don't know what it is."

"Do you think Athrolan will be changed?"

Keplan found he could not meet the man's eyes. "I think everything will change."

Φ

The 42nd Day of Glasmord, 1272

"I brought something for you," Azimir announced, plopping on to the seat across from Rih and Bimet. She was surprised to see only one of the signs was wrong. He slid a drawing across the table. "You mentioned how many Deaf people were in your country, and I looked into it. Into how your houses are designed, with so many who can't hear. I imagine your room here feels isolating by comparison."

She glanced at the drawing. It was poorly done, but she caught the line of a door jamb and a pulley system very akin to what they used in Ban. She raised her brows. "I find it amusing that it takes you looking at floorplans and schematics to decide for yourself that, yes, it indeed must be isolating."

He cringed. "Ah, well, I've made an arse of myself."

She laughed and held onto the illustration while he tried to tug it out of sight. "It's fine, I'm happy you thought of it at all. May I keep these? Perhaps I'll commission a mason with the king's permission."

Azimir frowned. "You're hardly a prisoner here, you shouldn't need permission to redesign your room."

"No, I shouldn't, but palaces belong to the monarch, and here he is king." She showed the illustration to Bimet, who smiled and tucked it away. "So to what do I owe the honor?"

Azimir snorted. "It's hardly an honor, I'm just the master to your Kajimet."

"Your grandfather was king of Mirik, even if he destroyed the place," Rih pointed out.

"We don't discuss that in our household," Azimir admonished before grinning playfully. "I thought you might like to see something alive, after the winter we've had. Coming back from home must have been difficult. Figured lunch was easier to talk over, than walking." He hesitated. "Was I wrong?"

"Chewing makes lipreading impossible, but walking isn't much easier, since we're not facing one another. Let's just be grateful Bimet is here."

Bimet rolled her eyes, signing and voicing at once. "If you think I'm not ordering the finest meal they've got on Master A'hane's coin, you're fooling yourselves."

Azimir laughed and waved over a footman standing at the fork in one of the paths. The order was simple—distilled water from the warehouses and a plate of meat and cheeses. When they were through, he turned back to Rih. "So, how do Athrolani greenhouses compare to Banis?"

"Regrettably, they can't. Though I have only seen the tops of the trees in ours, I can confirm even those are more lush than the whole of Athrolan." Bimet shot her a warning look and she finishing with an apology.

Azimir crowed. "Don't worry, I've got no horse in that race."

"You did bring us here."

"Well, it's not a slush pile, now is it?"

Rih dipped her head in a warrior's forfeit. "It's lovely, honestly. Just different. Everything is carefully divided. Clear plaques. Tidy branches. Ban's gardens—those I have seen— are overgrown, tumbling, a symphony of life."

Azimir's smile was gentle, almost longing. "I'd love to see that. I love green and growing things."

Rih's brows arched, but she waited to respond until the meager plates of their food arrived. "I didn't take you for one who liked plants. More just swords."

Azimir laughed. "Small wonder. Most folks just think I'm simple and sword-headed. I probably am, most times. But our mother gave us each a potted plant when we were little, said it would teach us patience and care."

"And did it?"

His dark eyes were steady as his hands rose into the perfect signs. "You tell me."

Rih's cheeks warmed, and she was grateful her darker skin hid most of the blush. The benefit of being raised by a courtesan was at least she was familiar with euphemisms.

"Do you wish me to leave?" Bimet asked.

Rih shook her head as discreetly as she could manage.

Azimir's eyes lit with curiosity. "I hadn't said anything just then. What did she say?"

"She asked if we wanted to be alone," Rih explained, still not meeting his eyes. *Please. I so enjoy our friendship.*

"Of course not," Azimir answered, smile still gentle. "I wouldn't want a miscommunication."

She stared at him for several heartbeats. If Bimet was right, the boy exhibited more self-control than most men she had met. "I'm glad. Our conversations are what I enjoy the most."

"Good, me too. Battle wasn't terrible either. What was that club you were using?"

"Atlatl. Not a club, more the handle to a projectile. Those big darts." She bit her lip. "I'm just not nearly as good at shooting as I am at clubbing people, it seems."

"I prefer close combat as well." He pushed the plate toward her, patting his stomach. "I'm stuffed, the rest is for you two."

Rih caught the shadows in his cheeks, fainter than any in the city, she imagined. She felt her stomach answer. "Do you think Athrolan will starve?"

He looked away, brows curling together. "People have already starved. People were killed in the floods. In the fight with the priests. People keep dying."

"Do you think it's his fault?" The words were treason, but she did not care. Treason seemed to be what she was best at.

"I don't think it's because he's king." He fiddled with his napkin. "But perhaps because of what he is."

"You believe it too. Like the Swordbearers."

"Not like the Swordbearers," he countered. "But yes. I do. What about you?"

"I want to believe. I want to think all the terrible things happening in the world have a reason behind them, a reason beyond just human imperfection and malice." She steeled herself. "If I'm married to a god, then surely there's something mighty in store for me."

Azimir's eyes narrowed on her, moved to Bimet, then back to her. "There's not regardless?"

Rih deflected with something coy, but her focus was on his observations, both of Athrolan and her own future. *Perhaps it's time to reach out to his mother.*

Their lunch wound on, despite the obvious lack of food. Rih taught him all the signs for the plants in the greenhouse, though he caught her making up a few that she had never seen before. By the time she and Bimet returned, it was almost evening.

A letter waited on her desk.

She made sure her study door was locked before slitting the seal. It was a plain scroll, decorated with the simple ribbon of a casual friendly correspondence. *For the amount of these I receive, you'd think I'd have more friends.*

Dearest R,

I'm glad our dear M caught you on the road. In times like these it's good to be reminded of friendship. I've been meaning to write to you since I was posted here (do forgive the reused parchment). My days have been long, and — as you well know — during war the nights always last forever.

But I've met a lovely woman who goes by Ajat.

I was hoping you would look into her family — I plan to ask her to wed, but I was hoping to know a bit about the family mine would be joining before setting my best tile.

Do write if you know anything about her that would shadow my humble honor.

Yours, in rain and sun,

Sefer Vam

Rih slid the scroll onto a stand and peered closer at the thin, battered vellum. Whoever wrote this knew enough of her conversation with Majilah Ag. *So is this Ajat the Mirikin woman she spoke of?* Sefer was a Banis name, one she recognized from her ever-changing list of distant allies. *"Do forgive the reused parchment."* She raised the lamplight and set the scroll just before it. Sure enough, what looked like a shopping list had been inscribed, then rinsed away.

Meat

Onions

Nettle tea

Amber rosin

She frowned. Amber rosin was expensive and rare and used only by imperial musicians. She went down the list again, writing down the first letter of each item. *Monareka Elang.* So whoever now went by Ajat had a previous name. A Border name. And Mirikin ties.

She tucked the information into her drawer of notes, under the stacks of letters from Vi-baln and Mosil. Next, she drew out a blank scroll and clipped it to her writing board.

> *Dearest Mobeka,*
>
> *Forgive my lack of correspondence of late. I hope you've fared safe during these times. Your cousin has been a bright spot for me, but I fear we aren't as close as we could be — you know her best — would she be open to friendship, despite our differences?*
>
> *I have finally chosen which colors I wish for the hat I promised to commission, but I also thought I might send something matching to my cousin back home. I fear for bandits, however, and Mirikin patrols. Do you have a secure route? If you're too busy I do hope you'll refer me to another craftsman.*

Her coded deception was hardly as careful as his had been, but this letter had far fewer hands to pass through. She reached for the string to the bell outside her study to call Bimet. Her fingers paused on the silk cord, eyes fixed on the figure in her study doorway.

"Your Majesty." Somehow, her hands did not shake. Whatever it was he wanted, she would face it.

Keplan stepped in. His mouth stretched in what she supposed was meant to be a smile. "I knocked, but I realized you couldn't hear. Would you like me to call for Bimet? I fear I don't know enough of your signs and I doubt they can be used one-handed."

Rih's gaze dropped to the limp arm at his side. His left shoulder hung a bit lower than the right. "Can you write?"

Keplan watched her hands. "You'd like to write?" When she nodded, he smiled. "My penmanship leaves much wanting, but if you'd rather, yes."

Relieved at the excuse, she put away her traitorous letters and found two wax tablets. She slid one across the desk with a stylus. *At least we're still in my study with a heap of polished wood between us.*

He gestured to the chair opposite her questioningly, sitting only after she nodded again. He wrote a few lines, then held the tablet up, smile awkward and expectant.

> *These past few months must have been bizarre for you. I thought we might start over. I want you to feel at home.*

Rih scanned the words. He had not lied—his penmanship was closer to bird-scratch than Banis.

> *It is hard to feel at home here. I feel as if I have nothing to set roots into.*

> *A royal entourage is hardly nothing, my lady.*

She winced. Perhaps her words were too candid, too rude. She recalled his temper and Azimir's bruises. If she could not find the strength to argue with Athrolan's boy king, how would she ever face the emperor?

> *Surely, I don't have to explain the dangers of a city full of strangers and a temperamental ruler. I might be a princess to you, but I wasn't always. Just as you weren't always the king I see here.*

He read the words, then sat back in his seat, face thoughtful. "I rode into Ban with little more than the clothes on my back and the ragged pony beneath me. I entered those gates—the ones hung with your family's colors—in shackles, without friends or family or an understanding of who I was, who I could trust." His lip trembled too much for her to decipher the words, but she suspected he faltered into silence.

She started to write that he forgive her, but he held up his hand, continuing on the tablet:

I realize that, for you, this seems no different. Forced marriage can feel like imprisonment. It did to me, too.

I hope you don't find my query rude, sire, but I saw a man leaving your infirmary. A common man, with dirty boots and a long yellow beard. He spoke with Azimir, and it looked as if he wept for you. Is he why you never came to my bed?

The king read the words, his dark brows knitting like thunderheads over the colorless sky of his eyes. He looked up at her, then back at the words, as if in disbelief.

This man, were his eyes green? And was he just barely taller than Azi?

She had not been close enough to see his eyes, only the redness on his cheeks and the shaking in his wild, gesturing hands.

They are the same height, and I did not see his eyes. But his shirt was blue. Bright, for Athrolani fashion.

Keplan's eyes closed tightly, shoulders heaving in a slow breath. Was he angry? Frustrated?

I have not visited your bed because you seem to have no interest in such things and I'm not a monster.

He cracked a tired smile.

Leastwise, not that kind. But that man is the reason I still draw breath. He is the reason I took the throne to prevent war — however ironic that is now. He is the reason I came back two weeks ago, and not the man who could have.

You speak as if there are two sides to yourself.

Aren't there to all of us? Who we want to be, who we fear we are?

It was her turn to sit back and think. Of course, there were times she was divided, times she questioned her own choices, worried she was not all she wished to be. But never had there been a side of herself she feared.

I suppose in some ways, yes. But I am rarely so divided.

You're lucky, then.

The bitterness in her bones wanted to scowl, wanted to throw every curse at this man lamenting his hardships as she sat before him, as good as shackled by the ring on her finger. She caught the tremble in his hand, though, and the tears in his eyes were just as salty as hers, as the ocean just below. He wanted to start anew, and though she could never trust him, she respected the suffering he endured, so different and yet similar to her own.

I'll prove that you mean peace. It was not something she had believed marching from Ban, not truly. Not with the fire of war burning in her blood. She was quite tired of men's complaints and whims, but it wasn't often she saw them vulnerable. She reached a tentative hand across the desk and pressed it to his before writing again.

I doubt either of us understand, truly, what choices led us here, to this palace, foreign and suddenly home to both of us.

He stared at her hand, then her words, still and silent for several breaths before he responded.

After all you've done for me and my kingdom, I think it's you who should have "mercy" emblazoned on your hand. I'm sorry for the fear and isolation this marriage caused. I caused. I've been told I'm a difficult man. It's a curse, being pawns.

Majilah Ag's gleaming eyes flashed in her mind, and Rih worded her next line carefully. It was an innocent comment, if he was less clever than she assumed.

You mention pawns. I often liken politics to tiles. War, too.

"Do you play?" The gleam in his overly large eyes told her she had not miscalculated.

Quite well. And you?

I've been looking for a partner. Neither of us wants this, but it should not make us enemies.

When she looked up from reading his offer, his eyes rested on hers, and his red palm was extended.

She raised her chin and took his hand.

CHAPTER FOURTEEN

The 47th Day of Glasmord, 1272
The City of Ceir Athrolan, Athrolan

HYLIER ARRIVED JUST BEFORE midnight. Muck coated one of his boots and despite the unseasonably warm evening, he wore a cloak. "Glad to see you're awake," he remarked, by way of greeting.

Keplan emerged from his bedroom, robe trailing after him. "I wish I weren't. What happened?"

"Traipsed across most of the city, got robbed by a street urchin and fell in a puddle trying to get my purse back—my key to my chamber was in there."

Keplan winced. "I'm sorry. We'll put you up if you need it."

Hylier shrugged. "I'll ask the barkeep to let me in. He has a key for emergencies. I was at the Inspector's Guild asking after our dear Greton. That place is a cesspool. Half of them are God-sworn now and attempting to enforce the rule on anyone who so much as sets foot outside without a red glove." Hylier faltered. His exhaustion was clear, shadowing his eyes. "Anyway, I was given this by one of the Swordbearers imprisoned there."

Creases in the cheap parchment made the handwriting almost illegible. Keplan held it to his nearest lamp, one hand working to undo the tightly folded circle. His nose wrinkled in distaste at the salutation.

> *Your esteemed divinity,*
> *We now understand why you balk at our words, but we pray you will cast your mercy on us, even for a single evening. Our prophetess wishes to set eyes upon you. In return we will gladly discuss relinquishing our hold on your city.*
> *If you agree to these terms, meet us in peace at the alley between Cherry Twist and Widow's Weep.*
> *With hope and faith,*
> *Mel Domar*

Keplan glanced up from the sigil scratched at the bottom. "The Swordbearers are requesting an audience."

Hylier scoffed. "They think they're going to come up here and we're not going to imprison them?"

"We wouldn't, if they did—that's poor warmanship, eh?"

Hylier's blue eyes rolled back in mockery. "You're going to fall back on that when they've usurped half the city and blown the other half to fire and back?"

Keplan shook his head. "I think everyone has had plenty of my not obeying etiquette and being a miserable child. Myself most of all. Besides, they invited me, not the other way about. It's just above the naval docks."

"You mean to go? I know you have a friend there, and that's where you used to buy dust—"

Keplan glanced up sharply. His feet yearned to trace those routes again, but this was business, and as much as his heart ached, maintaining his tremulous grip on order in Athrolan took priority over falling into his former lover's arms. "I didn't need the recitation," he replied dryly. "But company would be nice. I'll buy you breakfast in the morning."

"You pay my wage, sire. Technically you buy all my meals."

Keplan grinned, already fishing out his plain attire. "Fair enough."

"Do us both a favor," Hylier suggested when Keplan emerged, dressed in common garb. The guard handed him a poorly dyed glove for his right hand. He already wore a matching one on his own. "And here, I'll tie a sling. Enough folks were injured that no one should spare you a glance."

Neither spoke as they moved through the halls, down the stairs to the higher officers' quarters, and into the street that ran to the south gate. The cold air stank of smoke. The cobbles were more uneven, upset from whatever trembled under the earth.

They rounded a bend and Keplan's weak steps slowed. There was no line drawn in chalk or blood between the districts still controlled by the army and those under Swordbearer rule. There was no need. Warriors in white tunics strolled through the markets, lounged on street corners, played ruddy five and tiles at the mouths of the largest roads. What laughter he heard was sharp, more teeth than tongue.

Keplan longed for familiar night air and the bright sounds of the city at night. Instead, most stalls they passed were boarded up or in ruins. Those that were still open hung a flag with the Swordbearer's sigil. They passed a store selling pastries and Keplan paused to buy one for each of them. It made their progress less suspicious, and his stomach was tired of broth. The price was triple the usual, but it had been weeks since he tasted wheat. *I suppose the Swordbearers brought something useful.*

"It's odd," he confided to Hylier. "They've seen portraits of me, seen me in person enough. None ever recognize me."

"You're not as awkward-looking in person. Close," Hylier joked, "but not quite."

Keplan touched the strong bridge of his nose. If only he could disappear into anonymity's cloak for longer than an evening. Half of him wondered if the people would thank him for the favor. "I always loved these when we ran errands for the Hare," he said, waving his pastry and punctuating the recollection with a large, noisy bite.

Hylier winced at the sound, finishing his own bite before responding. "I love places like that. It's what I miss about Marl Galin. Outside of Manor Black."

"Why are the folk who live there the only ones who don't call the town Marl Black?"

"It's not a badge of honor, hailing from an exile's ward. I don't remember much of when it all happened — my father was Daymir's age and close to him, but he shared little. The man's almost an uncle to me, save for the fancy titles."

"Or lack thereof," Keplan quipped.

Hylier snorted. "Exactly."

"I didn't know you two were so close."

"Not so much of late. I respect him. Deeply. He made hard choices despite his honor and wealth, and I admire that."

"But?"

Hylier drew a long breath. "He holds fast to his ideals. Not what's right. And the man in that room up in the palace is no longer him. Just an echo."

"I'm sure, to him, his ideals are what's right. Very few of us knowingly commit evil. The definitions just vary."

Hylier hummed noncommittally.

"Do you think you'll return home?"

"When?"

"When you're done here."

"I wasn't aware my job was finite. Kings always need information."

But what if Athrolan no longer had a king? What if the Swordbearers won? He shook the thought away, absently wondering if it was his or Hylier's. "Surely you'll retire someday. Family?"

"I'd love a family. And a good house—maybe outside the city, somewhere green and quiet and with good folk." He shrugged. "I enjoy where I am now, aside from the murder."

With every step deeper into the Slummer, Keplan's heart pounded faster. His hands shook, and he was aware of every stray, lingering thought that unwound from the press of overcrowded houses. His body longed for peace, for something to sand down the sharp edge of pain and the chatter in his head.

Hylier raised a hand, pointing to the narrow alley. They were a few streets down from the Wise Hare, a part of the Slummer Keplan knew of but rarely visited. The aqueduct arched over the series of teetering buildings, outdated architecture hidden under decades of repair. Water dripped from overhead, sprayed from chinks in the aqueduct's marble blocks. A lantern flickered at the end of the street, but the alley turned, the golden light truncated by a battered wall roofed with poles and a draped sail pilfered from the docks below.

"Just around this bend, yes?"

Keplan did not answer. Minding his feet and his tongue might make all the difference down here. Hylier seemed to agree, as they both fell into uneasy quiet. He paused at a wall erected from what looked like a pallet. The captain paused and knocked. After a moment a gruff voice muttered something from the other side.

Hylier glanced at Keplan, his usually easygoing features tense. "I've brought He Who Sees All. He wishes to speak with your prophet."

Silence reigned. Water hissed from above, a fine manufactured mist. The puddle around Keplan's boots bore an oily sheen.

The person curled in the lee of the broken wall stirred and blinked up at the two visitors. "You looking for something to ease the night?"

"No, thank you for asking," Hylier replied easily.

Sweat burst across Keplan's neck and chest. *Yes. Please. Something to make the next few months fly past in a blur of distant, unimportant memories.*

"I've got 'whal tear from Berr—hard to come by. How about a pack of leaf, help you do your business and have time to spare? Or a box of dust, folk speak bad of it, but surely you'd enjoy if you tried—"

"I did try and did enjoy, too much!" Keplan snapped. "I'll give you money to leave me be, though."

Hylier grabbed the king's arm before he could hand over the coin, his other hand knocking on the pallet again. "I'm sorry, Master. We'll be through in a moment."

When this was over Keplan would be grateful for Hylier's improvisation and his seamless drop into speaking to Keplan like an equal. Now his mind was occupied with too many thoughts, the majority of which were chanting in the dust-dealer's direction.

The pallet creaked then swung up and out, catching Keplan's left shoulder as he tried to push through into the darkness. He swore.

The man beyond peered at him, black eyes narrowed. It was the Nenev.

Keplan tensed. "You weren't jesting."

"Can we get in?" Hylier asked. "Street's no place for anyone this time of night."

The pale man ushered them in with an exaggerated wave of his hand. "Please, be my guest. The help will be by in a moment with your choice of drink. We have swill, swill, gutterwash and swill."

Keplan cracked a grin. "I've always been partial to gutterwash myself. Hylier? How about you?"

Hylier's blue eyes narrowed on the man. "I'm fine without, thank you. We're here on business."

"You're here 'cause she said you could be, no other reason. You'd have never gotten as far as Welp Street had she not."

"You've changed your tune a bit," Keplan remarked, taking the grungy bottle from the man's hand and pouring himself two fingers. It would take the edge off the gnawing in his mind, and he needed his wits. Between Brentemir, Domariigo, and Daymir, bantering with an acerbic zealot was familiar, at least. "Time was you'd never speak that way to a god."

"Time was," the man quipped, "you'd never admit to being one."

Keplan's grin broadened and he was rewarded by a flash of a mirthless smile on the other man's face. "Is there a required amount of small talk and barbs we must partake in before I see her?"

"Hardly. You'll scarce get anything from her now. It's almost as if since we arrived, since you realized what you were, she's gone quiet." He sighed and settled onto a battered trunk. "She's sleeping."

"We came all this way —" Hylier began.

"You came across the city and it wasn't even raining," the man countered. "Shut up and sit."

In spite of himself, Keplan was beginning to like the man. *Other than the fact that he crippled my arm in an attempt to murder me.* "So. You're Mel Domi?"

"Yeah. Mel'iend before all of this."

A mental echo trailed his words, worming into Keplan's consciousness. He peered closer. White-blond hair, sallow-milk skin. Faded gray ink peeking from a headband dyed red on the right and green on the left. Something else flashed through his mind, a memory, not his, but close. Those features softened by boyhood. Screaming metal and fire. Howling, biting wind. "You helped my mother. Years ago." The math of ages and years faltered at the man's apparent youth. "You were their prince?"

"I'm about as princely as you are a god, in the traditional sense. But yes." His pale lips quirked. "She and I stole a steam engine."

"You trusted her." Keplan allowed himself a grin. "So. I'm here. Are you willing to discuss releasing my city?"

"Discuss, surely. But I think we both realize it's more complicated than that."

Keplan's gaze dropped to the boxes piled everywhere. He could smell the blood and fire through the damp canvas hiding the arsenal. *Bombs.* "Relinquish your war-weapons. Everything but your personal ones. Stop your terrorizing of my people. You can stay, so long as you're peaceful. Believe in me or not, I don't care, just keep it to yourselves."

The Nenev followed his gaze to the boxes of clay spheres. "That's family technology. We don't share it with anyone."

"Then ship it to the palace, care of General Domariigo. Surely you trust your uncle."

He snorted. "He left me for dead. But very well. I'll send it over in a week."

"You'll hand it over to the King's Guard tomorrow."

Mel stared at him, black eyes unblinking. He scratched at the irritated flesh around the stump of his horn. Keplan realized the red on his headband was his own blood, not dye. "Deal."

"Why the change of faith? You believe in me, then you call me a blasphemer and try to kill me."

"I believed in your mother. In our prophet. In you. Now I don't know what to believe."

"What, you had faith in a god until you realized he was real?"

"I believed in god until I realized he was just a man. Just a human."

Keplan sighed. "I'd beg to be 'just' anything."

"Dismount that high horse. We're all just people. In the end. Horns or divinity or fancy titles, in the end we're all just meat waiting to die and praying we matter."

Hylier's eyes widened and he looked away. The man's usual bright mood seemed to have little place in this dark room.

Mel's head tilted, and Keplan caught a trailing mental whisper. "She'll see you now."

When Hylier moved to follow, the Ageless man's arm jerked out. "Nope. Just the god. We'll leave the door open so you know we're not gonna off him. Though, honestly, poisoning the wine would have been easier."

Hylier blanched and stared at Keplan's half-drunk glass, clearly not reassured by Mel's dark chuckle.

"It's fine, Hylier. She can't hurt me." He slipped through the door, blinking as his eyes tried to adjust to further darkness. The room smelled of rosemary. Rags piled in the corner of the otherwise empty room. "My lady?"

The rags shifted, and a gnarled, bony hand slipped out. The finger beckoned. When he knelt before her, a mat of gray hair parted and he caught a glimpse of a moon-pale face folded in a thousand wrinkles. Her chilled hand fumbled at his knee. At the touch her shifting stilled and her wide eyes blinked at his.

Something cold caressed his mind. Not dread or resolve, but something else. The cool of the ocean, of death.

"You poor thing."

"It's nice to meet you," he offered, though the words sounded ridiculous in the dark room, passed between seer and god. "Do you have a name?"

"Oh, I did once. My sisters gave me one, I imagine. Been years since I needed it though."

"Where'd you come from?"

"Berr. Tiny place—"

"Tut Kunis. I saw it in a dream."

"They chased me there, the Mirikin army did. Didn't know about your mother until she stole our sea, left nothing but naked salt."

Despite everything he had seen in his mind, in the space between life and death, the thought of power of that magnitude set his guts writhing.

"But you knew most of that, and the rest doesn't matter. That's not why you're here, why your parents are here."

"They aren't," he corrected.

"Oh, they will be. Time's confusing, the way most people see it as a path. It's not. It's a landscape just like the earth, and we can travel wherever we wish if we've a mind. Most people don't. Makes them dizzy." Her wrinkles rearranged into the topography of a smile. "So tell me why you think you're here."

"Here in this room? I just want to know why," he whispered. "Why I'm alive at all. Why I have these thoughts — why I'm privy to everyone and everything and — fates — if I'm supposed to do something useful with all of this information, why can't I stay sane and sober long enough to do so."

"You already know."

"My parents made a mistake."

She snorted. "Hardly. They gathered the pieces of the world and removed the prototypes from power, set it all up for you, tidy like. Their only mistake was living so long and not telling you how to finish the job."

Keplan frowned. "Finish the job? I'm not the mistake?"

"All the power they gathered, their own and that of the gods your mother ended, it's got to return to the world if any of this is to continue. It's smothering without air, withering without its blood."

"My blood, you mean. The power can't flow back until I'm gone, I die, then?"

She wagged a hand at him, head tilting. Her breath smelled of rotting flowers. "If it were that simple, don't you think I'd have let you by now?"

He sat back. "Let me?"

"Listen to you, parroting my phrases worse than Mel and Nen. I grow so sick of it. You and I exist here, in this world, but also there, in the space between this breath and the next, where time is passable like the mountains. Every time you threatened to stay, I'd kick you out. Nothing so spectacular as your mother's absolute defiance of death. More just keeping the lid on you."

"So if it's not my death—"

"Not just that. You're an artery, clogged with nonsense and too much hubris, clotted like the one they pulled from Jun's heart when it gave out on him."

Keplan had no idea who Jun was, but he realized it probably did not matter. "And I've got to unclog? That's the strangling?"

"You go back to where it all began and rip yourself open, blow wide and release all this power—mine, yours, your parents'—back into the world. There, all fixed." Her gaze was distant. Almost absent, but closer to preoccupied. "You've got all your facts. Now just choose."

"Choose what? Whether to return the power? Either I do and the world goes on or I don't and it doesn't. That's not a choice."

"Just a few moments ago you were wishing for oblivion. I can hardly blame you." Her eyes fluttered shut, and when Keplan opened his mouth to ask another question, Mel shoved the door open. "Out."

Keplan emerged, brows furrowed.

"Not the answers you expected?" Mel quipped, words dissolving into a cackle.

"Those were hardly answers."

"My statement remains."

Keplan shook his head and pointed to the door. "If that's all?"

Mel nodded, wiry arms crossed. "I'll expect your man tomorrow. Make it afternoon, I'll be too ale-sick before noon."

Keplan did not dignify the demand with a response, he merely slipped back out the door and into the damp alley. Hylier did not speak until they had safely left the Slummer. "Did you learn anything?"

"I did. About what I am."

"And what's that?"

"A glorified blood clot in a fat man's heart."

Hylier snorted. "Some prophet."

"She told me how to fix the world. Finish what my mother started."

Hylier's face brightened. "That's more than you've had in weeks."

"She said it's a choice. I just don't see how." Keplan raked a hand through his hair.

"Were you hoping for permission to let the world slip into nothingness?"

Keplan could not bring himself to lie, so he said nothing. Instead, he shrugged deeper into his cloak. It was dawn, but the city streets smelled as foul as they had hours before. Neither spoke again.

Φ

The 49th Day of Glasmord, 1272

Rih's muscles burned with exertion. Another dart embedded itself in the target across the room. The other training hall was crowded as Fess and Curiel did hand combat drills, but the crossbow range was empty. As much as Rih wanted to learn Athrolani hand combat, the battle with the Swordbearers told her exactly how out of practice her atlatl aim was. *Besides, Menna's in there.* She had no doubts the other woman would gladly take the excuse to injure Rih.

Her second dart was closer but still well outside the target's vitals. *"Rih, this could kill you. Doesn't that scare you enough to stop?"* Tears flooded her eyes and her weapon fell from numb fingers. She knelt, gripping the loose sawdust and hay scattered across the floor. In Ban, she could have gone to the funeral gardens. She might have dipped her fingers in oil and walked through the rich flowers and trees, swollen and lush from feeding off the dead. But Il-fald's body would not be there. Instead, it would be tossed into the mud pit that served as Stytown's spring, rotting body folded into the muck for all to see her dishonor. Il-fald deserved more. Her fingers clenched to fists. Grief shook her jaw and chest in a scream.

A hand brushed her shoulder and she recoiled, arm rising unconsciously to block. Instead of a blow, a gentle hand gripped hers. When she blinked her eyes clear, Menna crouched beside her.

Rih rocked back on her heels, as much to put distance between them as from surprise. "What?"

Though it was clear Menna had no idea what the sign meant, her tense face formed what might have been a smile. Her hair was combed back and braided neatly. They were close enough that Rih caught the sharp scent of the other woman's fresh sweat.

She said a few words, then frowned and tried again in Banis. "You can read my mouth?"

Rih nodded.

"Did you injure yourself?"

Rih shook her head once.

Menna looked at the two darts, then the atlatl itself, cast on the floor. "You don't strike me as someone who'd have a fit because your aim was poor."

Rih glared at her and shook her head again. Whatever the woman was getting at, she wished they would get there soon.

Menna's shoulders heaved in a sigh. "I'll leave you be. I know you do not owe me time or focus, especially after my words. But I would like to make amends."

Exhaustion weighed on Rih. As much as she wanted to turn away and proclaim she owed Menna nothing, she also knew diplomacy mattered, and like most situations, the weight of that fell on her. She was tired of rude people. She was tired of racism and oppression. But she was also tired of lines. She folded her legs so they were kneeling, facing each other.

Menna flashed another nervous smile. "What I said was wrong. Though I thought my reasoning fair, it wasn't. You did not set those fires. And I know the choices soldiers must make, the orders they are forced to carry out. Your people are no more different than mine." She frowned. "Well, you are, but not any lesser, I guess. I wanted you to know that I'm sorry."

Rih did not move for a moment. She wished Menna had chosen to write this instead of the awkward interaction here, but perhaps she never would have read the words. After a breath, she offered her hand.

The other woman's smile was broader this time, and she took Rih's arm before standing. "I hope the rest of your training goes better."

Between grief and Menna's utterly unexpected overture, she was in no headspace to continue practicing. Besides, if the bright noon light filtering through the high, narrow windows was anything to judge by, she had been in the courts for a few hours already.

She put away her weapon and was leaving the courts when a train of porters blocked her passage. Their brows beaded with sweat despite winter's chill as they carted the crates down the hall.

Commander Fess stepped up beside her. "Those are firebombs from the Swordbearers," she explained. "I guess His Majesty reached an agreement, if tentative, with them. Their end was relinquishing all but their personal weapons. And to cease their enforcement of their beliefs."

Rih jerked a thumb at the dimly lit hall and the ornate double doors through which the boxes were carried. It did not look like an armory to her, or even a treasury.

"Old royal quarters," Fess explained. "His Majesty has been using them as a study of sorts, I suppose." She flashed a grin and slung her towel over her shoulder. "I'd best be getting back before my stench fells any of you."

Rih laughed but did not fall into the crowd that streamed from the hall for lunch. Instead, she brought her weapon back to her room. Her nerves were too tight for relaxation or rest, but neither of her handmaids were present. After a quick bath, she slipped on a plain outfit and set out down the hall. On her second circuit of the building, she paused outside the elaborately decorated doors of the former royal wing.

Why does Keplan live in the same wing of suites as we do if he could have these? Rih wavered at the corridor's threshold, curiosity unfurling. There were no guards — the majority had been moved to the palace walls in the wake of the battle. More, still, joined the Banis forces in keeping the peace in the city itself. "I don't suppose they'd begrudge the king's wife a few moments of curiosity."

The door handle was cold under her fingers, but unlocked. The rooms were dark but far from dusty. She expected sheets and curtains covering everything. Instead, four broad desks filled the center of the room. Easels with designs stood beside.

She brushed a hand over the nearest desktop, examining the sketches. They were meticulous depictions of the weapon the general forfeited weeks before. Her memory flashed with the Nenev Swordbearer, finger poised over the trigger that would end her. She shuddered. Dealing death should not be so easy as a single finger.

A notebook lay open, and she paged through. Mostly it held notes on the weapon itself and its history, but another, toward the back, held a list of what the projectiles themselves contained. Her gaze dropped to the stacks of crates along the far wall. She did not have to imagine the destruction. Its evidence was knotted in the king's flesh, the threat hung over her mind whenever she recalled the battle.

An advantage. Rih glanced at the door before lifting the lid of one of the crates. The clay was rough and warm under her palm. Energy thrummed through her at the prospect of raining fire down upon RoBal. Ban never adopted the black powder technology from the east. With an army several times the size of any of their neighbors, they did not need to. The vision was lofty, perhaps. *But in my world, so is liberty.*

The air changed, and she whirled to face the door. Nehla stood in the open doorway, face flushed, smile bright. "I've never been to this side of the palace! Is this an old storage wing?"

Rih froze, trying to flip away from the list without seeming nervous. Nehla was curious, surely, but it was uncanny how often she arrived just in time to interrupt her plotting. *Or glimpse my correspondence.* Realizing the woman expected an answer, she shrugged. "I think it was the old royal wing. The queen's old chambers."

Nehla spun in the large room, mimicking an Athrolani curtsey and the first steps of a traditional dance flawlessly. "Can you imagine living in a room this size? Multiple rooms?"

Rih laughed. "No. Seems like wasted space, most of it."

"These can't be Tzatia's," Nehla commented, tapping the sketches with a graceful hand. "This is His Majesty's hand. I recognize it from all the missives and negotiations."

"You read them?"

"I saw them in Vi-baln's study, when I was tasked with being your handmaid. I thought it odd that a king's penmanship would look so..." her fingers faltered and she looked up, voicing, "common?"

Rih showed her the sign, nodding once Nehla repeated it correctly. "Rumors aside, very little about him seems typical."

"Divine, you mean."

Rih did not answer. Like many in her generation, she was raised without gods, in the shadow of their death. The emperor had been eager to fill that role, and the Banis, terrified, let him. But that did not make Rih devout. "His Majesty asked for the general's weapon during one of the war councils — to study it."

Nehla's eyes widened on the open crate then, and Rih winced. It was too late to flip it shut without the deceit being obvious. "Those are the bombs. I didn't see it, but we heard them from outside the walls while we waited for you. The smell and smoke." She shuddered.

"How can he have these scattered about in here? One was dangerous enough," Nehla remarked. "In the wrong hands—Athrolani or otherwise—they could add to all manner of war machine."

That's exactly what I hope for. Rih made a show of shutting the crate before lying, "I just was curious. As a soldier I'd never seen destruction dealt so easily."

"We ought to go back to your rooms, Kajimet. I don't think they'd appreciate us nosing about in here."

"I saved their capital!" Rih protested.

"So you've stated. Thrice. Today." Nehla sighed. "This is also the kingdom that raised a pauper to the throne and canon-blasted its own people over disliking the heir. Don't mistake gratitude for safety."

Rih laughed, and by Nehla's expression, the sound was too loud for the narrow hall. "Usually Bimet is my caution and you're my fun."

That brought a smile to her handmaid's face, but she spared a final distrustful look for the crates before following Rih out.

When they arrived at Rih's room, Bimet was waiting, thin face lined in concern. "Kajimet, I worried when I couldn't find you." She turned to Nehla, not trying to hide her distaste. "We need to be more careful than ever, Nehla."

The younger woman threw her hands in the air with a smile. "I'm careful. The Swordbearers are loosening their hold as we speak. Besides, holing up in here does no one any good.

Speaking of…" She turned to Rih. "I haven't been able to visit my family. Might I have the afternoon off? Now that the curfew and threat is gone—"

"Go," Rih offered. "I'm sure they're worried for you as well."

Rih moved to her privy, grabbing the single jug of wash-water she was permitted a day. She set it on her hearth to warm and caught Bimet staring at her. "Is everything all right?"

Bimet stared at her, expression reserved. She chewed on her lip for a moment before confessing, "There's something I need to tell you. I believe in your cause, in rebellion, in freedom from His Eminence. I do. But I fear you're too optimistic."

Rih rose, uncertain. How could her only true ally lose faith? "You're joking."

"You think Il-fald's death was a joke? Or the town you condemned to burn to death?"

Anger flashed up Rih's spine. "I don't think their deaths were a joke! But this is war. A rebellion is war. That's how it is on the battlefield."

"This is not the battlefield. You're stuck here, above all punishment. Delegating damage."

"Delegating? When was the last time you saw me delegate? I've got to keep an iron fist on this, lest we're discovered."

"None have succeeded in this. For very real reasons. And if you do, what afterward? You anoint yourself as Empress of Ban and start where he left off? You cannot rule it all. Not unless you want to become just like him."

Rih stepped back. The words stung like a smack across the mouth. "I thought we might adopt something akin to Mirik's governing —"

Bimet sneered. "That cock-headed boy got to you after all. I'll leave you to your foolishness, then." She stalked from the room, and a moment later Rih felt a billow of air as the door slammed shut.

Bimet's words soured Rih's excitement at finding the bombs. Without Bimet's help, how could she ever borrow one long enough to study or send to an ally who might reproduce it? She recalled the bright burn of fury at Il-fald's death. The perverse delight that seared her body in battle. Her wash-water bubbled over, steam billowing from her coals, but she was frozen. Perhaps it was not just the emperor's features she inherited, but his ruthless touch.

Φ

The 2nd Day of Vurgmord, 1272

Doctors may have suggested Keplan stay bedridden, or leastwise, comfortably relaxed, but his body surged with restless energy. Another day of staring at the ceiling waiting for someone to visit would drive him back over the brink. Even the fluttering thoughts clustered at the cracks in his window and the gap under his door were not enough of a diversion.

He moved from window to window, tugging curtains back and lighting desk lamps. According to Fess, the distilleries were working well enough for immediate needs, and much of the military was carting snow from the hills beyond. He paused at the nearest mirror, eyes lingering on the reflection there. It did not move, save for when he did. He draped a cloak over it for good measure before continuing his pacing.

What Keplan cared more about now was removing the priests entirely and strengthening Athrolan for whatever storm was coming. Returning power to the world was well and good, but how would they survive until the kingdom was stable enough to continue without him? He did not know how to prepare for a magical onslaught or the impending natural disasters, only war.

A heavy knock startled him from his pondering, and he flinched. Every loud noise was another firebomb exploding. A crack of a revolver blasting his chest open. An aqueduct crumbled above.

When his thoughts cleared, An'thor was standing in from of him. "Easier to find you when you're not perched on the rooftops."

"Considering everyone panicked over my impending demise, I'm amused to see how well everything functions while I'm supposed to be on bedrest."

An'thor snorted. "You know monarchs are figureheads unless they choose to do something with their power."

"And those who do are either revolutionaries like Brentemir or dictators like Jamun-Ilta. And usually it depends on who you ask."

An'thor stared at him, black eyes unblinking.

"What?"

"I was wondering how many people had spoken his name. The emperor."

"He's just a man."

"Is that why you force informality on all of us? 'Domariigo,' 'Barrackborn,' 'Fess.'"

"I think it's foolish to pretend we're anything else." Keplan raised one of the notebooks, waving its pages at the general. "While you're here, I had a question."

"If I answer, will I get my revolver back?"

"Soon. I have to finish a few more schematics." There was nothing about the general he trusted anymore, and relinquishing the only firearm in Athrolan's possession into An'thor's hands made his nerves flame. "This would be easier if you allowed any of your books to be read."

"What'd you want, then?"

"We've put our hands on the Swordbearer's firebombs."

An'thor's features tensed, and he shifted into the memory of a ready stance. "I hope they're locked in the armory where they belong."

"What if I made them larger?" There was a trembling in the floor, faint, almost enough to be imaginary. It shook the blood in his veins and put his every nerve on edge. *Or perhaps that's just Domariigo's attitude.* "I imagine hiding your creations makes it easy to exercise your advantage. So I repeat my question — if I made fireshells large enough for a cannon, what would that look like?"

"Bombs."

"Excuse me?"

"You're asking me how to make bombs." Pride underscored the general's voice.

"Athrolan is at a disadvantage. We can't feed ourselves, half our military is repurposed with bringing wagons of snowmelt down from the hills, and every neighbor is starting to distrust us."

"Not Ban."

"I don't know the last time you trusted someone, General," Keplan remarked, "but that's not what it looks like.

That's being manipulated into a tidy place of compliance. Like you did when you put me on the throne."

"So instead you're going to horde yourself atop a pile of weapons you have no right to as warning?" An'thor fell into bitter silence, attention dropping to the notes scattered across Keplan's desk. "What's all this?"

"Notes on my visions. Dreams. Things I saw while I was unconscious."

His albic finger traced the writing, pausing on certain words before trailing down the rest of the page.

Keplan squirmed, mind naked before the general. If An'thor were on the list of people Keplan trusted to know his inner workings, he was at the bottom. "Nonsense, I think, most of it. Nothing the prophet didn't say. Whatever it is that's coming ensnared both our minds, twisting until there's no sense to any of it. I guess we should just count ourselves lucky I'm not spouting divine prophesies."

"Why aren't you?"

Keplan's babbling trailed into uncertain silence. "What?"

"Think of all you could do — reigning as a god-king from his mighty throne."

"It'd be a lie."

"So what if it is. These people can't govern themselves — look at where it's gotten them. You could be leading this kingdom with a fist of iron — I gave you my weapon, gave you the technology, but now your body is broken, your kingdom in shambles, and you're squirrelling threats like a mad old man. Act like you own the place."

"I don't own Athrolan, Domariigo!" Keplan snapped. "I'm a steward to the land and people, like every monarch before me."

"Steward? You believe that? You realize how many people would drop to their knees before you now? After that little display to the Swordbearers? You accepted their scripture. And half the city swore fealty to you while you lay," his black glare dropped to the notes under his hand, "tupping your maniacal twin in some pretty field."

Keplan stepped back, embarrassment and frustration churning his stomach. He sank into the heaving, the heat, the sickly gnawing. "I thought they'd listen. If you wish to talk about displays, let's discuss the fact that you were too busy chasing after some Ageless boy to fetch my body. Or that my wife had to smuggle soldiers through the gates to save our city because you couldn't be arsed. Or that there's a trail of bodies and the boot prints in the blood look suspiciously like yours."

"I don't need to explain myself to you," An'thor rumbled. "I've been here long before you, and if you can't relinquish your silly attachments, then I'll be here long after you're just a colorful paragraph in Athrolan's annals."

Perhaps An'thor did not feel the same pressing certainty that something was coming, perhaps no one in the city did but Keplan. The ground shuddered, books precariously balanced on the surrounding shelves thudded to the floor.

An'thor's eyes narrowed. "Still think they're wrong?"

"That's not me!" he protested. "I can see it, feel it, but it's not me. It's the earth. She bucks and writhes. Death throes, strangled—" His red fist slammed on the table. Panic threatened to overwhelm him. The ground spasmed a last time, glass rattling in the windows, coals spilling onto the flagging from the hearth.

His door slammed open, four guards entering, weapons raised. Hylier stood at their fore, tired eyes shadowed with concern. "Sire, are you all right?"

He glanced between the guards, their weapons, and An'thor's sour face. Fleetingly, he thought of telling them no, the general had threatened him. *Don't tear her asunder again, Wardyn.* He forced a smile. "I'm fine, thank you. Just a bit startled by the earthquake."

"If you insist, sire." Hylier's eyes narrowed on the general. "There's an inspector from the city here to speak with you when you're through."

Keplan fidgeted. *Inspector Greton?* "Of course, show him in. The general was just leaving."

An'thor opened his mouth as if to protest, but instead, slunk sullenly out the door. Were it not for the hard line in the general's neck, he would have looked defeated.

"Show him in, please."

Hylier hovered in the doorway before stepping inside and closing the door.

Keplan dared not flash him a grateful smile or a nervous glance. He sank back into his chair, hoping he still looked imposing without the copious state furs. *Or a working limb.* Longing for dust spread sweat across his skin, and this was not the time to appear nervous, no matter what the inspector had to say.

The man who stepped inside was young, closer to Keplan's age than Hylier's. The king's eyes lingered on the man's broad shoulders, the red blush to his light brown beard. "Your Majesty, thank you for seeing me."

"It's my pleasure," Keplan replied without thinking. Pleasure was perhaps a bit of an exaggeration. It was too late to backtrack. "Your help in keeping my city safe is appreciated, especially in these trying times. I only hope I'm able to return the favor."

"I'm Inspector Greton. His quick gaze darted to the guard at the door. "What I've come to you with is of a very sensitive nature. Perhaps best received alone."

Be polite. Welcoming. Anything but murderous. "Whatever you have to say deserves to be heard by the captain of the King's Guard. Please, sit."

"Very well." The inspector shifted, settling the long black coattails of his uniform behind him as he sat.

"Would you like tea? Wine?" Keplan asked.

"No. I've been entrusted with investigating the murder of one Peraan Goen of Littie's Green. I believe the barmaid Nikola Korier brought the matter to your attention."

"There were larger issues at the time, so I regret I did not follow through with her concerns right away."

"Or at all." The words hardened the air between them, and every nerve in Keplan's body rose to attention. "Do you know why I'm here?"

"I hope it's to inform me that in the process of solving the man's murder, his network has been uncovered. Though I regret the way his life ended, you have to understand anything involving a former enemy to the crown is of interest to us." Words flew from his mouth with a speed just shy of panic. *Easy there.* He forced a smile onto his face. "Forgive me, I've been on bedrest for days and your visit is a welcome diversion."

"Indeed." Greton's brown eyes leveled on Keplan. "Sire, we did uncover some interesting connections — not between Peraan and others, but rather between his death and attacks on notable figures."

Ice pierced Keplan's chest, but he dared not speak. Instead, he schooled his hand into stillness and attempted to put an expression of surprise on his face. Anything other than dread or guilt.

"A dust-dealer I spoke with saw someone dressed in fine clothes in the Slummer the night Paraan died. Said the man was drenched in blood. This is near where, later, Peraan's missing personal effects were found."

Apparently, Sha was not the only one suspecting who visited the Fussy Fat Hen every few weeks.

"Additionally, a palace maid noted that a jacket that matched the description of the murderer's was missing from your wardrobe the week following. Next is your attack on Master Azimir A'hane—the same type of attack as Peraan's. This was, of course, following his country's acceptance of the Swordbearers you decried.

"Lastly," he continued, "there is the matter of the murder of Duke Tzavanir."

"Murder? I thought that was an accident," Keplan finally interjected. "He broke his neck riding at home. A tragic accident, but an accident nonetheless."

"He was visiting Fort Godbane on business, and upon closer investigation, I believe it was an assassination instead. There was bruising in the shape of handprints."

"I see." This time when the floor pitched underneath him, Keplan knew it was only his imagination, the sensation of everything he worked for tilting out of his reach. *If I confessed but told him I couldn't be arrested, I had to keep Athrolan safe, would he believe me?* "You fear there's a murderer in my court?"

"This is not a matter I take lightly. Athrolan was built on honor and tradition, on strength and morals. My family has been inspectors since the position's birth. This is my city as much as it is yours, sire — perhaps more — and I will not have murderers walk free. Even if they're kings." He met Keplan's eyes. "Even if they're divine."

"Excuse me?" A shadow nagged at the back of Keplan's thoughts. Despite the twisting fear in his chest, he never actually thought someone could level the accusation against him. "You're accusing me of murder?"

The inspector scoffed, but it was mirthless. "We can't, not until it's proven, not until we know you're guilty. Let me be perfectly clear." He leaned forward, eyes ripping into Keplan. "I know you're guilty. I've sat across from hundreds of people like you, and I promise each one thinks it was justified, thinks they're above the law. I saw you raise that red palm in the market square and knew without a doubt you had killed."

Keplan sat back, hoping his working jaw looked betrayed, not nervous. "I agree with you."

Hylier gaped at the king, but Keplan refused to so much as blink in his direction.

"I have killed. I grew up killing. Rabbits. Deer. Grouse. Hunted since I could raise a bow." He gestured to his left shoulder. "Won't be able to now, I suppose. Though it wasn't something I enjoyed, I was good at it. But let me be clear, too." He raised his gaze carefully to the inspector's. "I have never killed a person. Yes, I stood in the middle of that market square and spouted scripture deifying me. I raised my bloodstained palm and promised no mercy should they defy me. I stripped myself bare before them, weaponless, asking them to demonstrate the mercy they claimed I'd have. Markedly ill-planned, I'll admit. But do you know why?"

Greton did not speak, and though his forearms bunched with hatred and denial, there was a glimmer in his eyes that spoke to fear.

"Same reason I took the throne. Same reason I raced across the country in the dark to meet an exile in a bar. Same reason I married a woman who brought me to be tortured. I. Want. Peace."

The inspector's head tilted, and he examined the skin about his nails. "I assure you, all avenues are being examined. It's the Silver Apron and the only thing looser than their spending is their lips. Someone saw you. I just have to find them. When rumor of my visit here hits the streets, they will come forward."

"I'm not liked, Inspector. Perhaps you've noticed," Keplan confessed, pitching toward recklessness. There was a relief in this all coming to fruition, even if the fruit were bruised and overripe. "A king is no better than any other man, and if undergoing an investigation, however misled, makes our city safer, I will gladly endure the embarrassment." *Unassuming,* he prayed. *Innocent.*

"If you claim to be innocent, who would you have die in your stead?"

Keplan almost winced at the accuracy of the question. "I haven't trained for years to solve murders, Inspector, but were I looking at someone clearing the path to the throne, I would look first at those who began a civil war over it."

The inspector drew a breath and rose. "You know my thoughts, Your Majesty. I wish we lived in the world you so prettily describe. But I think you and I can agree the world is a far more complex place that that. Good evening, Your Majesty."

Keplan did not watch him go. Instead, his mind fixated on the memory of a tight cell and interrogator's blades. Surely, Athrolan would not treat him the same, if only because he was king. He had long since stopped caring whether anyone knew he was guilty. *But if I'm in prison or executed, who will rule? How will I return the earth's magic to her?*

Neither he nor Hylier spoke while they listened to the fading thump of Greton's receding steps. Somewhere a bell tolled. Evening was an ushering mother, easing the city folk into the end of the day. Waves crashed through him, over him. Blood, slick and dark like the oil clogging his harbor, coated his skin each time he surfaced. The final tile he cast in this murderous game would be ugly and irrevocable.

CHAPTER FIFTEEN

The 2nd Day of Vurgmord, 1272
The City of Ceir Athrolan, Athrolan

KEPLAN PACED HIS ROOM. A small part of him, one currently struggling to keep its head above the churning guilt, told him this was not a solution. Not a true one.

"If you're committed to this, we have to act quickly, sire."

"As if I don't know that," Keplan snapped.

"If you'd like to do this alone, I can come back when you've been arrested," Hylier warned. There were no teeth in the words, however, and he ran a hand through his hair. "Who were you implying? When you said you weren't the one who started a war over the crown?"

"Oh, any number of people."

"I can really only think of two—one of them is somewhere between here and the cold end of the earth, and the other is a terrifying nightmare."

"It just came out," Keplan whispered. "It was something he said earlier today and I—"

"First thing we ought to do is start speaking like we know you're innocent. Even here, even when no one can hear us. It'll make everything more believable." He slumped into the chair the inspector had vacated shortly before. "And we will need to act soon."

Adrenaline rushed through Keplan's body, and he rose to pace his usual route across his parlor. "And do what?"

"We have one advantage still."

"What's that?"

Hylier's long fingers fiddled with his insignia. "I kept the ring. The one Daymir gave to Peraan."

Keplan's focus sharpened. "So we might use it to steer them in another direction? You can't be suggesting we frame a man who's losing his mind. Even I'm not that cruel."

Hylier looked away. "No, I suppose not."

Keplan glared at him in mock annoyance. "I'll ignore the skepticism this once."

"You strangled a man to death, sire, and we're trying to frame someone for it so you'll keep your crown. If I didn't know the details, I'd march you down to the provost at the City Guard this minute." Hylier sighed and leaned his elbows on his knees. "So who did you have in mind?"

"Your confidence is overwhelming. I thought we were going to act like I didn't do any of that," Keplan drawled. His weak legs trembled, and he settled back in his chair. Something had nagged at him since he spoke with An'thor that afternoon. A shadow he was only now recognizing. "When An'thor was here earlier he said something, said if I couldn't let my 'silly attachments' go, then he would be here long after I was just history. What attachments did he mean?"

"You said someone might have borrowed Daymir's common name. Do you think Domariigo would go that far?" Hylier asked.

Keplan's heart faltered. *Would he murder someone I was close to, to keep me in the palace under his careful eye?* "Undoubtably. Whether he actually did remains to be seen."

Hylier pressed his head to his knees as if to stave off rising nausea. "We can't possibly be considering framing the general. The man who has fought more battles and killed more people than most of us combined."

Keplan looked up. "You said they had to deserve it, Hylier. Someone who's murdered at least once to get me on this throne. Someone who would murder again, easily. Someone who has far more blood on his hands than I do, if only we can prove it."

Hylier's brows rose. "You already sent your former commander into the icebound north. You plan on imprisoning the most notorious general Athrolan's had?"

"He's hardly skilled anymore. The man's a drunk. He hid the queen's rotting body for weeks. And I wish that was the worst thing he'd done." Keplan rubbed the bridge of his nose. His head pounded with the press of thoughts, the weight of Hylier's own anxiety and exhaustion. The man was almost as tired as Keplan himself.

"How do you know?" Hylier's pale brows tucked together, two delicate arches over the open gates of his eyes.

He's pretty, Keplan noted. *Not my particular taste, but pretty.* He rubbed his temples again. "I can smell it on him." He was astounded, really, that others did not perceive what he did, the turmoil of thoughts, the cloy of scents. He wondered if others thought the same about Rih and her lack of hearing.

"That testimony won't hold, sire. He's a dangerous man and I need to be careful. If I had known being the captain of the King's Guard might entail breaking into the rooms of one of the most terrifying men I've known, I would have reconsidered."

Keplan's snort was as mirthless as Hylier's barked laugh. They were quiet, neither speaking, just staring—Hylier at his hands, Keplan at the flagging. "I'll call him at tenth bell tomorrow. He'll be well into his drink by then and we'll ramble enough to waste time. Don't know what I'll tell him, but I'll keep him busy for an hour or two. Will you report back afterward?"

Hylier shook his head. "Best not. If we're being watched—and surely, we are—then I'll go home afterward, as if it's a normal evening."

"Your next guard's report is due the day after tomorrow. Unless something goes wrong, I won't see you until then. Is there anything you need?"

When he met Keplan's eyes, his were wide. "Whatever's left of your mercy, sire." He wavered for a moment longer, then nodded and disappeared without another word.

Φ

The 3rd Day of Vurgmord, 1272

In all of his years, Hylier had entered countless houses. Some where he was invited, starched jacket and bitter tea scalding his tongue. Others where he eased into the comfort of a friend's chair, welcomed with laughter. Others, though, he slipped into as a shadow, easing like evening into corners and behind doors.

He had never been so terrified.

Like most raised before the Gods' War, Hylier was weaned on stories of An'thoriend. Most of those stories were epics, sagas where the general was a brilliant light of justice in an unjust history. As a child, he had believed them and steeled his soul with their hope. Now the captain's blood sang with warning. He was no longer a child, and An'thoriend had never been a hero.

He wandered through the gardens, hands laced behind his back. When he reached the arbors, decorated with their full foliage, he ducked into a shadow and pulled his jacket off, balling it under his arm. Next, his cloak flipped to reveal the ragged gray interior. Most captains could afford repairs, and while employed by the king himself, Hylier made more than most captains. Instead of using a tailor, however, he hand-stitched rags and scraps, muddy petticoat scraps or tattered washrags. He fastened the ties, a far cry from the bright buttons on his jacket.

The shades of gray and dingy cream blended into the water-stained marble as he inched up the wall. His strong hands gripped the window sill and he paused, eyes closed. Wind through the trees behind him. Water dripping from the roof onto gravel edging below. A *thunk* followed by creative curses as a maid in the lower levels dropped something heavy. No hobnailed pacing. No popping of a cork or sloshing of liquid into a glass. Hylier levered himself up, elbows locked while he listened again. Still nothing.

He eased over the sill and brought out the thin metal strip he kept tucked in the seam of his cloak, slipping it between the frame and style. A gentle tug of the thread attached to the end bent the flexible metal enough to catch the latch and raise it. The window clicked and he smiled. Like most in the palace, it opened outward, and a minute's shimmying allowed him to slip around the open casement and into the dark room.

The hearth looked like it had not been lit in a decade. A rumpled bearskin lay at the foot of a broad armchair. Two stained, chipped glasses lay beside it, one covered with a layer of dust. The bedroom lamps no longer even had candles, and chests and boxes cluttered the bare flagging, save for a path to the privy. If he had to, he would brave the low stench of stale vomit, but he preferred to start his search in the parlor.

Where would I tuck evidence? Hylier stifled a chuckle. It was like asking a farmer where to place the best copper mine. He lifted a stack of books from a chest and eased the lid open. Officer's logs from the past two decades moldered inside, accompanied by a few sets of training clothes that the captain highly doubted still fit the general. He replaced the lid and arranged the books the way he found them, matching their edges up with the dust.

Turning back toward the study, his heart leapt onto his tongue. A figure stood just by the bedroom door, silhouetted by the dim city light from the window.

Neither he nor the person moved. "General, forgive me, I—" His voice drifted into silence and he peered closer. It was almost enough to pull a proper chuckle from his chest. "I don't know the last time he wore you," he marveled at the stunning armor on the rack. It gleamed in the faint moonlight; he now saw the inlays of turquoise and white lacquer, still bright and bold. He dared not see if the ring fit on one of the gauntlet's fingers. Bringing the thing crashing to the floor was the last thing Hylier needed. Instead, he slipped into the study, turning his attention to the desk and shelves behind.

Beneath a stack of missives and an empty jug that smelled like wraith was a box. Hylier hooked one finger beneath the lid. The velvet interior was faded, worn and eaten by insects in some spots. He tilted it toward the faint residual light from the window. Nausea climbed up his gut. A collection of objects rolled in the bottom. The first was a lock of light gray hair, brittle and wiry from age. The faint scent of decomposition clinging to the velvet interior told him it had probably belonged to the queen. Two rings—one Nenev in style, the other delicate and Athrolani with its filigree and mimic of a kokoshnik. Sure enough, the base was inscribed with the sigil of Felden. Brown dried blood filled the delicate Athrolani filigree. The bottom dropped from his stomach. There were a dozen ornaments in the box—some he recognized, others he did not. Perhaps his concern at having a murderer sit the throne was misplaced.

His skin threatened to jump from his flesh when the bells overhead boomed the time. *Eleventh bell.* He was dawdling. He let silence return in the wake of the bell's toll. He listened to the overloud billow of his own lungs. Floors above creaked as servants moved things about the upper storage levels. And hobnailed boots clicked their way down the hall.

The same boots were used by officers, especially younger ones, but none had that uneven stride, the drunken stumble. And none would pause outside the general's door to fumble with a key. *No.* His grip clenched around the box. Its contents were evidence enough of what would befall him if he were caught. Keplan may have claimed to be a monster, but the general had always been one.

Hylier dropped the ring into the box, shoving it back onto the shelf. He bolted for the bedroom window. An'thor's chamber door banged open and he let out a weary belch. Hylier paused on the sill. There was no time to latch the window behind him. Instead, he tucked his knees and flung himself from the window.

Φ

The 4th Day of Vurgmord, 1272
The Village of Jai, Ban

Thunder did not wake Ajat. Instead, it was the roar of fire and the rumble of hooves. She lunged from bed, back already aching. Sefer stumbled up after her, tugging his tunic over his bare body. Their eyes met in the dark. "I'll check the east gate."

She nodded, pulling her own clothes and boots on. Adrenaline only set her groggy mind in stark relief. One foot braced her crossbow as she drew it back. Beneath the floorboards the earth trembled. She burst from her room and peered through the window at the end of the hall. *Smoke.* Fire. She dunked the towels from over the bath door into the tepid water before ripping them into strips. "Ikel!" she bellowed.

The shout brought her cousin stumbling into the hall. "What?"

"I'll get the children." She shoved the piece of towel over her mouth and pushed Ikel toward the ladder. "Go into the basement. Against the wall. Where's Jani?"

"He had duty, but—"

"Go." She tugged the children's door open and scooped Kas into her arms. "Issa. Up, sprout."

"Ma—?"

"Ma's waiting downstairs. Put this over your mouth and nose."

"Prairie fire or something?" she asked, with all the infinite wisdom of a child.

"Or something," she echoed.

Kas curled against her, barely waking when she tucked the towel between the hard edge of her shoulder and his face. Her other hand tightened on the grip of her crossbow. "Quickly now."

She pushed them down the ladder into the root cellar large enough to shelter a single family from tornados and prairie fires. *Or something.* Ajat emerged from the rel, tying the final strip of fabric over her mouth and nose. The eastern sky glowed orange, flames gnawing at the rain-soaked wood of the gate. Through the smoke—red, then black. She squinted, pulling her hood up. Even over the crackle of fire she caught shouts, whistles. Then a horn blared from the opposite side of the town. *Mirik.*

She swore and sprinted toward the west gate. "Attack!" she called. "West!"

Another five paces and Jani burst from a side road, face pale under streaks of soot and grime. "Ikel—"

"Safe, cellar," Ajat panted. "Gate?"

"Holding." They pounded around the corner together, Banis whistles trilling on every side. At the west gate they skidded to a halt. Grappling hooks wedged in the logs of the walls, and Mirikin soldiers dropped into the town.

Ajat caught sight of one of Kemmer's own agents— Eraka Oland. They knew each other well, their goals often overlapping. Watching the looping swings of the woman's broadsword, Ajat wished that could have been the case this time.

She let out a whistle of her own, high and sharp. "Oland!"

The knight ripped her blade from a Banis soldier's collarbone and whirled. Her green eyes narrowed on Ajat's and she rushed forward, sword rising. "I found her!"

Ajat raised her crossbow and aimed. The bolt thread itself through the meat of the knight's armpit. Ajat slid under the cover of a wagon, searching for Jani while readying her crossbow again. Across the square Oland screamed and ripped the bolt from her flesh.

Blinking through the sting of dust and smoke, she brought her bow up, felling the next soldier who breached the wall. Jani emerged from the town bathhouse behind Oland. His spear blocked her first blow and shattered under the second. Her blade crunched into his head and he fell, limbs twitching as life fled. Bile rushed up Ajat's throat. The gate exploded in a flash of fire and boiling water. Scalding water pelted the ground as the mechanism blasted into the air. The knight staggered from the force but kept hold of her sword.

Ajat fumbled for another bolt, but pain pricked her throat. She slowly looked over to see Sefer crouched beside the wagon, glaive pressed to the sliver of throat between the wet rag on her face and her collar.

"I'm on your side, Sefer. Trying to stop the war."

His expressed did not change. "Up."

A Banis call went up, gurgling into wet silence at another thud of the knight's sword. Shouts became screams and weeping, the crackle of flames from both gates cutting the soft night air. She wriggled from under the wagon, dragging her crossbow in her off-hand.

"Honest, Sefer —"

"Tutor indeed. Oland!" he shouted.

No.

The woman stilled, shoulders relaxing though her weapon did not lower a breath. "Sefer. Finally. Thought you were going to sleep through the whole thing."

Sefer chuckled. "Never miss the fun. East gate guards were better trained than I thought, though." He glanced at the disarmed and dead. His gaze settled on Ajat and his smile dimmed.

"I'm trying to stop this war, same as you," she explained. "This is ridiculous."

The knight shook her head. "We're not trying to stop the war, Elang, we're trying to win it."

"You say shite, I say shit," Ajat ground out. "And it's Rekajat Monre now." She bit her lip, steeling herself for the risk she was about to take. "Kill me if you want, but tell Hetmir A'hane she ought to write to Athrolan's new queen."

"We don't need their lily-white city —"

"Whatever lies you've got, you can spin to her yourself," Oland snapped. "She'll be glad to know where you defected to."

Ajat scanned the blood-soaked ground, picking out familiar features. Her crossbow was jerked from numb fingers. The intimate warmth of the hands tying her wrists told her it was Sefer. Unwilling, her gaze darted to Jani's body heaped at the bathhouse door. His right eye stared, empty. The other half of his skull was gone.

"I'll get them bundled up for the march if you'll torch the rest," Oland suggested.

Sefer looked between the town and Ajat for a second. "No need. We got what we came for. They'll be too busy mending their walls to follow us."

The Mirikin horn blared again. Once briefly, followed by a second trailing note. *Victory.* The rope yanked Ajat forward and she stumbled once before breaking into a slow jog. Behind her, wood cracked and squealed as the east gate fell.

She thought of Jani. Of Ikel. Bound behind her, her fingers twitched open, as if releasing a prayer.

Φ

The 6th Day of Vurgmord, 1272
The City of Ceir Athrolan, Athrolan

The scent of clean sawdust warmed the air. Keplan closed his eyes, taking another long breath. Even if his injuries had not kept him penned in his room, he doubted he would have braved the stables before now.

The stall before him lay clean, empty, awaiting its occupant. It was foolish to have ridden Moly into the city. Surely An'thor's remount would have managed the slippery cobbles. His hand brushed the ragged divot on the top of her stall where she had nibbled the wood away.

She was not meant for stabled life. She belonged in the woods, on the Felds. Long, easy rides interrupted only with birdsong.

"It's hard. Losing them."

Keplan glanced up. An'thor leaned on the wall of the next stall. A curry comb dangled from one steady hand. His clothes were plain and dusty. The horse behind him whickered, bobbing his gray head. "How many?"

The general looked down, features surprisingly calm. "I'm a very old man, Keplan. They've all been from the same line. I raised their first grandmother from a foal. She was sweeter than any warhorse had a right. It's funny how much their temperaments mirrored what I needed. Some were runners. Others fighters. More than I'd admit were stubborn and lazy."

"And they were all called Theriim?"

"That's their lineage. Each had a name, of course, but after a while they all become Theriim. Names don't change every time we do." He looped a sinewy arm under his mount's neck. "His dam was the only one ever died from age alone."

"What's that fellow's temperament like?"

An'thor's black eyes flicked up. "Hard to say. Living here, you lose a bit of that relationship. There were times I'd ride every day for a year. Other than drills I'm never in the saddle anymore."

"I miss it too," Keplan noted. He wished he could have spoken to Hylier before now, wished he was not ignorant of what happened the night before last. Surely he would know if something had gone wrong. "What do you say the two of us take off and leave the throne to Blackhouse. Come back in another two decades to see what she looks like."

An'thor's smile was slow, tired. "I think I've missed enough of her years. Plus, it wouldn't feel right leaving her such a mess."

Keplan stared at the hollows of An'thor's cheeks and his drink-blotched nose and brow. Lank hair. *You look like me.* It sent a stab of guilt through him. "Moly was stubborn too. And she loved the outdoors but loved food more. I was just wishing she spent her last weeks in summer fields, but honestly I think she was happy here in these warm walls, fed and cared for."

"Should we all end thusly," An'thor intoned, raising his brush like a goblet. "Heard the inspectors think you killed Peraan."

"Wondering how much else we had in common?"

An'thor snorted. "Just wondering if the rumors were true."

"I didn't do it, but I hope whoever did goes free. I consider it a favor."

"Perhaps. Ends and means and all that." An'thor fixed him with a thoughtful look. No caps covered the raw, sanded stumps of his horns. "You visited the Swordbearers."

"I did."

"The Nenev boy—"

"Mel Domi. Your nephew."

"His name's Mel'iend." Pain flickered over the general's face. "I'll let you return to your musing."

Keplan scanned Moly's stall again, but its emptiness only made him hurt worse. He made his slow way back to the palace. The air was crisp, still, but its bite was tired from weeks of gnawing. Perhaps their months of hunger would soon be at an end. His shoulder ached, as did his back from the stiff way he carried himself now. Still, his mind longed for stimulation, conversation, anything to draw his attention away from the looming information the prophet imparted. Instead of right, he bore left, following the hall around to the royal suites in the palace's rear.

The room was still, hardly touched since he ordered everything set. Stacks of books on religion and philosophy towered around him, waiting for him to delve into what, exactly, he was. That seemed moot now, knowing what he had to do. What he was did not matter. When he first learned who his parents had been, the grandiose childhood he could have had was what stung most.

The life he missed most, though, was the one they worked to give him. Woods. Shelter. Love. Peace. Every move he made seemed compounded with violence. He strode to the stacks of crates, yanking the lid from one. They were clustered in straw, nestled like eggs for the market. He lifted one out by its leather strap and carried it over to his desk before settling into a chair to stare at it.

The door opened and his gaze flicked up. Rih and her translator stood in the doorway. His wife's dark eyes were wide, focused on the object before him.

"It's safe," he promised. "Just don't bring a torch too near."

She approached, head cocked. "They're elegant in a way. Simple."

"Do you like war?" he asked.

She frowned at him, shifting her weight. He could have sworn it was an archer's ready stance. "It's familiar to me. I understand it. How armies move. Why. Where to aim to cause the most damage. Both on a body and tactically. I don't love it, but its intricacies are the only thing I truly trust."

Keplan cracked a smile. "I understand that, in a way. Not war — war is a confusing mess for me — but how people think. Why they act as they do. It's lonely when no one feels something the way you do."

"Or hear it," she countered with a grin. She pointed to the fireshell. "Are you planning on making more?"

"No. wondering what to do with them, actually. Monarchies are like bombs."

"Because they kill?"

"Because they serve one purpose. And once it exists, no matter who lights it, the result is the same."

She stared at him, then looked down at his red hand. "Even if he wants peace?"

"I'm trying to make this kingdom into something it's not, and I keep failing because no matter what I do, I'm still king. There's still a monarch. The whole thing is broken."

"That's how I feel about Ban." Her long fingers reached out, trailing over the hardened clay. A shadow flickered across her features and her lips thinned. *Do not speak the word —*

Keplan leaned forward, as if he could grasp her thought as it slipped from his mental claws. "Do not speak what?"

She stilled and met his eyes. Her gaze was wary but level.

No matter how much candor he requested, this was not home to her. Even the seeming familiarity of her confiding was calculated, a tile flipped and another laid.

"There's something I've been thinking about, since the priests," he confided. "Honestly, even in Ban I noticed it, but I didn't have the context for it, really, until I came here."

Rih leaned back, head jerking to signal him to continue.

"Athrolan is old. And I don't mean she has a rich history and strong foundation or deep roots. I mean she's decrepit. She's wasting away. Like the queen, she's rotting in a stagnant room."

Rih's nose wrinkled in distaste, and he wondered if she knew that ugly piece of how the queen died. "Seems as if the whole world is, too."

Keplan nodded, mind whirling. "I think I'll be glad one of us, at least, understands war before the end."

"Surely General Domariigo is a boon, even if he's only lived half the lifetimes he claims."

Keplan snorted and tapped a fingernail on the clay. "I'm afraid he's a bit like this." A knock sounded and he glanced up. Rih's gaze followed his.

Hylier stood at attention in the doorway. "Afternoon, sire. I have that report whenever you're ready."

"I was just leaving," Rih interjected. "I heard you were no longer on bedrest and thought I would see for myself."

"You're welcome any time," Keplan offered, belatedly realizing it was true. "As I said—I think I'll need your counsel."

She curtsied, and she and Bimet filed out.

Hylier bowed as they left but waited until they were well down the hall before shutting the door. He gestured to the dusty couches, forgotten by the windows. "Mind if we sit somewhere a bit more comfortable? Where that thing isn't staring at us."

Keplan snorted, rising. "It's not a creature, Hylier."

"Don't care." Hylier waited to sit until Keplan had chosen a chair and settled into it. "How have you been?"

Keplan shrugged. "Well enough. I see you survived An'thor's chambers."

"Narrowly, I'll have you know. Came back early—or maybe I'm just slow—and I had to jump. Lay in the gardens covered with moldering leaves while he paced, drunk, above me. Leg's still stiff."

Keplan winced. "I'm sorry. Honestly, you never should have been drawn into this whole mess."

"It can't be helped now." Hylier looked down. "I found something while I was there. Helped me make my peace with our choice."

"What's that?"

"A box. Had some of the queen's hair in it. A ring with the Felden sigil, and a pendant with the duke's. The former still had dried blood in the jewel work. I thought he was knocked from his horse."

"Apparently not."

"At least you never kept tokens," Hylier's eyes flicked to the desks across the room, "that I'm aware of."

Keplan snorted. "I think the nightmares are token enough. But he didn't see you?"

"No, I think he was too distracted by whatever you two spoke about. Kept swearing 'they just made a mess of it.'"

Keplan scowled. "At least Peraan's ring will not seem out of the ordinary with the other two. Eerie."

Hylier winced. "There were more. Other seals I didn't recognize and more basic, common ornaments. Close to a dozen. He's not a man I'd like to cross."

"Too late," Keplan remarked, looking out the window. "I've been trying not to dwell on it ever since. Fates, I'm not made for this."

"Made for what?"

"Intrigue. Ruling. I'm familiar with secrets, but not of this caliber. Give me the gossip of who's tupping whom from the Silver Apron any day."

"That why you were in a staring contest with a fireshell?"

Keplan glanced at the weapon. "Contemplating Athrolan's future. I know it's a disaster, but I can't see a way out."

Hylier rose. "Why don't I put our friend there away and you and I can disappear into the city for distraction."

Keplan shook his head. "Not until the investigation is done. I can't risk someone pointing and shouting that yes, the king was the person they saw ripping that man's throat out."

"Must you speak about murder so flippantly?" Hylier grimaced, cradling the fireshell carefully as he tiptoed over to the crates. He raised the lid and deposited the bomb back in its nest. "Funny that they put all that silk beneath them and not all around. Seems like one could fit more than nine in each. Not that we need more."

"What do you mean?" Keplan craned his neck. "Each one has thirty."

Hylier held up a long length of fabric. Keplan shoved himself up and stumbled over to the crates. Sure enough, the lower layers of fireshells were all replaced with wadded undyed silk.

"Did they come that way?"

Keplan leaned back against the desk. "I wasn't here when they arrived. Haven't opened them until today."

"So either Mel acted like the scum he seems to be, or you've a thief in your castle. Honestly, I can't say which is more likely."

"Either way." Keplan glanced at the door. "I ought to start locking this place."

Hylier paled. "You weren't before? You realize—"

"I do now, Hylier. And that's not what concerns me." His colorless gaze flicked to Hylier's concerned blue one. "A handful of fireshells destroyed my market square. What are they going to do with hundreds?"

Φ

The 7th Day of Vurgmord, 1272

Rih ducked into warmth of the fabric shop, closing her eyes and drawing a deep lungful of acrid dye and clean wool. When she opened them, Mobeka was bustling toward her. "It's lovely to see you again, Kajimet! What a long winter it's been without you gracing our aisles."

Rih laughed, taking the woman's offered hand in both of hers. "I was so glad to hear you were ready for my commission." She glanced back at the two Banis guards. "The rooms are tight here — why don't you find some hot tea and I'll send Bimet for you when we're through?"

After a cautious glance at the seamstress, both guards fell back but did not leave. "We'll wait here, begging your pardon. City's too dangerous for that, Kajimet."

Nehla waved a hand at them. "You know each of us has blades hidden under our skirts — this is my cousin's place and I won't have your filthy armor getting on jade-cost silk." She punctuated the brisk order with a bright smile and handed over a few Athrolani coins. "I promise I'll shout if something happens."

Rih hoped her smile was not overly bright as she turned back to Mobeka. "Might we sit somewhere?"

The seamstress led her over to a long, low sewing table and pulled the padded seat out before taking the plain wooden one opposite. "I was surprised to get your letter, actually. The city has been such chaos the past months."

Nehla dropped a kiss on her cousin's head. "I'll go say hello to the boys. Sewing was never my skill, just the results."

Mobeka chuckled and squeezed her hand. "They'll be glad to see you, I'm sure."

Rih sank onto the cushion, forcing her tense shoulders to relax. Here she could speak freely. Bimet stood a step behind but was hardly needed. As soon as the door to the apartment beyond was shut, Rih answered. "An opportunity arose and I couldn't wait. You said there was a safe route?"

"Of course. All merchants know lesser-used roads. Needs don't stop just because war makes things difficult." She smiled.

Rih shifted, making sure her hands were shielded from anyone entering. "What I have is dangerous. It will need to be packed carefully, each wrapped in silk. That's where I thought of you."

"How dangerous?"

"You heard what happened to the market square?"

Mobeka glanced at Bimet, as if looking for corroboration. "I see. And where do we collect these?"

"I have two armor chests in my chambers and another two in Bimet's. Locked. Packed well enough for a walk across town, but I wouldn't trust a jostling wagon."

"Will there be another?"

"I hope another two—"

"Rih!" Bimet protested. "His Majesty saw us there today. It's only a matter of time before he notices. He may have already!"

"His Majesty?" Mobeka glanced over her shoulder. "You might have mentioned that, begging your pardon. We're here with official papers and all, but our position is still tenuous."

Rih narrowed her eyes on the other woman. She felt for her, but rebellion called for sacrifice, like any war. "Does it change anything?"

She mouthed, hands rising, then falling before forming any discernable sign. "No, I don't suppose so. But it will cost you—there will be guards to bribe."

Rih produced a small purse of Athrolani gold. "And another upon delivery."

"I've got wagons going out in a week and another train at the end of the month, if nothing changes. The latter one is headed to the capital."

"What about a place called Jai?"

She frowned. "You didn't know?"

Rih's heart clenched. "Know what?"

"That was one of our usual stopping points. Just a week ago, half the town burned. Mirik attack. Apparently, there was a deserter there. Now Ban has barred any entering the city until they figure out who's to blame."

The informant. Rih would have bet the finest riah.

"Do you have a friend in another city?"

Rih frowned, examining her hands as if they might jump up and answer her questions on their own. "None that I'd trust with this yet. Unless—" She met Mobeka's warm eyes. "Your wagons go into RoBal itself, yes?"

"Indeed."

"Then these will be delivered to Stytown. The Tower of Jet."

Bimet's hand rested on hers. "Are you certain? The heart of the city is the most dangerous place for such a thing."

"There are so many shipments, no one will notice. We have bribes. Besides, they've got to be there eventually. I'd rather they were waiting for us when we attacked than not at all."

"It just seems so soon."

Rih pushed aside the nagging feeling at the back of her mind. It was too soon, but she could not sit on chests of fireshells for the next year until everything else was in place. The momentum of war was a heady concoction, and she still dreamt of her battle with the Swordbearers. "I've decided."

"To whom will I be sending your commission, Kajimet?" Mobeka asked.

Rih grinned. "Majilah Ag, the Valen Queen."

CHAPTER SIXTEEN

The 9th Day of Vurgmord, 1272
The City of Ceir Athrolan, Athrolan

THE INSPECTORS CAME AT sundown. Keplan sat in his parlor, an untouched dinner plate before him. The letter that morning inviting him to the hearing had indeed said fourth afternoon bell, he just did not expect them to be so punctual. The knock was loud enough for half the hallway to hear, but he took his time folding his napkin. "Yes?"

Hylier was not on duty. Instead, a young woman entered, hand on her pommel. "Sire, two inspectors are waiting outside the throne room. Official business."

"Of course, Corporal." He peered at her face. "Forgive me—"

"It's my first week, sire, no need. It's Kirbe."

"Thank you, Corporal Kirbe. Can you send a runner to your captain, please? Let him know they're here."

"Right away, sire."

Anxiety made sure he was dressed for this occasion hours before, but he still paused to arrange his weak arm in its sleeve and run a shaking hand over his tamed hair.

Dressing was more difficult with it covered, but he did not miss his mirror. *Were I the Banis emperor, they'd have to request an audience.* Were he the Banis emperor, everyone would know he was a murderer. He drew helpful thoughts close, the calm curiosity from the guards outside, the steady faith of Azimir across the city. Perhaps this is how he avoided madness. *Not with dust, but with acceptance.* Inspectors were another matter.

His guards fell in around him, escorting him to the large, cold room. Winter filigree of snow and frost settled on the glass dome overhead. Keplan settled himself on the throne, wishing there were cushions for his thin frame. Scribes and guards ranged about, but this was not a court affair, and the room was otherwise empty.

"Show them in."

"District Inspector Hasian and Inspector Greton, Your Majesty."

Both wore the long black jackets cut in a modern style, though he suspected the buttons were not always so shiny. "It's good to see you again, Inspector Greton. Welcome. And District Inspector Hasian, it's good to finally put a face to the woman helping me clean up this mess." He hoped his smile was gentle and did not show his father's teeth.

"Thank you for receiving us, sire, at such short notice. We are here to submit our evidence regarding the murder of Peraan Goen."

"I have been troubled by this case, indeed, and happy to observe my city's workings, but I wasn't aware every murder investigation came before the monarch."

"They don't," Greton snapped, adding a hasty, "sire," to the end when his superior glanced over pointedly.

"When the murderer abides in the palace and is directly under your employ, we thought it prudent."

Keplan's flinch was real, and he made a show of lacing his gloved red fingers through his green. "I'm deeply troubled by that thought. I suppose it's foolish to ask if you're certain." He offered a sad smile. "It's your job to be certain."

"It is, sire. If I may begin?" When the king nodded, the woman turned to Greton. "Your testimony, Inspector."

"When this case was first brought before us it was portrayed as a simple robbery. It is clear now that it was an assassination. Peraan was found dead in the South Fountain of the Silver Apron district of Ceir Athrolan proper in the early morning of 38th of Lumord. His throat had been ripped out, and a bag of his personal effects stolen. His death has uncovered others—ones that were not presumed murder either, at first.

"The damage done to Peraan's flesh indicates a person of great strength who was able-bodied," his gaze flicked up to Keplan's for a breath before returning to his paper, "at the time. Though the Silver Apron is a busy district, the murder took place quickly and in the small hours of the night. No one witnessed the crime itself, but a person was seen, bloodstained, in the Slummer district drinking wine and buying dust shortly after the victim died."

Victim. Peraan did not deserve the word, in Keplan's mind. Mirrel did, torn apart in her own courtyard. Azimir did, blade to his throat in his stables.

"Peraan's bag was found later in the Slummer, having been washed from an alley during the flooding. It was intact, but the time and rain had washed any fabric, handprint, or hair that might have led us to the murderer sooner. Our search continued, however, for one piece of Peraan's personal effects still missing: a ring, of which he was very proud, from the former royal estate of one Daymir Blackhouse."

Keplan leaned forward. This was the part he did not know. He may have scattered the clues, but how they found them and what the inspectors ultimately decided was a mystery. "But you've found it now?"

"Indeed," the district inspector answered. "Between Peraan's connection to the unfortunate attack on Master Azimir A'hane and bruises on Duke Tzavanir, previously thought to have died of a riding accident, we suspected someone within the court, or even a royal themselves, was responsible."

"Me, you mean," Keplan noted. "I don't believe we need to be coy here."

The district inspector stared at Inspector Greton, eyes narrowed. "You went to him?"

"I thought he'd confess. Everyone claimed the man was nervous and rash. Besides, his words led us to the murderer, didn't they?"

Keplan hid his tiny smile of glee with his hand. *Oh, that wasn't a sanctioned visit?* "My unorthodox behavior aside, Greton, you said you've found the murderer?"

"Indeed. During our investigation, we uncovered a witness who claimed to have seen a cloaked rider on a pale horse follow the duke into the woods that day. Upon your own urging, sire, and that testimony, I obtained a writ of search from the Commissioner of Palace Affairs and the Palace Steward himself for both your chambers and those of General Domariigo."

"You searched my things?"

"Indeed, while you were recovering in the infirmary. Of course, there was nothing to find, other than a strange taste in minimalist decoration."

Keplan snorted. "I'm afraid this first year has been a bit too distracting for me to truly sink into the finer aspects of nobility."

Hasian's eyes crinkled in checked humor. "I regret to say, however, that we found this in the general's rooms." She produced a small box and unfolded the wax paper protecting it. Its plain lid hinged upward.

Keplan peered inside. Nestled between the countess's ring and the queen's hair, beside a handful of other gruesome mementos gleamed Peraan's ring. Something shuttered closed on his heart at the image. *I did that.* "I see. And the others?"

"Belonging to other nobles and those associated with the crown. Moreover, letters were discovered in his possession between himself and the victim that implied the general hired him to systematically remove those who might influence you. He was using the alias 'Dam Ornsen,' a known moniker of —"

"Daymir Blackhouse." Keplan dropped his head in his hands. *Even Azimir was an influence?* He knew the general had little interest in the excitable young man, but assassination seemed a bit far. "I admit, I'm stunned. I suspected he did not have my best interests at heart, but to reach this far? Why murder Peraan, then?"

"I believe he was tidying his own loose ends, as it were."

"Of course, we pressed further into the testimony that placed a man of your build and age in the Slummer and were, indeed, able to find a witness as to you own whereabouts that evening. Inspector Greton?"

Lead thudded into Keplan's gut. He was drunk, weaving between houses and clambering aqueducts. There was no end to who might have seen him reckless and guilt-ridden.

The younger inspector ushered in a cloaked man, dressed in his finest common clothes. "State your name for the scribes, please, Master."

He removed his hat and patted his curls into order. "Firas Smythesen, of the Slummer. I own the Wise Hare." His eyes were fixed on the district inspector, hat clenched in his hands.

"And you're here as witness in the case of the murder of one Peraan Goen?" Greton asked. It was a formality, so there could be no misinterpretation.

"I am."

"If you could tell both the district inspector and the scribes what you told me? Surely His Majesty remembers."

"Perhaps not," Firas admitted. "There was a lot of drinking. On the night of the murder — the 38th of Lumord — I was with His Majesty in my inn. My sister was murdered the morning before — a lot of that going about then, it seems."

"And the claims to seeing the king in bloody clothes buying drugs?"

Firas winced. "I said my sister was murdered. His Majesty helped scrub the blood from my courtyard walls himself. She was like a sister to him."

"And he stayed late into the evening, then?"

Firas's cheeks flushed pink, but he raised his chin. "Indeed. And I was grateful. I needed the comfort. Do you need to know which position we preferred that night as well, or —"

"That's enough, Master Smythesen," Hasian interrupted with a sigh. "I hope you forgive us the indignity. And do you swear your words here are true and offered without coercion?"

Firas finally met Keplan's eyes. "I do so swear."

Keplan would have given anything—even his precious, fleeting sanity—to stand beside Firas, palms pressed together, and swear his everlasting devotion. Perhaps a few moments during a murder trial was all fate permitted him.

"Then by the Inspector's Code, I formally accuse General An'thoriend Domariigo of the Northlands of murder in the case of Peraan Goen, murder in the case of Duke Tzavanir of Ceir Pardelan, murder in the case of Countess Fiena of Felden."

Greton's eyes locked on Keplan's as the list wound on. Vehemence blazed in his eyes.

Keplan did not muster feigned betrayal at the verdict placed on the general, but his shock was genuine. His blood thundered in his ears and his body felt more alive than it had in months. Looking at Firas was like looking at the sun after decades of darkness, brilliant and aching and full of tears. Keplan did not blink.

"Sire?"

He turned back to the district inspector. "Forgive me, this is all so sudden."

"I asked if you wished to tell him yourself before we take him."

"What will become of him?" Keplan asked. Libraries could be filled with everything he had yet to learn about the laws and customs of this kingdom.

"He will be imprisoned for a year, after which time a committee—including yourself, as king—will decide his ultimate fate."

He looked down and drew a breath. He did not want to tell the general his fate. He did not want to watch the anger in An'thor's eyes or hear the accusation in his gravelly voice. *I've condemned the man in my place. It's the least I can do.* "I will. And I thank you for the consideration. He was always a confidant, and this momentous betrayal aside, I believe I owe him the dignity."

"If course, sire. We will await your orders to bring him in."

Keplan glanced at the door to the throne room. "How many guards did you bring?"

"A city patrol, sire. Why?"

"I fear you'll need them."

They bowed themselves out, Firas leaving first. By the time Keplan emerged from the throne room, his former lover was lost to the night. He thought of running after him, falling to his knees to beg or thank, or simply stare. *Why did you come to my bedside? Why did you lie before the inspectors for me?*

Instead, the king walked to the general's door alone. The halls were quiet, the last of the evening light fading from the windows.

Hylier met him at the door, panting. "I came as soon as I heard. I can go in with you."

"Stay by the door. I'll call for you and the city guards. This is something I need to do myself."

The captain nodded and stepped aside as Keplan knocked.

After a pregnant silence, the door jerked open. An'thor peered out at him, white brows curling together in a frown. Bloodshot vessels were a faint brown haze over black sclera. "Wardyn?"

Keplan's fist clenched, nails digging into his red-stained palm. He had not woken with the plan to burn every bridge that brought him here, but today was a day for fire. "Evening, Domariigo. May I come in?"

An'thor's frown deepened, but he stepped aside. "You want a drink?"

"I would, thank you."

"Why are you here?"

Keplan perched himself on a chair, not answering until the general produced the offered drink. He took a careful sip before looking up. "Athrolan is changing. I know you hope to bring her back to the glory you remember — the white walls, the towering palaces, the warren of tunnels and armies as far as my gaze reaches. But Athrolan doesn't need gods. She doesn't need the Rakos' fire and the Laen's thunder. If you look at her streets, at the trade in the markets and what little food is on her plates, it's not ours. And it's not from the gods."

"It's from that bloody treaty you signed with Ban."

"Actually, it's not. You've helped raise me this far, given me invaluable opportunities. And for those I am grateful. But I'm in lands you've never navigated. Her golden age is past. Her people don't care about palaces or gods. They care about each other; they care about food and safety. I'm not ruling for you. I'm ruling for them. I need a general who will walk beside me. Not slash a path he thinks is right."

Perhaps it was the steel Keplan borrowed from Rih's spirit. Perhaps it was his old candor. An'thor straightened in his seat and his eyes sobered. "You're asking me to resign."

"It's complicated. But I'm not asking."

"Who will replace me?" Deadly calm froze the general's words.

"I'm not certain yet, but I was thinking Rih. She's got more mercy than I do lately. I haven't asked her yet, but as of now, you no longer have control over the Athrolani army."

An'thor's placidity shattered. "You bastard! I'm what made this city what she was! I forged every alliance, I guided Xavier's hand, Tzatia's hand, even from beyond her borders when Athrolan faltered I was there, in the night, to protect her from her own missteps!" He surged to his feet, hands shaking, cracked, stained nails clawing at the air between them. "I made Athrolan! Not you or any Banis whore. Me!"

Keplan waited until the man sputtered into silence. "When I arrived here, Domariigo, your hand had guided her straight into civil war. Your protection forced one of her most beloved queens to rot alone, disrespected and forgotten, in the soiled bed where she died." He rose. "Athrolan has had enough of your guidance."

"Who carried the Nenev into battle that last time? Who saved your mother from her father's genocide?" An'thor snarled. Spittle flew from his thin chapped lips, flushed purple with anger.

"I believe she did that herself." Keplan's chest clenched. Holding so many contradicting truths, so many lies would take all of Keplan's sanity. He wondered if that was why the general's hands shook. If that was why alcohol was the only peace he could find now. Keplan rose. "You want honors for what you've done? Then accept them for putting me on the throne. You literally killed to have me here, so best not falter now."

An'thor paled, his white skin turning sallow under his faded tattoo. His dark gaze darted to the bookcase, undoubtedly searching for the box. "What?"

"You're being arrested by District Inspector Hasian for the murder of Peraan. And Tzavanir. And Fiena."

"I didn't kill him!" An'thor spun, tossing his glass with a snarl.

It took all of Keplan's willpower not to jump when the glass shattered in the hearth beside him. Keplan's soft voice cut through the rattling as An'thor tore apart his room. "I know."

The frantic rummaging stopped. An'thor's age-yellowed hair swung with each denying shake of his head. His horrified growl wound into a frantic scream. "You don't shed blood! Even the prophesy said you wouldn't!" Hobnails scraped stone as the pale old man turned.

Keplan realized that was, in fact, what An'thor was. Old. Wan. Tired. Ill. Keplan leaned forward, murmuring, "I'm not arresting you for his murder."

When An'thor's tirade did not continue, he elaborated. "Surely the city is, but I'm not. I'm arresting you for Mirrel. For Fiena. For the queen's doctor. For what could have happened to Azimir. For the people whose futures you broke and trinkets you took and everyone who met their end by your hand whether it wielded blade or bullets or pen."

"The city should be terrified of you, terrified you'll see their secrets, see their evil, hopeless ways."

"Enough, Domariigo."

"This is my home—"

"Not really. It's not even mine. It's home to whoever comes after us, whoever treads in these faded, broken boot prints. You know that. I think you've always known. Or feared it. This world isn't for you, hasn't been for a long while now."

An'thor sagged against the doorframe. Something lit in his black eyes, something bright and burning and unfamiliar in the wan, drawn face. "What will happen to me, then?"

"Prison for a year. After I don't know. Perhaps death." Keplan shrugged, wincing at the creaking bones. For a fleeting moment, Keplan felt sorrow.

An'thor's pale hand wiped his mouth. He did not shake. His eyes did not rove, searching escape or retaliation. There was no dignity left in him, nor pride. "Call the guards, then."

Φ

The 11ᵗʰ Day of Vurgmord, 1272

A bubble of warmth and noise burst across Keplan's shoulders. His body trembled with the memory of slipping into another bar, dust bright in his mind.

Hylier jerked a nod at the bar. "Fireale? Gutterwrack?"

"Wine. Dark."

Hylier frowned. "People don't drink wine in a bar—"

"Then water or tea, whatever." He waved at the man and turned to find a table. The tail of his long hair was tucked under his usual felt hat. In the wake of the Swordbearer's attack, many of the city folk began sporting color gloves— even indoors. Whether it was to display their devotion or some societal rule dictating common folk mimic a monarch's idiosyncrasies, he did not care. His were plain, as usual, but unremarkable compared to their bright crimson.

Keplan slid behind a table where he had a good view of the room. *Relax.* He forced his back to loosen until his right shoulder was not located beside his ear. He found a smile slipped onto his face watching Hylier pause to dance a few steps with a pretty brunette on his way back, two drinks held high. It earned him a playful slap on his backside, which the captain answered with a wink.

"Here you are." Hylier settled into a chair across the table and pushed a full mug over. "I know you're not into the strong stuff. It's the house's winter mead. Pretty good, if you don't mind sweet."

"I don't." Keplan sniffed. "Autumn, wheat, wildflower honey."

Hylier's brows rose. "I didn't know your powers extended to drinks. Though I suppose sussing ingredients is easier than delving into people's minds."

"I used my nose," Keplan retorted, and took a long draw. He narrowed his eyes on the man. "You always want to be a soldier?"

"Hardly. I mean, I enjoy it well enough now. I hated training. Instructors did not appreciate my cleverness."

"That's why I was asking. You're quick. And seem unchallenged by most things you take on. Flirting included."

Hylier laughed. "I enjoy fun, is all."

"I don't know if I'd recognize fun if I woke up beside it," Keplan explained.

Hylier's arm swept out to encompass the room. "Well, sire, meet fun. Fun, this is His Maj—"

Keplan made a shushing motion but laughed nonetheless. "I'll go by Lan out here. Always did."

"See, aliases are fun."

"I was under the impression they were for murder."

Hylier's mirth faltered and he drew a breath. "Right. Sometimes yes. Let's not be claiming killing is fun, eh?"

"Agreed," Keplan muttered, taking another sip. "So, will fun begin with a lesson in flirting with pretty girls?"

"Depends what you're looking for."

"Clever wit—just someone to talk with for an hour or two where I'm not pretending." *I'll always be pretending.* He saw it in Hylier's eyes, but the captain refrained from voicing it.

The captain grinned. "I understand that. I like someone who can keep up with me. I've been easily bored before."

Keplan scoffed. "I'd imagine there's a fair few who think you can't keep up with them."

Hylier had the grace to blush and shrugged. "You going to dance, or should I order you another?"

"No dancing. Least for me." He propped his chin in his hand. "There wasn't much dancing back home. Music, yes, and Ma would dance a bit, I suppose, but like me, her voice is closer to wailing gulls than song."

"Cards, then?"

Keplan's memory flashed with Rih's words about tiles, carefully curated and so unassuming. His rash words to An'thor about Rih replacing him as general held more water than he initially thought. "Please."

Hylier ordered a few fingers of a sickly-sweet brown liquor and produced a battered deck of cards from his coat pocket. Over the next hour he proved a far better player than Keplan.

After his third mead, Keplan wondered if he may be drunk. He peered at the mug before him as if he suspected it of stealing his belt purse. "Except no one uses belt purses anymore," he lamented.

"Thieves' Hand: you've got three chances to beat me or I take the pot." Hylier threw down a stack of cards. "What was that about a purse?"

"N'one uses purses anymore," Keplan slurred. "Just pocketfolds. I walked out of the woods with archaic fashion and don't know if I'm embarrassed or annoyed."

"Go with the former."

Keplan frowned at the cards. "I'll never win."

"Three tries," Hylier reminded. "I've seen a game turn in one."

"With someone as unskilled as I am?"

"Can't you just—" The guard wiggled his fingers and a borrowed memory of Brentemir doing just that to his mother two decades before flickered beneath his thoughts.

"No. I can hardly control it on a good day and certainly not in a crowded bar. I'm bombarded. It's why I turned to drugs—you remember the drugs," he reminded conspiratorially.

"I do. You know, I think people like your bad fashion. Returning to your purse dilemma."

"My bad fashion—you're doing a poor job selling that gold rook's egg there, Hylier." He tossed down two cards he hoped added up to seventeen.

Hylier grinned and shook his head. "Two more tries, boy-o."

"Don't 'boy-o' me, I'm a king."

"Not tonight, you aren't. Kings don't lose at ruddy five in a bar."

"Watch me," Keplan muttered. Another two cards.

Hylier did not bother to tell him they neither added up to seventeen nor were valid to play during the contest phase of the game, but his smile said enough.

Keplan glowered, shoved the rest of his cards away, and called for a fourth ale. *Or is it my fifth?* "We're playing tiles next."

"Tiles? I've never played—"

"So it'll be just like ruddy five but you'll be losing instead of me," Keplan countered.

"Pay this round and you've a deal."

"I've paid for every round, as you're technically on duty." He frowned. "Drunk on duty, I might add."

Hylier wagged a hand at him. "I'm just the distraction."

"Evening, boys." A low voice cut through the banter and a tall woman slid onto the bench beside Keplan.

Keplan smiled at Sha's familiar warmth. "Evening, Sha. Didn't think I'd see you in here."

"Are you avoiding me?" She gasped playfully, flicking her bright blond wig over her shoulder.

"Hardly—don't you patronize the Hen?"

Her expression darkened. "Veska's not the tender there anymore. Some cobblehead took over, tossed most of us out for paying too little for our rooms. I tell you—no amount of money will buy you bread if there's no bread to be had."

"I'm sorry to hear—fates, manners. Sha, this is Captain Hylier—"

Hylier dismissed his late introduction. "We go way back, same neighborhood when I first arrived here. Is it Sha or Rheman tonight?"

"Sha if I've got my hair on," she answered with a sly smile. Under the table her leg brushed Keplan's. "So, what's our merchant son forgetting this evening?"

Hylier's eyes flicked to Keplan, drink making his tells more obvious. "Forgetting he's a merchant's son."

Sha snorted into her wine. "Wrong bar for that, though," she continued, voice dropping, "I'm glad to see you're not buying from Jolly Jeck anymore, as much as I miss seeing your face."

He winced. "I think it's best for everyone I'm no longer Jeck's patron."

"Rather," Sha agreed dryly. "Care for a dance, either of you?"

"You know me, won't pay for it."

"I only start charging when the bedroom door closes, Dill, and you've got to be the only soldier who takes that part of the conduct seriously."

"I'm up for a dance, though I promise I'll be terrible," Keplan offered.

"Perfect, you'll make me look charitable." She tugged his hand until he followed her out into the cleared area of the room where a dozen other couples already pranced to the off-tune flute. The song easily rolled into another and she draped one arm over his shoulder.

"My arm, I—"

Before he finished, she tucked his weak hand into the broad Banis belt. "That all right?"

He grinned and laced the fingers of his other hand through hers. "Thank you."

She stood at his eye level, dark gaze roving over his features but never leaving his face. "So does your handsome friend know you're not a merchant's son?"

"He's my personal guard. So yes. How'd you know I wasn't? I never told you—did I?" His times at the Fussy Fat Hen were a haze of saturated images too fast for him to properly untangle.

"I'm a student of disguise and costume, I notice when it doesn't quite fit. Besides, our conversations later were clear enough."

Keplan felt a flush pink his cheeks. "You think others notice?"

"Oh, surely, some. But not enough, and they don't care enough to make a fuss. They might know you don't fit here, but that doesn't mean they've gambled on who you really are. Plenty of folk don a persona for the night. You and I just take it another step."

"Sometimes I wonder which one's the real one. Who I really am."

Sha's smile was sad. Lantern light glanced off the sharp lines of her cheeks. "For most of us, sweetling, they both are and aren't at once. Most never truly fit where we are, no matter the hair and jacket we choose." She hesitated, then leaned forward and ghosted over his mouth with a kiss. Longing tugging his stomach. It wasn't the dizzying lurch caused by Firas's grin. Her lips were soft and invited more, but he pulled away. "Not tonight, Sha, I'm sorry."

"Maybe I'm just having fun."

"Maybe my heart's just too distant," he countered gently. "I understand if you'd rather dance with someone else, given—"

"I'm interested in more'n work, you fool," she teased. "Why don't you play a round of tiles with me, since you were so boastful to Dill, and we'll call it an evening."

"Fair," he agreed with a laugh, and led her back to the game.

Two hours later he rubbed his temple with one long finger and groaned. "Sha, I never would have agreed to this had I known you were a master."

"Master, hardly!" she protested. "Most clients enjoy a game or two, so I've had a lot of practice."

Dill's grin was wicked and he leaned forward. "With tiles, or..."

She batted at him with the sleeve of her jacket, now bundled on the table. "Ladies never tell. Who taught you, anyway? You seem to know half the rules and have made up a dozen others."

Keplan let a grin ease onto his face. "A stunning golden riah in the Banis palace stables."

Sha snorted and rolled her eyes. "Small wonder they made you king—you lie as good as any noble, even if you can't dance worth a Berrin bone."

He laid another tile down, watching as Hylier countered him, and Sha took the pot for the third time in a row. His purse was light, his stomach full, and his heart quiet. Loneliness nagged, but it was a gentle melancholy worth feeling for a while.

A large sailor thumped into the booth beside them, black braids still salt-stained. She waved for a bartender and caught Sha's eye. "Hello again."

Sha's smile brightened tenfold. "Chamon! I thought you were gone another three weeks!"

"King called us in on account of the God-tuppers and the general getting the axe. 'Nother fish-shat barricade, I imagine. I'm tired of bobbing in still waters."

Guilt flashed through Keplan at the woman's words. Knowing his choices had far-reaching consequences was one thing. Hearing it from the candid mouth of one of his subjects drove the point further home than he was used to.

Sha's eyes darkened and her smile was just for the sailor. "I know the feeling." At the sound of Keplan's next tiles hitting the table, she flushed and glanced back. "Lan, Dill, this is an old friend of mine, Captain Chamon Zhe. Chamon, this is Captain Dillane Hylier and his errant drinking partner, Lan Guardsen."

Keplan offered his hand in greeting. "I think we're about ready to totter off to bed, you two ought to catch up."

Hylier made a lewd, if discreet, gesture, and Keplan kicked him under the table.

Sha squeezed Keplan's hand in thanks and helped them gather their playing tiles. "It was lovely to talk tonight, though. If you're ever back in this area—"

"I'll find you. Thanks for the dance." He followed Hylier's weaving way through the clusters of tables and out into the soft air. He tilted his head back, breathing deep the smell of the stone and lantern oil, salt and ale. His city. *Home.* His gaze, unsupervised, wandered to the road leading down to the Slummer. His heart ached with the echo of Sha's words, her expression when she saw Chamon.

"You want to go somewhere else?" Hylier asked, following the path of Keplan's attention.

He lied for me. And if Rih's observation was correct, Firas had been at his bedside. Was it at Firas's urging that no one told him, or out of pity? Keplan heaved a sigh and turned back toward the palace. "Not tonight, no."

Φ

The 13th Day of Vurgmord, 1272
The City of Mirik

The path wound through the thick trunks of the red Mirikin trees. Bren tilted his head back to sniff the air. It was a beautiful morning. Orange backlit the boughs. Somewhere a stream trickled. He hiked upward, toward the center of the island, that sacred place, the navel of the world. A cold finger trailed down his spine and his steps quickened with the knowledge he had somewhere to be.

Rumbling grew behind him. His legs ached and he broke into a run. Rushing water turned into a roar. The hill became a cliff and he was scrambling up, up, palms torn by the rough brown rocks. When he hauled himself over the lip, his hands before him were sunken, wrinkled, and corded with tendons and veins. He shuddered, mesmerized and sickened at the new liver spots dotting his flesh.

Now he realized — he did not race toward something. He was running.

The Gate stood before him, the slab of black rock cracked, worn by rain and moss as he had left it years before. It was little more than a picnic spot, a meeting place for young lovers or thieves.

The sky glowed, the sun must have risen during his flight.

He staggered closer. The slab was not the Gate, instead it was a tombstone, broken, exposing the corpse beneath.

Bren's heart faltered at the familiar black hair. "Alea!"

Instead of pine and soil, sickly-sweet rot drifted on the wind. The brilliant glow through the trees was not dawn. It was an inferno.

He fell to his knees, scrabbling at the earth as if by freeing her it would make her less dead.

Her eyes flew open, silver blazing through black, rot and darkness marbling her skin. She screamed, lunging, and his world turned inside out.

Gasping, Bren flung himself from his bed and staggered down the hall to the ramparts. Sobs heaved his burning lungs. *Breathe,* he commanded himself. Stone bit into Bren's elbows where he leaned on the wall. Bitter air tugged at his sweat-drenched clothes, but even in the chill the air was sticky with salt and rank with the cloy of old cookfires. Below, the harbor sat empty. *How did it come to this?* His wife was leagues away, probably leaning on her ship's rail, staring at the stars on the sea. His Spy Master had all but resigned to fight a war he never foresaw. *And the only piece left of my sister is tethered to a throne I swore Keplan would never see.*

Overhead, clouds gathered. He watched them churn, stomach tight. The weather was wrong. Everything in his bones — the soldier, the reluctant sailor, even the superstitious — told him these were death throes of something mighty. Two decades before he had stood on the ramparts these replaced and watched the world mend. The islands half a dozen leagues away had rumbled and burst into being as his sister dissolved the barriers between worlds.

He still did not pretend to understand. The air smelled so fresh then. Vigor replaced withering. But now something had changed. Or rather, something had not. It was as if the blood flow had not crossed the boundaries, as if by pressing the fragments of the world together, their connection to life, or whatever it was that kept them all desperately clawing forward, had scarred over.

Atrophy.

"You miss her." Alleanthus propped himself on the wall with a soft sigh.

Bren lifted a shoulder in a shrug. He did not know which woman his son spoke of, and admitting that would be more telling than he cared for.

"She's reached the coast by now. Should be a bird any day now," Alleanthus continued.

Kemmer, then. "I suppose you're right. I hope the waters were kind. Storms are more common this time of year."

"Weather's been odd though. Never seen a winter so sullen."

Bren nodded. "I wish she would see my reasoning."

Al heaved a second, deeper sigh. "You know I don't agree with you, not wholly, on this."

"I know, I just—I have this nagging sense that something's coming. Something's wrong, I—" His words died and he peered against the night. A flicker against the clouds. Not lightning but fire. "There, did you see that?"

His son leaned forward, but fatigue, not curiosity, pinched his eyes. "I don't see anything."

"There!" Bren insisted. "The clouds."

"It's snow lightning," Alleanthus protested.

Apprehension tightened Bren's stomach. Despite the hot air, gooseflesh dimpled his arms beneath his shirt. "It's over Le'yne. I dreamt of her. It's why I woke. She was screaming, calling for me—"

"You've dreamt of her every month for as long as I can remember!" he lamented. "I remember Mother pulling you away from the ramparts countless nights. I found you asleep up here half a dozen times. How many times did you take a rowboat and go out there just to bob in the water, staring, until dawn?"

"Al, this is different—"

"How many times?"

Bren looked away.

Alleanthus straightened. "I'm going inside. I've a meeting with the Berrin ambassador tomorrow and I'm exhausted." He paused at the landing just below, jaw clenched. "Don't be a fool, Father. You've spent so much time in the past you've failed to notice the present."

Bren did not answer, and when he finally turned to look, his older son was gone. His focus swiveled back to the dark and distant island. He knew what he saw. Lightning flickered across the sky in cool white. This was fire, writhing through the clouds, winding like wind, like a bird.

Like Arman.

Distant rumbling drifted across the water with the scent of salt—not the fresh ocean smell from just off the harbor. This was something else, a deeper, older note, underscored by stone and fire. "Toar," he whispered. His knees creaked as he rushed down the stairs. He did not bother with a cloak, though he knew once out on the water he would regret the choice.

It took half an hour to navigate to their personal berth on the northern tip of the docks. Without the looming warships, his own schooner looked quite tall. He nodded to the guard and strode up the gangway. By now the guards and dockhands knew better than to ask, than to question. He ignored their pointed glances and set about casting off.

Regardless of his son's accusation, Bren had set foot on Le'yne only once before. Several years after his sister disappeared into the south, he slipped out to the island. There amidst black stone he hoped to find something, anything that might bring her back to him.

Wind hissed through the frozen grasses, gray against the black night. Bren let the boat bob for a moment, listening to the slapping waves against the lacquered wood before pushing the bow onto the gravel strand. The place felt entirely different this time. His boots hit the beach and he paused, listening for an echo, a welcome, perhaps. *I have to be mad to sail this far on a whim and a flicker of light.* His gut told him, though, that more than madness drove him across the waves. Some may have forgotten the oldest deities, those that came before the gods of his childhood. He had not.

"Alea?" His whisper was loud against that of the wind, and just as lonely. He dragged the boat higher before trudging up the narrow path in the ragged black cliffs.

Each bootfall tugged his mind backward into memories. Waving goodbye as Alea embarked for Athrolan. Finding her body on the strand. *Step.* Dancing with her, poorly, in the Athrolani palace. Hunkering under the tents at Fort Shadow, watching the rain. *Step.* Watching her rip lightning from the sky as they sailed across the Iron Sea. *Step.* Looking up at her eyes for the first time as he knelt before her in the woods. He swiped at his cheeks. Somehow, under the pressure of war, their two years together crystalized into something purer than most of his other relationships.

"It's not real!" Kemmer shouted at him. "The only reason why your adoration lasted this long is her absence makes her perfect! You don't have to compromise or get angry like you do with every other relationship. Your love for her replaced your faith in the gods and it's just as ignorant as it was then."

"Faith isn't ignorant!"

"Yours is!"

A stair crumbled beneath his boot and he caught himself on a ledge. Stone ripped the meat of his palm and he spat a curse. *Focus, you brute.* He picked the worst of the grit from the wound and hauled himself the last few paces to the clifftop.

Time ought to have softened the stones, coaxed grasses from the roads, weathered the wood to gray slivers. Le'yne had not changed. Despite the wind, the air was close, stale, as if the breeze circulated but never brought fresh air in. *It's how the rest of the world feels, too.* Strangled. Stagnant. He turned slowly in the central square. Thunderous energy threatened to pluck the taught string of his body.

It was not a human voice that growled through the night, but something bitter and full of change. "Evening, Harvest Pig."

Blood of a Hundred Queens

CHAPTER SEVENTEEN

The 13th Day of Vurgmord, 1272
The Isle of Le'yne

EVERY HAIR ON BREN'S graying head rose. His boots stilled their turning. Jaundice-gold eyes flickered in a shadow that once belonged to ruins. Then sickening darkness peeled from the black around it and formed familiar shoulders and ragged hair. "Arman?"

"Barrackborn." Coals bloomed with the breath in each word, then faded back into darkness. The air around them flickered with fire. "Wondered if you'd see us."

Us. "She's here too?"

Arman stepped into the square fully. Fire and stone etched the suggestion of a body, but more for the empty space where organs and bones ought to be than for any true corporeal form. With the crackle of firewood settling into embers, he jerked a nod to the hill beyond. "Much as I am."

Bren staggered up the hill, following the cluster of ashes and charred bone that left soot streaks but no footprints. He expected embraces. Remarks about how gray their hair had turned or the lines on their faces.

The hall loomed from the clotted clouds, silhouetted with the shuddering fire flitting through the air. He could not shake the sense that he did not walk behind Arman so much as through him. The hall door stood ajar, and a slick trail of oily water led inside.

The years had not been kind to the building. Mold and mildew's earthy rot clung to every corner, and the stench of low tide lingered in the air. Glowering fire licked at damp lichen, and hunks of peat and frozen grass clustered in the center of the hall. There was ferocity in the sacrilege of building a campfire in a temple. *I guess it's not sacrilege if the temple's yours.* He reached to pull his cloak tighter, belatedly remembering he had not brought one.

A moist heap of mildew and algae bubbled up and out until it took the shape of a hunched boneless back and naked scalp. Finding her took twenty years, but the slumped figure across the fire made him wonder if she was still lost to him.

He eased closer, crouching, then shuffling forward on his knees. The stone under his worn hands was achingly cold. His teeth chattered and hoar frost rimmed his watering eyes. He stopped his advance when his longest finger was a breath from the gleaming black claw sprouting from her mildewed bone. "Sistermine."

Her lidless eyes rolled up with a squelch. *Brentemir.*

His laugh tumbled across the inches between them until, dusty, it resembled a sob. "I looked for you."

I know.

Bren leaned forward, but as much as he longed to touch her, his animal self was repulsed, horrified. Drowning had always terrified him. Hundreds of questions flitted through his mind, but none seemed important anymore. How did you ask a titan gone to seed whether she was happy? How she passed the twenty years since they last spoke? Whether she had found peace? The answer to that last one crouched on the flagging before him.

"Why are you here?" It did not escape him that, after decades of searching, he only found her when she wanted him to. There was no sudden whim that would drag her back into his life. "Is it Keplan?"

Bone crunched and smoke billowed as Arman turned to him. "So you've seen him too, spoken with him?"

Is he all right?

Bren winced at the bellowing in his head between the avalanche and typhoon of their voices. "He's king of Athrolan, though I imagine you knew that."

"Raven told us."

Bren glanced up. "As in the former commander? When did you see him?"

"Before now," Arman answered, frowning. "Time is slippery, like our forms. But we were traveling from Neneviir and he saw our fire. Told us Keplan was king. That your plotting?"

"An'thor's," Bren countered. "I tried to keep him safe, off the throne. Alas, I'm realizing with my boys, too, that they've become their own people when I wasn't looking." *When I was looking for you.*

Boys? Something that tasted of longing dusted the air with snow.

"Two. Sons. Alleanthus and Azimir. Azimir's almost a year younger than Keplan, actually." Every conversation, every shared childhood milestone they never shared, pressed on the space between them. Bren's breath was thin and gasping.

Is he all right? Alea repeated.

How did you explain to a mother that her son was temperamental, married, and accused of murder? That he almost died at the hand of the priest devoted to his existence? *You let him do it like the coward you are.* "Did you come to get him?"

We came because the world is ending and where else do we go but here, where it began?

Bren shuddered at Arman's stone-rattle chuckle. "I imagine you've noticed."

Bren shrugged. "Mirik is at war. Athrolan almost was, twice. Those who aren't starving fear for their lives." He had rehearsed this reunion countless times, yet here he was, discussing politics like he sat opposite any other dignitary. He pounded on the stone with a frustrated rumble. "I'm not telling you news you could hear at any bar!"

The cold sharpened around him, frost turning to icicles. *If you think we could enter any bar and ask the news looking like we do, then these last year haven't been kind to your mind. What aren't you telling me?*

"This is ridiculous, acting like this is fine, like you aren't rotting before my eyes, like you still have bodies, like you're still the people who left twenty-one years before. Like I haven't spent my life praying I'll see you again only to find this! Pretending you'll board a ship and walk up to the palace gates of Athrolan to have tea with your maniac son."

What he could barely call Alea lunged at him. Cold erupted in his chest. Decay writhed in his nostrils and lungs. Lightning exploded in his eyes, dancing across the soft gray of his brain before flickering over his skin and retreating. His body shuddered with intimate condemnation.

Guilt clawed like vomit up his throat. His mouth was too busy screaming to apologize, but her fury lessened a fraction.

Stillness held Bren for a moment, an apology in itself. She was a starless sky, and he nothing.

It lasted seconds, surely, but when his vision cleared the fire was low, and neither of them were anywhere to be seen. His spirit was too weak from relief to gather the shards of his broken heart.

Φ

The 17th Day of Vurgmord, 1272
The City of Ceir Athrolan, Athrolan

Rih watched the guards take An'thor from the palace. His shoulders were slumped but his jaw clenched. Age-yellow hair blew away from his face. *Am I missing something, being so young?* How could one have lived so long and not see beauty in humanity's frailty and imperfection? The defiant line of An'thor's back, the certain one of Keplan's in the courtyard, showed her the faint steps the emperor must have taken.

Beyond the walls, a train of wagons rocked east. Two thousand soldiers were scattered across the Banis grasslands, hearts hammering with the same devotion and ferocity as hers. Looking out at Athrolan's harried king, she wondered at their similarities. There was beauty in the undiscerning violence of the king's actions.

Keplan turned and his stare settled on hers through the misted glass. He raised a hand. An'thor was jerked onto the street. Another twenty guards fell in around him, but Keplan's eyes remained on Rih.

She had moved to the orchid alcove when Azimir found her a few minutes later. "That was hard to watch," he began without greeting.

"I didn't know you were there."

Azimir shrugged. "Like you, I didn't brave the wind. Just watched from the stables. I'm honestly not certain how to feel." He paused. "Is this all right, my signing? If you'd rather call Bimet—"

She pressed a hand to his to still the nervous words. "This is fine. Just slowly and with confidence."

Azimir's cautious smile broadened. "I'll try that."

"What's making you feel uncertain?"

"An'thor. He put my name on an assassin's list. Simply because he thought I—or my father, more likely—would influence Keplan against him. Or perhaps temper the monstrosity he hoped Kep would become. But I was raised in the shadow of heroes, and one of them was him."

"I think I'd know how to feel. If someone sentenced me to a life of pain not from hatred, but from indifference."

He glanced up from her hands, eyes dark and soft. "I'm sorry you're here, when you hate it."

"I'm not. Out of all the ill fates, I chose this one. I love home and miss it deeply, but the way it looks now, it's a world where I don't fit. A child of so many things and none of them entire." A wave of grief swept over her, for Il-fald and for everything the woman had symbolized to Rih. *I don't fit here, either.*

"I understand that." When her brows raised in invitation, he continued, "My father—he's entrenched in history. Mostly because of his sister. Toar, there wasn't a month that he didn't bring it up or develop a new attempt to find her. Keplan distracted him, but now that he's on the throne it's almost worse, as if the Dhoah' Laen will drag Keplan off the throne like an errant market boy, and then we'll all be happy."

"He says it a lot—we'll be happy again. But I've been happy, and Al's been happy. And my ma, too. But I look at this world—Mirik, Athrolan, Ban, even—these mighty nations decaying from within, people lost and starving and dying and I don't understand how these men don't see it. They want to bring glory back? Well glory brought us here. I'm tired of glory. Of heroes. None of it's real. Not really. Not to the people who matter. The people left behind." His shoulders slumped with fatigue. "I'm rambling."

"You always ramble." Rih turned away, heart pounding. If he had reached into her mind and drawn out the threads of everything that drove her to start the rebellion, his words would not have been truer. She moved deeper into the alcove. Smoky glass shielded the lamps, and pools of water, heated until they steamed, humidified the air. *People in the city drink boiled seawater and here, orchids have steam baths.*

When she looked back, his dark brows were dipped in a frown.

"Did I say something to offend you? You look sad."

"Thoughtful," she explained. "Your words in this room speak to my heart. I miss Ban. I miss my sisters-in-arms. I miss my rude, arrogant cousin. I miss the bathhouses and the brilliant green of the thousands of gardens. I miss the smell and the heat. My heart aches because the very things I seek to save and protect might be destroyed."

His fingers traced a broad, waxy leaf before he signed. "Destroyed because of our parents' war?"

Aim. Breathe. She thought of Majilah Ag, of Il-fald, of every woman who gasped her last in Rih's arms, every starving child in Stytown. Bimet would say it was too soon, but the wheels of war churned ever on, and Rih would have to move or risk being crushed beneath them. "I fear they will be lost when my rebel army takes RoBal."

Azimir stared at the pool before them, lips motionless, hands still. His steady eyes told her he did not for a moment think she was joking. After the space of several breaths, he voiced, "The network across Ban is yours, then?" When she blinked at him in surprise, he smiled. "I was in the market, caught a couple signs that were unfamiliar. But I pieced enough together to learn that someone is trying to topple Ban. It's the benefit of everyone thinking I'm a yammering blockhead. They think I don't notice."

"It's my network, and I planted the seeds before I ever came here, before I knew about Keplan, when the marriage in question was to you."

"How many allies do you have?" His questions were not mocking, but cautiously curious.

"Majilah Ag, queen of the Vales, for one. And a few thousand of the Banis troops. My cousin Mosil, the Banis ambassador to Mirik." Her instincts burst to life and her hands stilled. Bimet would be furious.

"It would have been so much easier had we married." He looked at the orchids, expression distant. "There'd be no secrecy. I know you have no interest in sex or heirs, but all I want is to talk with you. To sit in silence when the light grows dim. To laugh and debate and stand side by side. It might be incredible hubris when you have no interest in the last god this world will ever see, but—"

"Are you asking me to marry you?"

"I don't think so." He raked a hand through his hair, and she could see him, decades from now, lounging in her study in RoBal, ranting about something inconsequential. "I wish to be useful to you. I wish to help you carry whatever load you'll have, whether you're a refugee or the Banis empress."

Blood thundered in her chest. "Is this an elaborate request to be my ally?"

He dropped to one knee. "An ally, surely. But your friend. Your champion. Whatever path you take won't be a life of peace. But you deserve it, after everything you've done and witnessed. And I find myself wanting nothing more than to give you that. And be beside you for the fleeting tranquility and the sea of blood."

A proposal was something she never thought to see and never particularly wanted. But here was a man, a clever one, one who made her laugh, asking if she kindly would consider him not as a husband, but as a partner. "I accept."

His tan face broke into a bright smile and he rose to embrace her. When he pulled away, though, concern once more laced his features. "Have you told Kep?"

"His entire platform is peace. Even if he's failed in that. He might have allied with Ban in a time of war, but he's pointedly remaining neutral. And he hates Ban. I still can't believe I told you."

"I wouldn't have told me at first either. Yammering blockhead, remember?" His grin faded. "He hates Ban, and when you're done with it, it won't look the same. I imagine he'll appreciate that."

"Azi, this entire movement, it's carefully orchestrated, every move calculated—"

"I won't tell anyone. Not unless you ask me to. I meant what I said about being your champion. Your friend."

"There is one thing." She drew a steadying breath and loosed her mental arrow. "I have an offer for your mother."

Φ

The 19th Day of Vurgmord, 1272

"There's something for you, sire." Hylier poked his head into the study. "From your priests."

Keplan glared, yanking the folded letter out of his captain's hand. "They aren't my anything. I doubt they'd even call themselves that."

Hylier snorted and sat uninvited in the chair.

The parchment was old, dingy, as if previous ink had been blotted out to make room for this message. No greeting, just a line.

She's asking for you.

Keplan's gut growled with dread. "I have to go."

Hylier heaved himself up and reached for his hat.

"Alone."

He frowned. "I don't care if you're the most terrifying thing on those streets. I'm not letting you walk into the Slummer all by your lonesome. I don't have to follow you in, but I'm going too."

It was too much of a hassle to argue, and frankly Keplan did not want to walk into a trap. *Who knows the city's opinion of what happened with Domariigo.* Still, something in the note nagged at him. It was as if the prophet's thoughts were so heavy, so strong, they flavored the paper beneath Mel's pen. He pulled on his jacket, more for comfort than warmth. "Just to the door."

Barkers shouted that the king would dismantle the government next, like Mirik. Others claimed he planned to make Azimir the next general. One argued the king was not innocent, but An'thor had taken the fall to protect him.

Keplan shuddered. Neither spoke as they walked, and he wondered if Hylier felt whatever it was that tainted the letter. Maybe the man had lived a life so full of joy that he did not recognize despair. *Has anyone?*

Mel greeted them again, but this time no drinks awaited. Cheekbones were crags on his sallow face. "That was quick."

Keplan did not answer, just shot Hylier a glance that commanded solitude, and pushed into the room. It was much the same, though there were a few new blankets.

"Hela." Her name sprang unbidden from his lips.

"Gods' Blood."

"Mel said you asked for me." He knelt beside her, reaching.

"A painful life doesn't leave much in the way for kindness, eh? Just look at yourself." One thin hand ran up his own weakened arm.

"The symbolism is a bit heavy. Even for someone as melodramatic as me."

Chipped brown teeth punctuated her smile. She pushed herself up, entire form trembling. Keplan knew better than to help. She settled finally, a few inches higher than before. "There. Do you remember what I told you?"

"About returning the power to the world? I recite it every evening before bed," he whispered. "Not really, not aloud. But I remember."

She shook her head. "What I tried to tell you through Nena'phe. Through Mel, though he's bad at making friends. What I hauled my withered self all the way here to get you to hear."

Keplan sat back. "You went to war over it, which I disagree with."

"They may have gotten carried away, but the world is listening to you now. They think you have a plan. All those pretty dreams in your head," she tapped his temple, "you can let them out now. And they will listen."

"I've never liked scripture." She beckoned, and, with a scowl, he began. "The One True God will rise where the worlds meet, from death and birth, from chaos and order. His blood pools, drowning the world even as it gives it life. Though he will bear the marks of hate, he will be unable to raise its tools. Then the bit about mercy and hands and wrath."

"But there's more. You never let them finish. 'He will cast aside mortality once when death is chosen for him, once when death is begged of him, and once when he chooses death for himself.' She will wither and die without blood. Blood that began you, began us."

"My parents. And you. And me." Certainty slid into his chest and he drew a ragged breath. "We have to end."

"Oblivion."

"Why ask me? Why when you could simply step from a bridge, from the harbor gates, or find a knife, a rope. There are a hundred ways to end your life, if you wished. I know. I've thought of them all in the small hours of the night."

She looked away, then her pale, bulging eyes met his. "There's one last thing. You came to me weeks ago seeking answers. And I gave you what you asked for, if not what you wanted. Now I've had time to think. Time to judge you further. I see what you're doing. You mean to bring peace. Like your errant general begged of you — you will rip it from the world."

"If I have to."

"You wouldn't plan for the future if you were meant to let the world wither."

He smiled. "No."

"How do you hear thoughts best? Touch?"

"It helps with objects. Never tried it much with people. The few I've touched have been in passion — romantic or otherwise."

"Killing, you mean."

"Yes."

"Words don't do it justice, words you won't believe. You have to see it. There are echoes of the Laen's power still in me. I'm offering you the answer you seek about what comes after. What you are. But in return I want you to take my life." He barely felt her paper skin as she pressed her brittle hand to his limp one.

Images exploded in his mind. Everywhere. Everywhen. Life surged in him. Blood burst from the riverbeds, overflowing, hot and rich and healthy. Millions of birdsongs rang in his head, thoughts racing and plunging and full of the frantic madness of simply living. His body flushed and hardened with the vitality of an entire world.

Her fingers clenched, and he spiraled inward, through their skin and wound into the lace of her capillaries. What did his mother's look like? There, in the center, was a silver seed, pulsing with her heart, a forgotten embryo of power. *Ma pulled the souls from the gods.* Hela did not deserve that. No one did. Instead, Keplan tugged the seed. It loosened, tendrils gripping her soul for a moment before loosening further. He tucked it into the weakened flesh of his mental palm, blazing emerald in his mind's eyes.

The sensation of tendons and trachea beneath his grip flashed, but he pushed it away. *Mercy.*

When he opened his eyes, her head was cradled in his lap. Her breath was faint but there. He might not be able to save himself or his parents, so entangled with their titanic power, but he would permit himself this one tiny mercy.

He rose and slipped out before she woke. Mel glowered at him as he shut the door quietly. "She's asleep, thank you."

The Nenev returned to cleaning the barrel of his dismantled revolver. "I want to thank you."

"For?" Keplan asked.

"Seeing my uncle for the monster he really is. Not many look past the shiny legends."

Keplan snorted. *I just recognized myself in him and acted accordingly.* "I guess legends never impressed me all that much."

"Well, whatever the reason, thank you." He spun the revolver's barrel. "I don't expect we'll be seeing much of each other after all this comes crashing down. One way or another."

"No, I don't imagine so." Keplan stuck out his hand on impulse. It did not matter that the man was a fanatic, that he pulled the trigger that cost Keplan his arm. "Luck and love go with you."

Mel's grin was crooked as he took the hand. "You too, God's Blood."

It was only when they were out of the Slummer that Hylier asked, "What did she need?"

Peace. "There's such power that once belonged to the world—my parents'. Mine. Hers. And I'm the one who returns it."

"She returned her Laen powers to you?"

"Not me exactly." Keplan glanced at his hand. He wondered if his flesh looked any different inside, where energy still buzzed. "I'm just carrying them for a while. Safe keeping, you might say. Until the end."

Hylier looked away. "I thought that wasn't going to become a habit."

Keplan stopped, colorless eyes fixing on the captain. "I didn't kill her. She asked me to. It would have been a mercy. But they aren't the same, not by a longbow shot."

"I suppose there's a difference between mercy and murder, in the end."

Keplan's blood hummed, and his skin still flamed with hope. "Just depends on the hand you use."

Φ

The 23rd Day of Vurgmord, 1272

Rih adjusted her new hat and shifted in the saddle. It was not often that she rode, but like every Banis child, she grew up on the back of a riah. Ahead, Azimir bounced along on his cob, trying in vain to have a conversation with Bimet.

Keplan's letters had been unexpected, but the request even more so. *Please meet me at the Tomb of Madness to the south of the city. Noon.* Other than the incident with the dog, she had yet to be outside the walls. The trees pressed in, spindly white trunks like bones jutting from the earth. Even with the bright sun, winter was unwilling to relinquish its hold. At least the soft wool was warm, if a little itchy. Her eyes settled on Bimet. Since their time in RoBal, the woman had changed. Withdrawal into reservations and fear. Rih shared her fears, but somehow Bimet could no longer see the way through them.

Another twist in the road and they emerged on the bare hilltop. Blackened trunks ringed the weathered stone of the monument.

Keplan perched on the top, legs crossed, looking out at the city below. His face was as thin as ever, but there was a light in his eyes she had not seen before. He was smiling. "Morning, Your Highness."

Bimet turned quickly, dropping her horse's reins to translate.

Rih responded before slipping off and tying her mount to a tree. She climbed the rest of the way on foot, pausing at the base of the monument. "Is there room for all of us or are you coming down?"

Keplan dropped, landing clumsily. He settled himself at the base in the same fashion, waiting to say more until both she and Azimir sat alongside him. "I'm sorry for the odd request. I just couldn't think down there anymore. And I knew I needed my wits for this."

Azimir nudged her knee with his. "Go on," he signed.

Bimet caught her eye and shook her head. The woman's lips thinned with displeasure. "Not yet."

Keplan looked between the signs. "Would someone enlighten me?"

"There's been a lot of turmoil lately. But I had a favor to ask of you. As your ally." She swallowed. "As your wife."

"Does this have to do with the missing fireshells?"

Fear pulsed up Rih's spine and she dared not look at Bimet. He was just testing. There was no way he knew. Rih did not move. Not even an eyelid flickered. Her long fingers curled, twisted, then tapped her temple, her lips. "I don't know what you mean."

"Over a hundred are missing and my personal guard noticed several Banis textile workers removing chests from both your rooms and those of Bimet." He placed his red hand over his green, the image of patience. "No one carries bolts of cloth or last year's summer dresses that carefully, Rih. I'm at a bit of a loss—my wife is stealing weapons from me. Orchestrating a rebellion. Might be bedding my cousin while I'm not looking."

Despair sank in her gut, and she fought the urge to shut her eyes and end the conversation. The distant contempt she felt for An'thor, all his plotting laid bare as he was hauled from the palace, now turned on her.

There was no point in pretending anymore. She was a soldier, a warrior. She knew when a new battlefield dictated a change in tactics. "All I knew was you had powerful parents and were seventeen. I gambled on a foolish child king. I thought the isolation here would make me invisible. If nothing else, I thought I might be able to seduce you into my cause. Enough to turn the bloody tides in my favor."

"Keplan, listen to her." Azimir leaned forward, finally interjecting. "We came to ask you to help. She means to topple Ban. And she already has the Vales."

"I'm not bedding Azi," she retorted. "But he swore fealty to my cause. I penned a letter asking his mother's support just two days ago."

Bimet's fingers were hard on her wrist. "You did what?"

Rih turned to her interpreter. "I know you've cautioned me to be careful, not to trust, not to move too quickly, but Bimet, if I don't move, we'll be trapped here forever."

She felt Bimet's gaze on her, but she met Keplan's overlarge colorless eyes. "Half your moves are a disaster, an unplanned but necessary dismantling. I see it because I'm weaving the same thing for my own people. You don't have a general—give me half that power, a quarter, and I'll win every battle Athrolan faces, just let me help my people. Fates!" She waved her arms. "You tolerated Domariigo for far too long, and I can promise I'd make a better general than a drunk murderer."

"Do you know why I asked you here?"

She shook her head.

"Athrolan is too bogged in tradition. It's killing her just as much as my blood is killing the world. I think I'm ready to be done with traditions entirely." His ice-chip eyes flicked to Rih's dark gaze and he lifted his chin. "What happens when you reach RoBal? If you win?"

She had yet to see the vicious and terrified boy she married. It was as if he died on the battlefield, leaving Keplan behind.

"When," she corrected, the sign gentle. "We will win."

"What happens to the Emerald Throne?"

She frowned. "I've brought us this far. I'll see it through."

"In my infinite hubris I thought I was the only one who could fix this mess. I was wrong. My parents' mess is mine, but this one? This is all on Athrolan." His face was unreadable, eyes distant glaciers in the snowfield of his face. "There's another battle coming, one humans can't fight. Like you, I know it's one I can win. But there will be nothing left of me."

Azimir blanched. "You don't know that. You can't. Your father lived through two deaths already—"

"And so did I. Apparently we get three."

Rih set that information aside to ponder later. "That leaves Athrolan without a king. Again."

"I'm not what Athrolan needs. She doesn't need a god on a throne, casting mercy and wrath in turns until the world topples. You saved us from the Swordbearers. From war with Ban. It wasn't my faith, my choice. It was your strength. Your planning. You allied with Mirik when His Eminence couldn't. I brought as much violence to the throne as I did peace. There's a world I can see so brilliantly in my mind."

Tears trickled down his cheeks, pausing in the hollows of his scars. "The plains are golden with grain. Not Banis grain, but not Athrolani. The ocean is filled with fish, clear and dark and treacherous. The Berme's Eye is filled with fishes and kelp. Marshes overflow with life. Writhing with abundance. Of course, there's pain—you can't have life without pain—but it's just the usual ache of existence. Not this clamor, this scrabbling. I can feel the air on my face. The whole world, it teems."

Beside her, Azimir squeezed her hand.

"Is it memory or the future?"

"It's not a memory." Keplan repeated the second sign. "What's that one?"

She did it again. "It's our word for fate, or future. It's closer to the meaning for promise."

"It's a promise." Keplan smiled. "Is fifty thousand enough?"

"Pardon?"

"The entire Athrolani army. The navy too—that's another twenty thousand." He slipped the signet ring from his hand gently and offered it to her. "Take my throne instead of my hand, and wreak fire over every man who ever spilt blood that wasn't his own."

Disbelief swirled in her chest, billowing her heart almost like hope. *He can't be serious.* She did not trust him, but perhaps together, they could carve a suitable world from this dying, poisoned thing. Beside her, Bimet's pinched face paled with resigned horror. "Unite them under one crown, under one woman's rule, one woman's strength."

"You've thought about this," Azimir whispered to her.

"When you appeared on the road that day, begging for help. I know there's a line of heirs, but in that moment it was only us. I knew if Keplan died someone would be forced to wrestle the reins from General Domariigo." Her entire body trembled. Ban was one thing. This was something else entirely.

"You've proven you know what you're doing, certainly more than I have. You see the same future as I do. And you've already begun carving a path. What do you say?"

The ring was cold in her hand, even after resting in his palm. She ran a thumb over the sigil. *Dream bigger.* "I swear to honor her, as long as I reign."

CHAPTER EIGHTEEN

The 23rd Day of Vurgmord, 1272
The City of Ceir Athrolan, Athrolan

KEPLAN'S NEXT WORDS DROWNED in screaming. Beneath them, the ground shook. Every shudder released something in him, a popped joint no longer stiff with disuse.

Loose pebbles jittered across the exposed bedrock. He pressed his hand to it. Magma surged far below, pulsed in an approaching rhythm.

"What is it?" Azimir asked. His blocky hand rubbed at the back of his own neck. Did his muscles feel the tension in the earth? Rih looked between them in concern.

"Someone's screaming." Keplan looked to Rih and tapped his temple. "In here. It just goes on and on."

Trembling came again, stronger. Trees quaked on the surrounding hillside. Dead leaves and seedpods shook from their anchors. To the east, clouds clotted the sky.

The uncertain feeling when he glimpsed a mirror was nothing compared to the uneasiness in his shoulders. Lightning crackled through the black thunderheads and they billowed higher. *Thud.*

"All right, that I heard." Azimir hauled himself up, dropping his weight as if he stood on a ship's deck. He offered Bimet's reins to her, but the translator spat at his feet, jerking the leather from his hands. She did not sign her hissed words, nor could Keplan hear them, but he caught enough to know it was a curse.

Rih's hand was hard on his arm. Her fingers moved rapidly but calmly.

Azimir glanced over, shouting the translation from the tree line. "She said there's more to discuss, we ought to keep this to ourselves for the time being."

Keplan nodded. A roar went up and they all ducked. Gouts of flame lit the roiling clouds from within.

"Toar, what is this? An attack?"

Uneasiness was replaced with certainty, with longing, with a thunderous need to protect. Keplan grimaced. Those were not his feelings, but he knew them. They formed the lace inside his bones, the salt in his blood. "These are the heroes everyone prayed for."

Keplan flung himself onto Theriim's back, grateful he took An'thor's horse that morning. His knees pressed and the charger took off, scattering fallen gold leaves and dry soil as they pelted down the hillside. He bent lower, red hand fisted in the gray's mane. A scan of the aqueducts told him nothing had fallen yet, no towers were toppled.

By the time they burst from the trees and onto the swath of fields surrounding the city, ice crystals filled the bitter air. Another man might think this was judgement, dealt for his disregard of tradition, his condemnation of An'thor, or any number of terrible choices. Salt hung in the air, rank, as if low tide had exposed the decades of sludge and navy trash at the bed of the harbor. On the tail of it came the scent of burned flesh, dead earth. The cloy of scorched hair. Keplan's stomach roiled and he clenched his teeth against a surge of bile. *Thud.*

It was not his voice screaming, he realized. But a voice he knew intimately, a voice that sat in his head more often than not. One that murmured lullabies off-tune when he could not sleep.

Air whipped without any proper direction, uncertain and anxious. Atop the city walls soldiers attempted to wrest rusted weapons from their sheaths. Keplan dragged Theriim's head about. Black oily smoke wound from the eastern tree line, where the road disappeared between twisted boles. Putrid water trickled up from between the road's cobbles, from beneath the palace foundation.

"Something's in the trees!" The cry arched from the ramparts and soldiers massed above. Torches appeared, and arrows were lit. Hylier's bright hair gleamed as he shouted orders. Metal screamed, new rust raining across the cobblestones as the gate groaned shut. Guards milled, faces pinched in fear, eyes vacant. *What's wrong with them?*

"Stop!" Keplan drove Theriim toward the east gate, but no one seemed to hear.

Azimir's cob thundered up beside him. The young man's face was streaked with sweat and his cheeks were bloodless. "Kep, turn back!" A wet splat heralded his cousin losing his lunch.

"It's not an attack!" he insisted.

Azimir wheeled back, motioning for Rih to follow him toward the gates. A Banis whistle sounded. Azimir's voice cut over the clamor, translating as they thundered toward the city. "Open the gates!"

Frustration knotted Keplan's stomach. His bones knew. His blood answered. Through the stench of rot and creosote he caught the comfort of his childhood hearth and his father's cooking. Two figures appeared on the road. Theriim shrieked, shying from them. *Thud.*

The journey from Neneviir on horseback would have taken months, but they did not ride. With each step the man's feet turned to stone, then back to blackened flesh. Every step sent convulsions through the earth. *Thud.* Infection raged where his sallow skin was not burned. Cold cracked stone covered the hand knotted with hers.

Black lines radiated across Alea's frozen skin. Long hair hung lank over her abraded scalp. Horror twisted Keplan's gut, but not because of what he saw approaching. Leastwise, not out of disgust.

"It's not an attack," Keplan whispered, though no one could hear over the moaning wind. It whipped around the figures, ripping features from them as water vapor and smoke, replacing them a second later. He tumbled from Theriim's bucking back and staggered forward on foot.

Keplan met them on the outskirts of the cemetery. His father's too-hot hand gripped the king's limp left wrist, thumb rubbing a circle like it had when he could not sleep as a child. He fell into Alea's arms, heedless of the sickening softness of her body or the magma burbling in the cracks on his father's hand. Saltwater dampened his jacket where his mother's face pressed into his shoulder. Whatever battered organ still served as his heart shuddered and broke. *Ma.*

Φ

The Northern Banis Coast

Ajat wiped sweat from her face. The air was cool, still damp with rain, but the march strained her joints. Fifty years was a bit old for marching, in her mind.

Her eyes bored into Sefer's back. Betrayal did not bother her. Not from an emotional standpoint, at least. Only logistically. *So did Kemmer put a strike on me, or was it Bren?* Either was likely, but for entirely different reasons. Kemmer concerned her more.

They crested a hill and turned west. The Banis coast dropped away to the north, rolling dunes dotted with reeds and flushed with color. She raised her nose and breathed the rich salt. She had missed the ocean.

Beyond, backed by the clouds that would bring that afternoon's rain, was the Mirikin fleet. The few ships made decades before against Berrin attack now numbered several hundred. She squinted, but the haze concealed which bore the brilliant vermillion pennant of the Hetmir.

Noticing her steps had slowed, Oland glanced back at her, brows knit. "You all right?"

She scowled and did not answer, but picked up the pace.

He dropped back to ride beside her. "It's not personal. Promise. Just a job."

She added a bit more venom to her glare. "You torched my cousin's village and crushed her husband's skull to find me. You might not consider it personal, but I will."

"I still enjoyed our time together, our nights—"

"I'd stop, unless you want vomit on your horse's pretty hooves." She spat a dusty glob onto the ground to punctuate her words.

He opened his mouth, then shut it and nudged his horse back into place. Ahead, Oland let out a whistle, and they cut north along a packed trail through the dunes. Below, pulled onto the strand, sat a rowboat.

A plain canvas tent stood beside it, undyed to blend into the white sand.

There's the orange flag. Ajat fixed her hard gaze on the fluttering strip of fabric that denoted who, exactly, waited for her. Sand hissed from around her boots, and the ropes around her wrists bit at her skin when she stumbled over the soft ground. The other handful of prisoners fell into a narrow line as they wound through the dunes.

"For the Hetmir!" Oland called.

"For freedom!" The answer went up from the guards ranging around the tent. A canopy was strung over the tent's entrance, a small cookfire built just outside. A stringy hare was stretched on a spit, fat and juices sizzling onto the tired coals.

Ajat rolled her eyes. She never understood armies. Comradery was one thing, but trusting someone and holding them above others simply for their rank in a fabricated hierarchy would never be logical. They stopped under the awning and she relaxed in the momentary shade. The hot breath of Banis summer was fast approaching. Even the flowers knew it, beginning to crisp under the sun. Another month and the rains would be gone altogether.

Sefer emerged from the tent and beckoned to Ajat before following her inside.

A single low lamp sat on a large camp desk. Fishing nets covered the tent's windows, woven loose enough to permit light and air. The Mirikin Hetmir herself sat at the desk, strong features gripped in concentration as she scanned her maps. Her gray-laced auburn hair was raked into a tight knot at the back of her neck.

She glanced up, then turned to look at her prisoner fully. "Reka, I'm glad to see the Banis wilderness didn't swallow you entirely." Her eyes lingered on the new details of the tattoo. "Took us a fair while to find you."

"Ajat, Ser," Sefer interjected.

"Excuse me?"

"Her name's Ajat. She had a ceremony—"

Kemmer waved his words into silence. "Regardless, you found her."

"Did you come looking for me yourself, or did Bren send you after I told him where to shove his elitist ideals."

Kemmer's gray brows arched and she leaned back. Her sharp lips pursed. "You referring to his opposition of our war?"

"Some causes are worth fighting for," Ajat insisted. "I think he's been locked in your precious tower for a bit too long to remember that, though."

Kemmer heaved a sigh, rubbing her forehead. "You're right, of course. I scarcely recognize the man he's become."

Ajat allowed herself a moment of empathy and a smile. "I miss him too. Who he used to be."

Kemmer glanced up, as if recalling that she had an audience. "So what made you defect?"

"I didn't defect. You're fighting Ban and I'm simply seeking a way to protect the people most at risk of dying needlessly. You know Oland killed my cousin's husband? A man more suited to tracking and laughing with his children than war? I thought you were freeing these people, not making them victims of your bloodlust."

Kemmer did not meet her eyes. "That's regrettable. I'll speak with her. That does not change the fact that you disappeared from all contact, assumed another identity, and began trading Mirikin intelligence with some straw-made movement. I can't overlook the fact that you essentially committed treason, Reka."

She surged to her feet, hands pounding on the folding desk, heedless of the ink and pencil she smudged. "My name is Rekajat Monre. I am cousin to Ikel and ally to Kahma, soldier in the Fifth Arc. Close to three thousand soldiers is not a whim, Kemmer. I am here in Ban not to stop your war, but to topple the Banis empire. If you took a moment to actually listen to me, you'd see our goals aren't in opposition at all!"

Kemmer sat back, long arms folding over her narrow chest. A smile quirked on her face after a moment of silence. "Ajat." One hand rose, opened. "I'm glad we agree."

Ajat stepped back, frowning. "What?"

"I wanted to be sure. While you've always worked for Bren, I know you've often struck out on your own. Had your own agenda. I just wasn't certain what it was this time."

"So you know about the rebellion brewing in Ban?" Skepticism cooled the relief, but she could not help her shoulders dropping from their guarded position.

Kemmer lifted a scroll from a pile at the desk's corner. "I received this a few days ago. I had heard rumors, both from Banis prisoners and from my own agents, like Sefer. But we had to be sure. Such information is dangerous in the wrong hands and can't be unspoken."

Ajat stared at the scroll. "May I?"

"Please."

> *Hetmir Kemmer A'hane*
>
> *It may strike you as odd to receive a letter from the wife of the Athrolani king, but I hope you share your son's patience. We have not met in person, but let this serve as introduction. I am Rih-elte, Kajimet of Ban, and wife of His Majesty Keplan Wardyn.*
>
> *I write to you with a proposition. You seek to topple Ban, to end the slavery and inequality upon which the*

empire has been built. So do I. Over the past year, I have developed a network across my country and extending into Athrolan herself as well. A network of soldiers, of women and our allies, who wish for liberty.

I am lucky to count among my allies Majilah Ag of the Vales, Ambassador Mosil-ten Ebal, a man I know you've dealt with often in the past. And, of course, your own son, Azimir. Truthfully, I now count him among my dearest friends.

Ajat's brows rose. She did not know Azimir well. No better than any distant aunt. But it struck her that the impulsive, optimistic boy had struck such an alliance with the woman who might be the next Banis empress. She scanned the closing remarks and returned the scroll to Kemmer's hand. "Azimir's growing up."

"He takes after you, it seems," Kemmer grinned, rising to her full two-pace height. "I always hoped one of them would."

Ajat grimaced. "Did you respond?"

"I did. And this morning a bird came from Athrolan. An'thoriend has been arrested for murders. As in, more than one."

The bottom dropped from Ajat's gut. She did not particularly like the man, but he was an incredible warrior, and she admired his independence. *I'm not the only one who often had their own agenda, apparently.* "I think Keplan well and truly lost his mind."

Kemmer shook her head. "None of his decisions seem to make any rational sense, I agree, but I just hope he sees some larger picture. God and all."

"Gods are dead." Ajat heard the lie in her voice even as she spoke. She felt something that night, as Ikel carved her skin, as who she had been was stripped away, replaced by the fresh flesh of something entirely new.

"Well, one isn't," Kemmer argued. "His temple is erected in Mirik already, just beside his mother's."

"So who's Athrolan's general now?"

Kemmer's grin was wolfish. "Message bird came from Azi yesterday. Made no mention of a general, but it sounds as if your rebel leader has temporary command. Twenty-eight hundred soldiers aren't much against the Banis army, but fifty thousand will be."

Ajat drew a long breath. "It'll be soon, then. There's no way the emperor won't piece this together now."

"I said as much in my letter. We await her move. And her ally, Majilah Ag, should arrive with the last rains to treat with me. Can I count you among us?"

"Always."

Their strong arms locked around one another, Kemmer's dry lips brushing Ajat's cheek. "Welcome home, Ajat Monre."

Φ

The City of Ceir Athrolan, Athrolan

Ice covered the windows. Across the suite the hearthfire blazed. Keplan eased into the room, delicate boots sliding on the sheer ice glazing the stones. The door clicked shut behind him. "Ma? Da? It's me."

Light bloomed through the doorway as he stepped into the parlor. The hulking shape hunched in the hearth raised its hand in greeting.

The privy door was shoved open by a wave of cold seawater.

"I'm sorry it took me so long—the army's been a mess since An'thor—" He stopped himself. "I guess we all ought to start at the beginning."

"*Your face,*" Alea's voice crackled through his head.

He frowned, one arm brushing his cheek as if to whisk away crumbs. "I always get jam—" Sorrow lurched in his stomach. "Oh. I don't know where to begin. I was mistaken for a Mirikin spy. Something about the nose, I guess." His smile flashed.

Alea's waterlogged bones and cartilage flickered into the echo of her own strong nose. *From Azirik. "I'm so sorry."*

"It doesn't matter." Keplan's body dragged with exhaustion, but there was something else. Finality. A relief of his own. "You're here. This world might end. Or not. And it's up to me."

"*We left, searching for answers too, you know. We didn't have them all.*"

"I wondered. I saw you once in a dream, I think, but a true one. There was snow."

"*Neneviir. We went in search of a woman.*"

Keplan wished they had faces he could memorize as they spoke, wished for a moment they were simply his parents, the way he recalled them, and not fathomless titans. Perhaps, like them, he said goodbye to that in the woods a year before.

"*What about your arm?*" Alea's low voice pressed into his skull, trickling like she did through stones.

He scowled. "The priests you chased here— Swordbearers. One of them carried a revolver like An'thor's. Shot me when I wouldn't let them erect temples to myself on every corner."

Arman's laugh crackled through the room. "Fools. Religious folk always have been." Water splashed at his coals and steam hissed through the room. "Honest, Alea!"

"You went east and north—what were you hunting?"

"You, at first, and then Alea's vision kept getting worse. We knew it was connected to your power or what you might be. Ended up just leading back here the long way around." Bones settled like logs as he shrugged. "I saw Neneviir though. Fascinating, that."

"Did you find any answers?"

"Some. Mostly where we had to go next. Then we found Raven in the Northlands — you sent him to an icy exile. He told us you were king and we knew we had to come back."

"I'm sorry," Keplan whispered. "I know you didn't want this for me."

"It was foolish. My fault."

Arman's flaming skull turned to the oily puddle. "We both chose to keep him ignorant. Of us. Of what he is."

Keplan waved the impending argument away. There was so little time now, it seemed. It should not be wasted on faults or regret. Whatever choices had brought them all here, back to this palace on these cliffs, were long past. "Whatever I am, my existence is an infection. I had those dreams too. Visions. Violence. My blood choking the world."

"Did the prophet tell you why?"

He nodded, settled onto a chair by his father's warmth. "You joined the world but left scar tissue, almost. Perhaps when you brought Da back. But so much of the world's power is caught up in your life forces that without it, the world is suffocating. And I'm the clot, the pinched artery. We're caught in this place like a sheep's tail bound until it withers and drops. She said once I return your power, life will flourish again. She showed me." He smiled, reaching a hand out. "It's beautiful. Do you want to see?"

Water trickled upwards, lit from within by tiny blooms of lightning. It engulfed his hand, freezing and tickling with energy. A stone grip pressed to his limp hand. He closed his eyes and brought the images to the fore.

"Surely dying isn't the answer," Arman murmured when the vision faded from their minds. "Surely you can just act as a conduit. Step out of the doorway."

"The prophet said I have three deaths. This would be the last one. Both times something dragged me back from the brink." He had not let himself dwell on it.

Alea's cold ghosted his arms with a mother's worry. *"Both? My baby, no."* Saltwater beaded on his scarred cheeks.

"After the battle, with my shoulder. And in RoBal. Before I knew, before I ever came here. Interrogation."

The fire raged, sparks scattering across the floor. "Son —
"

"It's over," Keplan promised. "I'm here. I made it here. And I did find happiness for a while. Peace."

"That's all we wanted for you. Peace and happiness and a long, simple life."

Heartache pierced Keplan's smile. "I still dream about it. The low common room at night when the last patron is gone and the fire is low. When the music still drifts in the golden night air and Firas, as exhausted as he is giddy, dances to it. And, in the ways that dreams are timeless, Mirrel's there too. Upstairs or in the kitchen come morning. But there."

"Who's Mirrel?" Arman asked.

Keplan blinked and sat back. Of course, they did not know. "Mirrel, she's — she was — my friend. I suppose."

"A lover?" Alea's form uncurled further at the word.

"More like a sister. When I hear or read about siblings, I think of her. Her brother though—I loved him. Love him still. They owned a bar in the city. It's a small place in the slums, but old, with exquisite carvings on the pillars. I left there after I learned about the throne, but..." He shrugged, then trailed off. He wondered how similar the Hare was to his grandmother's Cockerel.

"It's still home," Arman finished.

"What happened? You speak as if they're gone."

"Mirrel's dead," he stated, but the downcast of his eyes and the softness in his face told her his tone was gentle. "Just after I was crowned. She was murdered. Murdered because I am king."

"And this man—Firas?" Alea faltered. *"Did he love you back?"*

"I think he started to. Wanted to. Their father guarded you, Ma." He looked up, finding the brightest clusters of lightning. "He died guarding you in the final battle. Smythesen."

"Kal Smythesen," Arman rasped. "A friend. He told us his wife was pregnant again just before we rode out."

"Well, that's Firas." Keplan shifted. He thought this would feel odd, but it was simply a relief. Perhaps discussing his romance would have been more awkward had his parents been corporeal. "Someone should tell him."

Alea shuddered. "We don't know you'll die, love. You may yet live."

"When are we going to do this? And where?" How was not a question he was ready for.

"We're in a place beyond time, I think," Arman explained.

"Everywhen," Keplan agreed. "I've seen it. Been there. It's the in-between place. Between here and oblivion."

"When is up to you," Arman promised. "Where I think we know."

Keplan looked up. Chills raced up his body, but it had nothing to do with the power rolling off Alea. "Gods' Blood. Their isle. Beside Le'yne."

"I imagine there are kingly duties you ought to see to." Alea's voice tasted bitter.

"A few. I relinquished the throne yesterday, actually. Just before you arrived. My wife — a political marriage — is the Banis Kajimet. She'll take the throne. And be good at it." He was too tired to explain her rebellion, the details, the thousand intricacies between their parallel lives. "Tell me about the journey. What did you see? And Daymir — what did he say when he first saw you? He's regent, actually."

Arman's chuckle rolled smoke through the room. They spoke long into the night, Keplan perched in the perfect temperature between them, laughing, gasping at all the right moments. After all their months apart, this was the fireside story he missed the most.

Hours later, with the moon setting and dawn closer than dusk, he returned to his rooms. Hylier dozed on the couch in the parlor, and Keplan slipped past to his study.

"How're you doing?"

For a moment Keplan did not recognize Hylier's sleep-scratched voice. "I didn't want to wake you."

"I'd be a terrible guard if I slept through someone sneaking into your rooms."

"You'd be a terrible guard if you fell asleep on duty."

"I'm not on duty," he grumbled, sitting up with a theatrical stretch.

"I know." Keplan's grin faded. "I'm all right, I suppose. Tired. Too much energy."

"And your, ah, parents?"

"I'm not sure. It's hard, I imagine, to find your child has become everything you feared they would. But I think they both realize I always would have. Even if I had stayed. I'm just grateful I lived a bit before."

"Returning the power, you think you won't—"

"I'm tired," Keplan reiterated. "I'm looking forward to sleep."

Hylier did not ask whether the king referred to now or to death. He just rose. "Letter came for you, sire."

Exhaustion dragged at his shoulders, but Keplan shook his head. "If it's more hate, I'll toss it in my glass and drink it down with a splash of wraith. I've given up caring."

"And with that, on the 23rd day of Vurgmord, 1272, a true king was born," Hylier drawled. "I'm going to head home. I'll be here tomorrow. For whatever happens. You know, as chaotic as your reign has been, I see hope in it. And we need that."

Keplan's smile faded as soon as the door shut behind the guard. He lit the lamp by his desk, extinguishing the others until he was cocooned in a ball of light.

Someone—Hylier probably—had laid the cease-fire with the Swordbearers, still unsigned, on the desk beside Mirik's latest missives. Already his eyes ached and if he never read through another doctrine, another missive, another list of supplies, he would die happily. A new envelope perched atop the mound of disregarded duties.

It was plain and stamped with the mark of several runners as well as the Dockyard Postal Guild. The handwriting wasn't any Keplan recognized but lacked the uniform loops and curves of a trained scribe. It almost looked like a youth's. The seal was the cheap colorless wax they sold in beads at most markets and post-houses. It snapped open beneath his fingers.

Lan, I'm sorry we haven't spoken.

Keplan's heart thundered into painful waking. He almost did not dare read further. *I need air.* He slipped from his study, from the bubble of bright orange light, and to his bedroom's balcony. The paper, still acrid from being pressed a few days before, hummed in his pocket.

His hand hovered over the letter, but he forced it away. The longer he waited, the longer he could pretend it was written in love. Written with the tenderness the man's hands had held all those months before. *A year,* he realized. *It's been a year.* Did Firas know, too? Did he count the days?

All of Ceir Athrolan lay below him. White stone shone under fading moonlight. Waves glittered, bobbing the battleships awaiting orders in his harbor. *My harbor.* He could have owned the world, and he would trade it all for the letter tucked in his jacket. He settled on the cold stone and began to read.

> *Lan, I'm sorry we haven't spoken. I'm sorry I turned you away.*
>
> *In my grief, I didn't think a man like you could understand this life. The life Mirrel and I led. I was wrong. I see what you're doing — not the meetings and orders and silks that fill your days now. But the ripples. Perhaps you understood even better than I did. It's why I testified.*
>
> *Mistress Ja-ila on the corner opened her home to teach us Slummer rats Banis. I asked her to teach me to write Trade first. I thought about dictating to her, then about not writing to you at all. But I wanted you to*

know, from my own words, my own hand, that I miss you every day.

I thought about what you said. You've got to have quite the pair to march in and think I was going to fall into your arms, to think that anyone could overlook your crown. And then I thought about your quiet wit, so sly I'd be surprised every time. And I thought about the way you fell into sex like a starved man, like it was the only thing keeping you tethered to this world. And I thought about how you were the first person besides Mirrel that I let in, that I let see me scared and lost.

I miss your strange, quiet smile. I miss your stubborn dedication. I miss your insight, as if the whole world was before you and you could draw pieces of it at will. I know the knowledge in your mind could fell a nation or raise gods. I know you're sacrificing your mind, your body, to keep this dying world alive. I know you have a thousand worries greater than my heartache.

But I still listen for your footsteps on the stairs.

The rending of Keplan's heart drowned the torrent of thoughts welling from the cityfolk. He wished he had a fraction of the faith in himself that Firas seemed to. Had his mother faltered until his father's faith solidified? A flash of anger, betrayal, the image of her screaming, lightning lancing toward his father's sullen sneer, told him it had never been that simple between them.

He learned to write so he could remind me where I came from. There was another reason, echoed in the promise of the last line, the open ending without signature, but his chest ached too much to hold it.

If he had a lifetime, it wouldn't be enough time to process Firas's words. The air trembled with the peal of bells, marking dawn.

Φ

The 25th Day of Vurgmord, 1272
The City of Ceir Athrolan, Athrolan

An'thor rapped on the bars. Within the cell it was dark. "You know this is a mistake!" he called into the low hallway light. Like his countless previous pleas and bargains, it went unanswered. Drops plinked from the pipes above. He paced, boots clapping against the damp stone. Even the two days in the palace under constant surveillance as he put his affairs in order were preferable to this.

Unintelligible voices drifted from the guard station at the end of the corridor. A clunk as the gate ratcheted open and footsteps. Then a ghost appeared just outside his bars.

One pale horn jutted from white blond curls on one temple, a healing stump knotted the other. He offered a nod, jaw clenched in anger or something else An'thor did not recognize.

He then leaned against the bars. "What the fuck are you doing here, Mel'iend?"

"Thought this would be a suitable place to visit. I'm told you don't get out much anymore."

An'thor growled. "That's how prison works. And that's not what I meant. What're you doing in Athrolan? In the capital? With that pathetic band of fanatics?"

"I thought you'd appreciate my choice to ally with the highest powers. It's very Nenev of me, yes?" He struck a pose.

"Preying on people who are too scared to know better?" An'thor spat. "Cults are hardly the highest power."

"I saw the truth in her words echoed in the world, the dying earth." Mel'iend's shoulder shuddered in a shrug. "No one knows scripture like a zealot, uncle, and our scripture is history. It's time you returned to your studies. He hears thoughts. Sees truth. His blood is the vigor of the world. And every shudder of the earth echoes his pain."

"You don't have to convince me that he's something shiny and special. Convince him if you can. I tried and failed. He refuses to own his power, to bend this kingdom to his will."

Mel chuckled, draping a hand over the bars, black eyes scanning the metal like a lover. "That's the single thread that runs through all your actions, uncle. You're a puppeteer with a twisted sense of good theatre."

An'thor's lip curled. His skin crawled and the boy's words wormed through his too-sober mind. "What I do, I do for Athrolan. I do for these pathetic people who can barely burble without direction!"

Mel snorted. "Uncle, their failures are arguably because other beings kept meddling, using humans for their muddled, selfish ends. You're proof, murdering so you can control a god."

"None of these people were worth being executed over. I've killed hundreds more in battle. So have you, as have most people here. Even his parents. Did you come here to let me out? Tell me you've asked for a pardon?"

"Sure." Mel's face opened in the broken gash of an overly bright smile. "I'll pop open this gate and gesture to the streets. 'Pick any direction,' I'll say." His smile shuttered into a glare. "You sent me to my death two decades ago."

"I told you to—"

"You left me for dead!" he roared. "I was a child!"

An'thor staggered against the bars, unable to look at his nephew. He had taken physical blows that hurt less. "You wrote me often enough for me to know you were too young for war and too much of a coward to trust."

Mel turned to look at him, a handspan between their pale faces. Bloodshot sclera shone at the edge of the fathomless black. "You know what I did? I was invisible in my inadequacy. I read the books left up in the attic, shared stories with the other children too weak to matter. Told them about the Dhoah's power and beauty. And when we'd had enough?" His yellowed teeth bared in a grin. "We blew the whole palace to oblivion. And it was simple and easy and terrible. Froze the whole lot of them in their beds. Shot those we had to."

The Swordbearer lunged, thin, wiry arms wrapping around An'thor's head, pressing his throat against the cold metal bars. His other hand rose and An'thor heard the heavy click of a hammer cranking back.

"Pick a direction," Mel'iend crooned.

"What?" An'thor choked out.

"'I don't care which, as long as it's not ours.' Isn't that what you told that little boy in the snow?"

An'thor winced as he swallowed past the biting iron squeezing his windpipe. "Don't stop until nothing looks familiar," he ground out.

Mel's whisper was in his ear now, just beside the cold front sight nuzzling his temple. "New gods. New kings. New nations. New laws. I don't know about you, uncle, but the world doesn't look very familiar to me."

An'thor squeezed his eyes shut. He was too tired for shame or regret. "Toying was never an attractive trait. Just finish it."

"I spent so many nights planning revenge on you. But honestly?" Mel laughed, then the barrel was gone and the unyielding arm loosened. He eased the hammer forward again, and slipped the revolver back into his holster. "It was way better in my imagination. I get nothing out of tormenting a sad old man stuck behind bars."

"So you're just going to leave me here?"

Mel backed down the hall, winking. "Seems fair to me."

The door rattled shut behind him, and the cell plunged once more into dank silence.

Φ

The 26th Day of Vurgmord, 1272

"You have no idea what you've done!" Bimet's hands flashed wildly, her face set in a horrified snarl. "There are people watching you, people who've watched you from the beginning and who can bring your entire movement crashing to the ground!"

Rih ripped the hat from her head with shaking hands. "I don't understand—this is what we've been working toward. I came here to take his army! I'm just happy I didn't have to seduce the man to get it."

"It's too soon!" Tears streaked Bimet's angry face. "We aren't ready! Ban isn't ready."

The words were like a dart to the chest and Rih staggered back. "I thought you were my ally."

"I believe in everything you are, everything you love, Rih. You are my Kajimet. My empress. But this is a mistake. News will be out before nightfall. You could leave tonight and they'd know you were coming before your horse's hooves hit the cobbles." She clasped her hands before herself for a moment, whether to center her thoughts or keep them from shaking, Rih did not know.

"I'm sorry. You've been my temper for so long. My friend. But I've been so isolated here, finding someone who listens and supports me as well as you was rain after summer." Rih reached out to her interpreter. "Please."

Bimet stepped away, but the movement was calm. "I know. I just need some time to think. To plan. I'll send Nehla up with your supper." Her eyes flashed. "And be careful what you tell her. We don't need them knowing any more than they already will."

"I know, Bi. I hope night brings you peace."

"And you."

The room seemed colder in her absence. Rih brought her long rolled map into her bedroom, laying it across the polished floor by the afternoon light cast through her balcony doors. The ink was faded, but her marks were new. She tugged a dart from her quiver and scattered the tiles she and Bimet used as markers across Ban. One piece for Kemmer. The dart tip slid the tile to where the Hetmir's armada waited off the Arc of Zunu. A second for Majilah Ag, who would be arriving in RoBal in three weeks. Rih pointedly chose the prairie cat, etched in black. Another for Mosil, for Ki-elte and her three hundred students. Soon the map was dotted with allies. She rubbed the final tile, the bright green lacquer filling the carving of the horse's skull. There were only a few moves left to make. She slipped the piece into her pocket and stepped back.

Her bones ached from the trembling earth, and her stomach was tight with the pervasive stench of smoke. She returned to her study and glared at the scroll stand. There were a hundred things to do, but she could not bring herself to act. The entire city seemed caught in her same looping restlessness.

Perhaps it's theirs. She understood the terror of the Dhoah' Laen and the Earth Shaker. But she was not frightened by them. She had stared into the eyes of too many predators to fear them. The might of the ocean, the heat of the earth, those were things she understood the way she understood battle. They were the rolling change of the world, brought to form.

Another letter was due to Majilah Ag, though, and so she sat and drew out ink and paper. *And to those in the capital.* Tomorrow would bring a long, complicated meeting with the king. Her gaze dropped to her hand, the heavy, garish ring on her finger. *Rih-elte. Kajimet and queen of Athrolan.* It did not sit right, not yet, but perhaps it was an acquired taste.

It was dark by the time she had finished all her correspondence. She set the scrolls in the basket by the door for the evening runner and paused. The room was cold. The lamps unlit. Her stomach told her supper should have arrived at least half an hour ago. *Maybe Nehla was busy. Or Bimet forgot to tell her.*

Frayed nerves hummed in her arms and she glanced at the door to the servants' quarters, then at the plain soldier's spear on her weapon rack.

She rolled her eyes and headed through the door. She was being paranoid. The stairs were steep, winding in a spiral down two floors. No lamps were lit, save for the very end of the hall. She peered at the names across the doors.

She drew a breath to clear her throat, then stopped herself. It was early evening. The quarters should be lit and bustling as shifts changed. Feeling the scrape of her slippers on stone, she crept forward. *Go back upstairs and get a weapon.* Il-fald's voice rang in her head and she winced.

A shadow moved in a darkened doorway and she froze. There, something dark on the pale flagging within. She inched forward, hovering in the doorway a moment. Every soldier knew the smell of blood.

Adrenaline flooded her body and she ripped the lamp from its hanger and shoved inside. Clothes littered the floor and the bed curtains were ripped, dragged across the floor. Rih's jaw tightened when she realized they were not dyed red, but bloodstained. She lifted one corner enough to glimpse Nehla's face. Her open mouth was a mess of torn flesh and purple blood. Rih did not have to look to know her hands were missing too. *Imperial Silence.* The ultimate blow from the emperor's men.

She let the curtain fall back into place, fury erasing any caution. A sob wrenched itself from her chest, aching and more familiar than her laughter just a few days before.

She did not know what Nehla might have told them, but Rih had to assume it was everything. But Nehla had not known everything. *Bimet!* Rih dashed down the hall, turning left and scanning the ugly Athrolani letters until she found the familiar Banis name. She kicked the door fully open, lamp held out, as much a weapon as a light.

Bimet's room was empty. A chair was splintered, desk drawers open and in disarray. But there was no body. *They have her.* She wished she could jog through the barracks and find Il-fald at her dimly lit desk in the sly hours of the morning. Perhaps if she closed her eyes, prayed hard enough, sacrificed something to the bitter Athrolani wind, it might carry her home.

Fury faded. A familiar path lay ahead, beaten in the earth by a thousand sandals before her, stained with sweat and blood and tears of failure, of defeat. *What about the women who come after me?*

"A woman is of a single mind." Her breath heaved as she returned to her room and locked the door. Clouds gathered over the ocean, black and snarling. She flung open the lid of her chest, digging until she found the small personal grooming kit. The fire bloomed then flickered into darkness as she dumped the kettle over the coals.

"She wakes for the Empire. She rides for the Empire."

Purple pooled at her feet when she undid her wrap. Her tunic dropped a second later. She swung the double doors wide, letting the layers of silk billow. The wind was biting, bitter and foreign. She knelt before her map.

"Her blood and heart and mind are Ban, breathing and alive."

The wooden handle of the razor was familiar, heavy in her hand. She was not wife to His Majesty Keplan of the Hartland and Athrolan. Tiny shorn curls dusted her shoulders. She was not daughter to the Emperor of Ban and the Jade Forest, Jamun-Ilta the Holy Emerald Throne. The scent of shaving oil and blood from each inevitable nick were bright in the fresh air. She dropped the razor to the pile of clothes and stepped onto her balcony.

"A warrior has a single mind."

Naked, bathed in the rising storm, Rih-elte laughed.

CHAPTER NINETEEN

The 25th Day of Vurgmord, 1272
The City of Ceir Athrolan, Athrolan

AZIMIR HURRIED DOWN THE manor stairs, pulling a robe over his naked body. His steward stood bleary-eyed in the foyer, taking someone's cloak. Instead of Keplan's gangly silhouette, Azimir glimpsed Rih's lean shoulders.

"Master A'hane, she insisted."

"It's fine. She's welcome any time," Azimir promised. "Rih, are you all right? It's midnight."

Low lights gleamed off her hands. They were steady. "You said you would be my peace when I couldn't find any."

He gestured down the hall to the parlor beside the dining room. "Master Illos, would you put a kettle on for tea, please? That's all we'll need." Switching to signing, he turned to Rih. "I'm afraid I don't have the pan or herbs to make Banis tea."

He had seen her wide-eyed expression once before, during battle. "I'll have it soon enough."

Despite the exhaustion dragging at his eyes, warning shot up his spine and he asked again, "Are you all right?"

"Nehla's dead. Bimet captured. As we speak, surely there's a riah bound west for RoBal."

Azimir felt the blood drain from him and he settled onto the seat beside her. "Toar, Rih, I'm sorry. What do you need?"

"I will need everything, every ally, from the mightiest soldier to the smallest child if I'm going to win." She drew a breath and Azimir watched the light gleam from her newly shorn skull.

"You're going soon."

"Majilah Ag will be in the capital for peace talks in three weeks. We will meet her there. And I need the world to be whole."

Azimir sat back, heart hammering. "What?"

"I'm not a person of faith. I'm Banis. We prayed to no one, no one but the false god on an emerald throne. False gods and war seem to be my lot in life now. There are thousands of different ways to lay a board—a philosopher once tried to write them all down, from first tile to last. He died at ninety-seven, work still unfinished. But there is only one way to end a game, and I know the moves when I see them." She held her hand out, dropping a game piece into his palm.

It was still warm from her skin, and he held it a moment before looking at the face. A horse's skull, painted green.

"You think Kep is the final piece?"

"I think we both are. I think all of this is. The three most powerful creatures to walk this earth are all in Athrolan, and I've been handed a crown just before I ride to take another. Those aren't coincidences."

"No, they aren't." His hands shook, but each sign was careful. He voiced occasionally, adding detail where his rudimentary signing vocabulary failed him. "I don't know how I will fill the days enough, so that I'm not consumed with worry. I know you have weeks of marching and planning and meeting my mother."

"I'm used to battle. Not like this, perhaps, but enough."

He rose from his chair, clenched a fist, and seemingly forced himself to sit again. "That's not what I mean. Of course, I worry about you, even though I know you are best equipped to protect yourself. I just feel as if I'm losing the two people I love most. I wish I could go with you."

"You could, if you wanted —"

"I think Keplan needs me more."

"I think so too. But afterward, whatever it is, you'll find me. You'll help me rebuild and I'll help you grieve."

"He might not die."

"But he might. And even if he doesn't, the name Keplan Wardyn will." She reached across the distance. "Mind if I stay? Just to talk, until dawn?"

He let their fingers lace for a moment, a pact, as official and weighty as the one she signed that morning with Keplan. "What else are best friends for?"

It was dawn when Illos stepped into the parlor to wake Azimir. "Master A'hane, His Majesty the King of Athrolan is here to speak with you." The steward's eyes pointedly did not even inch toward where Rih lay asleep on the couch. Her hand was still out, fingers curled in the ghost of a word.

Azimir stretched, hissing in pain at the tension in his neck. He wondered if she signed in her sleep, like so many spoke. He groaned, rubbing his eyes. "I'll see him in the dining hall, and I beg of you, please bring tea before I die."

The steward bowed himself out, a tiny smile in place.

Keplan was already seated when Azimir stepped in. "You look as bad as I feel," he remarked.

"Rih stopped by last night. We were up for most of it."

Keplan's eyes narrowed on his cousin, and after a moment his lips quirked. "I thought you looked at her a lot. She's not mine, if that's what you're worried about."

"She's not anyone's," Azimir whispered. "Though I know what you mean. And we didn't. Don't. We're friends. What did you want?" His heart was too heavy for conversation, but something in the shadows under his cousin's eyes made him force exhaustion from his gaze.

"Just to talk." Keplan shifted. "Have you had breakfast yet?"

"No, but I'll call for two, if you'd like." When his cousin nodded, he sent a message down to the kitchens. He was exactly where he needed to be, but he sorely missed Mirikin food. *Never thought I'd long for a crust of bread.*

"How are you doing?" Keplan asked.

"Oh, well enough." Azimir feigned disinterest. "Been a dull few days. I met with my family's steward about the manor. I think Da's furious I'm essentially in charge. He's worried the place will be in disarray. Oh, and Rih's off to war and the Dhoah' Laen returned as a cloud of lightning."

Keplan's laugh sounded more like a cough.

Azimir snorted. His jaw worked as he tongued his teeth with nervous energy. "So, did you talk to them?"

Keplan's flickering frown told him he did not need to clarify of whom he spoke. "Yeah. Through most of last night. I guess they're resting now. They didn't answer my knocks but I could hear the fire through the door—" His head dropped to his hand, shoulders shaking with sobs. "Part of me honestly thought I'd go back to that little cabin in the woods, and they'd be there. Just as they always were. Fates, I can still see their bodies, their faces when I look at them, but every time it's like a ghost, fading into nothing. And I don't dare take a breath to think about my own end and what'll be afterward, so I just barrel forward. Can't close my eyes. Too many images, thoughts. I think them being here opened something. Or maybe it's the prophet's power."

Azimir glanced up, forcing boyish energy across his face. "Anything useful in those visions? The outcome of the next Slummer iguana match?"

"Iguana?"

"Large Banis lizard from the northern islands. Poisonous and easily irritated. Made twenty on a frilled fellow the other night." A pang went through his chest. "I do feel bad for them."

Keplan rolled his eyes. "No. Nothing like that. Just blood. The future. You know, my usual fare. A world where people do not bear the scars I do. I wish I had time." He heaved a ragged breath. "I want to rescue the people like me. Before they need rescuing. What I wouldn't give for someone to break down that door and drag me bodily from their blades. Or to wake up and have the only thoughts rattling around my brain be mine, and mine alone. The echo in here would be incredible."

Azimir surged forward, panic drumming in his chest. This was the conversation he had been avoiding. "We don't know you'll die, we don't, that's not what the prophet said. It might not have sounded pleasant, with all the violent imagery—"

Keplan looked away. "It sounded fatal. My mother ripped open the soul of the world. I might have to cut it afresh.

Flood the wounds with life. Hope when it heals it heals whole. Connected." He shrugged. "But, you know, with magic."

A laugh sprang from Azimir's chest.

Keplan glowered. "I don't think it'll feel that funny."

"Kep, I love you, but sometimes you just ought to see your face. So stoic and weighty, then you say things like that." Azimir let out a last chuckle. "Besides, there's only so much talking about you dying that I can stomach. Gives me the winders."

"I'm sorry. I'm sorry for all of it. My reactions. My panic. Our fight. I could have killed you."

"You're not much of a wrestler." Azimir's smile was weak but genuine. "You heard about Rih going to war?"

"I read her note this morning. It's a nightmare."

"I just feel like it's too soon. Too much. Not her rebellion — well, partly — but both of you. I can't lose you both."

"You sound like your father."

"Toar, I mean it, Kep. You don't even know how you're going to do it. Just wait."

"I hoped to stabilize Athrolan before, but you saw them." Keplan's voice was a low rumble. "They're not even human anymore. We barely survived winter. The other cities are clinging to life. Mending the world is complicated. They started the job, but I've got to finish it. I think I'll know how when I get there."

"I don't know if they make instructions for gods." Azimir had never seen Keplan so still. Without tics or manic pacing.

"I need a favor."

"My sword is yours, you know that. Just ask."

"Not as my ally or the Hetmir's son." His eyes were bleached of feeling as much as color. "As family."

Azimir sank into his chair. Whatever he feared, it seemed worse. He nodded, then repeated. "Just ask."

"When it happens, it'll be on the islands. The gods' island. Whatever began there will end there. And I don't know how it will end. It's not something befitting a grand battleship, and besides, Rih will take half her ships west and you're as good a sailor as any Mirikin—"

"I'll take you." Azimir wondered if the earth quaked under Keplan's boots too or just his own. "I'll row you there."

Keplan lapsed into silence, staring at the fire. Their friendship began with babbling, overbearing questions, uncertainty. There were a score of things Azimir knew he would wish he said, wish he had asked, a dozen stories he ought to recount to fill their last few days together. But only one thing found its way from his heart to his mouth. "Just ask."

Φ

The 28th Day of Vurgmord, 1272

Rih's body hummed with energy. The hills beyond Athrolan were massed with troops. She waited in the barrack courtyard, bouncing on the balls of her feet. Of course, there were those who balked at her orders. Those who had enough of the changing command. They marched south or stayed in the capital. Many of the Banis soldiers she had brought from the capital were gone as well, and surely more would disappear during the coming march. She wondered if they were the ones marching Bimet home. *Stay strong, Bi. I'm coming for you.* Rih's hands scraped against the cold stone, the only sensation grounding her.

Keplan appeared beside her. He held up a wax tablet with a faint smile.

I came to wish you luck.

She smiled back, but it was as if she already looked at a dead man. He always fit so poorly in the role of king that now, without it, his imprint on the kingdom was already fading. *Except for the starved, the thirsty, and the dead.*

Do they know yet that you're to be queen?

She smudged out his words.

There are rumors. I'm letting them fly. When we win, when the world is whole, then they'll know. I asked Lady Gella to come to rule as steward. We'll see how she feels.

She'll say yes, but not out of joy.

Keplan hazarded.

There are a dozen fewer nobles who would gladly take the duty. I don't want someone ruling if it's what they crave.

Well, no one hates it more than me

She glanced over at him, at the overlarge eyes, the pale moon face in the early light.

You and the emperor have so many similar steps but for opposite reasons. You both thought you were destined for the throne. He because he deserves nothing less, and you because you deserve nothing more. He is a man who thinks he's god. You're a god who wishes to be a man.

She was rewarded with his faint smile.

When do you leave?

I'm waiting until the missive arrives at every city. Azimir's rowing me there in a few days. Ma and Da, they're traveling the way they came. I'm glad, though, in the end. That I met you, that I could help you. And that you found Azimir. Everyone needs a friend so faithful.

A flag rose below, a brilliant green horse racing before a tall white tower. It was her personal sigil for now. Her armor burned on her, and she found a bright grin on her face. She offered her hand, soldier to comrade. He tugged his glove off, and his skin was cool, no warmer than the early spring air around her.

"Love and luck go with you, Rih-elte."

"And with you, Keplan Wardyn."

Φ

The 30th Day of Vurgmord, 1272

Cold air nibbled at Daymir's bare hands, but it was not winter's cold. The bells had been tolling for days. Perhaps longer. He pushed his boots deeper into the soil. He missed having a garden. *And solitude.* The boy had come again that morning. He came every few days. Sometimes they spoke, but more often he settled across the tea table, content with silence. It was a kindness, Daymir knew, but not one he appreciated.

He tipped his face to the overcast sky, relishing the wind as it mussed his hair. Its iron gray had faded to white, though he could not recall when. Footsteps approached from behind him, but he did not turn. *Make them look.* He was not ready to give up the sea air, for them to remind him of things he would rather they did not.

His name is Keplan. Just as sure as he remembered it now, he knew it would be foreign to him in an hour. He did not really mind anymore. This quiet in-between was more familiar. It's why he slipped out more and more, perhaps, though he rarely recalled deciding to don a cloak and stride from the palace.

Below waves thundered into the cliffs. The air was thick with salt, with a bitter, familiar tang. He had missed that in the mountains. He leaned back against the headstone behind him, the sun-warmed stone seeping warmth through the thin fabric of his housecoat.

"Morning!"

The bright voice was not one he recognized. He rocked his head back on the stone to look. She was old, as old as he, perhaps, though whether he was forty or eighty he was not sure. "Morning, mistress. Am I intruding?"

"No, but I rather imagine I am." She settled in a peasant's squat beside him, skirts of her plain sarafan tucked up. Her wool hose were embroidered with bright blue fishes.

"Not really. I mostly talk to myself these days."

"Hela." She stuck a hand out. Her eyes were gray, though they gleamed as if once, they held a secret.

He took the hand. Someone had called him something. *Blackhouse?* But that did not seem to fit in the space between his tongue and teeth. "Ornsen. Dam Ornsen, I think. Are you from the city?"

"No. Haven't decided where I'm from yet." She jerked her head at the hills behind, at the long road winding and the red swollen buds on the trees, just beginning to think of leafing. "We have a friend in common. Keplan."

Daymir frowned. "I assume he's looking for me?"

"No, but he suggested I ride with you a while, since I was headed east."

He looked back out over the ocean. His bones ached, his back was stiff with the raw ocean air, as much as he loved the scent. "I didn't know I was going anywhere."

"Only if you want. I'm headed toward the mountains. Winters are long, but I'm looking forward to not having to listen to anyone yammering for a long while."

He laughed, and the way mirth burned made him wonder when he last had. "On that we can agree."

"What do you think?"

Athrolan had been home for so long, but when he looked over its towers and streets now, even through the waving glass of his window, they were unrecognizable. He missed his orchard. His study. He missed solitude. Groaning, he rose, thinking a silent apology to the headstone's owner as he used it to lever himself upright. "Tell me—Hela, was it?—how do you feel about a little town called Marl Black?"

Φ

The 35th Day of Vurgmord, 1272,
The Village of Jai, Ban

Soot marred what little of Jai's walls still stood. The grasslands were more Banis than Athrolani, and the weather warm. Rih slipped from the saddle. She hated that this destruction was because of her, because of her allies. Even for a greater good, blundering armies wreaked pain wherever they went.

A familiar figure stood under the broken gates. "Rih!"

"Kahma!" She rushed into her friend's arms, squeezing tight, smelling the warm grasses and sharp sweat. She pulled back to sign, "I didn't know you'd be here."

Kahma's face fell, and it was then that Rih noticed her cheeks were streaked with tears, and her eyes were bloodshot. "My brother died. I was permitted to come here to help his wife—with a full riding, of course, to look into the Mirikin threat."

"Mirikin did this?"

"I guess it was chaos. Mirikin came in to extract an informant and a deserter. The Banis soldiers here took the opportunity to attack those they thought were traitors—whether for your cause or the Mirikin, it's hard to say."

Rih rubbed her face. She was exhausted. The Athrolani army strung out behind her. It would be hours before everyone would even arrive or make camp. *How do we hide something this size in the grasslands?* The Banis never had to hide their soldiers. The threat was often enough.

She shoved the concern aside and nodded toward the village. "What do they need? We have medics. Medicine. Precious little food after the Athrolani winter, but what we have we can share."

"Just rest for now." Kahma smiled, hand resting on Rih's shoulder. "There's someone waiting for you."

On the far side of the village, under the copse of acacia trees, was a cluster of tents. They weren't the elaborate, curtained Banis, but plain, serviceable canvas. The largest bore a vermillion flag.

The flaps were bound open in the warm air, and a handful of Mirikin soldiers clustered about a table. One, a towering woman with bright, brassy armor, glanced up as Rih approached. She dipped her head to the man at her right and met Rih at the tent's opening. "Welcome. I'm Hetmir Kemmer A'hane." Her iron gaze followed the signs for a moment, but she did not ask. "You must be Kajimet Rih-elte."

Rih expected someone like Majilah Ag, as stunning as she was dangerous. Kemmer A'hane looked tired. White streaked her auburn hair, and freckles covered her lined face. She was beautiful the way an old city was — with life written on her streets. "I'm honored to meet you, Hetmir A'hane. It's actually Her Majesty now. Queen of Athrolan."

Kemmer's pale brows arched. "That's news."

Rih nodded, reminded of her own youth, her own inexperience. She would need Kemmer and Majilah Ag in the coming months, perhaps even more than she did now. "It's informal for now. You heard about the Dhoah' Laen and the Earth Shaker?"

"And my nephew. Yes. I wish I could have met him."

The older woman nodded toward the prairie outside the walls. "Well, I'm glad to meet you. I was worried the whole journey here. There are at least half a dozen patrols we've lost the trail of in the past month. The fields are rife with Banis scouts."

"And only half of them are mine." Rih flashed a smile. "If you've the maps we can discuss our plans now over dinner—"

"You must be exhausted. Once your arse hits the chair, you'll feel every league. Please. I'd rather know you first. I like to know who's beside me in battle."

"As do I, but we have little time. Our actions were spurred by the capture of my translator and the death of a handmaiden." The wounds were raw still, and she winced at the pain of opening them again. "Let's speak this evening. It will take all night for my army to arrive anyway."

Kemmer snorted, thin lips quirking. "They always leave the slow plodding out of the epics."

"If they didn't, I doubt we'd listen to them at all."

"I understand it now," Kemmer mused.

"What's that?" Rih looked from her interpreter to the Hetmir.

"My son's devotion to you."

"Devotion?"

"Everyone needs their guard. Their support. Lyne'alea had hers in Arman. Arman had his in the other Rakos. Keplan surely had one. He's yours."

"He wrote you about me? Before, I mean?"

"A month ago, when you first began to trust each other. He was torn. Thinking he had to choose between the two of us. He asked for my permission to marry you."

Rih laughed.

"By your reaction I assume he already asked?" Kemmer held her gaze.

"He didn't, really, in the end."

"No? My son is not often one to back away."

"I'm already married and have no wish to do it again. He changed his mind, I think. He did propose, but it was an offer of friendship. Undying, lasting, simple friendship." She met Kemmer's eyes. "Between queens, I think you'll agree that's harder to come by than romance."

Kemmer's smile was bittersweet but genuine. "Go, bathe, rest if you need it." She reached out, stopping Rih as she turned away. "And welcome home, Your Eminence."

The title did not fit, but Rih wondered if one day she would grow to fit it. She wondered if she wanted to. The bathhouse was hastily repaired, but scented oils and thick steam brought tears to her eyes.

The crowded Athrolani horizon, with its hills and cliffs and pale, unfamiliar faces, crowded her heart and her mind. Perhaps this was how Keplan felt, too, inside the confines of his own skull. Now her sandals beat the packed clay, and the baths were crowded with her kinfolk.

Hot water engulfed her, and fingers stiff from holding reins worked dirt and sweat from her skin. By the time she emerged, she felt weightless and at least a few years younger.

Her tent had been erected beside Kemmer's. The emblem from her first journey to Athrolan was replaced, if hastily, with her more fitting new sigil. *If they didn't know Athrolan would change hands when this march started, they'll know by the end.*

Her hammock was already made up, and all she wanted to do was fall into it and never come out. But revolutions did not run themselves. She was almost dressed when she noticed the red flag by the tent flap that served as a knock.

Draping her wrap over her shoulders, she lifted the fabric.

A Banis courier stepped in, kneeling for a breath before looking up. "Your Highness, I brought—"

"I can't understand you through the panting. Take a moment." She took her own untouched glass of water and pressed it into his hands. They were clammy. Shaking. Even the strength in his face quaked under the weight of nerves.

Rih glanced outside. The skies were still clouded. Dark. She had not realized how often the capital was rocked by weather. When she glanced back, he was already speaking again.

"—I had to. But the roads aren't what they used to be." He raked a hand through his dark hair.

"Where did you come from?"

"Package came from RoBal." He had not touched it since dropping it on the floor in his bow, and he seemed unwilling to hold it for the few seconds to hand it to her. "It's from His Eminence."

A chill flashed through her, despite the soft air and long minutes in the baths. Even gifts were not to be trusted.

It was wrapped in oil cloth, meticulously folded and sealed with the stamp of palace runners. She lifted it, gauging the weight before setting it beside the tea tray and lifting the lid. Acrid perfume seeped from the sawdust and straw packing. Jasmine? No, plumeria from the western coast. She pushed aside the straw enough to glimpse dark flesh gone ashy with blood loss.

Rih recognized hands as well as she recognized faces — she knew how each person used them to speak to her, how long fingers flared, how strong ones curled. Even if she did not recognize the tiny bronze ring and jade sigil on the first finger, she would know Bimet's hands. Left over right. Her tongue felt as if it, too, rested on a bed of salt and sawdust.

There was no letter, no message, no note. Only a tile, cupped in the right palm. She slipped it free. It was from one of the emperor's sets — cast in copper heavy with verdigris. Tiny rubies made up the horse's skull.

"Find me a translator, then rest. It's a long way from RoBal." Rih could not meet his eyes. It was no coincidence to receive this package just days before the attack. The emperor expected her.

She slid the lid back onto the box and cradled it under her arm before slipping from her tent. Whatever relief she felt at arriving in Jai was wiped from her body, erased from her thoughts.

Kemmer was still crouched over maps, though her hair was now loose, and a thin robe covered her loose training clothes. She glanced up just long enough to register who stood in the doorway before launching into a diatribe Rih did not bother to try to decipher. Instead, Rih slid the box onto the Hetmir's desk.

"He knows."

Kemmer frowned, lifting the lid with her smallest finger. Her face paled further, and she let the lid drop shut again. "Whose are these?"

"My translator's."

Kemmer's gray eyes flicked to meet Rih's dark gaze. "I'm sorry."

"He's a fool to think this wouldn't happen. No one's power is absolute," Rih insisted. Her hands shook with rage, with horror, with grief.

Kemmer was careful. Organized. Reserved. Rih longed for Majilah Ag and her calculating viciousness. She forced herself to focus through her fury, catching her interpreter's signs a few moments late.

"Your Eminence, this is Ajat, my informant here in Jai. She's a terrific scout, but her skills shine best on packed earth rather than on the ocean. She'll aid you in RoBal."

Rih looked up. The woman was Border, with long dark hair and light brown skin. Her nose and cheeks were tattooed with a bright red and black butterfly. Other than the scar knotting one eye, her gaze could have been Azimir's. Rih's brows rose, but she extended a hand. "Call me Rih or general, please."

"Ajat Monre. I'm honored to be here."

"I'm grateful you came."

It took a moment for Kemmer's officers to assemble, but soon they were ranged about the long desk. When they had, Kemmer settled in her camp chair, eyes fixed on the unrolled maps. "My armada awaits just off the coast, and my army marches west as we speak. By the time they reach the walls of Zunu, we'll have joined them."

"Our issue with all the cities is the walls," Rih noted.

"How can you think to take down those walls—I've stormed keeps with walls half that made of stone," a narrow-faced woman interrupted.

"I'm sure General Rih-elte was about to explain, Oland," Kemmer admonished.

Cheeks hot, Rih bent over the map, pen poised. A red dot marked the capital. "I brought cases of fireshells for you. Ours await us in the city."

"Fireshells?" Kemmer leaned forward, curiosity lighting her eyes.

Rih grinned. "Black powder, like what's used to fire your cannons. But wrapped in a sphere of clay, with a wick. Light the wick, toss it—"

"No more walls."

"No more gates, at least," Rih offered. "The Swordbearers used them to attack Athrolan and I've rarely seen such quick devastation. When will you attack?"

"Night, at year's end."

"That gives us enough time to arrive and for them to send reinforcements."

"I fear they won't," Rih glanced at the box resting on the desk before her. "They know we're coming."

Kemmer's grin broadened. "Of course they do. They think you've gone rogue, stolen the Athrolani troops, and are marching to help us on the coast. One of our informants has been double-crossing us for weeks. Instead of killing the man, we just told him false information."

"You know there'll be a trap laid at the Arc of Zunu," Rih warned.

"Probably, yes, but we're not the point anymore. Your war is bigger than ours." Her hand rested on Rih's forearm. "We've the entire Mirikin navy. They'll be hard-pressed to end us all. Tell me your strategy for the capital."

"There's no way we'll hide most of the Athrolani army." She glanced up to Curiel. "I managed fine with a few hundred Banis, but there's nothing subtle about sand-white faces in Ban. Some of you we can disguise as slaves brought in through Majilah Ag's contacts, but we'll need enough of us in the city to open both the main gates and the palace gates to allow you in."

"How do you plan to do that?"

"RoBal means 'Seven Springs' in old Banis. It's built over six hot springs—it's why we've a bath house on every corner."

"Why call it seven if there are only six?"

"The seventh spring is devoted solely to watering the imperial gardens. Another is outside the city limits." She pointed to the dot on the map. "Another is beneath the gate and powers the mechanisms. That will be our first target. The piping system is a bit complicated, but the runoff tunnels are large enough for people. Most soldiers have to chase urchins out. We'll go in at night."

"What's the second target?"

"Another group—mine—will get in through the gardens. They're large enough to hide us. Once the main gates blow, we'll attack. Fireshells can get us inside, but they will have to be well placed."

"I know someone who works at the main gates, but he's the head of the fourth guard," a young man responded. She caught the hint of blocky eastern features under his Banis skin.

Rih frowned. "I wanted to attack at night, fourth guard might be too late."

Kemmer moved her hand into Rih's view. When she looked up, the Hetmir smiled. "It'll take all night to get in and for the army to be within charging distance."

"Then we'll attack at dawn." Rih chewed on her lower lip. Momentum pushed her, urged her on fiercer than any baniol's copper spurs. But Kemmer was right. Doing it properly was better than quickly. "Let's say we take advantage of your friend."

"Mu-bat."

"Mu-bat. He plants the bombs on the gate's mechanism. That gives my army our entrance. Majilah will have left the capital by then on her way to attack the third city of the Golden Three. I sent her a letter before we departed. She hasn't answered, but as soon as she free of the capital's confines, I'll surely get her response. The palace gates are next."

Kemmer frowned. "Breaking a few pipes will do that?"

Rih kept her contempt of Mirikin and Athrolani plumbing to herself. "Not just the pipes—the pressure can kill a man. We release it at once and you'll have steam a hundred paces high. The entire city was built around them, dry, then the masons directed the water into its new path. It's akin to bleeding a gazelle."

"Messy," Kahma noted.

"But deadly." Rih tapped the palace. "Once we're into the palace we'll need disguises to find a way upward."

"You can't just storm it?"

"A dozen doors and twice as many keys lie between the entrance level and the Emerald Throne." She sighed. "Mosil is my route in."

More marks were made on the maps, others rubbed out. She might have brought thousands of Athrolani troops, but her rebellion rested on a handful of Banis civilians and soldiers. Tiny rubies pressed into the flesh of her palm as her grip tightened on the emperor's tile.

Midnight came before they laid aside plans and pens. There was nothing more, no amount of planning would confirm victory. *Please, Keplan, don't fail me now.*

Kemmer's broad hand rested on the maps. "Very well. Oland, inform my fleet we'll rejoin them tomorrow and to prepare for the journey west."

Rih glanced at Kahma. "Send word to Majilah Ag, to Mosil, to Ki-elte. Tell them I'll see them soon, tell them it's time." Her hands shook, but it was with fury and certainty, not fear. "Tell them I'm bringing the war home."

Φ

The 41st Day of Vurgmord, 1272
The City of Ceir Athrolan, Athrolan

It was a letter Keplan had composed a thousand times in his head. Emotions picked out in relief against the horror of a billion thoughts. It was not long or flowery. He was certain there were misspellings. Smudges. Written over weeks of fear and bloodshed, faint hope, and a sliver of longing. But every word was wrung from the shuddering blood in his veins. Not the gods' blood. Not the human. Just his. But it was also impossible. When Firas could not read there was a finality, a barrier. It was almost snowmelt. Not even a year ago his feet were tripping northward, bound for pain and glory.

Keplan's hand inched toward the top drawer, but he forced himself to his feet. "No." His fist slammed on the desktop. "Fates. It's a grip, love. It's not even that I want it. Because I don't. But my blood gnaws for it. My mind hungers, worse than anything I felt in Ban. I don't notice and before I know it, I'm leaning over the stuff. Breathing. I could breathe with you. Not these horrible gasping sobs. Actual breath. Actual air. I can't remember the last time the air smelled real."

A tune twined through the open window and he slipped into his bedroom. It was wordless, just something composed on the spot. Unlike his letter. A thought slipped between them, a confession, an invitation. He raised a hand, resting it on the memory of the other man's shoulder. The wish of a hand ghosted over his waist and he smiled. Perhaps it was not the thoughts or the monstrous blood that made him mad.

"Gods can fashion the earth at their will. Heard prayers to them and answered every single one. So tell me why I can't will you here. Not much of a True God, eh?"

The tune died in a flurry of happy greetings. Keplan let his arm drop. "Maybe another night, then."

The letter that slipped from his pen that night was not poetry or even proclamation. He was not even sure it was he who wrote it. Keplan stared at the parchment. Were this a drama or a Banis puppet show, the desk would be littered with crumpled drafts. Instead, his pen had hovered over the blank page for the past hour. How did one simultaneously ask for love and explain they would die in the next week? He wondered, all those years ago, what his mother had said, what she told her friends and family and Arman?

I know I've asked too much already. I know stumbling into your bar a year ago begged more mercy than I deserved. I'm begging you to have a little more, and grant me goodbye. I was never meant to be king. I was never meant to sit on this human throne and blunder our way out of war. I did so because I was tired of bloodshed and tired of watching your world crumble. But I didn't do it because I was good at it.

I long for the peace of the Hare. I hope that's what death is like. But I can't imagine it without Mirrel's bustling energy. I hope the hearth is still warm. I hope you've found someone to help. I wish it could be me. I'd trade a year of the finery here for a single day sweeping the floors.

In a few days I travel across the sea to the Isle of the Gods. What power is left to them will pass to me and then to the world. Returning the power, the life force, to the world may, very well, mean my death. It's a romantic notion, made simple because none of us really understand how it will work or what will happen in those minutes, those hours. All we know is it will end them. And probably me. There's a chance, a small one, but one I'm praying for, that it won't. I guess I can only hope it doesn't hurt.

Tears blurred the words flowing after his pen, but his heart did not need to see. He just hoped Firas would forgive the handwriting. He hesitated over the last few lines. He saw what the possibility of his mother's life did to Brentemir. That was a prison he wished on no one.

For once the thoughts in his head were not foreign, were not pressing in from the hundreds of people he failed or saved. They were his. He paced his room, breath coming in frantic gasps. Silence. He deserved his last night as a king, as a man, as whatever mess he had become, to be peaceful. Even after all the terrible choices he made, he deserved silence at the end. He tore through his desk, riffling through papers and letters he had forgotten about or never answered. It was as if he searched through a dead man's belongings.

Guilt flashed through him at the thought of how much Rih would have to clean up. *Maybe the palace will topple and it won't even matter anymore.* He supposed when one inherited one nation and sacked another, a dead god's unanswered missives might be the least of her worries.

"Where is it?" he snarled, slamming a drawer shut and narrowly missing his thumb. Surely Azimir had come through and cleaned his chambers, or a maid, perhaps. Someone with his best interests at heart. Everything seemed to come easily to the younger man. Even kindness. Empathy might overwhelm his mind, drive him to numb himself with drugs, but Azimir simply basked in it. *Selflessness.* He hated them for it. If he faced a long, glorious life, it would be different. If he faced decades of ruling Athrolan, this would be a mistake. But these few days ahead were his last, and it no longer mattered whether he were sober.

His bedroom was next. The chest at the bottom of his bed was piled with his common clothes, half still speckled with mud, the others wrinkled beyond repair. There, at the bottom where he had hidden it, was a box of dust. He cracked it open and slumped on the floor, tapping a scoop out onto the wooden chest top. Relief was close, but still his nerves ignited, burning away any peace he gleaned from solitude. Perhaps the closer he came, the further his mind seemed from normalcy.

He dipped his head and inhaled silence. He leaned back, heart thundering in relief. His blood heated and hummed, and he settled in to enjoy the quiet sounds that came with existing in a flesh body. Did his parents miss this?

His mind trundled down Athrolan's muddy streets, through the drifting mist of the Slummer, through the lamp-oil haze that blanketed the naval docks. It was only when he heard the creak of the sign outside the Wise Hare that he realized his feet, unsupervised, had followed his heart. Stink clung to his jacket more in this weather. Loneliness underscored even the scent of Slummer runoff.

Firas's words scorched his heart, burned down his throat like elixir, like medicine. It would be cruel now to stumble in, for his bootfalls to clatter up the attic stairs. He just did not know who it would hurt more. Part of him wished for the pain of it all, for the ache of sex and goodbyes and love, just to say he experienced it, just to know what living felt like before he no longer could.

The door clapped open and a young boy stepped out, emptying wash water into the gutter. Keplan stepped closer, tugging his letter out. "Boy. You work there?"

The boy stepped back, washbasin held between them like a shield. "Who's asking?"

"Give this letter to Master Smythesen, will you?" He added a coin to his palm. "It's from an old friend."

The boy eyed the coin and letter, then grabbed both, retreating inside without another word. Keplan tilted his head up to the spitting sky, breathing the smells for a moment. He could not afford to dawdle, but this was a place he wanted to keep, the place he wanted to think of last. The common room's glow spilled across the cobblestones and flooded Keplan's face.

For a moment his eyes met Firas's.

He sank back into the shadows, heart thrumming in his throat. Maybe he did not care how much it hurt his own heart, but he had done enough damage to Firas to last three lifetimes.

"Who's there?"

Keplan stumbled backward, knees cracking on the stone before he found his footing. By the time the bartender had rounded the corner he was pelting into the mist. Part of him — most of him, if he were honest — wished to run into the street, under the teetering walls of the tall Slummer houses, stacked brick on rotting brick. He would climb the Wise Hare's stairs and wordlessly fall into bed.

"Make me forget it, forget everything."

His racing steps brought him up to the arching towers over the harbor gates. If he woke tomorrow in Firas's arms, he could never cross to the Isle's desolate shore. Given a true taste of what he could have, he would never give it up. Even for the world. Life was a funny thing — he spent so long indifferent, unaware of his mortality and therefore uncaring of its beauty. He had never wished for death, though, other than under interrogators' knives. He had times when he didn't care if he lived, but he never came so far as to seek death. *I will.* Soon he walked, opened armed, into her indifferent maw.

He was too afraid to even run. His hand gripped the moss dotting the stone beneath him, yanking at the tender blades until the green stained his palm.

"I'm the only person who really knows what you're feeling right now."

He didn't look over. The reek of seawater and cold rotted flesh drifted, even with the brisk wind. "I suppose you're right. And Father. Funny, the things you never think you'll inherit."

"You've got my hair and nose, too, don't worry." For a fleeting moment her laugh sounded closer to a mountain stream than a swamp, and Keplan glanced over.

"I love you. My whole life you knew me best, and I never had the chance to truly see you. Not till I left. Not until now.

But I still love you, and no matter what I see before me, I'll remember you as my mother. Both sides. Both women."

Her gaze, if it still could be called such, lingered on his blown pupils. She looked away, tears peeling the loose flesh of her cheeks. *"I think, against all odds, we did a lovely job with you."*

"Careful. Boasters soon will meet a bitter end."

She elbowed him, exposed bone digging into his skin for a moment.

"But not tonight." He let his head drop to her shoulder, breathing the scent of sea and decay, of wind and distant rain. The snap of lightning mixed with crushed moss.

Φ

The 49th Day of Vurgmord, 1272
The City of RoBal, Ban

Damp leaves and compost pressed on the slats over Rih. Gooseflesh raced along her arms. The wagons had stopped lurching hours before but her stomach still churned with nerves. There was no turning back. There never had been. Something tapped her wrist twice, paused, then once. The west guard tower had called the hour before dawn. She shifted, fingers seeking the latch underneath her. It clicked under her touch and the wagon's bottom dropped open, spilling her onto the soft earth of the imperial gardens.

She drew her first breath of clean, fresh air with relief. Their journey had stunk with the wagons' cargo and the greasy smell from the celebration dinners of Majilah Ag's peace treaty.

She rolled from under the wagon, scanning the dark woods around her. The wagoneer had parked them along the wall separating the northern gardens from The Jewels.

Around her others tumbled from the narrow spaces hidden by the wagon's false bottoms. Kahma was already distributing weapons hidden against buckboards. Rih's blood warmed at the familiar grip of her soldier's spear. A quiver of atlatl darts went across her back and the weapon itself looped onto her belt.

"Kahma, you and I will take another four women up to the imperial sanctum. Kol, you and your group cut through the slave quarters. Free as many as you can, but be on the lookout. Jasetti, you take the rest southeast toward the stables. There's a side door there for the draft horses, where we came in."

"Can't say I'd recognize it from under the manure," she joked.

Rih snorted. "Well it's the only gate out of here, save for the palace entrance. It's flanked by a series of palms. Once through there you'll have to make it to the palace gates. Try to make it before the city gates fall. Before they suspect anything. Remember, if possible, give the sign to those you encounter. Many may yet be our allies. Best not do the emperor's work for him and kill each other." She glanced up. Through the dense branches the sky was a soft purple. "It's time."

Kahma's hand rested on her wrist. "A woman has a single mind."

Impatience nagged at Rih's heels, but she tightened her jaw and nodded. "A woman has a single mind. She wakes for the Empire. She marches for the Empire. Her blood and heart and mind are Ban, breathing and alive. A woman has a single mind." Around her a hundred women whispered or signed the words. A still moment passed at the end, then they sealed the prayer with "Liberty."

Half an hour later, Rih was tucked in the shadows of the bonsai fountain, draped in branches and leaves. Two guards rounded the trail ahead, and Rih clenched her teeth to quiet her breath. These were the last two to make the round before dawn. Her chest ached at the fatigue in their features, at the limp set of their shoulders. War's toll was taken from all sides.

Her hand tightened on her spear shaft as they passed. She slipped from under her camouflage, pausing to be sure they had not heard. She held her stance as another of her soldiers emerged from the path ahead of the guards, raising a hand in greeting. Her hand opened in the sign for rebellion.

One guard's hand tensed on his sword, the other spat on the ground. Three leaping steps and Rih's spear tip drove down into the hollow between his clavicle and shoulder. The other guard jerked as Kahma's blade opened his throat.

They dragged the bodies into the brush, covering them with boughs and leaves. A swipe of her sandals removed most evidence of the scuffle. She slipped to the next bole, watching the flicker of movement as the others followed suit. Sneaking in through Majilah Ag's contacts would have been safer. Easier, even. But this was far more direct. Warning tapped in the back of her mind about why none of them had responded. The double guard surrounding the city, however, was the reason, she chose to believe. *You're being paranoid. Not even the emperor would risk his alliance with the Vales.*

She dropped to a crouch and ducked to the next tree, inching toward the palace. Ahead, the ramp gleamed. Several teams broke off, making for the quarters tucked along the base of the palace walls, where their armor or disguises waited in the shadows.

A flurry of movement broke out at the edge of the trees. *The other guards.* Any moment she expected to feel the ground shudder as the gates crumbled. She paused for a moment to brush a hand over the horsehead tile design on the ramp, but she did not know whether it was for luck or in promise.

The ornate folding wood doors at the top of the ramp were shut, the full story of their elaborate carvings stretched before her dark eyes. *The rise of the empire.* Her gaze lingered on the face of Ban's last empress at the bottom. Her skull was pressed into the ground beneath the new emperor's sandal.

Rih's lips curled in a mirthless smile. *Soon, sister.* She beckoned Kahma forward. The soldier crouched, pressing a clay cup to the wood. Her eyes were unfocused as she listened. Overhead the clouds' bellies were cut bloody with sunrise. The soldier glanced up and nodded once.

Rih rolled the doors aside, leaving them wide. The corridor beyond was deserted. Rolling her neck and shoulders, she slipped into the palace. The others would take care of the lower levels, and once the gates were open, Curiel and her allies in the city would take the rest. *But you, Jamun-Ilta, are for us.*

The corridor turned and her steps slowed. Pressing to the wall, she tugged out the tiny leather-bound mirror tied to her armor. Angling it against the dawn light pouring through the windows, she checked the next hall. "Deserted," she signed to the women behind her. They were several levels below the imperial sanctum, and the halls would usually be crawling with guards, but Mosil must have made good on his promise.

"My cousin will meet us two levels up in the dignitaries' wing," she explained. A glance at their collective armor told her it was too worn, too dusty to pass as palace guards, let alone imperial ones. "Be prepared to fight our way in."

Kahma grinned. "That's what I've been waiting for since you first spoke of liberty."

Tears blurred Rih's vision at the sight of her sign, the sign of freedom, loosed in the palace halls. She rounded the corner and broke into a jog. A glance out the high, narrow windows told her the gate was still shut fast. Concern soured her stomach. Wind eddied across the stone and she breathed the familiar scent of perfumed fountains and damp clay. She slipped up the next set of stairs to the wives' suites.

"Go," she signed to one of her women. "Every door with a red tassel on the lamp outside their door. We'll push ahead. Meet us above with Mosil."

The women took off down the hall, knocking faintly at the first door.

Rih watched her go, longing heavy in her chest. *I wish you could see this, mati. I wish all your sisters could too.* Her limbs throbbed with their blood, though, the blood of every woman whose body made the Banis walls, whose blood dyed the emperor's war sash.

Kahma tugged her hand. Already women and men were emerging from their rooms, faces lit, slim, concealable weapons slipping into sashes and folded silks. Each one who met Rih's eyes steeled her soul. She let herself be pulled away to the smaller private stairway at the end of the hall.

The woman froze, hand in the air to halt. Then two fingers extended. Two guards waited for them at the top. Her free hand slipped a long wooden needle from a box at her belt. It was wickedly sharp, discolored green at the tip. She popped it into a slim tube and pressed herself to the wall, counting silently. On three she whirled around the corner and shot up the stairs. Before her first victim finished falling down the stairs, her second poison dart found its home, and his companion tumbled after.

While others dragged the bodies into one wife's room, Rih followed Kahma up the stairs. The dignitary's wing stretched before them. Now came the difficult part. *The part Bimet's death may have cost us.* They crept through the halls, weaving south, then west until they turned a corner.

Rih's nerves calmed at the sight of Mosil's silhouette at the end of the corridor. "Ally," she told her guards, breaking into a soldier's trot. Her cousin did not turn or even sign a greeting.

Her eyes narrowed on his arms, still by his sides. He jerked, then slumped to the floor as the curved blade of a glaive was pulled from his kidneys. Behind him, Bimet straightened, weapons gripped in her two whole hands. For a breathless moment Rih thought she would put the weapon aside, turn and join them. Instead, she raised the polearm to block the hall.

No. Rih hesitated, then lowered her weapon to sign. "Bi, I don't understand."

Bimet did not lower her glaive. Her body shook, and the shadows under her eyes could have swallowed the city entire. "You never did, Kajimet. You were coddled from the moment you became a soldier — not brought on the worst missions, not forced to march farthest. Permitted to become a wife instead of trampled into the dirt."

"Being excluded is not a privilege!" she argued. Precious time was slipping, and the light through the window screens grew ever brighter.

"Perhaps you had terrible choices, but at least you could choose. Do you know what I'd do for your life?"

"I think I do, now." Rih's heart broke. Not for the betrayal, but for her friend. "Why don't you help me? I know you believe in this, believe in our cause."

"But I don't believe you will win."

It was past dawn, yet the palace was still. Doors were locked. Window screens shut despite the warm breeze. Apprehension shot up Rih's spine. Perhaps Kemmer was not the only one heading into a trap. *She's just the only one who saw it.* "What about the gates? Our network? Where is everyone?"

"Your fireshells didn't even make it to the border. The palace has been locked down for days. The baniol's tunics will be red for years to come. His Eminence's war robe will never need dying again."

"I have allies across the entire city," Rih retorted.

"You're a fool if you think they'll rise up now. You should have seen it, Rih." Awe opened Bimet's features, but it was not made of joy. "Don't you smell it?"

Rih did now, under the heady perfume of lilies. The tang of blood, the slick of rendered lard. She rushed to the nearest window, yanking open the screen. The bodies of hundreds of female soldiers piled in the open square between the palace walls and the barracks. Their hair was long, their clothes Valen. The smoke drifting over RoBal the was not from Majilah Ag's peace supper. It was from the pyre of her slaughtered army.

All Rih's rage at Bimet's assumed death roared to life. "What did you do?"

"I arrived two days before she did. I told Vi-baln everything." Bimet seemed unable to look out at her handiwork, and Rih could barely understand her through her chattering chin. "I'm so sorry, Rih. I had to. I wish—"

Rih would have preferred apathy. She would have preferred cowardice. Anything was better than shame, than guilt she felt compelled to comfort away, even in the heart of an enemy.

"A war is begun by making enemies, but it is won by making allies." Minata Kaz was right. Rih did not survive the army, the Purple Throne, or even Athrolan by dividing.

A door opened down the hall. Vi-baln's golden robes shone in the bright light. He ambled toward them, drawing up beside Bimet, seemingly unconcerned with the soldiers fanning across the hall. He stroked the back of Bimet's neck with one large, smooth hand. She shuddered, the fight leaving her eyes. His thumb circled her throat for just a moment, just enough to remind them both who owned RoBal.

CHAPTER TWENTY

The 49th Day of Vurgmord, 1272
The Isle of the Gods

WAVES CRASHED AGAINST THE garnet beach. Alea watched as two figures disembarked from a rowboat and pulled it above the high-tide mark. The shorter drew his cloak tighter against the wind and moved to wait on a boulder. The other stared into the tangled forest in the heart of the island before turning and making his way along the strand toward them.

"He's here," she called to Arman, the brown stone beneath her already waterworn from her pacing. Her mind existed both in the never and always, but one thought overrode all: her son's face had scars. Her fist clenched. A tower fell somewhere in the ruins beyond. This is how kingdoms ended. Fury and vengeance. The boulders clustered by the tree line reddened, sheaves cleaving off at the inferno in their heart. *"Did you see his face?"*

Flames flashed white, then gold. "I did. I can't imagine —
"

"Makes you want to let the world rot. You don't do that to a god. Not to him." The waves roiled, lightning blossoming over the sand in frustration.

"Ma?"

She turned, the seaweed and salt solidifying into a mass capable of embracing. Keplan's jacket mildewed under her touch. She brushed her hand over his cheeks.

"I could fix these," she whispered.

"They don't need fixing, Ma. Certainly not now."

Her head tilted, mirroring his. There was no need to speak. Not in that they understood everything in one blink of Keplan's too-large eyes, but in that it was too much to convey, and the world's sand was running from its glass. *"I wish so many things."*

His smile was filled with more hope than sorrow, and he reached out to both of them. "And they'll be true. Maybe not for me, but for someone. Ever since I knew the truth, I've been trying to save the world, or even just my corner of it. But this, this is the first time I know I can actually do something. That I know my actions have an impact. I feel like I'm actually supposed to exist. That I wasn't a mistake."

She trailed lightning down his face. *"You could never be a mistake. Even if ending the world meant creating you, I'd do it again."*

He pressed a kiss to her cheek. "I love you, Ma."

Unable to speak, she pressed her consciousness against his before pulling back. Heat bloomed behind them and Keplan turned.

Sand melted to glass under Arman's steps. The towering flames around him reduced enough that one hand cooled as it reached out. Gleaming white marble clenched Keplan's shoulder. "There are so many things I wish I had the chance to teach you and to learn from you. So many."

"We just have now. Now has to be enough." Keplan squeezed, seemingly unaffected by the coal of Arman's palm.

"I always had to sink into my power," Arman suggested. "Surrender."

Keplan nodded, then looked up with a frown. "How badly does it hurt? I've come close but never —"

"Much, but it's quick." He flashed a smile to Alea. "But my deaths never lasted as long as they should."

They exchanged another few words, then Arman stepped away, hand out to hers. "Milady, it's time."

And it was. Her ice sizzled against his flame and she backed into the ocean, eyes fixed on her son. Of everything she had done and made and said, she was most proud of the battered man on the beach.

The ocean surged and her feet splatted on the tops of Le'yne's black cliffs. Across the ocean gleamed Mirik's distant lights. Despite the waves, the scuttling clouds, it was as if time stopped. She recalled a different night, a different journey down those stairs.

But this time she would not be alone. Flames exploded beside her and she offered him a smile he surely felt more than saw. "*It's probably silly to ask if you're ready.*"

"It is. But I am."

Together, they wound up the path, into the hall and down the spirally stairs. Water flooded after them, stone and ash crumbling in their wake, blocking the way back.

Arman's burning form served as a light, but Alea did not need it. She trickled down the walls, through the earth, between every stone and crack in the foundations of Le'yne, of the world. Finally she could stretch. She shuddered, Arman's echoing shiver shaking the ground.

The cavern was dark and empty, devoid of pool or gleaming bundle of souls. She wondered what happened to them so long ago, loosed with nowhere to go. *"Here's where it began. As good a place as any."*

"I'd argue it began in Vielrona, with your hand on my chest and searing pain."

She settled into the hard stone, fingers laced in Arman's, or rather, entwined in the heated air and writhing dust that served as his bones and flesh. "But how we are now began with your death and a walk across the ocean."

Hot air swirled like his breath on her neck. "What would have happened, I wonder. If you hadn't. If you had left me there. Respectfully buried me. Sent a letter to my mother. Married Daymir."

Alea snorted, rheumy eyes rolling. "We'd have lost the war. Or it'd be harder won. Perhaps another of the Rakos would be tapped to channel that power."

Stone rattled against steel in his laughter. "Nonsense. I am the only Earth Shaker, the most powerful."

It was a flash, a fleeting glimpse to an evening years before. Arman, slumped on the flagging of Fort Stone, giggling and drunk. *Fates, we were so young.* Of all the men surrounding her then, however, not even Arman had seen what she was. How could one go twenty years of living together, raising a child, weathering winter and spring floods, and yet never know a person? Perhaps no one had known her. Perhaps knowing a person, truly, was impossible, even for oneself.

Rock cracked, chucks of ceiling shattering on the cave floor. "How do we do this?"

"I did it once, with the gods. I imagine it's much the same." The feeling of timelessness, of nowhere, grew. Her mind reached deeper into Arman's power, scorching and white and

full of sound. Power pulsed as she drew it up, out of herself, tugging twisting magic like threaded roots. Another pull and the branches of power came loose. Blackness curled on the edges of her consciousness.

The whirling, raging constant of him pressed against her now, closer than they ever came when they still possessed physical bodies. *"Thank you for always being here."*

"Thank you for listening. For laughing. For everything you did. I know I didn't always do right by you, but fates, I tried."

"It was enough. This life, it wasn't perfect. But all of it, even the pain, was enough." She yanked a final time. Power exploded in the cavern, black power roiling with gold. Sound and light flared. Then there was nothing.

Φ

The City of RoBal, Ban

Sunbaked walls loomed over Ajat's head. She pushed hair from her eyes, hating how the mud clung to her every inch. She tucked herself farther under the shack roof. Damp burlap scratched at her skin with every motion.

An urchin with Sefer's face tossed a net in, just under the draw bridge. He pulled the net out, glance darting between the top of the wall and Ajat. Two rocks plinked from his hand.

Two guards.

The net cast in again.

Ajat was good at waiting. The sun slunk lower, and she fished out a piece of dried meat to quiet her rumbling stomach.

Sefer scanned the open gate again, caught her eye, then slipped away into the squalor that clustered along the road.

Ajat stretched, rolled her neck, and eased to her feet. She trailed along the moat, peering into the water as if looking for some treasure to sell or food to eat. The minutes between the guard change and the gate rising were few, but she could manage. She slipped down the moat's bank, mud coating her legs, and ducked under the bridge.

Her way into the gatehouse was hidden by dusk and the hulking mass of the bridge, at least for the moment. Under the bridge's shadow was a packed bag. She pulled it out and set off across the moat.

In the legends, Banis moats were filled with crocodiles or snakes. Some on the coast even claimed to stock theirs with sea monsters. The true threat of the RoBal moat was the stench. Tucked at the base of the bridge's hinges was a small culvert. Thick muck from deep within the city spilled through, and Ajat steeled herself.

Banis infrastructure was coveted in most nations, but there was a problem when you no longer cared where your waste and sick pooled. She bound up her hair and, holding her bag above the worst of the scum, pulled out an air bladder and sandals with hooks under the ball of each foot. She filled the air bladder with humid air and slipped the sandals on, wincing at the squelch of fates-knew-what between her toes. Feeling along the base of the wall, her fingers caught on the thick bars of the grate.

The last few wagons for the day trundled overhead and dirt rained onto her. Every movement sent water sloshing against the red clay. It did not matter that she knew no one could hear over the din of the city, she felt eyes on her, knew ears were trained to listen to even the slightest sound. A press of another finger and the latch came loose. Metal clunked and she eased the grate off its latch and opened it.

Drawing her last deep breath of clean air, she pressed the bladder's straw to her mouth and dove into the sewer.

She squeezed through the opening, dragging herself through the mud and scum until she reached the larger pipe that ringed the city. Here, at least, the pipe was large enough for her to stand, even if muck and scum oozed around her waist. She pulled herself upright, her pack with its precious contents going on her back. One hand ghosted over the pipes running along the walls, feeling the heat emanating from some. Others were no warmer than the surrounding clay. Each hot pipe was marked with stripes of colored paint. Her eyes found the red stripe in the darkness and she forged ahead.

Filthy water dragged at her legs. Her sandals' hooks helped her grip the scum-slick bottom. The stench of waste and trash and mildew brought tears to her eyes, but the thought of opening her mouth to breath flooded her throat with bile.

The red pipe curved right, the others cutting deeper into the city. Another twenty paces and the tunnel arched around a massive pilon. *The gate.* A ladder led from a round door in the floor above. The pipe, too, followed the pilon up into what must house the gate's mechanism. Light filtered through the floor slats, and in the slivers of light she caught the glimmer of teeth jutting from the clay. RoBal's massive walls were cemented with secrets as much as mud.

Water rushed through the surrounding pipes, but she heard no footsteps overhead. By her count she had another two minutes before the new guard shift arrived. *Sixty breaths.* Hand over hand, she hauled herself into the gatehouse. Four breaths to scan the room. Massive gears stretched into the darkness. Pipes led to and from. In the far corner was a valve that was fed by the spring. Her gaze dropped to the empty corner under the valve. *Deershit.*

Mu-bat was meant to have brought the crate from the weavers the night before. *No crates or no Mu-bat?*

She scanned the gears, mind whirling. Perhaps keeping it open would be enough. Grabbing the stool, she broke one leg free. Noise no longer mattered. Thirty-nine breaths left, she clambered up the largest gear and shoved the stool leg into its workings.

Footsteps creaked in the hall. Low Banis voices. Her gaze dropped to the open cover down to the sewers. The broken stool beside it. She could make it, but they would know. *Make it count.* Ajat shifted into a crouch, one hand holding her body taught from the gear. Her body ached with adrenaline. Shadows loomed in the door, then two soldiers entered. She dropped.

He coll with the impact and she used her momentum to slam his head forward into the floor. The lamp he carried shattered, oil and ash and fire spilling across the floor. A warning whistle shrieked through the air. She rolled free and came up, panting, blinking sweat and mud from her eye. The second guard's knife skimmed past her face. She twisted with the blow, hand blocking a breath too slow. The blade bit into the meat of her hand. She snarled, glaring at the two fingers tumbling across the floor. A vicious ache throbbed through her hand. He pressed his spear tip against her throat. "Talk."

There was no time to talk. The room stank of ash and blood, the smell of war, of the ruak. She grinned.

"What?"

"Ash and blood."

He spat, eyes not leaving hers.

"We used to call on gods in times of transformation. We'd use ash and blood. I call the lifeblood of the world, spirit who ends us, who guides our arrows. Stripped." She extended her mangled hand from her chest, opening to the sky. In the space it took for him to frown, she lunged, thrusting her bleeding fingers into the broken lamp. Her world imploded in flames. "Remember your name, he who bleeds the earth."

Φ

The Isle of the Gods

The gods' city was nothing more than ruined brown granite. Keplan trailed through the memory of streets, the suggestion of a market. He expected skeletons. Scorch marks, even. Some evidence of the horror his mother caused. Keplan's tongue filled with ash and the salt of brine and blood.

He hiked farther in, steps carrying him up winding stairs, through crumbled arches. His parents were brontide in his blood. His reflection dragged at his bones, drawing him up, in, until he skittered out onto an open rooftop. It had been an amphitheater once. Or perhaps a throne room. Silver dusted the stone, emanating from a point near the center.

Screaming wormed through the air, his mother's inhumane voice wringing water from the very air. Brilliance burned away his vision. Blackness, hot with blood of the world, surged after. Energy flooded his body, pouring upward from the earth. It was pain, lancing with each image, each memory as his consciousness shifted to accommodate each new piece, new position, a weary body sinking into a clean bed and feeling every ache from the day. *How do you carry it all?*

"The thoughts? Or the duty?" He recognized his reflection's drawl. *"Or just existing?"*

"I knew you weren't gone." Keplan fell to his knees, hands pressing to the warm stone of the gods' world. Their foundations. *"All of it."*

"You can't."

Seawater and electricity crackled over the islands. Fire gorged on his flesh. The earth shuddered, cracked beneath his hands. Magma erupted, flooding between his fingers. Red copper erupted from his skin, not his father's scales or his mother's rot, but something wholly new. Lightning crackled. His body lit with flames.

Life pulsed, a flash, hotter than sun, than lightning, freezing with its intensity. It was a small wonder why the skin of the earth cracked with its own might. *I am he who bleeds the earth.*

Like a spine popping with a stretch, the earth opened. Stone melted, rivers boiled. Chalk dusted from Athrolan's cliffs leagues away. His body ached, power writhing from within, life in a womb he both did and did not have.

Mountains rose and wore to nothing. The Banis plains burned and were once more fertile. In the west, ships rocked against the shore, buffeted by tidal waves under a clear sky. He was the ocean air toying with Kemmer's rogue curls as she loosed another volley on Zunu, teeth bared.

He was the earth churning beneath RoBal's springs, heating the water to steaming as the city shuddered under the footfalls of thousands. Archers drew back, and his back ached against the drag of a thousand strings. In Berr, the sea roiled, fishes from the deep places surfacing, ripping junks in twain.

He was the marble toppling from the aqueducts in Ceir Athrolan, crushing the warehouses, the prison where An'thor awaited doom. Sobbing laughter bubbled from Keplan's mouth, and he surrendered himself to the sensation. Everything fell. Everything rose. Mighty billowing breaths.

Life was too much to bear, too much for a single soul, a single land, delicate stone crusted over the burning might of everything. Alea saw the foretelling of this, and in Mother's hubris, thought it him. He saw the ferocity of his blood, the hideous duty resting on his shoulders, and in his own hubris called himself a god.

I am no more god than she. Than Rih, than Firas. Than any child of humanity. They were right. No creature could carry this power, the weight of life. Not at once. *Not alone.*

Life fled his body, flooding after the pulse of energy, and for a perfect moment, there was oblivion.

Φ

The 1st of Lleume, 1273
The City of RoBal, Ban

Rih's knees stung as she was shoved onto the mosaic floor of Vi-baln's private audience chamber. She scanned the room, counting windows, doors, guards, anything that she could use to turn the game in her favor. There were few playing pieces left, though, and all were in his hands. Bimet fell to her knees by the Hand's dais, narrowed eyes focused only on her own hands clenched in her lap.

I would have sworn those hands were yours.

But if they were not Bimet's, then whose? Rih shoved the grisly mystery aside. Kahma dropped beside her, cheek bleeding from Vi-baln's smack. She cast a furtive look to Rih, seeking orders.

Rih shook her head once. Not yet. They would only get a single chance, so whatever their plan, it would have to be good.

Vi-baln's mustard-gold slippers passed before them, and she looked up.

"I was so flattered that Bimet here thought to include us in your little rebellion party. Hurt, of course, that you didn't think of me yourself, but alas." His smile was broad and full of hate. "From the moment my niece Nehla took interest in you, I knew you were one to watch. She was always too clever, playing the superficial, playful courtier." His lip curled.

Beside her, Kahma signed as much as she could, but Rih understood enough for horror to wash over her. Nehla had never been the one to suspect. *I'm so sorry. You tried.* If any of them survived this, she would owe a visit to Mobeka. And an apology.

Kahma's hands were moving again.

"His Eminence will be thrilled to hear we've quelled your ambitious — if poorly executed — plot before he ever stepped into his morning baths. It was close there, for a moment. I'll admit even I believed the Valen bitch for a while." Vi-baln had settled into his seat, crossed slippers inches from Bimet's tight face. "Luckily, Bimet is always happy to oblige me, ever since she was a girl."

Nausea twisted between Rih's ribs. At his feet, Bimet trembled. Air puffed past them, and Rih turned. The door was rolled aside as a veiled woman slipped in, head bowed over a tray set with an array of food. She knelt at the dais, tray raised overhead for him to eat from.

After months within Athrolan's famished city, Rih's stomach awoke with a burn. When she glanced back at Vi-baln, he was laughing.

"Hungry, are you? Best be used to it. I doubt they'll feed you before you're brought to the walls."

Time. They needed time. Curiel would be hard-pressed to storm the walls, but surely fifty thousand Athrolani swords would count for something. Keplan had to count for something. She pulled a smile onto her face. "Kill me if you want. Kill every last one of us. It won't save you."

Kahma broke into faltering translation, eyes darting between Rih's flashing hands and Vi-baln's predatory gaze.

"Empty threats won't save you, Kajimet."

"You recall the scripture, the one that drove me here months ago?"

"Vaguely. I'm not in the business of pandering to false gods."

Rih tilted her head. "Aren't you, though?"

"You think you know anything about the wrath of a god? You're nothing more than a lank-haired nag's dam." His expression soured and he rose, shoving the serving woman aside. He dragged Rih to her feet by the shoulder strap of her armor, fruit-sweet breath wafting across her face. "I can promise, you haven't even tasted a hint of its bite. Bimet knows. Her sister too—she was kind enough to lend us a hand. Both of them, actually."

Rih pulled saliva from her adrenaline-dry throat and spat it across his face. His grip loosened and she hit the hard floor, head cracking against the lowest dais step. Colors exploded across her vision and her world spun. When she could see again, Vi-baln's personal guards at the door were motionless lumps of silk, two of the women from the rooms below standing over them, weapons drawn and bloody.

Vi-baln was once again in his chair, hand pressed to the back of his own head. Fresh blood stained the neck of his robes. Bimet stood before him, body shaking. The blade of her glaive, however, was perfectly still, and pressed to the hollow of his throat.

Her free hand signed for Rih, though her eyes never left the man's face. "Her name was Fedar and she was my world. You promised nothing would harm her—any of them—if I brought you the rebel queen. It felt like dying, losing her. Like gasping, without air. Except, worst of all, I still had to go on living afterward."

The ground trembled. It was faint, nothing close to the quakes in Athrolan, but there. The second lasted longer. Maybe it was even closer. Dust eddied down from the rafters.

"Look, Empress." Bimet's face shone with a lifetime of justified fury. "It feels like you might win after all."

Rih stumbled to her feet, head pounding. "Bimet, I—"

"I'll find you later. I'd like a few minutes." All expression fled her face. She no longer even looked tired. Easing her weight to her other foot, she let the glaive bite through the thin skin over his clavicle. "He always enjoyed our time alone."

Rih backed toward the door, torn between trust and suspicion. But she knew countless women who walked in Bimet's sandals. The same fire screamed within their ribs. She yanked her weapons from a dead guard and shut the door behind herself.

The guards outside were dead too, and a dozen armed courtesans awaited her. The serving woman pulled the silk from her face.

Rih caught one glimpse of Ki-elte's bright brown eyes and collapsed into her tutor's arms. The shudder of laughter or weeping passed between them, then Rih pulled away. "I missed you."

"I've missed you, too," Ki-elte answered. "But you've an empire to overthrow and are a bit behind schedule. The guards all expect you, and they're at every door. But I trust you remember how to dress."

Rih grinned. "You'd be so proud—I even have a favorite hat." Someone handed her a kalas and wrap and she set to work. The clay shuddered, a tiny crack racing across the wall. She paused in tucking the last piece of silk. Rih followed the gazes to the windows opposite the Hand's ornate parlor door. Dust plumed in the air just inside the walls. A twitch of the bedrock followed, then boiling water shot skyward.

A hand dragged her back from where she leaned against the sill. "There's no time," Ki-elte scolded, ripping the silk from her. "You and the rest of your girls, with me." They wound upward through the warren of narrow slaves' tunnels and stairs, her thighs burning with every step. The ground continued to tremble, though perhaps it was the momentum of all surrounding her, all their allies in the streets.

Ki-elte pushed aside a curtain and they emerged in the foyer of the emperor's private bathhouse. Rih's arm whipped, muscles loose until the last moment when the dart thudded into a guard's ribs. His fingers scrabbled at the shaft as if he could extricate himself.

Rih leapt. Air swept her side as a blade brushed past. Another slid cold fire between her fifth and sixth rib. She wondered what they heard when she screamed. Panting, she ripped her dart from the guard. Blood spurted, and his limbs shuddered into stillness. Her shoulder blades ached with the effort.

Beneath them, the earth convulsed. It was a moan Rih felt between her ribs. A stretch after decades of slumber. No one had found her fireshells. She rolled from the guard's body in time to block a descending sword with her spear shaft. She kicked up into his gut and flipped her spear around to drive its tip into his belly. She flopped back, breath shallow. Hot blood bubbled from her side. It was an atlatl's dart, and there was no time.

At the end of the hall sunrise shone through the jade doors. She snarled and snapped the shaft off. She wiped a hand through her blood and smeared it across her brow and up her cheek. This was her battle. She shouldered the door open.

Sunlight shot stars through her vision. She jerked her spear free, chest heaving, blood cooling on her leather armor.

The opposite wall was open to the gardens, and no fewer than five pools were built into the floor. In the largest, along the outer wall, waited Jamun-Ilta the Holy Emerald Throne, Emperor of Ban and the Jade Forest.

Naked, without his face paint and finery, he was unremarkable. Annoyance pinched his broad face. "Rih-elte. I expected to see you at a sunset execution."

Of course he signs. She was never permitted to look upon him, not even his hands so she might understand him. "I'm a bit early. And it's not my execution."

"I gave you everything you could ask for. And this is how you repay me?"

"You gave us everything we needed. You gave us rage. You gave us knowledge. You gave us invisibility. And me? You gave me these things most of all."

Darkness pinched the edges of her vision and her knees locked to keep her upright.

"Honestly, I'm offended this is all you think it would take. Look at you. You're bleeding out where you stand. I can hear your lungs wheezing from here."

She laughed, blood and spittle misting the air between them. She grinned. He did not know she bled with the blood of a thousand queens.

Below, the city rocked. Geyser after geyser exploded into the air. Rubble rained from the billowing clouds of steam.

Uncertainty crept across his face. "We destroyed your little clay bombs."

"Those aren't fireshells, Jamun-Ilta." Steam rose from the pools surrounding him, bubbles rising faster, larger as the water heated from below. Every lamp globe in the throne room crackled and exploded. Shards rained across the room, drawing spider-silk lines of blood from their skin. The bathwater tinged pink.

"What is this?" he asked again, gaze roving between her and the miasma outside.

"You thought you could tame us." She tossed the tile into his bathwater. He watched it sink. "You thought you could crush us like you did our foremothers. Like you did the Vales. And here I am, covered in blood, just like all those before me. You may have been crowned by the gods, but they are dead now. And the new one has decreed your time is over."

The sky blackened, knotted clouds pulling strength from the rising stream. The ceiling overhead shifted, dropping even as the earth cracked beneath their feet. She wished the look on his face was fear. She had to settle for disbelief.

Pain radiated across her back as she ripped the atlatl dart from her side. She dragged a last deep breath from her collapsing lungs. Every step spurred her heart faster. Re-bel. Rebel. *Rebel!* The mantra became the tattoo of her footsteps; she launched from the tub's lip, bloody dart raised high.

They collided. Metal wrenched over bone. Blood sprayed her face. She pushed the dart deeper into the tender place just above his clavicle. Her dark eyes bored into whatever was left, rotting, of his soul. She forced her shaking, bloody hands to sign.

"The One True God chooses me."

CHAPTER TWENTY-ONE

The 2nd Day of Lleume, 1273
The Divine Isle

HOT WATER SLID OVER Keplan's skin. Comforting. Blinking, he found himself on a mound of warm black rock, hardened in whorls and currents. Steam rose from the cleft in the rock just beside him. Pulsing heat emanated from below, but it was soft. Quiet. A few paces away a clear spring bubbled from the earth, and it was in its trickling water that he woke. Nothing grew, but destruction bore fertile soil.

Tender palms raked a hairless, burnt scalp. New. Pink. He rolled over onto his naked belly, muscles protesting at the hard stone beneath them as he pushed himself upright. His body would not obey his command to stand or walk, but he could crawl.

Rough stone scraped his burnt palm as he cupped water to his mouth. He watched the spring trickle across the gnarled scar tissue obscuring the curls of claret and green. Clean. The air in his lungs was clear, but it lacked stillness. Now it had bite, ferocity, mirth. This is what the Laen had seen. *It's alive.* So was he.

A sound arched over the barren landscape from somewhere below, by the strand. A bird, perhaps. He propped himself on his stronger arm, the left still weak. *I guess I have no excuse not to exercise it now.*

"Keplan!" The voice came again, the word clear, if strangled with tears and perhaps more than a little laughter. Azimir appeared over the hill and broke into a sprint.

Keplan offered a weak wave.

His cousin stumbled over the undulating rock, avoiding the warren of steaming cracks. When he came to a halt beside Keplan, he was panting, clothes streaked with dirt and sweat. "Kep."

"Azi." His voice was hoarse, lowered from a thousand screams. "You stayed?"

Azimir sank to his knees and stripped his coat off, tucking it over Keplan's bare body. "I thought you might make it. After all of this. And if you didn't, if there was anything left, I thought I'd bring it back."

Keplan thought the stiffness about his mouth might be a smile and tried to broaden it. "None of us deserve you."

Azimir batted the compliment away. "What happened?"

Keplan looked around at the ruins on the next hilltop of Le'yne. At the Mirikin cliffs, half swallowed with solidified lava. "It worked."

"And your parents — ?"

"Don't." Keplan's stomach writhed with grief. "Legends paint pretty enough pictures. Truth needn't be a part of these. They're gone, and that's all." He allowed Azimir's hand under his elbow to lift him. "I feel like I ought to be dead."

"That's how you know you're not," Azimir explained with a faint smile. His dark eyes lingered on Keplan's head, on his face.

"I must look it."

"You don't look like you. That's all. Are you able to walk?"

"I think so, just a bit weak to try." He glanced at the Mirikin palace, tucked between new land and old ocean. He imagined he would recover there for a time before returning to his capital. He and Rih could rule in tandem, perhaps. His chest was tight, though, and his smile felt frayed at the edges.

"What is it?"

"Just thinking of going back. Of all that's left ahead. Returning to the throne. Explaining, after all of that, that I survived."

"What if you didn't?" Azimir's questioning gaze settled on him, and the young man propped an elbow on his bent knee.

Something opened in Keplan's ribs. "What do you mean?"

Azimir looked down. "The night before she left, Rih and I had a talk. About a lot of things, but some of it was you. I knew you might live. Call it whatever bit of intuition I inherited from the powerful side of the family. So we made a contingency. Athrolan doesn't need to know you lived. No one has to. If you realize you do want to rule after all, you want the Athrolani crown, it's in its case in your chambers where you left it. Rih will gladly rule a single empire instead of one conjoined. Go home, take up your kingdom, and rule beside the Banis empress for the rest of your days."

Keplan's mouth was dry, and he drank another handful from the spring before running a hand over his bare head. "And if I don't?"

"Then I stumble back home and tell Athrolan their king is dead. Their gods are dead. Proclaim the world is whole and new and alive again. You take the pack I put together and disappear. Rih left you some things too. They're waiting at the post office on the Athrolani docks, addressed to a Lan Guardsen."

"My parents did the same thing. Running." Shame burned in Keplan's gut. "Why does it feel like cowardice?"

"This time the job is done. Truly," Azimir promised. His face was lined with fatigue, as if the last hours—or days, perhaps—had aged him a year. "In a way it is. But you've admitted you don't want the crown. Admitted you're no good at it. We just thought we'd give you a choice if you survived long enough to make one."

Φ

It was dusk when Azimir climbed the steps to his family's manor in Mirik. Sweat and dirt stained his clothes, and his eyes were tired. He walked alone. Already he spotted riders setting out across their new single island as tentative cartographers.

Victory had been declared in their war with Ban, but the news was murky with talk of the new empress. The adjoining estates of the other commissioners were quiet. Azimir rapped on his father's doorframe. It was ajar, but the ambassador seemed transfixed with his untouched drink. "Da?"

Brentemir blinked and looked up. "Azi? I didn't know you were home."

"Just arrived. May I?" He gestured to the seat across the desk. His father did not answer, but after another quiet moment, he sat. He could still smell the stink of sulfur and seawater on his clothes and the tang of his own nervous sweat.

Bren still had not met his gaze. The little auburn still left in his hair seemed faded, as did his wan face. "I watched it from the harbor gates. Like I did the first time."

"It was incredible."

"You saw it in Ceir Athrolan?"

Azimir winced. Where did he even begin the lies? "No, I actually came to Mirik days before. I was the one who rowed Keplan to the island. He asked me to."

Bren stared at Azimir as if viewing a stranger. "I should have been with them."

"You had no place there, Da."

"And you did?" Bren's rumbling voice was scraped thin on the sharp edges of feelings he never bothered to file down.

"Toar, I cowered under my boat for the better portion of it." Azimir sighed, raking a hand through his hair. "When I was nine, you told me the story about the final battle of the Gods' War. The night before. Do you remember?"

"But this is war, and I'll probably die," he rasped, the notes barely in tune.

"You stayed up most of the night singing and dancing. A defiant vigil in the face of certain death. Well," he drew a long breath, "this was mine. Keplan was my Alea. Hero and mystery in turns. And just like her, now he's gone."

Bren stilled, and his eyes squeezed shut. "Gone."

"When you're a god, I don't think death is a strong enough word."

"Alea?"

Azimir shook his head. "I'm sorry."

Bren's head sank to his blocky battered hands. His shoulders shook. "They were all I had. The only ones who remembered what happened. The only ones who saw it through with me."

Anger flashed in Azimir's heart, but it was old, and he was tired. "Da, an entire world saw it through. All of it that we know of, really. You can't define your life by a single year. Even one as powerful as that." His fist clenched and he thought of a young man, burned and beaten, but miraculously whole, disappearing into the press of people in the city. "Keplan was never ours. None of them were. But

Ma's yours. I am, and Al too. Rih's mine, as much as she's anyone's. Say your goodbyes. But let them go."

Bren's shoulders shuddered. "I've spent my whole life saying goodbye to them, and yet I somehow still don't know how."

"I doubt anyone knows how to, in the end." He looked at his own hands, more his than either of his parents'. "The Swordbearers will be going on about this for a while now."

"I imagine so, yes." Bren cleared his throat with a frown, as if trying to remember how to be a man. "Where are you headed next?"

Azimir leaned back, mind already slipping through the window, boarding the ship to Athrolan. "The crown belongs to Rih now. I'll deliver it to RoBal with Commander Fess and Lady Gella." His breath shook as he drew it in, feeling the power in the words. "Athrolan is no more."

Bren looked down, a silent moment offered at someone's passing. Except this time it was an era that died. "Toar, I hardly know my place."

Azimir turned to him, arms crossing over his chest. "Stay home. Ride the new coastline. There's a crack in the earth where you can see its pulse." When his father glanced up, shocked, Azimir smiled. "The magma surely will benefit our fields."

Bren frowned. "Our economy rests on grazing, but with the fertile soils." He trailed off and met his son's eyes. "You're right. I belong at home. And when your mother returns, I'll be here to greet her."

Azimir's lips quirked.

"What?"

"That's the first time you've called her that. My mother."

Bren sat back. "How long did you know?"

"A lot longer than anyone realized. It just didn't matter," Azimir confessed.

Sorrow eased over the ambassador's features. "I'm sorry."

"For what?"

"You became a man when I wasn't looking. I realize how much I've missed chasing people I never..." He sighed.

"We've got years, Da. Decades if you stop drinking like An'thor."

Bren's smile was shaky but genuine. His sword hand retreated from the bottle on the shelf behind him. "I'll try my best. Do you leave tomorrow?"

Azimir nodded, rising from the chair. It was late and he was filthy. "I hope to stay in RoBal for a time. Maybe ride the empire a while. I always wanted to visit the jungles."

"I wish you a safe ride to Ban." His father rose, arms opening.

Azimir stepped into them and squeezed. "And I wish you a fair spring." He slipped upstairs, movements unconscious. He called for bathwater and settled at his desk. The moon rose as he penned his letter to Rih, and in the city below, a man who was once a god slipped into the night.

Φ

The 19th Day of Lleume, 1272
The City of RoBal, Ban

Even after weeks, Rih still did not consider the palace hers. She knew the halls better than most and the gardens better than that, but the hulking building was more a nuisance than a home. The piled rubble still being sorted and repaired was a startling splash of bright broken stone in the gleaming clay steps, garish even from the west guard tower, where she now stood.

The room was windowless, save for a narrow slit near the top by the door. The smoke from the pyres in the fields was stronger here. The door swung open and her focus snapped to the man limping in.

Mosil's face was thin but his color far better than it had been in the days just after battle. He bowed to her and gestured to the man shackled behind him. "Evening, Your Grace. I've the man you requested from Ceir Athrolan."

"Bring him in and unchain him."

Mosil ushered the prisoner forward and settled him in a chair. He unlocked the shackles before removing the hood from the man's head and stepping back.

Rih looked down into An'thor's dull black eyes. "Evening, Domariigo."

The Nenev glanced from her hands to Mosil as her cousin translated for her. "What is this?"

"I couldn't let Athrolan's best military resource crumble with half its streets," she informed him. "And you'll address me as Your Grace while you're our guest here."

"Guest," he stated, voice dropping with skepticism. "Something tells me this is a visit I can't refuse."

"I imagine this is better than your previous accommodations, though." She stared at the crumpled legend. "You'll have almost everything you need and some of what you want."

"And in return," he hazarded, "I'm your…what, strategist?"

Rih snorted. "I'm standing atop a fallen empire and you're in prison. I don't need your strategy." She handed him the leather tube protecting all of Keplan's sketches and schematics. "I need your war-weapons."

She stepped back, gesturing to the cot and clay tub on the far side of the room. "I'm sure your ride was a bumpy one. I'll come again tomorrow so we can discuss what else you might need."

He rose as she turned to go. "Wait. What if I say no?"

"Then I wait until you grow tired of counting the floorboards." She nodded to him and followed Mosil from the room. It was locked, of course, but no one noticed one more prisoner among thousands dragged to the tower on the other side of the gardens.

Rih wanted peace as much as Keplan. She smiled, hurrying down the tower stairs and into the fresh air of the gardens. But she was a soldier, and no one knew better the unrest that came in the wake of war. She had killed a monster, but its brethren were still loose in the world. An'thor and his mechanical mind would secure Ban's new liberty.

Across the city Stytown still flooded with the unchecked springs. RoBal was nothing more than an eye, bruised but still glittering. Rih had no interest in rebuilding the crumbled walls, content to let them gape, bones jutting from the cracked clay. New pipes would be laid, as would new laws. The broken government would die and maybe even the empire, in years to come. Kemmer would have more to teach. Rih drew a deep breath of jasmine and the hot summer night. One thumb rubbed the horse-skull tile in her pocket. There was much to learn, but Rih was of a single mind.

Φ

The 34th Day of Lleume, 1273
The City of Ceir Athrolan, Athrolan

Ceir Athrolan was unrecognizable. Brilliant red banners covered most surfaces, a sharp contrast to the turquoise pennants. When Keplan spared a glance for the swollen dome of the palace, his heart faltered. It was cracked open like a hen's egg, made brighter by the black draping every tower. *Mourning.* Mourning a king. A god. A boy who should never have been, should never have ascended the throne. He stepped off the gangway, wincing at the scrape of rough fabric on still-raw skin. He slipped into the crowd, another scarred man after war, another face tilted up among a sea of desperate, hopeful souls.

After the foreign press of Mirik's Jug End where he stayed the last two weeks, Athrolan's broad streets were almost lonely. Half the buildings no longer stood. The prison had been crushed beneath a toppled aqueduct. The gutters flooded with runoff from the new spring bubbling in the hills to the south.

Despite missing half its roof, the post office bustled with clerks and guards alike. He ducked under the scaffolding and into line. Gazes slid over him, past him, lighting on the new scars, not seeing the old. He found the expression tugging his mouth was a smile.

"And for you, Master?" the postmaster called, beckoning Keplan forward.

"I've a letter waiting for Lan Guardsen." A smile tugged its way onto his face. Aliases were for murder, but this time the victim was who he used to be.

The man frowned and peered at the shelves behind him, muttering the name until he found the appropriate section. "Ah, yes. Been here a while. Traveling, were you?"

"A bit."

"Staying home long?" he asked absently, stamping a few sheets of paper, then sliding them across for the younger man to sign.

"Not sure yet. Depends on the next few days."

The postmaster laughed. "I know that story. Said it myself forty years ago when I applied to be a runner. Been here since." He handed over the thick envelope and waved the next person forward.

The sunlight was brilliant off the water, and Keplan hiked the steep stairs past the naval docks. A new sigil hung from the walkway over the open harbor gates: a tower, half red, half white, crossed by a sheaf of wheat on a black field. *The province of Ceir Athrolan in Ban.* His grin returned. This was not the world he or his parents ever walked. It would be a better one.

His scar-thickened fingers fumbled the heavy seal for a moment before it loosened. Tucked in the waxed envelope was a stack of papers. One, a writ of passage to anywhere in the new empire. The next, a note to a sum of money — insignificant when compared to the Athrolani and Banis treasuries, but large for a common man. Lastly, there was a letter. Each was addressed to Master Lan Guardsen. A thrill thrummed in his limbs at the name.

He opened the letter.

> *Lan,*
>
> *It feels odd to write to you, not knowing if you'll read this or if you'll be dead. But I suppose I am not writing to who you used to be, who I knew you as. Rather, I'm writing to who you will become. If you have need of anything, any time, no matter how much time or distance has come between now and then, you need only ask.*
>
> *As I write this, Azi rides west. He and Commander Fess bring the Athrolani crown to me. I don't know yet what I will do with it. You must know that I meant it when I said I saw the same world you did, when I said I'd help make it. There will be more to come, so much more. I pray we succeed. I write that with a smile, you know. As I'm sure you're smiling now, reading it.*
>
> *You told me very little about your life in Athrolan before taking the throne. I just know that you wished to return to it. And that there was a man waiting. I hope you're reading this beside him. I hope you found there was a place still set for you.*

I know I could have done all this alone. But I also know it would have been harder and taken longer. And I am glad for your help, for your recovery, for your perspective.

We made each other better, in the end.

- Rih

He did not weep. At least, not until her final line. Sweeping potential lay before him, a vast untainted field. Perhaps it always had, but the night had been too dark, the storm too loud for him to notice. *"I hope you found there was a place still set for you."*

He tucked everything back and lifted the pack onto one shoulder. The city had changed much, but he did not need to mind his feet on their way to the Slummer. His heart still knew the cobblestones. The building beside the Wise Hare was abandoned now, the windows boarded. In daylight the lantern above the inn's stoop was not lit, but the sign groaned a welcome in the breeze. Smoke drifted from the chimney and it smelled of home.

He pushed the door open and stepped inside. Sunlight spilled over the floorboards, and Keplan shot a glance at the bar. It was deserted, and he remembered abruptly that the common room was only open in the afternoons, save for folks renting chambers above. Keplan doubted if the knots in his stomach would allow him to eat anything. Still, he slid onto a stool and set his bag aside.

"Be with you in a moment!" the deep voice rumbled from the kitchen.

Keplan's heart threatened to stop for good. He loosened the collar of his shirt as if it would somehow lessen the pressure building in his chest.

The Banis boy whirled from the kitchen, one hand gripping the severed neck of a plucked chicken, the other dusted in flour. "Sorry, Master, caught us in the midst of preparing supper." His dark eyes flicked from Keplan's scars to the bag at his feet, then back. He offered the flour-covered hand, then the chicken, then decided against a handshake altogether. "Gillus. What can we do for you?"

"I'd like to speak with Master Smythesen, please."

Gillus made a face. "I wouldn't raise your hopes on a room. Things are changing, Banis money and all that."

Keplan's heart sank. It was almost impossible to think of a home that was not the Wise Hare. "Tell him anyway, please."

Gillus raised his voice. "Firas!" When the bartender called through the kitchen doorway, the boy continued. "There's a man here to see you. Says his name is—"

Keplan shook his head.

"He's a traveler," the boy conceded. His full attention returned to Keplan. "May I get you anything?"

"Privacy."

The boy's curiosity inched over Keplan's face, but he nodded and returned to the kitchen. A breath and an eternity later, Firas emerged. His broad back was to Keplan as he set an armload of clean mugs on the counter and began to hang them.

"You wanted a room? What'd you say your name was?"

"I hadn't. It's Guardsen."

The mug clattered against its hook as Firas turned. There was no recognition in his green eyes.

Guardsen was a common name. Scars changed a person. *Years change them more. Even if it's just one.*

There. A glimmer, maybe of tears, probably of anger. Firas's shaking hands pushed the mugs away. His gaze roved over the mottled burn parting his shorn dark hair and his lanky bare arms, bare hands. It refused to meet his, however, brushing over every inch of him, save his eyes. When he opened his mouth, only a few strangled attempts at words emerged. He looked away and sagged forward, wiry arms bracing him against the bar.

"Firas, I'm sorry," Keplan whispered. "I don't mean to hurt you — though I imagine I've done nothing but. Always have." He smiled, but his body was too exhausted, too nervous, to pull it farther than his mouth.

Firas's shoulders jerked and he sniffed. "Why are you here?"

Keplan faltered. He expected a welcome, an embrace. Not questions. "It seemed the thing to do. So much of my life was fluid. Myself, even." He raked a hand through his hair, belatedly realizing it set it at odd angles. He swore softly and tugged it back into order. "When I was here, Firas, I knew myself. Maybe not all of me, but I could see the foundations." He shrugged. "I'm going about this all wrong."

"Going about what?" Firas scrubbed a hand over his face. The one beside Keplan's remained unmoved.

"Apologizing, I suppose."

"Showing up on my stoop when news of your death was literally rung from every tower, when the palace is decorated in mourning colors — fates!" Firas's fist slammed on the countertop. "You know how hard it is to grieve when everything around you is grieving too? Makes the loneliness deeper, biting. You realize you're dead?"

"Keplan is. But I'm not. Lan Guardsen, former barboy, former stable hand, came here to the Wise Hare, hoping his old job might be available. Or his room."

"Both are Gillus's," Firas countered.

"He said things were changing, something about money?" Keplan tried again.

"Building beside us is up for sale. Trying to scrape enough together to buy it. Expand. Her Grace is offering investments for smaller places such as ours and I'm hoping to apply, but that's not really important."

"If you had help," Keplan started. His mind flickered to the note in his bag. He would rather spend the rest of his night alone on the road than buy Firas's heart instead of earn it. That would be for tomorrow, if his tomorrow included Firas. "I just mean—"

"I thought you were dead. The whole city—world, actually—thinks you're dead."

"That was rather the point."

"Why didn't you tell me? After everything, after every secret I kept for you? You saw what I went through when Mirrel died. I hate it, but part of me wonders if she'll come bustling in after you. If there was some miracle, something your mother did. She brought back the Earth Shaker all those years ago—" He groaned. "I'm too sober for this."

"I'm sorry." Keplan looked down. "This was Rih and Azi's plan, actually. I never believed I'd survive. I had to free you from forever listening for my footsteps on the stairs."

Silence yawned between them, broken by Gillus's muttered Banis swears as something boiled over in the kitchen. Firas's lips trembled and he still refused to look away from some distant point in the street outside. When he spoke again, it was barely a murmur, but there. "'All we know is it will end them. And probably me.'" His gaze slid along the bar, inching toward the other man.

"There's a chance, a small one," Keplan prompted.

"But one I'm praying for," Firas rasped. His eyes fixed now on Keplan's shirt collar.

Keplan eased a shaking hand across the countertop until just a hair's breadth separated them. "That it won't."

Green eyes met blue. The silence billowing between them was softer. Listening. He did not dare break it. Whatever thoughts flashing through the bartender's mind were best left to percolate. Keplan eased himself from the stool and stepped quietly behind the bar. Firas did not move as the younger man took a mug and filled it with water. Keplan leaned on the counter beside Firas, taking a slow sip. The water tasted of stone. When he glanced up, Firas was almost smiling.

"What is it?"

"You. Here. It's familiar. I missed it."

"I missed —" Keplan's voice cracked and he cleared his throat.

"The drink," Firas quipped, laugh nervous.

The space buzzing between them was a lifeline. "I missed the way your brow knots when the first rays of morning light hit your face. I missed the way you dance, with so much enthusiasm that it doesn't matter whether you have skill, though you do. I missed the way you'd go from playful to world-weary then back again in a moment, just at the smell of smoke or the glint of firelight. I missed the way your body curled into mine and the way your hands traced every mark on me like they were your favorite city streets, not scars." He looked up, hoping his eyes were honest, not bloodshot or manic. "Of all the things I've lost since I lost my mind, I've missed you the most."

"Then stay," Firas whispered. "Forever's a long time, but it's yours."

Joy bubbled from Keplan's chest. He fell into the other man's arms, laughter escaping as their lips met. *Home.* When he pulled away, he plucked at the strap of Firas's apron. "I'll be needing one of these."

Firas's fingers curled in the short hairs at the nape of the taller man's neck. "I miss your hair."

Keplan dropped his head to press their brows together. "Give it a year or two. Then enough folk will have forgotten the pauper king."

"A year or two." Firas drew a shaking breath, expression sobering. "So much is going to change. This is a lot to carry."

"We'll figure it out," Keplan promised.

"Together." Firas's grin bloomed. "All right, get to work."

Keplan laughed and crossed the common room. The floor creaked beneath his boots and he swung the door open. Dusk was just beginning, the promise of a storm purpling the sky's edges. He stood, chest open, breathing the new air. With a last glance at the falling night, he lit the lantern and shut the door.

END OF RESTORED

ACKNOWLEDGEMENTS

The end of a book, whether we're writing it, or reading, is always a bittersweet moment. Concluding a series even more so. These characters carried me through so many strange and unsettling times, and it's fitting to set them loose on the world when everything is the most uncertain it's been in a long time.

I'm grateful to all the incredible people who helped see this series and book through, and while I could never name them all, here are a few:

Thank you to Mickey and the entire Creative Edge team for seeing this book and characters for everything they are and having faith in me. Thank you to Kat, for cheering me on and being my platonic soulmate in so many ways. Thank you to Marissa and Amy for all your feedback and dogged enthusiasm even while I was locked in the doldrums.

Thank you to the Sirens team, past and present, and to the Iceland Writers Retreat, for creating such a welcoming place when I needed it most. Thank you to all the incredible queer communities I've found.

Thank you, of course, to Brad for reminding me of the balance I need in my life, and for always supporting my wild ideas and tempering my workaholic personality.

And thank you to my dad, who introduced me to stories and to dreams, who taught me to greet adversity and hardships with a plan, and who taught me about graceful farewells, and most importantly, when to say them.

This book, this series, and all of them, are because of you.

-V

The taste of the ocean was the same salt as Nubon's blood. The waves beat in the pulse at her wrist, her throat, her thighs. Battered wood bit into her clenched hand. *Thirteen years and three days. I've heard the sounds of this sea for thirteen years and three days.* She absently wondered if the sounds of the womb she heard before were the same, an echo of this, much larger, water.

"It's almost dawn."

Nubon glanced at the man beside her. His sprawled stance lacked its usual playfulness. "Are you excited, *urhun?*" She had uttered the Berrin title for teacher a thousand times more than that for "father," and it held the same tenderness.

"No. Not today." His voice was as wave-beaten as the city bobbing at the horizon.

She heard Berinnal's streets from here, smelled the tar and kelp that kept the city afloat. The ships bearing the seven other potentials for the throne were visible, dark blots appearing occasionally through the morning fog. Nubon mentally ticked off her list. *Tua from the east. Buen from the south-east. Lebon from the south....* She continued, the words familiar in her mind, a touchstone she worried when her mind stormed. The snap of the junk's rigging dragged her eyes to the mast. The plain, dusky-orchid flag rose, the color of a warning sky. *And Nubon, from the north-east.*

A skiff slapped into the water. She followed Urhun down the ladder. This would be the last time they took to the sea together, at least, with her as his pupil. He pushed off from the ship, allowing her to simply be the passenger for the first time since they departed Berinnal a year ago.

"I think I'll miss this." She watched the knots of wrinkles in his beige face soften.

"I know I will." He paused in his rowing and looked at her as if her features were a map he needed to memorize. "Nubon Northeast. Remember everything."

"You taught me all I needed, I'm sure. I'll remember, I promise."

"You'll have to." Something darker shadowed the sadness in his voice. They could not speak about the week to come, the trials that would decide which of the eight scions could bear the weight of the Warlord's title.

Nubon forced herself to sit straight. Her tarred wooden armor was suddenly cloying. They were close enough to hear the smack of the others' oars. Close enough to see their faces were as apprehensive as hers. By the end of the day they would be enemies. Nubon looked to the city, glimmering like the inside of a shell in the sunrise. She wondered, for the first time in thirteen years and three days, what happened to the scions who failed.

Read the rest of Nubon's story in *Out of the Darkness,*
a dark fantasy anthology from Amphibian Press

ABOUT THE AUTHOR

V. S. Holmes is an international bestselling author. They created the BLOOD OF TITANS series and the NEL BENTLY BOOKS. *Smoke and Rain*, the award-winning first book in their fantasy quartet, became an international bestseller in 2018. *Travelers* is also included in the Peregrine Moon Lander mission as part of the Writers on the Moon Time Capsule. In addition, they write game content for Stone Blade Entertainment.

As a disabled and non-binary human, they work as an advocate and educator for representation in SFF worlds. When not writing, they work as a contract archaeologist throughout the northeastern U.S. They live with their spouse, a fellow archaeologist, their dog Rory, and own too many books.

www.vsholmes.com